The

LAST

TRUE

POETS

of the

SEA

JULIA DRAKE

LITTLE, BROWN AND COMPANY

New York   Boston

For my parents, with love

Copyright © 2019 by Julia Drake

Cover art copyright © 2021 by Neil Swaab. Cover design by Neil Swaab.
Paper texture © VadimZosimov/Shutterstock.com
Cover copyright © 2021 by Hachette Book Group, Inc.

Little, Brown and Company
Hachette Book Group
1290 Avenue of the Americas, New York, NY 10104
Visit us at LBYR.com

Originally published in hardcover and ebook by Hyperion, an imprint of Disney Book Group, in October 2019
First Trade Paperback Edition: June 2021

Little, Brown and Company is a division of Hachette Book Group, Inc. The Little, Brown name and logo are trademarks of Hachette Book Group, Inc.

The publisher is not responsible for websites (or their content) that are not owned by the publisher.

The Library of Congress has cataloged the hardcover edition as follows:
Names: Drake, Julia, author.
Title: The last true poets of the sea / by Julia Drake.
Description: First edition. | Los Angeles : Hyperion, 2019. | Summary: Inspired loosely by Shakespeare's Twelfth Night, teenaged Violet is shipped off to Maine after her brother's hospitalization, where she searches for the lost shipwreck that her great-great-grandmother survived and for answers about her family's long struggle with mental illness, all while falling in love.
Identifiers: LCCN 2018058556 | ISBN 9781368048088 (hardcover)
Subjects: | CYAC: Families—Fiction. | Shipwrecks—Fiction. | Mental illness—Fiction. | Love—Fiction. | Maine—Fiction.
Classification: LCC PZ7.1.D73 Las 2019 | DDC [Fic]—dc23
LC record available at https://lccn.loc.gov/2018058556

ISBNs: 978-0-7595-5499-3 (pbk.), 978-1-368-04941-2 (ebook)

Printed in the United States of America

LSC-C

Printing 1, 2021

The excitement and the uncertainty of the quest is more important than the treasure itself.

—Jacques Cousteau, *Diving for Sunken Treasure*

◇◇◇◇◇◇◇◇◇◇◇◇

I came to explore the wreck.
The words are purposes.
The words are maps.
I came to see the damage that was done
and the treasures that prevail. . . .
the thing I came for:
the wreck and not the story of the wreck
the thing itself and not the myth.

—Adrienne Rich, "Diving into the Wreck"

◇◇◇◇◇◇◇◇◇◇◇◇

What country, friends, is this?

—Viola, *Twelfth Night*

PROLOGUE

SHIPWRECKS AS A RECESSIVE GENE

Fun fact: my great-great-great-grandmother was the lone survivor of a shipwreck.

For a long time, my parents liked to point to this story as evidence of family strength. We're descended from *survivors*, they said. *Making it* is in our blood. We cling to planks off the coast of Maine, we don't freeze to death, and when we wash ashore, we marry, we procreate, and we catch lobster to feed to our children. Crying? There's no crying in shipwrecks. No need—as a family, we're not only lucky, we're lucky *and* we persevere.

My younger brother, Sam, and I grew up loving that shipwreck. Every summer when we visited our mother's childhood home in Maine, he and I descended to the rocky shore behind the house and imagined we were underwater explorers in search of the wreck of the *Lyric*. We wore goggles and carried empty glass bottles as oxygen tanks, scrambling across the rocks at low tide until we were frozen, grimy with sea scum. We dreamed of discovering the shipwreck ourselves, imagined gold coins half-buried in sand, jewels blooming in tide pools, hermit crabs fashioning shells from diamonds. We weren't just in it for the riches: more than anything, we wanted to find the ship's carcass, grown green with moss and flickering with fish. We wanted to see what kind of disaster our great-great-great-grandmother had escaped.

The *Lyric* was more than a sunken ship—it was our family's story, long lost to the ocean's depths.

∽

At the hospital, I joked my brother's stomach pump was his snorkel and my mother said "That's enough, Violet" so sharply the nurse dropped his stethoscope. Later, my father caught me by the vending machines chatting a little too close with a boy a little too old (Dad [bewildered, aghast]: Your brother's in the hospital and you're flirting with a *fully bearded man?*). By the time Sam woke up later that afternoon, his teeth gritty and ghoulish with charcoal, our parents had new summer plans for all of us: counseling for them, a treatment center for my brother, Maine for me. I became a bad sister and a bad daughter in an hour; an exile in just under two.

By comparison, the *Titanic* sank in two hours, forty minutes. Pretty impressive, to have sunk to the bottom even faster than the twentieth century's greatest shipwreck. Especially considering I was only sixteen. I didn't even have a driver's license, but I was an expert in the art of catastrophe.

PART ONE: WRECK

YOU'RE JUST SO **BRAVE**

The day I left for Lyric, I shaved my head. A prophylactic, if you will.

A week had passed since the Hospital Incident, and the middle of June bloomed in New York City, perfect weather for cones from Mister Softee and imagining your brother in the psych ward. I packed light for exile, ditching my usual leggings and liquid liner for two pairs of my dad's faded jeans, six Hanes T-shirts, one ancient tube of fragrance-free lip balm, and a heap of cotton underwear. Plane reading was Sam's copy of *Diving for Sunken Treasure*, which I kept on my lap the whole flight, unopened. Inside, I'd slipped the scrap of paper on which my mom had written the address for Sam's treatment facility in Vermont. My plan was to send him a letter, and after drafting in my head all morning, the best I had was, *Dear Sam, Sorry I couldn't keep it in my pants after you tried to kill yourself, fixing that now. STEP ONE: NO HAIR! Step two: Bad clothes! ps How's the maple syrup?*

My work, needless to say, required some revision.

The plane ride to Portland lasted forty-five minutes, and the flight attendant asked me how I was feeling four separate times. She put ice in my orange juice and slipped me Milanos instead of the off-brand biscuits she'd given to the rest of steerage. As I disembarked, she pulled me aside and told me, tears clinging to her thickly mascaraed lashes—purple, I noticed—that a niece of hers had gone through chemo last year.

"You're just so brave," she said.

I was so stunned all I could do was nod. She pressed two pairs of plastic wings into my hand and told me she'd keep me in her thoughts. As far as reinventing myself went, this did not bode well.

"Your hair!" my uncle Toby bellowed when I met him at arrivals.

He pulled me into a hug, and I bent my knees so I'd be the right height to press my face into his shoulder. Toby's flannel smelled cozy, like cotton and flour and yeast—from the bakery, I guessed—and underneath, the faintest hint of my mom's morning smell, before she left for the hospital (catch her after work and she smelled antibacterial, like Purell and latex). I pressed my face deeper into Toby's shoulder and clutched the plastic wings until they pinched my palm.

"You're okay, kid," Toby murmured. "I've got you."

Eventually, he pushed me back by my shoulders and made a great show of peering at me. Toby was nearly a decade younger than my mother, but his tan face was crinkled like an ancient gnome's, weathered and sweet. He had enough hair for the both of us, sandy, lank, gathered into a sloppy bun at the nape of his neck. He studied me until I looked down, uneasy with the attention.

"Nice kicks," I said. His plaid Converse high-tops were busted along the seams and splattered with coffee, the perfect match for my equally grubby white ones.

"Bad arch support. Save your plantar fascia while there's still time, kid."

I rolled my eyes. My plantar fascia was the least of my worries.

"I like the new 'do," Toby went on. "I like this whole new look, but the 'do, especially. The last time I saw you, you looked like— what's the word? A *celebutante*?" I grimaced. "Now, though, you look like a seal pup."

"I look like an ogress with alopecia."

"There's that Violet wit. Have you been practicing your scowl?"

"Thirty minutes in the mirror every day."

"Hm. Well. Practice makes perfect, I suppose. Which is exactly why my meringues always collapse. Listen, kid, at the risk of sounding very old," Toby said, "stand up straight."

I winced. The truth was that since the Hospital Incident, I'd been perfecting not my scowl but my slouch: step three of my master plan, after the hair and the clothes. I wanted to take up less space, or just *be* less: muted, quiet. Shrinking. Not my usual self. I had a lot of height to contend with, but if I hunched, I could pass for five foot eleven, maybe even five foot ten, instead of my real six feet.

Fine. My real six feet and one half inch.

At 72.5 inches, I represented less than 1 percent of the American female population. Growing up, I'd been every basketball, swimming, and volleyball coach's dream until they realized I had zero interest in athletics and zero talent to boot. I was interested only in theater—nay, *the theatre*, preferably of the musical variety. I tap-danced and soft-shoed and sang, dreamed of Broad*way* in my future. Not that it mattered now. My theater career had gone the way of the dinosaur long ago.

"C'mon, don't waste that height! You got the good genes!"

I straightened up and loomed over my uncle. As if to emphasize the difference in our statures, he stood on tiptoes to rub the fine layer of fuzz on my skull.

I shook him off. "I'm not a *dog*, Toby."

"But if you were, you'd be a Great Dane."

Count on my uncle to know just what to say.

❧

Lyric was four hours north, and we inched along the Maine Turnpike through tourist traffic and construction. I cracked a window and inhaled: it'd been three years since our last family visit to Maine, but that briny, sharp sea smell was exactly the same as I remembered. So was the feeling, as we got farther north, that civilization was slowly falling away. The tourist spots became dingy fishing towns; roadside buildings grew more and more dilapidated until they were just husks. Lyric was a small town, shaggy around the edges, lost and forgotten. Not to put too fine a point on it, but my parents had sent me here for a reason.

"Think of it not as a punishment, but as an opportunity," my mom had insisted. "With less distraction, maybe it'll be easier to turn off the romance channel."

I was already two steps ahead of her. After the vending machine debacle, I'd sworn off smooching and everything else that'd led to that moment: my wild hair, my love of tequila, my unrelenting insensitivity. My need to be at the center of all things. In Lyric, I'd be *less*. Maybe I'd even disappear.

"You're quiet, kid. I almost forgot you were here," Toby said.

The plan was working already.

⚬

My phone lost service just as things started to look familiar. We passed the weather-beaten sign for the Lyric Aquarium, the fishing supply store, the harbor. Past town and then into the pines, down the long dirt driveway to my grandmother's—now Toby's—house. I held my breath until we reached the bottom, a habit from an old game with Sam.

The house came into view just when I thought I'd burst. It'd been my grandparents' home originally, a turreted Victorian framed by the boat-dotted gray sea, weathered and damp and plagued by a serious mold problem. A family of raccoons had once lived in the turret's walls and chattered ceaselessly throughout the night. Against the water, though, the house still looked to me like Botticelli's Venus. I exhaled, dizzy.

"You want me to set you up a tent in the turret?" Toby asked.

"Not if the raccoons are still there."

"I believe Maude and her young have finally found greener pastures," Toby said. "You and Sam were so cute up there. Camping. Roasting marshmallows. Nearly setting the house on fire . . ."

"I'll stick with a normal bed, thanks."

"You've finally grown up, Violet. I'll warn you: getting old is expensive and boring."

"Boring might be a nice change of pace," I said.

I got out of the car and accidentally slammed my door.

Inside, Toby apologized for the mess, but I barely noticed, because one step over the threshold and *bam*, it was our last summer here. I was thirteen; Sam was twelve. For three weeks, he ate green apples and drank Earl Grey tea. I had a plastic choker that left a tan like a trellis around my neck. We shared the same room like always, but we didn't talk at night. He'd started grinding his teeth in his sleep.

In the kitchen, Toby poured me a lemonade and added a sprig of mint, playing a perfect host. Then he poured himself a beer. A pilsner. Light and crisp. I stirred my mint sprig like a cocktail straw.

"What, no booze for me, Uncle Toby?"

He shot me a look of alarm.

"*Kidding.* Relax." Beer was one thing from my former life I wouldn't be sorry to say goodbye to. At least, not *super* sorry.

"Violet . . ." Toby started. He had that look on his face like he wanted to capital-*T* Talk. Couldn't anyone take a joke anymore?

"I'm going outside," I announced.

I took off through the house, which wasn't messy so much as *stuff*-y. My mom always complained that my grandmother had been a pack rat—she died when I was five, and my grandfather, way earlier—and Toby seemed to have inherited that trait. There were books everywhere, a tchotchke on every available surface, a collection of foam rollers, nesting tables topped with tea sets, a million boots beside a boot dryer (in *June*), some Batman Legos on the mantelpiece, *so many books*, a single ice skate on that coffee table, and on that couch, a stuffed guinea pig inside a disassembled blender.

I passed through the den into the dining room, which was kind of tidy, except for a just-emptied puzzle that sprawled across the big table. The box showed a movie still from *The Wizard of Oz*. No place like home, I thought grimly. In the living room, a blanket of dust coated the brass telescope and the globe that I knew said USSR, not RUSSIA. I sneezed as I yanked open the sliding glass doors to the backyard.

For the smell of pines outside, I'd put up with the dust and a whole raccoon army. The view was spectacular—my dad's word, always. Past the overgrown grass and the weedy flower bed, the ocean stretched on endlessly. Moored boats bobbed below me and birds pinpricked the sky. Down the hill was the shore where Sam and I used to play. The boulders seemed to have shrunk, eroded, maybe, by salt water and sand. Or had the shoreline always been that small?

Toby appeared at my side. "Remember all the plays you performed on this lawn?"

"Don't remind me," I said.

"I've got great memories of you singing 'Greased Lightnin''
with a croquet mallet as a microphone. Sam sang backup."

"The horror." I shivered for emphasis.

"What? You were talented! *Are* talented."

"I don't really do that anymore," I said. "Perform, I mean."

"Why not?"

Because (a) singing only ends in disaster, and because (b) I
found more exciting extracurriculars.

"No reason," I said.

Toby took a casual sip of his drink. "Your parents mentioned
things had gotten a little wild in the city. Any connection there?"

What a fool I'd been to think we could avoid this conversation.
Of course Toby was going to bring up my former life. *So, uh, Vi,
what did it mean when my sister called, absolutely hysterical, and asked
if I could provide you shelter for the summer?* I knew Toby was being
nice, but I went rigid at my uncle's attempt to bond. Our relationship had heretofore been standard uncle-niece fare, pleasant and
innocuous: trips to the zoo and belated birthday cards featuring
too-slow sloths. I had no desire to talk with him about my Year of
Wild, nor Sam, nor the general brokenness of my family. What was
there to say, really, to him, or *anyone*? Sam *was* fucked up, and I *got*
fucked up. The end.

Toby was waiting.

"I don't know about *wild*. My slutting around was pretty run-of-the-mill. Sam, though. Finishing a whole three-quarters of a bottle of Tylenol? *That's* wild. Especially for him."

Toby whistled, long and low. I imagined how all the boats on the ocean would sink. A snapping mast here. A hull can-opener'ed on a coral reef, maybe. A strangling from a giant, hungry kraken.

"So that's a no on talking, then," Toby said.

"All I want is to disappear."

"Good luck doing that with a head like yours in a town this small."

I poured the rest of my lemonade in the pachysandra.

"Thanks for the drink." I really meant it, though I see now that's hard to believe.

Upstairs, in the blue room I used to share with my brother, with the stiff twin beds and the lamps filled with sea glass I used to count to fall asleep and the whole bookcase full of Nancy Drews, my phone said it was *searching.* . . .

I'd never been great at keeping in touch. A handful of summer-program friends gave up on me eventually, and even with friends in the city, I screened calls and let texts go unanswered. Maybe that had all been *practice* for this very moment. Over the years, without even realizing, I'd built strong disappearing muscles.

I switched my phone fully off, and *poof*, I was gone.

ASK ME HOW I'M **SAVING** MANATEES

With a single phone call, my parents had gotten me a volunteer position at the Lyric Aquarium, one of the more traditional tourist attractions in town. Apparently, if your great-great-great-grandparents once helped found a local aquarium, you *will* be hired more than a century later, even if you have no experience and just as much interest in fish. "Nepotism at its finest," I'd said to my dad.

"Maybe you'll learn something," my dad had replied.

"You do realize *Sam* is the one who loved the aquarium."

My dad had rubbed his eyes beneath his glasses. "Violet, I know this may come as a shock to you, but we're doing the best that we can. Just give the fish a chance, okay?"

"I just meant—" I didn't know what I'd meant. I'd just wanted to say Sam's name out loud.

My first day there was Tuesday, two days after my arrival in Lyric. In the dim kitchen that morning, I found a cinnamon bun and a note that read, *they're lucky to have you, xo, a ghost. ps toby's day starts at 5 but he says what's up. pps call your mother!* The icing was cream cheese and so freaking good that I licked the plate clean.

The aquarium was a fifteen-minute bike ride away, through

and past the center of town. I pedaled slowly at first, grateful that I could breathe in my dad's jeans, even if they were too short. I gained speed and was so relieved to be rid of heavy earrings and jangling bracelets, free from raccoon eyeliner and long, long hair. I pulled that whole look off, sure, but I'd never felt exactly myself in those clothes. At their best, they were a costume that made me the sort of girl you wanted at your party, and at their worst, my clothes were *wrong*. Case in point: I'd been underdressed for my brother's suicide attempt. I'd been wearing my tiniest pair of shorts, denim cutoffs, a nip of butt cheek visible when I ascended a staircase. A flimsy cotton tank top and no bra, nipples perky in the harsh hospital cold. I'd ached for a sweater, for a parka, for something that felt more *right*.

Something, it turned out, like men's jeans and a shaved head.

I was on the edge of town now, zipping past the outdoor store, Toby's bakery, the hot dog joint; the lobster shack, the movie theater, the Korean restaurant. The one grungy bar, the Lyric Pub, with its perpetually drawn shades. Then the gift shops, and tucked up on a side street, I knew, was Treasures of Atlantis, the so-called "Wonder Emporium" that Sam and I used to visit on rainy days. Once, I'd made him shoplift tiger's eye, and when he later confessed to Mom, I didn't speak to him for days.

Like that, the shops were gone, and I was at the docks, where I stopped to raise the height on my bike seat. Far off, a group of dudes in waders and beanies were unloading from a fishing trip—their boat was called *Sheila*. Sam and I used to invent boat names, and we'd finally settled on HMS *Promise and Discipline*. We were six and seven and Mom had just about died laughing when she heard it. "Gotta learn to sail before you name the boat," she'd said, and Dad'd said: "I dunno, I like the idea that they're the only kids in Maine who *can't*."

Seat fixed and almost there now, I was starting to get nervous. What would I do in an aquarium? I knew *nothing* about the ocean. Not like Sam. His favorite place in the whole world, besides the shore behind my grandmother's house, was the Irma and Paul Milstein Family Hall of Ocean Life at the Museum of Natural History (countless visits meant that the exact, interminable name was forever in my memory). When Sam was thirteen, he sent a poem he'd written about a jellyfish to a curator there, and she was so moved that she invited us for a private behind-the-scenes tour. I was fourteen and I remember, more than anything else, my hangover.

Sam reminded me of a jellyfish, actually: porous, wispy, faintly luminous. He was a city kid not equipped to handle the city, unable to stand the pace, the traffic, the crush. I thrived and he floundered. As a fifteen-year-old, he'd choose to walk an hour rather than take a fifteen-minute train ride. As a five-year-old, he'd hurl himself on the sidewalk in front of the subway entrance, dead-weight and screaming. Passing strangers covered their ears or shot my mom looks; I remember studying salt scatter on the sidewalk and singing "Sixteen Going On Seventeen" under my breath to pass the time. Once a tantrum started, Sam couldn't be reasoned with; we'd just wait until he screamed himself exhausted. Then my mom would scoop him up and load us into a cab, late for whatever birthday party/movie/child-psychology appointment we were headed toward.

Sam's official diagnosis was complicated. Depression, anxiety, and patterns of disordered eating that, his shrink believed, existed concurrently with certain aspects of obsessive-compulsive disorder. *That* mouthful, I felt, barely scratched the surface.

What about the way Sam seemed to flicker like a fluorescent light? Or how he occasionally hid in weird places—under a table, for example, or an out-of-the-way bathroom. And then there was the fact that, in spite of all this, he was perfect in school, every teacher's favorite.

At home, though, he was always the problem. Except for this past year, when I was.

⚯

The Lyric Aquarium had been imposing in my memory, but when I saw it that morning, the first word that came to mind was *rinky-dink*. The building was octagonal, once painted blue but now weathered the pale gray color of vitamins I'd gagged on as a kid. Inside, the foyer smelled of salt water and rot, and the ticket desk, a cheap folding table, was coated in a fine layer of dust. The main room's focal point was a touch tank that housed nurse sharks and sea cucumbers; another circular tank held rays and skates doing slow, morose laps. A marine skeleton hung from the ceiling, its bones suspended by fishing line. A sickly whale? An extra-large tuna? It was a little embarrassing that I didn't have a clue.

"Violet?"

A white-haired white lady in a black fleece and tall brown rain boots was striding toward me, trailed by a wolfish dog. This must have been Joan, the aquarium's director. She broke into a huge smile as she reached for my hand.

"Oh my goodness, hello! You're *so* tall! So grown-up!" she told me, pumping my arm so hard my bicep shook. "I know it's been a few years, but wow!"

"I'm sorry. Have we met?"

"Oh, you wouldn't remember, you were just a kid."

I looked between the dog and Joan and realized I *had* met them. I mean, I'd only been thirteen, and more focused on the hot volunteer than her, but—

"How're your folks? And your brother! You know I still have a poem he wrote during one of our Critters of the Deep workshops? It's hanging in my office. *From the small sea snail to the great blue whale, everyone has feelings.*"

Apparently, I walked in Sam's intellectual shadow in not one state, but *two*.

"We're so happy to have you. Our very own Rudolph! Your grandmother was such a lovely woman. She helped me with research from time to time."

"My last name's actually Larkin. My dad's."

"You'll always be a Rudolph here. You're the closest thing we have to a local celebrity."

The dog barked. "Oh, hush, Boris, life isn't a zero-sum game. He gets jealous," she whispered conspiratorially. I offered her a weak smile. Boris could totally have the local celebrity title.

Joan handed me an informational packet labeled LYRIC AQUARIUM AND OCEANOGRAPHIC EDUCATION CENTER TRAINING MANUAL and two electric-teal T-shirts with ASK ME HOW I'M SAVING MANATEES printed on the back. Before I could follow the shirts' instructions, Joan said, "Orion should be here any minute. He's our star employee—works here year-round—and he'll train you. Really, this is just so exciting. We wouldn't be here if it weren't for your ancestors!"

"Neither would I. Though maybe that'd be better for everyone."

She blinked, then burst out laughing. "What a card you are!" She chattered away about my schedule—"Just part-time, Tuesday through Friday, mostly be dealing with summer camp field trips, though we haven't had a lot going on, I'm sorry to say. . . . Frankly it's been a dead zone, there's a flashier aquarium about thirty minutes south and they just built a penguin exhibit, so . . ."

I flipped through the packet, skimming paragraphs on marine biomes, longshore drift, and thermohaline circulation. An entire section was devoted to "Maine's Natural Wonders" and listed the limestone cliffs of Fabian's Bluff; Old Sow Whirlpool, the largest whirlpool in the western hemisphere; the Desert of Maine. (*Not a true desert, but a tract of glacial silt!*) Did I really have to learn all this?

"Do you guys still do tide-pooling classes?" I asked. "I remember liking those with my brother."

"*Weellll.*" Joan's voice grew squeaky. "There've been some cuts to programming in the past few years. We've lost some funding, sadly, and a few of our educational programs have fallen by the wayside as a result. That's why we're closed on Mondays, you see."

"Oh." For the best, maybe. The last thing I needed on my conscience was a child banana-peeling on a sea star and cracking her head open on a rock. "What about the lobster demonstrations?"

"Good memory!" she said. "But, no, we don't do those anymore either. There was an . . . *incident.*" She made pincers with her hands and chomped at the air. "I maintain our lobster was provoked, but . . ." She shrugged. "We're a little light on the programming this year. But. So happy to have you on board. You're going to do great work here."

Boris raised his wolf-doggy eyebrows. He had me all figured out.

"I've got to go track down your paperwork, but please poke around! Explore. That's what we're here for."

Joan disappeared upstairs, Boris jingling after her. My poking around left me underwhelmed. The aquarium's star attraction was an (admittedly awesome) mammoth blue lobster named Louise, but otherwise, the exhibits were grim. Along one wall, a three-foot-long box of soil and scraggly grass was labeled REEDS AND PLANT LIFE OF THE MAINE COAST. There was an outdated chart of coral reef death titled HELP SAVE OUR ECOSYSTEM, a fairly standard exhibit on the Gulf of Maine, and beside that, SEA MONSTERS OF OLD, which featured some seriously bad artists' renderings of Cassie, the Casco Bay Sea Serpent. Even the small nook of a gift shop was depressing. It sold, along with china Cassies and Lyric Lobsterfest T-shirts, unconscionably phallic stuffed sea cucumbers with googly eyes, no less.

The only exhibit that I lingered over was the *History of Lyric* display, and that's because it featured my ancestors, the town's founders. A model *Lyric* steamship sat behind glass, gathering dust on its miniature deck. Beside it, a computerized map charted the ship's course by red dotted line—technology ripped from *The Muppet Movie*—across the Atlantic, until the line exploded a few miles off the coast of Maine. Tiny animated stick figures bobbed in the water. One flailed for shore. The screen flickered, then rebooted, sending stick-figure Fidelia swimming on an endless loop toward safety.

Sisyphean was the SAT word I was looking for.

I turned to a picture of my great-great-great-grandparents, Fidelia and Ransome, on their wedding day. A copy of this same photograph sat on the cluttered mantel in our living room, but I'd never really studied it. Now I leaned in close. Fidelia was covered in head-to-toe lace, long veil, high-necked dress, a bouquet of flowers spilling over her unseen hands, leaves dangling almost to her knees. Ransome stood beside her, top hat tucked under his arm. It wasn't in fashion to smile for photographs in those days, but his lips curled upward anyway—delighted, I guessed, at his good fortune. I didn't blame him. Even with all the lace, my great-great-great-grandmother was kind of a dish.

The informational plaque dated the photo at five years after the shipwreck. THEIR LOVE WAS OUR BEGINNING, read the caption.

I'd forgotten this was the unofficial town motto. Really great place to turn off the romance channel, Mom.

I was staring at the photograph and trying to figure out if I'd ever look that happy, let alone actually *be* that happy, when someone tapped my shoulder and said, "Hey, man."

I turned and two things happened at once:

1. The tapper realized I was, in fact, not a man;
2. I realized the tapper was, in fact, a man. Not just any man: the most beautiful man I'd ever seen. Though *beautiful man* hardly does him justice. Because the tapper was so much more than that. He was a Certifiable Smokeshow and Knee Buckler to End All Knee Bucklers.

He had shaggy brown bedhead, clear olive skin, and green-gray eyes; chapped pink lips, broad shoulders, and a full chest that stretched the cotton of his teal aquarium T-shirt. His eyebrows were truly gorgeous in a way I did not know eyebrows could *be*: slightly arched and polished, drawing his whole face into focus. A tattoo on his inner arm caught my eye, but he shifted to readjust a large purple lunch box he had over his shoulder, hiding the design before I could make it out. An eco-conscious tattooed eyebrow god? Yes, please.

The Knee-Bucklingest: he was *even taller than I was.*

Yes, I know. Didn't I just literally shave my head so that everyone would stay *away*? Hadn't I dedicated myself to turning off the romance channel? Hadn't I been so blinded by lust that I wasn't even able to *see* what my younger brother was going through, not even *in the actual hospital*?

But, but, but. If you had seen Orion Lewis's eyebrows. Born witness to their majesty. I'm telling you: you would have understood.

"Oh," he said, arching his glorious you-know-whats. *"Shoot."*

"Fake-out," I said.

He looked perplexed. "Are you . . . ?"

An excellent kisser? On birth control?

"Female?" I suggested.

"Working here."

I reminded myself of my priorities. Celibacy. Disappearing.

"Yes. I'm Violet."

"Ah. You're—wow. I thought . . ." He fumbled for words, and the strap of his lunch box strap pulled at his T-shirt, exposing a tanned, smooth shoulder. In another life, I would have sunk my teeth into that very space.

He gestured toward his hair. "Sorry. I thought you were a guy."

"Whatever." I shrugged. "I thought you were one, too, so."

He laughed a stammering laugh, revealing a gap between his teeth. It suited him, and I was glad it hadn't been fixed.

"If you're Orion, I hear you're the star employee," I said.

"I'm sort of the only employee. We'd be in trouble if I weren't the star."

"It's just you and me?"

"And Joan and Boris," he said. "Come on. I'll show you around."

He led me upstairs to a very fishy-smelling break room with a wobbly table, an industrial-size freezer, and a fat maroon sofa upon which the dignified Boris reclined, front paws neatly crossed. Aquatically fetal blobs floated in jars of green juice on the counter; the shelves were scattered with dried bits of coral and the crusty shell of a horseshoe crab. Orion weaved among cardboard boxes full of aquarium merch to rub the dog's ears, and Boris, that smug bastard, yawned at me in triumph.

Orion opened the freezer next and pulled loose a silver bucket labeled FEED. The smell of days-old fish filled the room. I shuddered, thinking of poor Louise's insides.

"Are you a bio major or something?" I asked him as he placed the bucket on the table.

"Nah." Orion took a folded paper napkin from his pocket and tucked it under the wobbly table before placing the bucket on top. "I'll be a senior. In high school. You?"

"Junior."

"The height tends to throw people. You probably know that."

I nodded. He unzipped his lunch box and removed a plastic bag filled with pearly-gray critters. Their heads were still attached, jelly black eyes peering at me through the plastic.

"Late breakfast?"

"Good stuff for the fish. I try to get them something special when I can swing it. You can leave the heads and legs on." He pulled a Swiss Army knife from his pocket and when he passed it to me, his fingers didn't linger on mine. *Good*—no funny business on his end either. I turned to the plastic bag.

"Um. Orion. What are these guys, exactly?"

He looked at me strangely. "They're shrimp."

Huh. Shrimp were usually pink and peeled, curled and dipped in cocktail sauce. I poked at the bag, as if to test for shrimpiness.

"I didn't know shrimp had *legs*."

"Really?"

"Sorry. I mean, I must've known that. I'm not really a fish person."

He looked at me sideways. "You *do* know we're working in an aquarium, right?"

"Yes. I know."

"So there are lots of fish here," he said slowly.

"Yes."

"So why did you get a job working at an aquarium if you're not a fish person?"

"Oh, well. I didn't exactly *want* to work here."

"You didn't?" He looked confused. This was going all wrong. Goddamn this shipwreck gene. I could never say anything right.

"My parents got me the job." Even I could hear how spoiled that sounded.

"Ah," Orion said. "So you're summer folk." He zipped his lunch box closed and shouldered it.

"No! Well. My mom grew up here. I used to come here as a kid. I'm from the city. But I'm not like a tourist."

"Portland? Boston?"

"Er. New York City?"

"The Big Apple, huh. I've never been."

"*Really?* Oh my God, you'd love it. Like—if you like the ocean—at the natural history museum alone, there's the great blue whale model, and the pearl diver exhibit, and the squid and the whale. . . ."

"Whereas here we just have the ocean."

"No, no, that's not what I meant. Though, come on, you *do* have to admit," I said, gesturing at the feed bucket, the jarred specimens, and the dog-hair-covered couch. Boris lifted his head. Why was I still talking? Why couldn't I stop? The words were bubbling up, unstoppable and ugly: "This place used to be great, but it's kind of depressing now, isn't it?"

"I guess so," Orion said quietly. He gestured at the shrimp. "You can bring those down after you finish dicing, okay?"

With that, he left. Boris trailed after him, woofing in disapproval. First day, and I'd managed to offend even the dog.

⚹

It took me an embarrassingly long time to dice the shrimp. I found Orion downstairs at the touch tank with one arm in water up to his elbow. Boris lay at his feet with his head on Orion's sneaker.

"I didn't know with the shells . . ." I said, placing the bucket beside him.

"You did fine," he said. With his bare hand, he took a shrimp between his finger like a cigarette and returned his hand to the water. The rays flocked to him, flapping at the tank's lip, splashing water over the side with their wings. They'd been the Eeyores of the sea world an hour ago, but now, with Orion, they looked almost mammalian, like a pack of tail-wagging golden retrievers.

"They love you," I said, standing next to him awkwardly.

"They're fish. They only love me for my food," Orion said shortly. I'd known him only a few moments, but I recognized thin skin when I saw it. I'd grown up with my brother, after all.

"About what I said . . . this seems like a great place to work." God, even when I was trying, I sounded sarcastic. My mom was right: I did have to work on my tone.

"I'm sorry," I tried again. "I think I'm really nervous."

Not perfect, but better. Truer, at least.

"It's cool," Orion said in a detached way that indicated just how deeply uncool I'd been. "I want to study marine biology in college. So. This is a good place to start. And money's tight, but we're applying for grants and stuff, and Joan's been really supportive of me. She doesn't let on, but she's kind of a bigwig in the science world. She's gonna write me a rec for college."

"Cool."

"Yup."

We watched the rays in silence. Boris thumped his tail. The bubblers in the tanks whirred; upstairs, I heard Joan's footsteps creaking. Talking with a new person was so hard without a drink.

"Do these guys have names?" I finally asked.

"Not officially."

"But unofficially?"

Orion finally looked up from the rays.

"You really want to know?" he said.

"Sure."

"Okay," he said, inhaling, a little hesitant, maybe a little embarrassed. "The darker guys are bat rays. That's Billy Ray Cyrus and Rachael Ray. That big tan one is Ray Charles. She's Raven-Symoné."

"Who's that far one? Ray J?"

Orion shook his head. "Sting."

I laughed so loud that Boris yelped. Orion patted him on the head.

"Who's this guy?" I said as a large sandy one silked near

us—indistinguishable, as far as I could tell, from Sting and Raven-Symoné.

"This is Link Wray."

"Like the guitarist?"

"You know Link Wray?" Orion sounded impressed. Good. Thanks to an appreciation for bad wordplay and my dad's record collection, I was beginning to climb my way out of the hole.

"You can pet them," Orion said. "Two fingers. That's what we tell the kiddos."

My fingers had barely skimmed the surface, when Billy Ray and Rachael Ray scattered. Sting all but pulled a U-turn to avoid me. I tried not to interpret ray rejection as a sign of how I'd fare with Orion.

"You need one named Famous Original Ray's Pizza," I said.

"What's that?"

"A New York thing. They're all over the city, in different iterations. People kept stealing the name, wanting to pass off Ray's pizza as their own. Ray's Original. Ray's Pizza. Ray's Famous. Original Ray's." I could keep going. Pizza had been my favorite drunken delight during my Year of Wild.

"Some urban mimicry right there."

"Come again?"

"Mimicry. Like, a striped octopus mimics the sea snake. For protection, not selling pizza, but the idea's the same. I'll show you a video sometime."

He lowered another shrimp in the water; either Rachael Ray or Billy Ray swooped toward him. I studied his inner arm, the small tattoo that was half-submerged in the tank: five horizontal lines, crossing through an open circle. I had my own stick-and-poke UFO on my rib cage, done by a friend in her kitchen in Brooklyn while her mom made us tacos.

"Is your tattoo a whole note?" I asked.

"Oh. Yeah." He wiped his hand dry on his jeans.

"And Link Wray—are you into music?"

"Yeah. Let's talk about your training."

Tattoo = highly classified information. Noted, no pun intended.

"I'm gonna start you off in the gift shop," he said. "Can you work a cash register?"

"Sure," I lied. I didn't want him thinking I was any more of a dumb turista than he already did. How hard could it be?

In my first day at the gift shop—which was a fairly slow day, I might add—I interrupted Orion eight times for help. *Eight.* I didn't know how to run a credit card, nor did I know how to take the membership discount. No, I didn't know if we had those Louise the Lobster sweatshirts in other sizes, let me ask Orion. I accidentally charged a beleaguered dad three times for a stuffed clown fish, then somehow managed to lock the register with his credit card inside it.

"So, when you said you could work a cash register . . ." Orion said, punching buttons to fix my mistake. The small child screamed.

"Excuse me," the dad asked, "but where's the penguin exhibit?"

Orion, for his part, was the prince of the aquarium. From my perch at the cash register, I learned he had an endless well of patience for questions: did horseshoe crabs have stingers ("Nope—they use those tails to flip over if they get knocked on their backs"), or did sea monsters really exist ("Never say never"), or why didn't the aquarium have sea otters ("Man, I wish we had them, too! They're so cute!"). He showed kids how to pet the rays just as he'd shown me, and even held up one tiny boy who wasn't tall enough to reach.

In the afternoon, I spilled a fresh cup of coffee on a new box of stuffed sharks.

"*Shoot*," Orion breathed. "C'mon. I'll show you where the mop is."

It is not an exaggeration to say that the most enjoyable part of the day was *cleaning* at the end of our shift. Orion put on Sam Cooke, one of my dad's favorites, and whistled as he went about his closing tasks. I mopped like I'd never mopped before, scrubbing what felt like years' worth of grime from the floor to songs I knew by heart. Maybe work wouldn't be a complete disaster. At least I knew how to clean, and at least Orion had good taste in tunes.

"Can I do anything else?" I asked Orion after I'd finished mopping.

He was counting the money in the gift shop register, mumbling under his breath. The music was louder in the gift shop. Sam Cooke was singing about how his baby done gone away and left him. I wondered, briefly, if my mom missed me.

"Orion?" I repeated.

He turned and held my gaze. In his green-gray eyes, the evening took sudden shape. He was going to offer me a ride home. We'd stop for milkshakes, and he'd tell me the story of his tattoo. We'd engage in some strictly platonic and wholesome activity, like fly-fishing, or a trip to the hardware store. *Shoot,* he'd say, laughing at my hardware-themed puns, *that was a good one.*

"Did you reset the totals on this drawer by accident?" he asked.

Oh. Just kidding.

"I'm not even sure I know what that means," I admitted.

"Never mind. It's cool."

"I can help," I said. I wanted so badly to be useful.

"No, really," he said. "You can really just go home. Really."

He didn't have to say *really* a fourth time.

I arrived home to find Toby hunched over his *Wizard of Oz* puzzle. "Care to lend an eye?" he asked, sweeping a hand over the heap of pieces.

I shook my head. My back hurt from mopping. My dreamy, off-limits superior thought I was a dope. *I* thought I was a dope. I missed Sam. I missed my parents. I didn't want a puzzle: I wanted salt and limes and somebody else's body. I wanted to forget myself the way I normally did—only, I was supposed to be different.

"I might go for a walk on the beach," I said.

"Flora and fauna can be a balm."

The beach was no balm. It was low tide, smelled like sewage, and was littered with rusted cans of Polar Seltzer and smashed Shipyard beer bottles, plastic bags plastered to rocks, one water-swollen Nike sneaker. The beach had never been pristine, but the water had always been clean enough for underwater tea parties and breath-holding contests. Sam and I got so cold our skin turned blue, but Mom could swim all the way out to the buoys and back. "Hardy New England stock," Dad said from shore, pulling his sweater tighter around him. He'd moved a lot as a kid—his explanation was always "my dad worked for General Motors"—but he'd lived the longest in Jacksonville, Florida, famous for strip malls, the Jacksonville Jaguars, and, apparently, the smell of paper mills. Whenever we complained about New York, he'd say, "Just remember, you could've grown up in a town that smells like sulfur and diapers."

Would I have been different if I'd grown up there?

In March, I'd been caught smoking weed during the school day. Not on school grounds, but close enough that it mattered. Immediate suspension, and that went on my permanent transcript. Colleges looooove that. My parents, who'd been pretty preoccupied with Sam, who sometimes called me their "little experimenter," did an about-face. Cue curfew, tattoo discovery, room cleanout. Screaming. Door slamming. All three of us trying to get the doormen on our team (Hector accepted my brownies, only to tattle on me *that very night*).

And every night, March, April, May, Sam lurked in my doorway with some dumb excuse. "Do you have a pencil sharpener?" "Have you seen my watch?" Like I didn't know exactly what he was after. He really thought he was going to make me feel better? Downtown was the only thing that made me feel better.

"No," I said. Then I closed the door so I wouldn't have to see his face.

I didn't have to baby him anymore. He was doing *better*. He'd gained weight. He played Magic with that one kid—Tim, I think? He was crushing his classes, though that was standard. He'd talked about joining stage crew. What a turnaround, we all thought, right up till his big date with Tylenol.

Sam had really needed the limelight, but my parents had their beam swiveled my way. And I was too busy throwing their love back in their faces to notice anything else.

I took my shoes off to wade, but the ocean was too cold and too gray, too weedy. How had Fidelia survived this water in March, let alone walked from the beach to town? I stared out at the ocean, imagining her ship somewhere beneath. I wondered which wreck felt worse: hers or mine.

Something in the sand caught my eye, opalescent and clawed. Abalone? A pearl? My breath caught. Maybe there *was* treasure on this beach. Maybe Sam and I hadn't been wrong to think so. I dug with the edge of a mussel shell, taking care not to cut myself on its razor edge. Even just a pretty shell, maybe. All I wanted was one tiny, pretty thing.

It was a tampon applicator, half-buried in the sand.

⸎

Toby had passed out on the living room couch. I moved the blender/guinea pig combo, put a blanket on him, and left him a note: *Violet would like to be alone right now but she wishes you luck with the puzzle. Tell her mom she'll call her later. Signed, a ghost. PS that cinnamon bun was freaking delicious.*

THE WREXPERT

The next morning, Joan was pissed about the coffee-covered sharks. Gift shop sales, particularly stuffed animals, brought in most of the aquarium's money. I offered to pay, but she just shook her white-haired head at me.

"Just ask for help with the register next time, okay? Me—Orion—anyone."

"I asked Orion."

"And he didn't help you?"

"No! He did."

"Not enough, then," she said skeptically.

"No, no, he was *extremely* helpful. I'm just inept."

Joan frowned. "Violet, some professional advice. 'I'm inept' is a phrase I never want to hear from an employee. I'm sure most bosses would agree."

She, Orion, and Boris spent a good twenty minutes in her office after that. I busied myself with the crossword and prayed no one would come in, because I still didn't know the price of a ticket.

"Did I get you in trouble?" I asked Orion when he reappeared.

"Nah. I should have trained you better. Let's go over the cash register, okay?"

He taught me. The lesson was disappointingly professional. He was so upset. I bet he never got in trouble.

"Don't let the man get you down, Orion."

"Joan's right. And I'm pretty sure I am 'the man.' "

"Wanna arm-wrestle for it?" I elbowed him, but he just looked down at my puzzle. I had the upper left, but after that, I was stuck. This was the point, normally, where I'd ask my mom or Sam for help.

"If you know one, shout it out," I said.

"You should probably . . . like . . . save that for your break," Orion said. "You can read the info packet if we're slow, okay?"

I slipped the crossword into my back pocket. Truly, the least I could do.

⁕

Orion more or less monosyllabic'd me for the remainder of the week, which was fair. Left to my own devices, I learned a lot about the Bermuda Triangle from the info packet and named the cash register Scrooge McDuck.

Friday night, I cleaned extra hard and slow, resisting my release into the world. It was my first real weekend in Lyric, and I had no plans and no friends. In New York, Friday night meant a flurry of texts and a train ride downtown, for sake-bombing, maybe, or concerts in Brooklyn, or to the bar that didn't card. Maybe we'd meet some NYU kids and they'd invite us back to their party. The beer was bad, but that wasn't the point.

I didn't miss any of it, but I also missed all of it.

I sprayed Windex on the glass *History of Lyric* display and wiped down the photograph of my great-great-great-grandparents. Their clean, shiny faces stared back at me, young-looking but wise. I leaned in close to them, and whispered: "What do you think, Fidelia? How long did it take you to feel happy here?"

"Who're you talking to?"

I whirled. Orion had crept up on me.

"No one. The photograph. Can't a girl commune with her ancestors in peace?"

"Ancestors?"

"They were my great-great-great-grandparents. Didn't Joan tell you?"

"She did *not*," Orion said. His eyes were suddenly wide. "You're *related* to them?"

"Well. Yeah."

"That's sort of awesome."

"I had nothing to do with it." I resumed my cleaning, embarrassed to have been caught talking to a plaque.

"Hey. Listen."

I looked back, and Orion was fiddling with the carabiner on which he kept his keys. I wondered if he rock climbed, or if he just had it to look cool. Who was I kidding? *Of course* he rock climbed.

"Are you doing anything tonight?" he asked.

I almost dropped my Windex. *I beg your pardon?* How did we move so swiftly from "Can you please save your crosswords for your break?" to "Hey, Violet, let's hang"?

"I have this friend. She's super into Lyric history. You wouldn't want to come meet her, would you?"

How silly of me. Orion wanted to impress a girl. Of course.

Even though I was lonely, I hesitated. I wasn't sure I wanted to be paraded around as show-and-tell to help Orion get laid. Then again, my alternative was puzzling with Toby, who started so early at the bakery that he'd be asleep by seven, leaving me alone with my terrible drafts to Sam.

"She's really nice," Orion said. "And for what it's worth, I'd really appreciate it."

"All right. Fine. But Fidelia and Ransome are pretty much just names to me. If your friend's looking for insider info, I've got nothing."

"Totally fine," Orion said. "Your presence will be more than enough."

I wished he didn't look so good when he grinned.

❧

Allow me a quick primer on the history of Lyric, Maine—at least what I knew before Orion introduced me to his friend Liv Stone.

Most of my information was family lore, recited anecdotally by my parents and gathered over many years. My parents themselves had relied on my grandmother's stories and the town's general knowledge, which is all to say I wasn't provided with a bibliography for the following.

Nevertheless: In 1885, my great-great-great-grandmother on my mother's side, Miss Fidelia Rudolph, née Hathaway, boarded the steamship *Lyric* for passage from London to Boston. A March nor'easter sank the ship off the Maine coast. Fidelia was the wreck's sole survivor, though it took a while for that to actually be *revealed*.

See, when Fidelia washed up on shore, she didn't go running into town screaming, "Guys, I'm lucky *and* I persevered!" Instead, she disguised herself as a boy and found work running errands in the house of Ransome Rudolph, my soon-to-be ancestral grandfather. I suppose he eventually discovered she was a woman, because, next thing you know, they were married. Together they made the town official, naming it Lyric after her sunken ship. Then they started laying the groundwork for their long line of descendants, that pesky shipwreck gene popping up every now and then.

Since the *Lyric* sank, there had been a few efforts to locate the ship. Theories held that the wreck lay in the outer islands somewhere, but what with unpredictable tides and lack of funding, there hadn't been any serious attempt at discovery. The *Lyric* may have mattered to this one town, but the wreck wasn't exactly the *Titanic*. Frankly, no one really cared that much. *Their Love Was Our Beginning* was where the story started and ended for most people.

Except my brother and me, ages seven and eight; and Liv Stone, age seventeen.

∞

Orion drove a minivan. Not just any minivan, he told me: Orion's car was the "original minivan," a 1980 Plymouth Voyager, complete with a wood-paneled exterior and beige leather seats. It was also extremely dirty. Half-drunk Arizona iced teas and energy drinks littered the floor of the passenger seat, and on the seat itself there were three empty M&M's bags, four crushed Coke cans, and an Icee cup tacky with melted blue sugar.

"Just shove that stuff onto the floor," Orion said, starting the engine.

I shoved and hopped aboard. "Sweet ride."

"Nothing flashy, but she works."

"Does *she* have a name?"

He looked sheepish.

"Wait!" I said. "Let me guess. Van Morrison. No! Van Helsing."

"Her official name is the Apogee."

"Good name." I sounded like I meant it, which was good, because I did.

"Thanks," he said, and I wanted to throw a parade to celebrate this moment of sincerity between us.

"So tell me about Liv," I said.

"She's one of my oldest friends," Orion said. He kept his eyes on the road and seemed like a good, if cautious, driver, but then again, I didn't have a license. "You know the town motto?"

"Is your love also your beginning?"

"Not quite." He laughed. Subtext: *not yet*. "Liv's got some cool ideas about the motto. About your ancestors' story. She's working at the Lighthouse Museum this summer, over on Bat Wing Point? You know it?"

"Yeah. Never been."

He nodded. "It's pretty cool actually. I'd never been, even, until this past year, besides, like, fourth-grade trips. Mariah's mom—she'll be there tonight, too, Mariah, not her mom, and probably Felix—has made a big difference. It's a good spot for Liv. She's super"—he opened and closed his hand, like he might find the right word in the air—"*bright*."

"Huh." Just because I was off the sauce didn't mean that I wanted to hear him fawn. I changed the subject. "*Orion*'s an unusual name. What's the story there? Are you named for the constellation?"

"My mom likes stars, I think. Liv says Orion's the son of Poseidon, though, so that's cool. She's one of those people who just like retains everything. She knows *so many facts*. She'd kill on *Jeopardy!*, you know?"

Seeing as I didn't have much choice, I tried to imagine the sort of girl Orion Lewis would fall in love with. Someone wood nymphy, I bet. I suspected Liv Stone had a curtain of flaxen hair, a wood-whistle clarinet, and an entourage of assorted woodland creatures. She was, without doubt, under six feet tall.

"Is that a *tape deck*?" I said. I punched the play button and a trumpet blared out at me, clear and fast and frantic.

"*Shit.*" Orion's hand shot toward the console and knocked loose a full, uncapped bottle of Snapple from his cup holder. Dark pink drink sloshed into his lap, and he swerved. An oncoming car honked. Orion careened back toward the shoulder, throwing his arm across my chest and slamming on the brakes. Somewhere in there, I screamed.

"Are you okay?" he asked.

We were safely pulled over. The trumpet was still playing.

"Swell," I said.

Orion's arm had me pinned against the seat, still. He had quite a wingspan.

"I'm so sorry. Are you sure you're okay?" His hand held tight to my right arm, his freckle-less forearm braced across my chest.

"You can let go of me," I said.

"Sorry." He uncurled his fingers. The pads of his fingers were squashed and square, nails bitten down to the quick. Blood rushed back to my arm.

Orion moved with mechanical precision. He turned off the music, then dabbed uselessly at his jeans with the hem of his shirt. He fished the offending Snapple bottle from the pedals, dumped its remains out the half-open window, and tossed the empty bottle toward the graveyard at my feet. Finally, he switched on his blinker and eased back onto the road.

"What the hell was *that*?" I said.

"Nothing. Just practice tapes."

"That was *you*?"

"Nothing serious. Just ideas."

"You *wrote* that?" My arm was still tingling from where he'd gripped me.

He bit his lip. "I dabble."

"Orion Lewis, are you in a *band*?"

"It's complicated." His hands were tight on the steering wheel, and from this angle, his tattoo was more visible than ever. Something juicy had gone down, I could tell.

"C'mon, man, you can tell me. My dad raised us on Bowie and Patti Smith and the Talking Heads and Joy Division. Music is liiiiife, man. Rock and *roooooolllllll*."

He looked at me sidelong. "You're ridiculous, you know that?" he said, but he'd cracked a smile. Mission accomplished. "Liv's brother and I used to play together. Jazz."

"Jazzz, baby! Did you guys break up? Oooh, was it because you fell in love with his sister? A Yoko situation? *West Side Story* meets 'Under the Sea'? Was there a rumble in the aquarium? Was there—"

"He died. Three years ago. Bike accident."

He lifted his chin slightly. I think I said I was sorry. I *hope* I said I was sorry.

"Don't worry," Orion said. "You didn't know."

What I remember next is struggling to breathe. The car had stopped on the side of the road, and we were by the woods. A local spot, he said, don't tell your New York friends. I was sitting down but I was dizzy. His friend was dead. We'd almost hit a car. My friend's friend had jumped out the window once. My brain was on the fritz. Was I going crazy? Lost marbles, like Tootles in *Peter Pan*. Was that—? We were almost in a car accident. I couldn't breathe.

Sam had tried to die.

Orion said something. Sam had tried to die. Orion's door was open. Orion and I had almost died. "Violet?" My thoughts were mashed potatoes, and Sam was in Vermont, learning to eat, like a baby. It was freezing. A noise: a hand shaking dice. "Violet, you okay?" I'm not blacking out, not high, def not an orgasm. The dice clackclackclacked. "Violet, it's okay." A skeleton, playing her own rib cage like a xylophone. "Am I dying?" That was my voice, cut with dice clacks. I spoke and my mouth moved against my thighs. That was weird. I'd folded in half, I guess. My eye sockets were in my knees. My arms cradled my head. I couldn't breathe. Purple and gold galaxies danced on my eyelids.

"I can't—"

Orion's hand was between my shoulder blades, the way you might calm a quaking dog.

"You're not dying," he said. "Deep breaths."

My teeth were chattering. That was the dice noise. The rib noise. My own teeth. Why were my teeth chattering?

"It's okay," Orion said. His hand spread wide and flat. "Deep breaths."

A breath shuddered through my body. Time passed. Each of Orion's fingertips touched my back. My teeth slowed. I thought of Mom, Dad, even Sam telling me it was okay that time I lost my apartment keys and cried. Time passed. Orion's fingers were like a tree frog's. I'd gone through a tree frog phase as a kid and in my head I recited different species until finally, finally, my teeth stopped.

I sat up and the world pitched.

"Slow," Orion said.

I went slow. I leaned against the seat and gazed up at the gray fabric ceiling of the minivan. My teeth clacked once and I steadied my jaw with my hands. My face was wet. I'd been crying. What the fuck had just happened? God, poor Orion.

"Sorry. My body—that was weird. God. Sorry. Your friend—"

"Do you get those a lot?" Orion said.

"What do you mean, those?"

"Panic attacks. My mom gets one, like, every tax season."

"No," I said, because panic attacks weren't part of my repertoire, I'd never had one. Why did cars have fabric ceilings? Why—oh—fuck. I understood what he was trying to say.

"I don't want to have a panic attack," I told him. My voice sounded exposed, young, and Orion's face was full of sympathy.

"Well, it already happened, so all you can do now is go slow. You okay?"

"I think so." I peeled my head from the headrest and looked him in the eye. "I'm sorry about your friend."

"I'm sorry—whatever happened there. Whatever I did to, um. For my driving back there. I'm sorry."

"Were my teeth chattering?"

"Like crazy. You want me to call someone? Or I can take you home—"

"Can we just sit here for a second?"

"For sure."

He got back in the car. We sat there. A breeze blew in from Orion's open door. My tears were drying on my face, and when I surprised myself with a yawn, the salt tracks cracked like riverbeds. I felt like I'd run six marathons and hydrated with iced coffee. I said as much to Orion and he laughed.

"I'd offer you some really old Grapeade, but I'm all out," he said, gesturing at the Snapple bottle.

"The grossest flavor," I said, and he laughed, I laughed, and it felt really good. Then my laugh went wacky, dangerously so. My teeth did a quick Irish jig. Christ almighty. Not even Sam had panic attacks. I would've heard about them. I rubbed my face with my shirt.

"Do I look terrible?" I asked.

"You look fine."

I flipped my mirror down. "I'm *completely* blotchy, Orion."

"You look good. Who cares if you were crying, anyway?"

He was right. Who cared? I slammed the mirror shut. "Let's go meet your girlfriend," I said.

"Take it easy," he said.

"Sorry. Not your girlfriend."

"No, *you* take it easy. Your body's done work just now. Just, like, be nice to yourself, okay?"

The thought had never even occurred to me.

"Oh—um—and—don't say anything to Liv about her brother. She doesn't like when that's the first thing people know about her."

"I'd never."

"I figured," he said, putting his hands in his pockets.

I don't know what it was, exactly, but that *figured* made me feel a little better. Like we were on our way to something. If not friends, then friend*ly*.

We walked through the woods and found ourselves on the edge of a rock slab, big as a baseball diamond, long and flat and sandy gray, a little yellow in the fading sun. We could see all of Lyric below us, the coastline, one street, no stoplights. Three people were grouped around an unlit inflatable lantern, two girls and a boy, and past them, the rock ended and the sky began.

"Wait'll the stars come out. Normally the fog rolls in, but I think it's going to stay clear tonight," Orion said. He walked across the slab, clipping his carabiner around his belt loop as he went.

"*Leeewis!*" called the boy as we walked closer. He had shoulder-length hair and was seated on his heels like a yogi. One of the girls was wearing a baseball cap and smoking a cigarette. The non-smoking girl had a choppy black bob, a nose ring, and a perfectly lipsticked red mouth. That must've been Liv. She wasn't a pixie princess, but she was certainly a babe.

"Felix is hoping you brought weed," the babe said.

"Better. This is Violet. She works at the aquarium."

"You're his underling? Pro tip: he's actually a softie."

"Thanks for that, Mariah," Orion said. The other girl took a drag on her cigarette and Orion turned to her. "She's Fidelia's great-great-great-granddaughter, Liv."

Something whacked Orion in his chest; Felix had pelted him with a flip-flop. Orion pelted him back.

"Boooooo!" Mariah screamed. "I take it back! He's not a softie, he's the worst!"

"Ignore them," Liv said, standing up and reaching out her hand. "They're just upset they don't have a project."

Liv Stone was not the bohemian fairy I'd envisioned. She wore all black—not in a Goth way, and not in a chic New Yorker way either, but in a plain, *black is my uniform* way. Her black dress was a sack that hung to her knees, and she wore black sneakers, even the laces and the soles, and a black Portland Sea Dogs cap. Her hair had been gathered into two thin braids, locks of hair escaping the plaits and sticking out like straw. The only thing flashy about her was a ring that sparkled on her index finger: a huge purple rock in a gold setting, so craggy and rough-hewn it seemed as though it had been ripped directly from the earth. I wondered if that rock had left behind a crater somewhere.

She crushed my hand in a strong handshake, and something thrashed in my stomach, finned and flickering.

Mariah said, "You want a beer? Liv's driving."

"Liv's always driving," Felix said. His right eye moved slower than his left. "That's why we love her."

"*A* reason we love her," said Orion.

Yes beer. No beer. *Take it easy.* I shook my head and sat between Liv and Felix.

"So what's the project?" I asked.

"Liv's a Lyric truther," Mariah said.

Felix waggled his fingers. His right eye was glass, I saw now. "Small-town conspiracy. Big cover-up. WooOOOooo."

"Full disclosure, Felix is extremely woo-woo," Mariah said.

"Mariah, you gotta let the woo-woo reveal that on their own schedule."

"Violet should know what she's getting into with you clowns," Mariah said.

Felix cackled. Orion grinned. Liv's expression was difficult to read beneath the brim of her hat. She brought her cigarette to her lips, inhaled, and the tip bloomed red with heat. Her eyes were wintry.

"I'm just saying," Liv repeated, swallowing her words along with her smoke. "The way this town rallies around this supposed *love story*"—here, she exhaled, and her voice dripped with disdain—"is bewildering. I mean, really. *Their Love Was Our Beginning?*" She scoffed, then looked at me. "No offense. I know they were your people."

"None taken."

"It's just so ridiculous"—"Here we go," said Felix—"so *ridiculous*, Felix, that everyone thinks Fidelia and Ransome's story was a fairy tale! Violet. Would you like to hear the big questions?"

"*Here's* a question," said Felix. "If two trains leave Chicago at six-oh-five p.m. . . ."

"They'd leave two *different* stations," said Mariah.

"If one train leaves Chicago, and one leaves another dimension . . ."

"But now you need the theory of relativity."

"Maybe Violet brought that," said Felix.

"Orion wants to kill us," Mariah said.

"Orion, don't be mad."

"Orion, we love you."

"Orion, ole buddy, ole pal . . ."

"For Pete's sake! I'm not mad! I just want to listen to Liv for fifteen seconds without you two putting on the Goon Show!"

"We all agreed to call us *Mastergoon Theater*, Orion," said Mariah.

"You're right," said Orion, rolling his eyes. "My bad."

"I, for one, *love* Mastergoon Theater," said Liv.

I really hated the smell of cigarettes.

Mariah hooked her thumb toward Orion. "See what I mean? The angriest he gets is 'for Pete's sake.'"

Orion put his head in his hands.

"So . . . the big questions?" I said to Liv.

"Thank you," she said. "To start: Why didn't Fidelia just write her family after she washed up on shore? Why did she disguise herself as a boy? Was she hiding from something, and if so, from whom? Why did Ransome just *give* this strange, beaten-up boy a job in his home? Think about how fucked up she must have looked. She'd just pulled herself out of the sea! And why doesn't anyone think it's weird that Ransome *married the woman he thought was a boy*? And why, then, would she choose to reveal that she'd survived the wreck, months later? Yet here we are. Over a century past, and still celebrating their love."

"Maybe they were, uh, gender-blind," I offered.

"In Maine in 1885? Yeah, right. Even if they were, trust me, that's not how people in this town are interpreting the story." Liv licked two fingers, clamped them around the end of her cigarette, then tucked the butt into the front pocket of her dress. "The things I do for you, Orion, you see this?"

"You're doing it for the *planet*, Liv, not for me."

"Are we done yet?" said Felix.

"The ship, Liv," Orion said.

Liv's arm shot out and she gripped Orion by his shoulder. My heart fluttered—because of them, or for them, I didn't know.

"The ship!" Liv cried. "How could I forget!"

"Liv, do you subject my mother to this every single day?" Mariah asked.

"Say more, Professor Stone! I sense I'm about to become a convert!"

"I will say more, Felix, thank you. Final question: Why hasn't the ship been found?"

"What, you think the wreck was a hoax?" I asked. That seemed extreme.

She shook her head. "Of course not. I just think the fact that no one wants to look for the ship is indicative of a larger problem. No one wants to address the fact that thousands of other people died. Everyone just wants to celebrate the love story. *Literally: no one wants to look for the wreckage.* Consider it a metaphor: no hunting for the ship, no hunting for the underbelly of Ransome and Fidelia's story."

I made a mental note to start encouraging people to *consider things a metaphor.* Also to use the words *underbelly* and *indicative.*

"My mom calls her the wrexpert," Mariah said.

"As in wreck expert," Orion said.

"Yeah, Orion, I think she gets it," said Mariah.

Felix clapped wildly. "This girl's gonna change the world!"

"I'm not *trying* to change the world," Liv countered. "I just don't understand why no one in this town will turn the rock over." She fluttered her hand along her acned cheekbones, and I went to gather my hair and touched only bare neck with dirty, rock-dusty fingers. The sensation was startling, like missing the last step on a flight of stairs.

"Anyway," Liv said. "It's cool to meet you. You must know a ton about your family."

"Hardly. I'm sorry."

"Don't apologize. You're perfect," Mariah said. She shot me an enormous thumbs-up.

"Tobias Rudolph is your family, right? From the bakery? We were supposed to meet, but he never got back to me," Liv said.

"Ooh, can you get us free blackberry pie?" Mariah gasped.

"Toby's my uncle, and maybe on the free pie. Sorry he never got back to you. He's not the most responsible. But you should come poke around our house if you want. There's bound to be some stuff lying around."

Liv's eyes widened. "Seriously?"

"Sure. I'll be at the aquarium during the day, but otherwise, yeah."

"I told my parents I'd see a movie with them tomorrow. But next Saturday? One week from tomorrow?"

"She'll show up," Mariah warned.

"Sure," I said. "I am embarrassingly free."

Felix propped himself up on his elbows. "I don't think you realize this, Miss Violet, but you just made Professor Stone's *life*."

Felix lifted himself into bridge pose, then did a back walkover.

"Show-off," scolded Mariah.

"Nice work, Lewis," Liv said.

She reached over and slapped a mosquito on Orion's calf. She didn't even stop talking as she did it, or warn him. Just slapped his calf and carried on.

ⅆ

The night grew dark and the sky fell in a starry dome around us, so panoramic and dizzying it hurt my eyes. I craned my neck back so far my vertebrae crunched. The conversation meandered, then puttered, and Felix and Mariah went to pee in the woods. I was left alone with Orion and Liv. They were playing slaps now, their hands hovering over each other, quick reflexes and stinging heat. I felt like I was in one of those tourist-trap vortexes where marbles rolled uphill. They weren't *together*, according to Orion, but I still felt like a third wheel.

"I'm gonna get a better look at the stars," I said.

"Just don't go too close to the edge. It's a far drop," Orion said, and Liv smacked his hands.

Away from Orion and Liv, I stretched my eyes wider, and then, when they couldn't go as wide as I wanted, I literally held them open with my fingers. I was weirdly aware of my eyeballs as *eyeballs*, moving and wet. I wondered if the stars were this good in Vermont. Mom and Dad probably couldn't see anything besides the moon, which was full-ish, waxing or waning, who knew. I wished that I were the sort of person who could identify constellations, point to the sky and declare, *Cassiopeia*.

"Glass half-full, Chatterjee."

"No way she'll ever say yes. You heard her—she *hates* a love story."

Felix and Mariah, talking in low voices, closer to me than they realized. Sound carried well across the rock.

"But their love story was our beginning!" Felix said. "Lewis is a fox. I'd keep him on the hook, too."

"You don't have her willpower. You'd make out with him after ten minutes."

"Poor guy has gone without action for *so long.*"

"Oh, fuck off, Felix, she doesn't owe him access to her vagina."

"That's not what I *meant*. Come on, Mariah, you know I'm a feminist."

"Fair-weather feminist, more like."

"Hi?" I called cautiously.

"Oh, shit," said Felix, "we forgot to swivel."

A phone flashlight popped on: They were on the edge of the woods. Felix patted the ground beside him.

"Sorry—I wasn't trying to—"

"Eavesdrop?" Mariah said.

"C'mon, Mariah, she'll learn about the Orion-and-Liv saga soon enough. I'm telling you, if we all just talk about this, get it out in the open . . ."

I glanced toward Orion and Liv. They had a way of being together that made me ache. During the Year of Wild, there had been lots of bedrooms, lots of tongues and mouths, lots of hands up my shirt and down my pants—but there hadn't been anyone who'd looked at me the way Orion looked at Liv Stone. There hadn't been anyone who realized I was being bitten by a mosquito before I did.

"How long have they been a thing?" I asked.

"A thing for years. A couple for never. The heart craves the familiar," Felix said.

"It's not really any of our business," Mariah said, not meanly, just to move us along. She gestured for me to sit and I joined them, feeling suddenly shy.

"So," Mariah said warmly, "where're you from?"

"New York City," I said.

"Ah! New York is my destiny!" said Felix.

"New York's not a bad idea for you, actually, Felix," Mariah said. "I read about this psychic a few years back who scammed the shit out of these rich New Yorkers. City dwellers are the true suckers," she said, sounding quite happy about it. "And what brings you here, Violet?"

"Um—my mom grew up here."

"She wanted you to experience the torture firsthand?" Mariah said.

"Is Lyric that bad?" I asked.

"Not if you have friends. Which you do," she said. She patted me on the knee, and I felt, in the best way, like we were in kindergarten, our friendship decided with one easy exchange.

"Yeah, at least you found us in this wack town, which is

evidence, Mariah, *that energy in the universe has a pattern and we meet the people we need to meet through its seemingly random energy.*"

"That was barely English, and correlation does not imply causation."

"She says I can't start a coven."

"I said you should think about what it means, as a man, to start a group that's traditionally female."

"But the whole point is inclusivity!"

"I really can't have this argument with you again, Felix."

"So we *are* arguing."

"God. No. What I'm saying is . . ."

In the dark, far from us and beside each other, Orion and Liv were so close they might've been one person.

⚭

When I got home, Toby was on the phone. By the all-too-familiar way he was mashing the heel of his hand into his eye socket, I knew he was talking to my mom. He saw me and practically threw the phone at me, saying, "Hold on, Margaret, here she is," before rushing off.

Mom (suspicious): Where were you?

Violet (trying hard to cooperate): Out with people.

M (long pause): What *kind* of people?

V: Heroin addicts, Mom.

M: Heroin's a huge problem in this country, Violet, particularly in Lyric. Toby volunteered for a while at the needle exchange, I believe. I'm sure he's got some stories to share. Would you care to talk about the dangers of opioids? What it does to a body? What I see every day at the hospital?

V: You're a pediatric surgeon, Mom.

M: My point exactly.

[*That* shuts Violet up.]

V: They were normal people, Mom. Kids from work.

M (sighs): I'm sorry. I'm just worried. Why did you turn your phone off?

V: I don't have service.

[silence]

M: We miss you here.

[silence]

M: We spoke to Sam last night. I think he'd really like to hear from you.

V: He hates the phone.

M: Why don't you write to him? You know how much he loves letters. You're not that far away from him, you know. You could even go visit. Toby would take you, I'm sure.

[silence]

M: Toby told me you're trying to disappear.

[Silence, shocked this time. Violet's forgotten this was her goal. How has she forgotten? She'll start now, on this phone call. She won't say another word.]

M: Honey . . . that made me so sad to hear. Disappearing? That's not you. You take up so much *space*. You walk into a room and people pay attention. Boys, girls, young, old. Not because of how you look, but because of who you are. Dramatic and charming and *big*. You have such a presence, honey. And when people look at you, you light up!

[Violet thinks of the perfect Halloween costume: Attention Whore. Maybe she could rig up a spotlight, somehow, and dress like a *Cabaret* dancer.]

M: Write to Sam, honey. We miss you. Don't disappear.

[Violet says nothing and hangs up softly, so softly she bets her mom doesn't even notice. Mission accomplished.]

∞

Toby was doing the puzzle. I hated puzzles. Especially this one.

"Why did you tell my mom I wanted to disappear?" I said to him.

"Because I was worried," Toby said honestly. "I'm *still* worried."

"Well, don't be. Just ignore me, okay? Better yet, just pretend I'm not even here."

IN WHICH OUR HEROINE SPENDS THE ENTIRE NEXT WEEK ATTEMPTING TO WRITE ONE MEASLY LETTER TO HER BROTHER

DRAFT #1

Saturday, June 18

Dear Sam,
Remember me, your long-lost sister?

DRAFT #2

Tuesday, June 21

Dear Sam,
Remember that Halloween we went as a pair of dice? It was such a good costume.

Today, I'm writing you from the Lyric Aquarium gift shop. Slow day. Every day is slow. I continue to be the world's most useless employee. This morning, a kid named Andy came in—he comes in a lot, according to my coworker. He's about eight, and a complete brainiac, and asked me what was effectively an exam question about the gender roles of the potbellied sea horse (NB: we don't even have potbellied sea horses).

When I didn't know the answer, he stared at me a long time and said, "How *did* you get a job here?"

Meanwhile, I've fallen into obsession with my off-limits coworker. He's totally in love with this other girl, but still, I find myself having some seriously vivid dreams in which he features prominently. Dream Orion has a delicious mouth.

I'm sure this is really relevant to your life right now.

DRAFT #3

Thursday, June 23

Dear Sam,

Remember this past spring, how you helped me sneak out? Both of us walking through the apartment together, timing our footsteps so it sounded just like you going to the fridge. You had to breathe through your mouth because your allergies were so bad. My clompy high-heeled boots dangled from my hand. I think of your face as you watched me leave, on the cusp of speaking. It was in May. Do you remember what you were going to say? What if you'd said it? What if I'd asked?

When I finally got to those parties, told them the elaborate tale of my escape, people called me Fun. *Even when my lipstick smeared across my face, or I fainted when I was too high, or I threw up. Violet, you're* FUN.

I didn't want to be Fun in Lyric. Fun was thoughtless. I wanted to disappear. I shaved my head. I wore the plainest clothes I could think of, like my disappearing uniform. I turned off my phone, like everyone in the world seems to think is the answer. In Lyric, I'd be a withering wallflower. That's why Mom and Dad sent me here, right?

Then, today, I was locking up my bike outside Toby's bakery. His blackberry pie is so good *and it stains your teeth purple, like your teeth in the hospital. I was locking up my bike, thinking of you, and someone drove by and yelled,* Sick ride, dyke! *and I yelled back,* REAL CLEVER, PAL, *projecting from the diaphragm like I'd learned on Broadway, so loud I wonder if you heard me in Vermont.*

These tourists on the sidewalk stared, and I was embarrassed, but it also felt really, really good to yell like that. To have people look.

Mom told me I could never disappear, and you know what? She's right. And at this point, I don't even think I want to.

So screw disappearing.

Disappearing sucks.

Life's a whole lot easier when you're Fun, anyway.

FUN'S NIGHT OUT: LYRIC EDITION

That same Thursday night, two hours after bailing on her correspondence and sneaking past her sleeping uncle, Fun sits in the back booth of the Lyric Pub with her new friend, Rus. Or was it Gus? Fun doesn't care—no one's carded her and Rus/Gus is handsome enough, so the night's off to a great start.

"You should come see my boat," Rus/Gus says, one hand on her knee. He smells faintly of smoke and engine oil, and he's bought her three tequilas so far. His beard is gray in patches. If the man by the vending machine was too old, this man is *definitely* too old. He hasn't asked Fun her age, but if he does, she's decided she'll say *nineteen*. Older, but not yet twenty. This feels like the right amount of lying.

The Lyric Pub's not exactly New York, but Fun's not complaining: Thursday night turns out to be karaoke night, which promises great entertainment. There's a vending machine in the back that sells cigarettes, which is funny. The table's littered with lime rinds, her lips sting with salt, and she's most of the way to forgetting herself. She's forgotten her brother (almost). She's forgotten the sharpness of her mother's voice in the hospital, or at least it's gone muffled around the edges. She's forgotten the nice things, too: dancing with her dad to "Rebel Rebel," how she and her mom would sometimes sit in the park, eat candy, and watch the dogs go by.

Rus/Gus moves his hand up her thigh. Fun is not alarmed. In fact, she's pleased. Everything is going according to plan: the drinks, the guy, the touching. She's done this a thousand times during the Year of Wild, disappeared into bedrooms while the party carries on outside the closed door. She's liked it. Hooking up always feels good. She's never done anything she hasn't wanted. She knows she's lucky.

"The boat's just down in the harbor," Rus/Gus says. "You want to come see?"

The edges of Rus/Gus's molars, up by his gums, are blue, like people of her parents' generation.

Okay, maybe Fun hasn't done *this*, *specifically* a thousand times.

"You okay, hon?" The bartendress is upon them, stacking her empty tequila glasses, looking wary. Her hair's in a greasy bun, and she looks like the singer of a cool lesbian punk band Fun saw once, black tank top, black jeans, strong arms. She's got that same expression her mother gets back home, when she looks at Fun, when she looks at Fun's brother. . . .

Nope. No. Don't go there. Don't forget: Fun's a regular girl with a regular family.

"Aren't you Toby's niece?" the bartendress says.

"No."

"I saw you in the bakery the other day."

"Leave us alone, Frieda."

"Fuck off, Rus."

Ah! It *was* Rus!

She turns to me again. "I need to see some ID."

Rus puts his arm around Fun's shoulders. Fun hands the bartendress an excellent fake that she ordered from the internet. Frieda doubles, and Fun sways a little bit, even though she's sitting down. Behind the bartendress, a man is setting up the karaoke microphones on a stage. The bar's getting more and more crowded, faces Fun doesn't recognize. Good. Fun loves a crowd.

"I have to run this," Frieda says. "Doll. You sure you're good? Is there anyone I can call for you?"

The bartendress's face is so full of concern Fun almost takes her up on it. Her uncle would be mad, sure, but didn't she want to be different? A call home would certainly be different. But if Fun goes home, the spell will be broken. She won't be Fun anymore. She'll just be Violet.

She'd rather go to Rus's boat, even if he does have blue molars.

"One more round," Fun says.

Rus kisses her on the cheek. Fun smiles. She's glad to be back to her normal self. It feels—if not *good*—then at least familiar. Familiar, she supposes, is its own kind of good.

Two singers take the karaoke stage. They've picked a song that Fun knows. She can sing along in her head, though she'd never sing out loud. She doesn't sing anymore. They're off-key, but swaying with their arms around each other, having a ball. They seem like best friends. Fun doesn't really have a best friend; she's too Fun for that. There is some strange feeling in the pit of her stomach—what is that? Longing? They're off-key, grinning, drunk. That one girl's cute. But that's not it. This feeling is like: nostalgia for something that didn't happen. No—nostalgia for something that *could've* happened, if Fun were a different person with a different life.

Rus watches her watch the singers. He thinks he understands.

"Let's get you up there," he says.

"No." Fun doesn't sing. Fun hates musicals. Fun's never heard of Broadway.

"Okay," says Rus. "No singing. How 'bout we leave, then? Right now?"

Rus has his hand tight around her wrist. Fun feels a funny jolt: her longing has turned to fear. How odd, she thinks clumsily, that she's never felt real fear in New York, but here, in this little town . . .

Fun glances toward the door.

"Don't tell me you're changing your mind," he says, like that is the worst crime.

His grip is painful and he pulls her from the booth. She's not Fun anymore. She's Violet, and like her mother taught her, she yells, makes a scene. She takes a glass from the table and throws it as hard as she can against the floor. He drops her wrist, Frieda yells, and Rus calls her a psycho bitch, and that's fine, just fine, because that's how she feels, plus which, she's already out the door and halfway down the street.

It's not even 10:00 p.m. Children are still awake, sitting with their families at the ice cream shop. Teenagers are loitering outside the movies, aimless, happy. Violet's running. She forgot her bike. She knows who she is but she feels away from herself. This happened sometimes in the city. She'd see things from above, her eyes separate from her head, her body half-gone like the Cheshire cat's.

She's just about to pass the general store, when she recognizes two people in the parking lot. Orion's carrying an armful of candy and Liv's got a pack of cigarettes. Violet freezes on the sidewalk like a scared little bunny. Maybe they won't see her. Orion gets in the van, but Liv looks down the sidewalk and meets her eyes. Gently, gently, she raises the pack of cigarettes in greeting.

Violet pulls a zipper across her lips.

Liv mouths: *You okay?*

Violet considers this. She can't remember the last time someone her own age asked her this, really asked her. She can't remember the last time she answered honestly. Slowly, she shakes her head no.

Liv points to the van, as if to say, *Want to come?* Violet shakes her head again, and then Liv does something inexplicable: she lays her hand flat across her own chest and presses.

Violet's breath catches. She's never really thought of her heart before. The heart's a muscle that works to keep her alive. Works to keep this other girl alive, too. Two muscles squeezing over and over to keep them upright, all for the purpose of this moment, right now.

They're standing far away, but Violet can feel Liv's hand on her own heart.

GO-BETWEEN

I might have written that whole night off as a dream. I might have, were it not for my loving, slightly unorthodox uncle, who burst into my room that morning before sunrise and cried, "I had quite an interesting call from Frieda at the Lyric Pub!"

I squinted awake. The clock read 4:02 a.m. I had a splitting headache, a series of singing cuts on my ankle—glass shrapnel, I figured—and a horrible memory of Rus's hand on my wrist. And something else . . . at the end of the night . . .

Liv's hand on my heart. For a split second, even through my hangover, I went fizzy and alert with the memory.

"Up and at 'em, tiger. Day's about to start at the bakery. Thought I'd give you a ride to work since I'm already up. Let you mull things over in the bright light of day."

"It's the middle of the night," I said, pulling a pillow over my head. The room pitched like a boat. I needed to be horizontal for at least another eight hours.

"The teenage girl who's been out drinking and subsequently terrified her uncle gets the worm. That's how that saying goes, right?" He yanked off my comforter. "Violet. Seriously. Out of bed, now. We need to talk. I'll meet you in the car."

Somehow, I managed to obey. I dressed and blundered outside, and we drove through inky darkness in silence. In the blue light, Toby's face wore a look of supreme disappointment. I leaned my head against the window and the night came back to me, stronger this time. Toby may have been disappointed, but I couldn't *believe* how badly I'd slipped up. I was supposed to be different, but last night had been a disaster. Exactly the same as New York. Worse, even.

Except the ending. The glass, the heart. That'd been different. Jarringly so.

"How do you feel?" Toby asked. His voice was quieter, calmer than it'd been in my room.

"Like shit," I said into the window.

"Frieda said you threw a glass."

"I'll pay for it."

"That's not my point. Were you—is everything all right? What happened?"

I considered this. Nothing happened. Everything happened. The answer lay somewhere in the middle, murky and difficult to articulate, especially with a hangover. I was so tired. I went with old reliable.

"I'm fine," I said. "I just overdid it. I won't again, I promise. Are you going to tell my mom?"

"Haven't decided. You sure you're okay? Why the glass?"

I wondered how much Frieda had said. "Am I in trouble?"

"Not in the traditional sense," Toby said. "You can't do this, Violet. I was terrified. *Am* terrified."

"I'm sorry," I said, and it sounded weak, but I meant it. Disappointing Toby felt particularly awful. He'd trusted me completely, for absolutely no reason at all, and left me baked goods and notes from ghosts. He didn't deserve what I'd put him through.

The car ride was short. We were already pulling into the aquarium's parking lot. Everything looked different in the dark, empty, a little sad. I wanted to be a better niece, a better sister, a better version of myself.

"I don't know if you're in trouble," Toby said slowly. "You're more in Serious Worry. I'm thinking mandatory puzzle hour every day after work. Structure and habit can be wildly transformational when one is spinning out. They've helped me a lot. We have more in common than you think, you know. That's a large part of why your mom sent you here."

"Not because she hates me?"

"Vi. Is that what you think?"

I fell silent, staring into the dark parking lot. I hated myself a lot of the time. I wouldn't blame my mom if she did, too.

"Violet," Toby said, in a soft way that made me feel like I was in danger of cracking in half, "your mom loves you so much. She thinks she failed you."

That was laughable. If my pub escapade had made anything clear, it was that *I* was the failure in the family. I didn't say that, though. Instead, sounding far more hurt than I intended, I asked, "If she loves me so much, why'd she ship me off here?"

Toby placed a warm hand on the back of my head, like I was

a baby. The simple kindness of the gesture almost undid me. Toby and I'd always gotten along, but we'd never really *talked*. I hadn't known he'd be so gentle.

"A change of scene. Space. A chance to gather your thoughts." Toby paused. "You should talk to her about how you feel."

"And tell her what a transformation I'm making? She'd be so proud."

"You'd be surprised," Toby said. "She's a really great listener if you give her a chance."

"What if she . . ."

"What if she . . ." Toby echoed gently.

What if she doesn't like me anymore? I was going to say. But it sounded so babyish. I couldn't talk about my mom anymore. It hurt too much.

"This is a punishment, right?" I said, pointing to the aquarium. "Being dropped off at work six hours early with a hangover?"

"Work? This isn't work. This is Lyric's hip after-hours spot, Club Tentacle."

"Ha-ha."

Toby shook his head. "It's not a punishment per se. A chance to clear your head, more like. Unless you'd rather come to the bakery. But the ovens are really hot, and I thought at least the aquarium would be cool."

"It is freezing in there," I said.

He reached into the backseat of his car and handed me a blue-and-pink windbreaker.

"Weird parenting move, Toby."

"Kid," he said, ignoring the dig, "next time you find yourself in a situation like that, you call me. No matter where you are or what time it is. Okay?"

"There won't be a next time."

"But on the off chance there is," Toby insisted. "You promise?"

"I promise," I said, but promising felt superfluous. I already knew that last night had been a turning point: a real one. I wouldn't go bananas like that again. I didn't want to. The Lyric Pub had been Year of Wild Violet's last horrifying hurrah.

"You have keys?" Toby said, nodding toward the aquarium.

"Uh-huh."

"Good," he said. "We're gonna keep talking, you and I. Open lines of communication, so to speak. Promise I won't make it too painful. In the meantime, enjoy Club Tentacle. I hear the rays can cut a serious rug."

※

In the dark, the aquarium was different. I waited for my eyes to adjust, then walked through the blue shadows toward the touch tanks. The world around me was still, but in darkness, underwater had come alive. The creatures in the tanks were brighter, their colors more vibrant, their movements agile and pronounced. Grapefruit-pink anemones waved their tentacles hello. Tangerine-spiked sea cucumbers breathed across the mossy tank floor. A chunky scarlet sea star shuffled across a rock. I touched a purple urchin and the urchin actually responded, catching my index finger in its spiny grip.

A feeling of wonder stirred in my chest. Maybe this wasn't what Toby had meant by clearing my head, but in the urchin's grip, I felt smooth and cool as sea glass. I understood, suddenly, why Orion loved the aquarium. Maybe I could love it, too. It had been so long since I cared about something.

And at the very least, the Lyric Aquarium was more scenic than the Lyric Pub.

Hours stretched in front of me. A deep de-scumming, I decided, would be good penance for last night, a fresh start. I tidied the gift shop, refolded the sweatshirts, scraped the grime from between Scrooge McDuck's buttons. I stocked the bathrooms and mopped the floors. I emptied out the industrial fridge upstairs and scrubbed fish juice from the insides, vacuumed Boris's hair from the break room couch. All of that, and I still had an hour to kill, so I lay down on the fresh couch to catch a quick nap.

I'd barely closed my eyes, when I heard a noise coming from beneath me. Not a noise: a harmonica. A song. I crept downstairs to investigate, keeping my footsteps light as I followed the tune to its source.

The sound, I understood when I rounded the corner, was Orion. He was standing in front of the far tank, playing harmonica to Louise the Lobster.

Correction: he was standing in front of the far tank, *serenading* Louise the Lobster.

He was playing a zipper-breathed, bluesy version of "Moon River," and while the aquarium may have been lackluster in some ways, its acoustics, it turned out, were fantastic.

The melody ached through the space so richly that I felt the song behind my eyes, my nose, and my mouth, that feeling of almost crying, of your nose brightening, pinging, prickling. A warm hum spread through my chest. The song was almost the same feeling as Liv's hand on my heart, all the way across the street. The notes buzzed through me, leaving me a little weepy, aching for someone I could call my huckleberry friend.

When the song ended, I erupted. "That was *beautiful*."

Orion spun, startled, and hid the harmonica behind his back. "Shoot. You're here early."

"Are private concerts a regular thing? Because if they are, I'm going to make early arrival a habit."

He looked embarrassed. "I play to her sometimes."

"Is this like a sing-to-your-plants sort of thing?"

"Sort of. It's dumb."

"I bet it's not."

Orion considered for a moment, and then launched into a half-mumbled explanation: "Lobsters don't have ears. But they emit vibrations. Probably for self-defense. Maybe for communication. You know how humming to periwinkles brings them out of their shells? I thought with maybe the vibrations of the harmonica . . ."

"You could talk to her?"

"It's not exactly scientific," Orion admitted bashfully.

He was like Doctor Dolittle. It was the sweetest thing I'd ever heard.

"Who *cares* about scientific? I love it. You sound really good, also. From a purely melodic standpoint. I mean, independent of communicating with animals."

He put the harmonica in his back pocket. "Thanks. I haven't played in a while, so . . . that actually means a lot. Hey, I'm glad you're here early. I think you're ready to move out of the gift shop and onto the floor. You want to learn about some sea creatures?"

I nodded. I wanted all the facts.

⚶

"Have you always wanted to study marine biology?" I asked him later that afternoon. It was so nice out, Joan had sent us both home early, but we'd decided to eat lunch on the picnic tables behind the aquarium. We'd sat on the same side to better look at the now-defunct Exploration Zone, a rocky shore ideal for tide pooling. In those tide pools, Sam and I had seen miniature worlds. *From the small sea snail, to the great blue whale, everyone has feelings. . . .*

Maybe I could show Sam the aquarium at night, one day.

"I was pretty shy as a kid," Orion said. "Animals were easier. We had so many pets growing up, like dogs, guinea pigs, bunnies, you name it. We had this wounded raccoon once for a few weeks before the shelter had space. My mom still feeds feral cats."

"I wish we had a dog. A really, really big one, you know? My dad feels too guilty in the city."

"Yeah, our last dog, Faye, was huge—a Lab-and-hound mix. She died in April, though. It's the worst part about having pets," Orion said simply. "Marine biology, though. Living here . . . I mean, the ocean's on your mind all the time when it's your backyard, and plus half the people in Lyric make their money fishing. But it'd be cool working here, regardless. The ocean's got so much to discover. I mean, starting with just the basics, do you know we've explored less than five percent of the world's oceans? Seventy percent of the planet is salt water, and we know, like, zilch."

"Sort of like the human brain."

"How so?"

I studied the carvings on the picnic table, jagged graffiti done with penknives. ALL U NEED IS LOVE someone had written, and beneath that, in Sharpie, someone else had added YEAH RIGHT.

"Well, like antidepressants, for example. Psychiatrists don't even know the science behind how they work. They just know that they do. Or don't, depending on the patient." Sam had been on so many different med cocktails that I'd stopped keeping track. "What about Liv? Is the truthing a new thing?"

Orion inspected his sandwich in thought. "She always liked history. As a kid, she was really into Rasputin. She went through a pretty hilarious Goth phase. Like, cat collars and black braces. Will and I gave her so much shit for that." He half laughed. "The truthing started round the time he died. Gave her a thing to think about."

I understood distracting yourself. Unfortunately, I distracted myself in significantly less intellectual and thought-provoking ways. Such as smashing glasses on the floor of the local pub.

"What was Will like?" I asked.

"Smart, like Liv. But less book smart. He liked taking things apart and putting them back together again. He liked music, not as much as me, but he played the sax, and we had this idea. . . ." Orion rubbed his hand along his thigh, steadying himself.

"We don't have to get into it."

"No, I was just thinking it's good to talk about him. It's not like I don't think about him. People don't normally ask, because they don't want to upset me. But . . ."

"It's not like you forget."

"Exactly. You're not going to remind me of anything I'm not thinking of twelve thousand times a day, anyway," he said. "But yeah. We had a harebrained scheme that we were going to build a boat and sail around the Caribbean. We actually started building it in my garage. Liv was in on it, too, kind of, would sit there while we worked. She thought we were idiots, actually. That we'd all drown if we ever finished the thing. But she kept coming."

"Do you love her?" I asked. I tried to keep my voice casual, which was tricky. *Love* was so far from my experience that I could barely say the word. Orion, though, didn't even bat an eye.

"I know it's a cliché. Best friend's sister. Girl next door."

"She'd probably have a field day taking that one down."

"Believe me," Orion said, "she already has."

"She's supposed to come over tomorrow. To research, or whatever."

"She told me."

I traced the heart on the picnic table, thinking of how they looked like one person that night on the rock. Orion's music, Liv's hand on her heart. *A saga*, Felix had said. I'd vowed to turn off the romance channel this summer, but what about helping other people *tune in to* the romance channel? That was . . . noble. Good. They both deserved a good thing.

"I could talk to Liv for you, if you want," I said.

Orion scowled. "You mean, like, *woo her*?"

"Sure."

"Terrible idea. Better to just be direct. Besides, she knows how I feel."

"Maybe not. Have you *told* her? Expressly? Been like, Liv, I like you, let's date?"

"Okay, no, but—"

"Real direct, Orion."

"It's hard!"

"Exactly! Which is where I come in. Subtly, obviously."

"Aren't we past this stage in our lives?"

"Dude, no. My parents met on a blind date in their thirties! This won't be some middle-school clusterfuck. I'm good at this. I set my best friend up with her boyfriend!"

Really, I'd poured them both shots and they'd taken care of the rest, but Orion didn't need to know that. I just wanted to convince him I could Yente the hell out of this situation. *Matchmaker, matchmaker, make me a match. . . .*

"Look, I'll show you photographic proof."

I pulled out my phone and swiped through pictures of my former life to find one of my (not-exactly-best) friend and her boyfriend.

"Wait," Orion said, leaning over my shoulder. Our faces were close, and our shoulders were touching. Neither of us moved away. "Is that *you*?"

Oh God. It was.

Orion snatched my phone and brought the screen inches from his face. Last night had been a good reminder of my former life, but I'd gotten so used to my seal hair that Orion had recognized me even before I had, dressed to the nines for a Year of Wild Party: a regrettable velvet mini-miniskirt (it was *December* and *freezing*), a Solo cup in one hand, spiked heel boots. I'd had blood blisters on the tips of my toes for weeks.

"*Shoot*," he said.

I grabbed the phone back.

"I mean that in the nicest way possible," he said.

"I'm sure."

"You look . . . I mean, *yikes*."

"How can you say you're not good with words, Orion?" I sneaked another look at myself. Actually, my lipstick that night had been kind of cool.

"Violet. Are you a secret party animal? Were you all up in the New York Club?"

"It wasn't a big deal. Just normal high school."

Just normal high school. That's really how it had been. Tall, loud, drunk, down = normal. I wasn't weird, at least not in anyone else's estimation. Sam was weird. Sam, smart, skinny Sam, who sometimes ate Splenda packets for lunch, paper and all (*so* fucking weird, my "friends" agreed, and I laughed, because if you laughed with them, you hurt less); Sam, who avoided the third-floor bathroom because the fluorescents were too bright and the mirror was warped; who once, in the second-floor bathroom (softer lighting, less foot traffic), was spotted slapping himself across his own face, hard. I thought of telling my parents about that one. The hitting, I mean. I didn't. Sometimes rumors are just rumors, like the one about me hooking up with the substitute math teacher.

Turned out I had it wrong: if you laughed, you hurt even worse.

Orion was still looking at me as though I were a complicated painting he was trying to figure out. There was nothing complicated about us, though. Sam imploded, and I exploded. We could have been a traveling circus act: the Fabulous Siblings Concave and Convex.

"You look better now," Orion said finally. "I mean, you didn't look bad before. Or now." I watched him flounder, and my heart squeezed. "You just look like you now. With this."

There was static. The romance channel. Searching.

"Don't let Boris hear you talk like that. He'll get jealous."

Orion laughed and the static was gone.

"So do I have your permission to talk to Liv?"

"Why do you even want to?"

"Good question," I said. "Um . . ."

I thought. I wanted to give him a real answer. It wasn't just about *me* being behind the scenes. It was about *them*. Liv's hand, Orion's harmonica. They were like two halves of the same whole, it seemed.

"You two make sense," I said finally.

"Yeah. That's how I feel, too." Orion sighed. "All right. I still don't think it's a great idea, but you can talk to her. Just be cool, okay?"

"Subzero," I promised.

He smiled again, showing that gap-toothed smile of which I was becoming problematically fond.

The whole truth of why I wanted to set them up didn't occur to me till later that night, when I was sorting through puzzle pieces with Toby, helping him build the border. It was true that Orion and Liv made sense to me. But I also just wanted to be near them, bask in their bug-slapping closeness. Their friendship seemed so deep that I could pencil drop inside and never hit the bottom—just float along between them, weightless and held.

ELEMENTS: INVOKED

Toby left the oven on Friday night. By morning, the house *reeked* of gas.

"Why are you baking in the *house*? At night? You own a freaking bakery! What are Liv and I supposed to do now?"

"Just show her the beach! Sometimes, Violet, a man just wants to midnight bake. And, *PS*, you're lucky I'm letting this social event take place. Only because you made such great progress on the puzzle yesterday. Well, also because I know the Stones, and there's no way they'd let their daughter rage at Club Tentacle." Toby threw open the kitchen windows and the screen door, then handed me a key lime bar. "How's that taste?"

Even through the gas smell, the bar was tangy and creamy, graham cracker crust spreading across my tongue like yummy Florida sand.

"It's very good," I said begrudgingly. "But we're supposed to be doing research. In the house."

"So to be clear, this isn't a hot date, then?"

"No. Literally, her friends call her Professor Stone. We're looking into Fidelia and Ransome's backstory."

"Sounds pretty sexy, if you ask me," Toby said, waggling his eyebrows.

"Never mind."

I took a second bar and trudged outside to wait in the driveway. What had kept him up so late, driven him toward midnight sugar and key limes? I wondered if he was lonely here in this big house, if he missed Maude the raccoon. I ate the second bar whole.

The day was off to a bad start. If I'd had Professor Stone's number, I would've flaked with one easy text. Instead, I just felt bonkers nervous, oversugared. I had no idea where we'd start looking for info on Ransome and Fidelia, even if we *could* go into the house, *plus* I had no idea what to say about Orion. Not to mention the whole hand-on-heart episode.

Liv arrived wearing the exact same outfit she'd been wearing both times I'd seen her: black sack dress, black sneakers, black Sea Dogs hat. Scarecrow braids. Big purple rock. Like me, she was a fan of the uniform.

"You didn't have to, like, wait for me," she said.

"I'm not," I said, and explained about the gas. "We can just go down to the beach until the place airs out a bit."

She looked skeptical. "How much walking will be involved?"

"Not much."

"Great," she said, "as long as I can smoke down there."

"Certainly preferable to smoking in the house with a gas leak."

Despite her coastal upbringing, Liv wasn't a natural

outdoorswoman. She lagged behind me, an unlit cigarette dangling from her lips, slower even than I'd been as a kid. I did my best not to giggle, but this Liv was so different from the Professor Stone I'd met. I had to admit it was refreshing to see her this way: she was less intimidating when she stumbled all over the place.

I heard a clattering behind me, and Liv swore.

"You okay?" I asked.

"Fine," she said.

She fished her yellow lighter from a tide pool, shaking off the water. At least she couldn't smoke now, I thought, but then she rubbed the lighter dry with the hem of her dress, turned it upside down, and cranked it across a rock a few times. She checked for a flame and found one. I'd never seen anyone do that. It seemed like magic, but she pocketed it like it was no big deal.

"Let's just keep going, shall we?"

I gave up on talking then. In the quiet noise of ocean and bird-calls, I brainstormed nice things to say about Orion: He played a mean harmonica, and an even meaner trumpet, supposedly. He communicated with lobsters. He had good creaturely hands and that battered carabiner. This carabiner/key combo, for some reason, seemed crucial. Like he was adult and earnest and responsible. Boyfriend material.

"You want to park here?" I asked, pausing on the edge of a pool, the deepest one on this stretch of beach. It had been Sam's and my favorite for that very reason.

"*Yes,*" she said. She settled onto a perch on the tide pool's lip and fumbled to light a cigarette in the breeze, tucking one leg over the other and regaining her regal posture.

I dipped my hand into the pool and pried loose a snail that clung to the lichen. The water was cold. Yards away, seagulls shattered mussels open by flying up high and dropping them for maximum impact. Liv exhaled downwind.

"Why do you wear that hat all the time?" I asked her.

"Why'd you shave your head?" she fired back.

"No reason."

"Me neither."

A plastic bag was being dragged in and out with the tide. In the training manual, I'd read about the Great Pacific Garbage Patch: a modern-day Charybdis, a trash-filled gyre twice the size of Texas. *Consider that a metaphor for this research date,* I thought. We should have just rescheduled. Toby was right—I had actually been making good progress on the puzzle.

"Violet."

"Liv."

"Are we going to talk about our run-in the other night?" she asked.

"I wasn't planning on it, no."

"You looked wasted," she said. At least she didn't mince words.

"I'm fine. Or I wasn't, but I'm fine now." I squirmed under her gaze and tried to reaffix the snail to the wall of the tide pool, but he wouldn't stick. "It's not a big deal. I'm not going to do it again."

"I'm not judging you." She paused. "I didn't tell anyone."

"Thanks," I said. I put the snail beside me. I hoped I hadn't killed him.

"Seriously. Are you okay?" Liv asked.

I shrugged. "I have a lot of stuff going on. Family stuff. My parents . . . they sort of sent me here to chill out. What you saw the other night, that was like . . . a past life."

"I see Felix has already brainwashed you, too." Liv stubbed out her cigarette and tucked the butt into her dress pocket like she'd done the other night. "The hat was my brother's," she said finally. "I know Orion told you that he died."

"That's . . ." I wanted to say I understood, but I didn't. I wanted to say that I was sorry, but that seemed so feeble.

"That's really, really sad." It wasn't much, but it was the truest thing I had.

"It was," she agreed. "It *is*."

"My brother—is—uh. He's . . . he's in a clinic. Treatment facility. For, like, troubled kids. He's got issues with depression. And food. Not like anorexia but, like, kind of? Sort of an OCD thing. I don't know. Right when school let out, he tried . . ."

I couldn't finish my sentence.

"Family stuff?" Liv filled in.

"So much family stuff I shaved my head."

Liv looked at the water. In profile, I saw she had a single red dot of a birthmark on her left ear, right by her temple and acne on her cheek that looked painful.

"You know, our names are practically anagrams," she said.

"Almost the same person," I said. Except her brother was dead, and mine wasn't.

"Are you and your brother friends?" she asked.

"Sure." I thought of the drafts of my letters to Sam, sitting on my desk. I had a brother, and she didn't. I had a brother, and she didn't. I had a brother, and—

"Yo, so what's the deal with you and Orion?" I asked.

To my surprise, she let out a guttural half scream.

"Sorry! Should I not have asked?"

Instead of answering me, she yanked off her sneakers, hitched her dress into a high knot across her thighs, and hopped in the tide pool. Before her legs disappeared in the water, I glimpsed a strong line of muscle down her thigh. Her hamstring curved like a comma. I had a fleeting thought, one I'd have trouble forgetting, that it was a nice line.

That I wished my legs looked like hers.

"Sorry," I said again. "We don't have to talk about him."

"No, it's fine. It's just bizarre having to, like, tell someone from the beginning. It's so *tiresome*. Mariah and Felix know better than to ask."

The pool was deep, especially for her, lapping at the knot of her dress. She gave the impression of being taller than she was. She trailed her fingers across the surface, leaving behind ripples. She looked like a naiad.

"We can go back to our brother issues if that's preferable," I said.

"Ha! Pass."

"Maybe it'll be nice to tell everything to an objective observer," I said. *Objective* was a stretch. The more time I spent with Orion, the more he told me about electric sea scallops and moon snails and Faye the dog, the more subjective I felt.

"Objective observer?" she said, raising an eyebrow.

"Objective. Swear to you."

She squinted, and I wished she'd take her hat off. Her face was hard to read. I touched the snail shell for luck.

"I'll give you the SparkNotes version," she said finally. "My brother died when I was fourteen. Orion and I kissed for about a month after."

"Grief sex."

"Grief second base," she said, and she blushed so furiously, so red, that I felt the heat on my own face.

"Now Orion wants to date. I don't."

"Why not?"

"Why do I need a reason? I don't. Isn't that enough?" she said. "I mean—sometimes I think I should, that's where the confusion comes in. Our relationship is pretty nebulous. There's a lot of history there. My brother, obviously. And my parents love him. 'He's a fine young man,' or whatever. They like basically have my dowry prepared."

"Really?"

"No, no, they're not that bad. Sometimes they are. I don't know. Sometimes I think they actually want Orion and me to get married and have babies. But we're in high school! He's going to college next year! Babies are repellent! Nothing *serious* could happen between us, even if I wanted it to. No one's being realistic about this. In spite of what everyone thinks—him, my mom, whoever—and in spite of what we might *look* like—Orion and I aren't a *love story*. We're friends. That's it."

"I love the way you talk," I said. The words erupted from me like a frog's tongue. "I just mean—you have a really good vocabulary. *Nebulous*."

She cocked her head. "Thanks. Look, Orion's truly one of the sweetest people you'll ever meet. When he was little, he used to ask that people make donations to Save the Whales instead of giving him birthday presents. I was asking for blow-up chairs and feather boas, and he was developing an ecological conscience."

"You wanted a feather boa?"

"A *pink* feather boa. With glitter. Talk about bad for the environment."

"It would've gone well with the cigarettes," I said.

"Those came later," Liv said. "Though I *did* think a cigarette holder was the epitome of glamour."

I imagined eight-year-old Liv wrapped in a silky feather boa and puffing away on a lacquered cigarette holder. *Focus. Wooing. Orion.*

"Orion buys the rays sushi-grade tuna, from what I can tell," I said.

"Exactly. He's almost *too* nice."

"Is there such a thing?"

"I think so. Don't you? People need, like, edges."

I didn't know if I agreed. I was almost all edge, and it was a problem.

"Besides," she went on, "I'm not even thinking about boys right now. I have this idea that a project—a discovery—will help me get into Oxford. I want to study history there. And if I can make a contribution to the field, get published, they'd want me more, maybe give me a scholarship. Not like I could afford it otherwise."

"I'm fucked for college," I said. "My English teacher says I was 'squandering my radical potential,' which basically means no one sucks more than I do. And I got suspended this spring. Bit of a blemish on the old transcript."

"Oh, *whatever.* Your sophomore year? Doesn't matter. Just write your essay about that and how you've grown tremendously. You'll still get in anywhere, probably."

"My parents don't see it that way." That was a lie: they told me they didn't care where I went to college. But sometimes, in secret, and even though I hadn't been in plays in years, I read about schools with good drama programs. The best ones wanted good grades, and, I suspected, no suspensions.

"What were you suspended for?" Liv asked, playing with the surface of the water.

"Cutting class and smoking weed."

"Ouch. How'd you get caught?"

I bit my lip. This part was super embarrassing. "I went *back* to class."

"You're kidding."

"I know, I know. It was so stupid. But I had chemistry and my teacher was kind of cool, always doing these weird demonstrations where he, like, turned sugar into living black ooze and made the whole room smell like caramel."

"Dehydration reaction," Liv said.

"What?"

She pulled a braid over her mouth, like she'd said too much. "Sulfuric acid makes carbohydrates break down into carbon and water and acid. Don't look at me like that, I just liked balancing equations. I'm sorry you got suspended. Can't your parents, like, donate a library somewhere?"

"We're not *that* rich."

"Yeah, but your mom grew up in *Fancy* Lyric. Your brother gets to have his breakdown in Vermont! Sorry, that was a dick thing to say. I really, really hope he's doing well. Sorry. Violet, that was really mean of me. I'm really sorry."

"It's okay," I said. "I think it *is* actually pretty swank."

"I hope he has, like, masseuses and a private chef. And let's be clear, I live in Fancy Lyric, too. Though we don't have a beach. Will you need loans for college?"

I'd never asked, which was my answer. "I don't think so."

"That must be nice," Liv said, but she didn't sound mean. She just . . . sounded like she thought it'd be nice. It was nice. *She* was nice.

Focus. Wooing. Orion.

"So, Orion told me you went through a Goth phase."

"Orion again!" She slapped the water in frustration, splashing us both, then brought her wet hands to her hips. She'd been in that tide pool awhile now. I wondered if she was getting cold, if her thighs were smarting, red.

"Did he put you up to this?" she asked.

"Objective observer, remember?" I said. I sounded so casual. I used to be an actress, for crying out loud. I could pull off objective. "It just sounds like he's really into you. I don't know the ins and outs of what he's done to, like, win you over. But if I were him . . ."

She snorted. "This'll be good."

Challenge accepted, Liv Stone.

Acting is hubris. You not only attempt to faithfully represent someone else's experience, but you do so in front of a (hopefully) full auditorium. What makes you worthy of being watched and listened to? How do you convince an audience to stay, rather than waltz out the door and hit the nearest bar? Forget a full auditorium: how do you convince one measly person that you're more interesting than whatever is happening on her phone? And if you can distract them long enough to do that, how do you overcome the seemingly insurmountable challenge of winning a complete stranger's affection?

Back when I acted, I decided that the answers might be found not in the words themselves but in the gaps around them. I thought a lot about punctuation, and in my head I even gave them personalities, like the colon was kind of dramatic, the dash even more so. A period could be stiff, but it could also be a pushover. I'd run two lines together, maybe, or hold a pause just a beat too long.

Those pauses were my favorites, when I knew people were watching. I thought of this pause as *gathering* the audience: as though every single person were part of a crop, or a wildflower, and I'd stretch the silence until I sensed another set of eyes, another, another, and then I'd wait another second because I could. This pause announced: I am here, but I will speak when I am good and ready. You, audience, will endure this pause—in fact, you will enjoy it—because *I am just that good.* I'd hold the bundle of them in my hands, an expectant bouquet, leaving them waiting, anticipating—nay, *longing*—for what I was about to say.

In that pause, they fell in love with me. They knew they'd come to the right place.

"This'll be good," Liv Stone said.

I stood up on the edge of the tide pool. I cleared my throat and gazed down on Liv. I remembered every speech I'd given onstage; every song I'd sung. I channeled Annie Oakley and Julie Andrews, Judy Garland and Eliza Doolittle. I remembered cadence, diction, controlling the diaphragm. Thesis, antithesis, emphasis. Strong stance. Clear voice. Eye contact. Projection, escalation. Feet planted, shoulders back. Act with your voice, not your hands. I straightened myself up to my full six feet and one half inch.

Then I gave Liv Stone, Lyric Truther and Hater of Love Stories, the most goddamn romantic speech she'd ever heard in her entire life.

I started out slow. "There'd be letters," I said, "good ones, too."

Ever so slightly, so that she barely noticed, I talked a little louder. I picked up the pace. The letters would be proper, I said, like sailors used to write their beloveds from sea. I'd weather storms and gales to return to her, my soul, my only. I was finding a rhythm now, and Liv listened, rapt. I paused, a key change, and spoke again, this time a little zany. I'd pitch a tent, I said, outside her window. We'd be like Romeo and Juliet, minus all that mutually assured destruction, of course, and I'd sing to her so she would not forget me, even in the dead of night. We'd be a love out of time and space, ethereal, destined, and her dreams would take shape around my song. I'd teach the hills to say her name, and the winds and the trees and water, too, so that that the elements would love her, so that everywhere she went, no matter where, she'd hear the world crying out for her, calling over and over:

"Liv Stone, Liv Stone, Liv Stone!"

There was silence after I yelled her name. A moment passed. Then, one at a time, sounds began to return to the world. The ocean exhaled. Liv cracked a knuckle. A seagull took flight, and as though what I'd said had come true, his wings seemed to beat her name through the air.

"Sounds like you'd do a bunch," Liv breathed.

Beneath the brim of her hat, I found her eyes.

"You would not rest," I said.

I looked a little batty, I knew. Foolish. But I couldn't help myself. I'd gotten so carried away. But I'd forgotten how much I loved being onstage, forgotten how much I loved the feeling of having to win someone over. And here's the thing: sometimes you can be foolish, and you can still be very convincing.

Sounds like you'd do a bunch, she said.

I held her gaze. Her eyes were gray and darkly changing, like the back of a whale mosaicked in light. Like smooth, clacking stones on a necklace I'd once loved.

You would not rest, I said, and I wondered what my eyes looked like to her.

Two things then happened at the exact same time: my heart fluttered in my chest, and Liv sliced her foot on a cracked-open mussel shell.

❧

We limped back to the house, Liv trailing blood like bread crumbs. Half-propped against me, she barely reached my shoulder. For once, I was glad for the extra height, glad for the reach of my legs and arm as I helped her across gaps. Inside, the gas smell was weaker. Toby'd left a note about a bakery emergency. We were alone.

"Don't smoke," I said to Liv. "Lest you immolate us all. Not to mention for your health."

"I'm injured, not brain-dead, Violet."

I left her scowling at the dining room table, holding a paper towel against her foot. Upstairs, I rooted through a medicine cabinet overflowing with old lipsticks and creams and potions, perfume long since turned to vinegar. Liv had smelled like smoke and grit and SweeTarts. At the aquarium, we had a small hunk of ambergris, a waxy gray substance that formed in the belly of whales, rare and sweet-smelling, earthy, used in expensive perfume. Ambergris. Gray amber. That was Liv's smell, and also her eyes.

She was pale by the time I returned with Neosporin, tweezers, and a box of Band-Aids from the previous century.

"You okay?" I said.

"I'm not great with blood," she admitted.

"Let me see," I said, pulling up a chair and reaching for her ankle.

"I try to not let anyone see my feet up close. They're really gross."

I rolled my eyes. "They're *feet*. They get you from point A to point B."

"You don't understand. They're . . . *bestial*."

"I promise you, I won't care. Just let me see, because you look like you're about to pass out."

I lifted her foot into my lap even as she protested. Her feet were, in a word, horrifying: enormous, with dead skin around the heels like snakeskin, scars of former blisters thick along the back of her ankle. Her second toe stretched way past her first, gangly and alienlike.

"You've got a nice arch." I wasn't lying. It would have made a ballet dancer jealous, the same comma shape as her hamstring.

"Thanks," she said quietly.

She stared at the puzzle, staunch and upset, while I dabbed at her foot with the damp paper towel. The mussel had slashed open the ball of her foot, drawing a razor-thin red line of blood.

"Does it hurt?"

"Stings," she said. "Um. Can you not tell Orion we talked about him?"

"Sure. Can you not tell Orion the stuff I told you about my brother?"

She nodded. She was all Neosporined and Band-Aided, and her wound had stopped bleeding, but she still looked a bit shocked.

"You sure you're okay?" I asked.

"I'm not going to *swoon*, Violet." She jammed on her shoe without undoing the laces.

"I promise I won't tell anyone about how damsel-in-distress-y you were," I said.

"Thanks," she said, softening. "You were very chivalrous."

"This same thing happened to me down there when I was a kid. Well, I stepped on a sea urchin. I should've warned you to be more careful," I said. "Sam used to say I was part shellfish. Like it had absorbed into my bloodstream."

"That's your brother? Sam?"

"Sam," I repeated, nodding. I hadn't said his name out loud in weeks, and I thought it'd be harder, or it'd hurt more. But it came out easily. Saying his name had felt *good*.

Liv was thinking, running her finger along her lips. "So if anything that's caught in there will absorb into my bloodstream, and this happened to you, too, then we're like blood brothers."

"Shellfish blood brothers."

"Shellfish blood-brother anagrams," she pronounced.

I didn't know what it meant, but I liked the sound of it.

✖

That night, I was in bed drafting another letter to Sam, when Toby peeked his head in. He was holding a thick red book against his chest, like Sam, hugging his binders in the halls at school.

"Knock, knock," he said. "How'd the hot date go?"

"Research inquiry."

"Tomayto, tomahto."

"The research inquiry ended in no progress forward and a minor foot injury."

"Oof," Toby said.

I toyed with the corner of my legal pad, thinking of Liv's foot in my lap, saying Sam's name. The Ransome-and-Fidelia truthing search wasn't off to a roaring start, but I wouldn't have called the afternoon a *complete* disaster.

This, given my genetics, was unusual.

"Toby, you can, like, *come in*," I said.

"Cool." He plopped on the near edge of Sam's empty bed, close enough that we could reach across the space and hold hands if we wanted. Toby shifted and the springs shrieked. I know, I thought, I miss him, too.

"Sorry, again, about the gas. Though I found this in the attic, which might make it up to you." He passed me the book. It was so heavy it hurt my wrist to take with one hand. The title was embossed gold, the cover plush, mottled leather.

"*Guide My Sleigh: A Rudolph Family History?*"

"Your grandmother went on a genealogical kick a few years before she died. I think she had visions of making a book as a Christmas surprise. Hence the theme. Take a look," Toby said.

The spine crackled perfectly when I opened it. The front cover showed an illustrated family tree, every relative represented by a red-nosed deer. Fidelia and Ransome's lineage trickled all the way to Sam and me, rendered at the bottom as little fawns. Just above us, two deer labeled Margaret and Tobias Rudolph slept beside a berry bush. I felt a jolt. I'd always known Toby was my uncle, but it was different seeing their relationship spelled out in ungulates. My mother and Toby were brother and sister. They'd grown up together. In *this* house. Her room was just down the hall.

"Bonus pics of you and Sam in there, from yours truly. *And* the playbill from *Peter Pan*, which I still regret not seeing, though I am grateful for your autograph." My uncle was speaking to the ceiling now, with his legs thrown up over Sam's headboard, coffee-splattered Converse against the clean wall. This never would have flown in our apartment. It was so clean that Sam and I called it the Museum, usually when we wanted to piss off our mom.

"Are you sure you and my mom are related?" I said.

"There's evidence in the back."

I flipped to the end, pulling loose the photographs of Sam and me that he'd stuck in the binding. Pictures of my mother and Toby had been arranged on the back pages under cellophane: In one, Toby looked about eight and was wearing a too-big suit, hanging on to my eighteen-year-old mother's arm at her high school graduation. In another, my mom passed off a white bundle to a goateed Toby. *Me.*

"Toby. Why don't you and my mom talk?"

"We talk."

"You practically sprinted out of the room the other night when you were on the phone with her. Did you two have some dramatic falling-out? Did you try and steal my dad from her, or something?"

"Violet, your dad's a good guy, but surely you must find it hard to imagine a scenario in which he's the linchpin of a love triangle."

"But you and my mom aren't *friends.*"

"I'd agree with that."

"So you *did* have a falling-out."

"No. Hardly. It's more . . ." He clucked his tongue, searching for the right word. My mom did the same thing when she was thinking, made that little plucking sound.

"Your mom's not my sister like you're Sam's sister," he said finally.

"What does that mean?"

"We're really getting into this, I guess. That's good. Open lines of communication and all that, just like I said." Toby rearranged himself to sit facing me, and the directness made me a little nervous.

"How much do you remember of your grandmother?" he asked.

I shook my head. When I was really little, my grandmother would slather cold cream on my face and Sam's, then dress us in her silk kimonos. She loved costume jewelry. Fake rubies, fake diamonds, the shinier and bigger the better. As a child, I confused her with Elizabeth Taylor. *Cleopatra* once came on TV and I shouted, "There's Grandma!"

"She seemed glamorous. And like . . . pretty baller to give her kids *her* last name and not her husband's."

"It helped that Dad's last name was Slerpinn."

"*Slurping?*"

"Slerpinn, one *e*, two *n*'s. Mom would've been Sterling Slerpinn, which was kind of a mouthful. But yes. A champion for women, possibly, but more likely just vain. She was glamorous, though, you've got her fur collection in that closet right there. She also had a lot of trouble, emotionally. She'd go completely numb and lose feeling in her right side. Or she'd say it felt like there was a pane of glass between her and the world. Once, she lost her vision. Back then they called it hysterical blindness. Today—and let's be clear,

I don't like to diagnose people and I am but a humble baker—but I'm guessing it'd be a symptom of a dissociative disorder."

That one was new to me, even with my doctor mom, even with all the shrink talk I'd heard over my life.

"What's that, exactly?" I asked.

"As I understand it, you have episodes where you feel like your body isn't yours. Like you're separated from yourself."

"Oh, I feel that way sometimes," I said, and all Toby said was "Huh."

"Did she have panic attacks?" I asked.

"Not sure. She might've. Why do you ask?"

"No reason."

"Okay," Toby said, like it was no big deal. I felt an overwhelming impulse to hug him, which of course I didn't.

"Getting back to your mom. She's ten years older than I am. Dad died when I was three, your mom was thirteen, and with a mom like mine . . . I mean, *your* mom practically raised me, Violet. We talk, but we don't talk the way you and Sam do. We never did. It doesn't surprise me that this is news to you—I think it's hard for your mom to talk about. She was basically your age and responsible for a kindergartner."

"My poor *mom*," I said.

"I resent that. I was a perfect child. Hey. When was the last time you talked to Sam?"

"I said goodbye the day before I came here."

"And before the hospital?"

"Oh. Um . . ."

I knew the answer, but I didn't like to think about that. The last time I talked to him, *before*, was right after exams. Midmorning. Mom and Dad were at work. I emerged from my room around eleven, and Sam was at the kitchen counter with orange juice and a crossword. I'd been angry then: his presence felt invasive, like he was waiting for me.

"I can't really remember," I said to Toby. Had I always been this much of a liar?

Toby sat up and clasped his hands, his face suddenly full of worry.

"Violet. I know I joke around a lot. But after that phone call from Frieda . . . if *you* ever want to talk about your brother—or just you—I'm here."

I'd never seen him look so serious, and it scared me. "Okay. Thank you. I'm fine."

"You're your mother's daughter, you know that?" Toby scooped a balled-up draft on the floor and flattened it against his knee. "What's this, your poetry?"

"Don't *read* it!" I leapt from the bed and snatched the paper away from him.

"Sorry," Toby said. "I should've known better. I'm private with my poetry, too."

"It's not *poetry*. I'm trying to write a letter to Sam."

"You say *poetry* like it's a bad word. Listen, I'm glad you're writing him. Writing makes your brain think differently."

"Yeah, except everything I write sucks."

"Have you considered the telegraph as an alternative to snail mail?"

"Ha-ha. He doesn't like the phone."

"Neither do you, I suspect." Toby kicked at another crumbled draft with his toe. "You know how to juggle?"

"What?"

He hopped from the bed and gathered five crumpled letters, then shimmied his shoulders like an Olympic swimmer getting loose. "Ready for this?" and before my neurons had even fired, all five balls were in the air. For a second, time froze, and crumpled legal pad stars hung against a white ceiling. He couldn't possibly catch all of them—he didn't have enough hands. I sucked in my breath, waiting for the trick—

Quick as they were up, they'd fallen, scattering across the floor.

"Me neither. But that doesn't stop me from trying. I'm here if you ever want to talk, okay?"

He kissed me on the top of my head on his way out. Without hair, the feeling was new, but it wasn't strange.

⤸⤹

In bed, I took a closer look at *Guide My Sleigh*'s family tree. We were descended from Ransome and Fidelia's son Sterling, whose son Edward had had our grandmother Sterling. Sterling sandwich, one male, one female. The book glossed over Ransome and

Fidelia—so much for helping Liv—so I flipped through the rest of the generations. The first Sterling had won some science award at Columbia, and his son Edward had married a girl he met at Coney Island, according to the *New York Times* announcement (I did the math and she was *definitely* pregnant). I didn't know that our family had New York history, too, and that my grandmother and grandfather were the ones to move back to Lyric.

I'd come now to us. My parents' wedding. Violet and Sam with deep-sea-diver glass bottles. The four of us on a boat, then the same with Toby replacing my dad. They must have traded off being photographer. The *Peter Pan* playbill, signed *Violet Larkin*, *i*'s dotted with stars.

I think Sam *had* been waiting for me that morning back in June.

"Have you gotten forty-three down yet?" he'd asked me as I made my way for the door. I tried to make our exchange as quick as possible; my friends were waiting for me in the park and I was already late. I didn't want to talk to Sam. I just wanted to leave.

"I don't do the crossword anymore," I lied.

"Oh. I thought you did. Sorry."

I considered him then, with his finished puzzle and his full glass of orange juice. Was he going to leave the apartment at all today? He was probably lonely, it occurred to me, and I felt a rush of sympathy.

"Are you glad school's out?" I asked, starting over.

"Are you?" he said.

"Yeah," I said, because I was a normal human being. Who'd admit in summer's first week that they were already stressed out by their phone, their friends, the free time? I hadn't tried that hard yet to get a job, despite my parents' insistence, but now I wished I had. I almost wished I could just go away all summer, to Lyric, maybe. I'd always liked it there.

"I hate summer," Sam said.

"Because you spend all day inside. It's a beautiful world out there, Sam! Get outside! Have an experience!" I sounded sarcastic, but I also meant it.

"It's too hot," he said.

"When does nerd camp start?" I said. He was going away, just for a week, to do an intensive course in ancient Greek and Latin, which he *loved*. I really thought he was going to have a good time.

"Two weeks. I don't want to go anymore," Sam said. "I'm just going to get homesick."

"Maybe you'll like it. Maybe more people will play Magic! Like Tim!"

"His name's Theo," Sam said. "It's going to be horrible."

"Yup, okay, you're right. Horrible, horrible, horrible. Everything will only ever be horrible. I'm going to the park, okay? See you later. If you leave, turn the air-conditioning off, or Dad'll freak."

"I'm not going anywhere," Sam said. He hadn't even touched his orange juice.

There was a paper pocket in the back cover of *Guide My Sleigh* that held my parents' wedding invitation, Sam's birth announcement, and a receipt for a fur coat cleaning from years ago—yup, classic Sterling Rudolph II. There was a note, too, on Lyric Aquarium letterhead.

Sterling, Thank you so very much for the wedding photograph, as well as your other generous donations—these will make the perfect addition to the exhibit! Do let me know if you track down those letters. I'd love to include Fidelia's own words, if possible. J.

The letter was dated over eight years ago, but maybe Joan remembered. My new shellfish blood-brother anagram would love Fidelia's own words, too.

Who knew? If we looked, maybe Liv and I might find some treasure.

PART TWO: SEARCH

SAPPHIRE OF THE SEA

First thing Tuesday morning at the aquarium, I found Joan in her office, deeply engaged in what appeared to be an archaic form of book balancing. I was nervous to interrupt, especially because I hadn't spoken much to her since that time she'd scolded me for calling myself "inept." Joan was always shooting around, either in her office on the phone, or rushing to help guests interpret exhibits, saying things like "prebiotic soup" or "geologic time," showing off sea stars in the palm of her hand.

Now, with a pencil clamped between her teeth and a red pen tucked behind her ear, she stabbed at her calculator so violently that her desk shook. Eraser shavings pebbled her yellow legal pad; she blew them clear to make a note with the red pen, which she then regarded, scowling. Sam's poem hung on the wall behind her, green construction paper with blue marker letters and a kid's drawing of a snail. Boris snoozed beneath her desk, oblivious to her labor.

"Sorry to bother you," I said. "Do you have a moment?"

Through her pink reading glasses, Joan's gaze was startled and blank, like she didn't recognize me. I knew this look well. If you interrupted my dad in his study, he'd blink at you, adjusting slowly back into the known world. My mother reminded us, over and over, of what a hard worker he was.

She pulled the pencil from her teeth. "Of course! Come in, come in. What can I do for you?"

This warm invitation was just like my dad, too. He'd move a stack of papers from his extra chair and run lines with me while his computer pinged and his phone buzzed. He probably lost hours of sleep as a result. Just another kindness I'd taken for granted.

"I found this the other day." I passed her the note I'd found in *Guide My Sleigh*. "I've gotten interested in Ransome and Fidelia. Or, at least a friend has. I'm helping her."

"Wow. Ancient history," Joan said, adjusting her glasses. "But believe it or not, I *do* remember writing this. Supposedly, your grandmother was in possession of Fidelia's letters—ones she'd written to Ransome and to their sons. We were redoing the *History of Lyric* display at the time, and Eliza thought I might be interested."

"Nothing ever came of it?"

"No, the letters never materialized. Sterling was a bit flighty. I'm sure you know." She gave me a wry smile and stood from her desk. Boris, awake now, yawned and stretched his front legs. "Let me see what I have here, though. Eliza never came back for the files, I remember that, because I reminded her about twelve times. . . ." She opened a drawer in the filing cabinet across her office, and I stole a peep at her legal pad. A scribble of cross-outs and dollar signs, red numbers being added to more red numbers. A lengthy to-do list columned down the right-hand side of the page. In the margin, Joan had doodled a ship being dragged down by an octopus.

I didn't even realize it was *possible* to work this hard for an aquarium. Boris shot me a look that said, very plainly, *Of course you didn't, you dope.*

"Aha!" Joan cried. She pulled a file loose and raised it above her head, victorious. "This is what we'd dug up. A lot of it came from your grandmother, actually. Did you know that Ransome was an amateur artist? She even had some of his sketches."

I flipped open the folder: there were enough newspaper clippings and photographs for a bona fide primary resource document bonanza. Liv was going to be so happy. I couldn't wait to see the look on her face.

"Thank you so much," I said. "I'll look for those letters."

"Wonderful. Anything else I can do for you?"

I stared at the ring of lipstick around her pencil. Boris raised his eyebrows at me, expectant.

"I want to help more around the aquarium," I blurted. "I know I'm new. But if you can think of anything I can do. I want to be more useful."

She broke into an enormous smile. "That would be lovely, Violet. I'm sure we'll think of something."

⚬⧫⚬

Downstairs, Orion was being trailed around the touch tank by Andy, our most loyal patron. Since the day I'd failed to properly explain the gender practices of the potbellied sea horse, he'd come nearly every day, often carrying a tome as thick as his torso. Andy, to quote his mother, was "a handful." Andy, to quote Andy, "preferred a good book to a playdate." I had little patience for him (in fact, sometimes I hid from him behind the gift shop counter), but Orion was good with him. Today, though, Orion seemed as wilted as Joan.

"Were you up all night dreaming of Liv?" I asked.

"Ha-ha. I've been here since five. Joan called. One of the filters on the turtle tank broke, so I was dealing with that all morning. . . ."

"If the odds of finding Louise were one in two million," Andy said, "what are the odds of finding six? In a six-month period?"

"But now I think one of the turtles is looking a little peaked, so I might have to take her to the vet. . . ."

"Or the odds of finding ten in a year?"

"But who knows when I'm going to do that, because we've got this camp coming in today—"

"Orion! I'm asking you a question!" Andy said.

Orion blinked down at Andy. "I don't know, Andy. That answer involves a lot of math." He looked at me. "Can you drive the turtle to the vet?"

"I don't have a license."

"Shoot," Orion said, and he looked so peaked I wanted to take *him* to the vet.

"Aren't you a grown-up?" Andy asked me.

"Not a very good one," I admitted. I thought of Joan, the pile of eraser shavings. Of the easy and stress-free day that stretched out ahead of me—arguably about as easy as Boris's, sleeping at her feet. Why hadn't anyone called *me* to come in early?

"I can manage the floor today, if that helps."

Orion hesitated. "Are you sure? The camp's a nature camp. They wanted a talk. Something science-y. I was going to give my usual spiel about Louise." Ah, yes. The usual spiel. How did he normally start that? *What's more uncommon: a blue moon or a blue lobster?* Surely the answer was lobster. Right?

"Can you handle them? Camps are good business for us, but most of them have been going to the other aquarium. Joan really wants us to start rebuilding our educational model. Especially since we can't afford penguins."

Those fucking penguins. They'd be my undoing.

"Sure," I said. "Not a problem." My palms were already starting to sweat.

"You're a lifesaver," Orion said.

"You're in trouble," Andy said as soon as Orion had left.

"What did I just volunteer to give? A talk?"

"A *science-y* talk. To a nature camp," Andy clarified, blinking up at me through his thick lenses.

"Dammit."

"Language." Andy put his hands on his hips and eyed me like a stern grandmother. "Have you ever even *left* the gift shop?"

"No, Andy, I'm actually a troll and the gift shop's my home and at night I sleep in a fort made of stuffed animals and sweatshirts."

Andy giggled, but that didn't make me feel any better. Orion had taught me some things, true, and the training manual had been way more interesting than I'd originally thought, but I still kept my interaction with visitors to a minimum. It was one thing to recite lines, it was quite another to *teach* someone about how starfish regenerated arms.

I was totally and completely sunk.

"Quick, Andy. How much do you know about Louise? Enough to give a talk?"

"I'm *eight*," he said.

Someone shrieked. A squadron of children in Day-Glo T-shirts barreled through the doors, their counselors dragging themselves in behind, wearing sunglasses and carrying vats of Dunkin' Donuts iced coffees: 1000 percent hungover. The kids scattered, pressing their palms against the glass of different exhibits, dunking their whole hands in the touch tank. My poor, sweet urchin friend.

"Where are the *penguins*?" one screamed.

"How are you saving manatees?" said another.

"Dumb shirt," one said.

"Cool hair," said another, and only then did I realize they were talking to me.

"Guys, c'mon," said the boy counselor lamely. The girl slumped against the wall and arranged her arms in a pillow for her head. It was like looking into a past-life mirror.

"Two fingers in the touch tank," Andy murmured.

"Two fingers in the touch tank!" I yelled, too loud.

"Violet, please don't yell, it startles our sea friends." It was Joan and Boris. The kids swarmed Boris, petting and petting, and he reveled smugly in the attention.

"Where's Orion?" Joan asked, gesturing to the chaos.

"I'm actually gonna talk to them."

"*Oh,*" she said, in a way that managed to convey extremely polite disappointment. "You were really serious about pitching in, weren't you?"

"Serious as a heart attack."

Joan grimaced.

"Sorry. Bad joke."

"Why don't I stay and watch?" she said warily.

"That's okay."

"No, really," Joan insisted. She pointed to the touch tank, where one kid appeared seconds away from diving in headfirst. "You might need a hand."

"All right, chickadees," I called, "circle up! Andy, can you help? Circle up!"

With help from Andy and Joan and no help from the counselors, I managed to corral the group into a circle in front of Louise. There were about twenty kids, and they couldn't have been older than twelve, the same age I was when I'd played a Lost Boy on Broadway. I'd been a good kid then, at least at the start of things. I'd listened to adults. The Broadway director had always said I was so well-behaved, but it hadn't occurred to me that I'd had other options.

"Good morning," I said formally. So much for being *myself.*

"Why are you so tall?"

"*Shhh*," hissed Andy.

I took a deep breath and pretended I was Orion. I imagined my eyebrows growing as shapely as his; my smile suddenly gap-toothed; my brain inclining toward the ocean. I understood tides. I loved Liv. I donated to Save the Whales and was steeped in the secrets of lobster pigment.

"Why are her eyes closed?" one kid asked.

I squinted. Twenty fidgety heads looked anywhere but at me: at their nails, their split ends, the rays circling behind them. With my index finger, I wiped off a mustache of sweat. A girl in pigtails mouthed, *Ew*, to her friend. Guess that one was watching.

Joan cleared her throat. Boris growled. All I could think about was Orion serenading Louise with "Moon River." I had to say something. *Anything. The spiel. Just remember the spiel.*

"Did you know," I started, not entirely sure where I was going with this, "that periwinkles come out of their snail shells if you hum to them?"

"Yeah, right," the pigtailed girl said. Someone else giggled. God, I was surely not this difficult as a Lost Boy. Joan glared at me over the preteens. This was not off to a good start at all.

"Okay," I started. "Maybe not. *But* lots of animals communicate with each other. Whales talk to whales, and dolphins talk to dolphins. We know a lot about lobsters, and one thing that we know is that they emit low-frequency vibrations—a humming sound, though the jury's out whether it's for self-defense or chatting."

I straightened up. I paused. I gathered.

"A demonstration," I said.

Then I did the only thing I knew how to do, even though I hadn't done it in years: I sang.

I wasn't *planning* on it. I started out just humming, easing my way into the notes. I focused on Louise for signs of life, a twitch of an antenna or a click of her blue claw. But the words just seemed to bubble up from somewhere inside me, from an ancient, prehistoric place. I strummed an imaginary a guitar, channeled my finest Holly Golightly, and sang to the tune of "Moon River":

"Blue lobster
Sapphire of the sea
Marine anomaly
With claws
Oh, crustacean,
You . . ."

The only thing that rhymed with *crustacean* was *bus station.* I opened one eye.

"Keep going!" Andy shouted.

"I'm out of rhymes. You. Help me out."

I gestured to the pigtailed girl, who ducked behind her friend.

"Anyone? Anyone?"

"Vibrations," shouted a kid toward the back.

I launched back into it:

"Oh, crustacean
With vibrations
A-humming and buzzing
You crawl 'cross the sand. . . ."

I stopped singing. All eyes were on me. No one was fidgeting.

"Here's what we're gonna do," I said. "We're gonna make our own songs."

A collective groan rippled through the crowd.

"Ugh, I know, it's so *miserable*, to engage your mind creatively!" That, at least, elicited a minor chuckle from Joan. "Bribe time: winner gets a super-sweet prize from the gift shop." I'd fund it myself. My mom had always said that bribery was a useful tool.

That got them moving. They broke off into pairs, and I passed out pens and spare crosswords as scratch paper. I assigned everyone to an exhibit that served as the basis of their song, then visited each group to guide them, helping rhyme *Gulf of Maine* with *overfishing drain*, or squeezing *phytoplankton* into the meter. The whole exercise was decidedly more *vague* than *science-y*. But it was *working*. The kids were having fun. So was I.

We gathered outside by the picnic tables, using one as an improvised stage. A trio of girls sang "Ode to Koi" to the tune of "Ode to Joy." Two kids actually wrote a rap about "Reeds & Plant Life of the Marine Coast" (*these eelgrass fields are dying off / the clam population is feeling the loss*). Joan even wrote—and performed— "Baleen" instead of "Jolene." Orion returned with the turtle just as the last group, two boys, climbed up onto the picnic table to present their work.

"Our exhibit was *Sea Monsters of Old*," the larger boy said, looking out at the audience. "And for our song, we used 'Don't Stop Believin'.'"

"How's the turtle?" I whispered as Orion joined me in the audience.

"Clean bill of health," he whispered back. "How'd things go here?"

The boys on the picnic table started singing:

"Just a small-town fish
Swimmin' in a deep, deep lake . . ."

"What is this?" Orion asked.

"This," I said, "is vaguely science-y."

"Shhhh," said Andy.

The boys sang on:

"Just some city folk
Tellin' us it isn't true . . ."

"I did what I knew best," I said, "which, as I warned you, has very little to do with fish. But the show had to go on, so . . ."

"They *wrote* these?" Orion said.

"Yours truly made some liberal suggestions."

"Violet! Stop talking!" hissed Andy.

He loves *me now*, I mouthed at Orion. Orion elbowed me, grinning, and I elbowed him back. He elbowed me, and I elbowed him, and we elbowed and elbowed and elbowed, our clumsy arms half dancing to this song that encouraged us to believe in the unbelievable.

⧓

"We could do a whole musical series," Orion said that night as we walked across the parking lot. We'd stayed late cleaning, and then just *talking*. Before we'd realized, the sun had set. I sent Toby a quick text that I was on my way, and he texted me back six donut emojis, which was a great sign for dinner.

"You write the lyrics," Orion said, "and I'll provide factual accuracy and harmonica accompaniment. Move things from vaguely science-y to actually science-y. Better than penguins."

"Let's not get carried away," I said.

"C'mon. You got any other song titles in there?"

" 'Twist and Trout'?" I offered.

" 'Cod Only Knows.' "

" 'Kelp!' "

"Like 'Help!'?"

"Uh-huh. *Kelp! We love sea otters* . . ." I trailed off. "Needs some work."

" 'Earth Angler,' " Orion said.

"Like 'Earth Angel'? That's terrible."

"That's why you're in charge of lyrics," Orion said. "Lyric's own lyricist. Didn't you say you sing? You'll have to sing for me sometime."

"Maybe," I said, climbing into the Apogee. The passenger-seat trash heap was so deep now it reached past my ankles. "Orion, have you heard of a recycling bin?"

"I know, I know. It's bad."

"I'm surprised you don't use a thermos, given your whole eco-friendly vibe."

"These aren't *mine*. I pick them up from the side of the road. Or the beach."

"You're kidding."

"You'd do the same thing if you knew how all this trash messed with habitats." I wasn't sure I agreed, but was flattered he thought so.

We were the only car on the road, and it was dark, dark, dark, away from the light pollution. Through the windshield, the stars were bright.

"So," he said. "I heard you broke Liv's foot."

"Wow. Some go-between I am. She beat me to updating you."

"She did. She liked you. I could tell."

The fish was in my stomach again, flashing his tail.

"I feel really dumb even asking this," Orion said, "but did you two . . . uh . . . talk about me?"

"We didn't," I lied. "Trying not to be too obvious, you know? Have to win the lady's trust."

"I wouldn't say *subtle* is your usual style, but that's fair."

"Can you put me in touch with her, actually? I found all these papers on Ransome and Fidelia she'd be interested in."

"You need *me* to set *you* up with Liv?"

"In a way. I'll do more relationship recon for you, too."

"'Cause you're so good at it."

"Don't bite the hand that feeds, Orion."

"Oh, *wow*," Orion said, pointing. "Check out that *moon*."

I dipped a little to catch a glimpse through the windshield. The moon was the color of strawberry jelly spread thin, and so close, slung low over the peaks of pines, their rise and fall like a serrated knife.

"It's pink!" I cried. "Can we pull over?"

"Forget pulling over," he said, hitting the gas, "we're getting up high before the fog rolls in."

⤬

He drove fast, but not fast enough. Up high, on the rock where we'd been the other night, there was only mist. Without the sky, the rock felt smaller, but without the others, it was empty, too. I was ready to turn around—we'd probably get a better view on the ground—but Orion said we should give it a minute.

"Sometimes it clears up."

I pulled Toby's windbreaker tight around me. The last time we'd been here, I'd had a panic attack. I tried not to think about that. I tried to be here, with Orion, platonically.

"Sometimes I think how crazy it is that the moon's gravitational pull *actually* controls the tides," Orion said.

"Seems too poetic to be real," I acknowledged.

"That's the ocean for you," he said. He bumped my shoulder with his. The temperature had dropped and his body was warm, radiating heat. When we touched, I shuddered.

"You cold?" he asked, and I shook my head. I hoped he wasn't about to, like, offer me his jacket. I wondered if he brought girls here all the time. Or maybe this spot was just his and Liv's. And at this moment, his and mine.

"Orion, as your official go-between, may I ask you a question?"

"You may."

"Have you ever been out with anyone *besides* Liv? You're a good-looking, smart guy. I imagine you could have a whole lot of success in that department, if you were so inclined."

He cupped his hand around his ear and grinned. "Say again? What was that, about good-looking, smart?"

I placed two hands on his chest and shoved. He fell back, stumbling.

"I mean," Orion said, "*been out* might be a little strong."

A grin played around his lips, and he shot me a sheepish *I've been laid once or twice* look that zipped through me. If we'd still been in the car, the empty bottles at my feet would have popped like popcorn.

"No one stuck, though," he said. "Now, I'm sort of like, why would I go out with someone I'm not really excited about?"

"Shall I give you a lecture in the pleasures of the flesh, Orion?"

"The lady speaks from experience."

"*Experience* is putting it mildly."

"You must have left behind some heartbroken dudes in New York," Orion said, and for a moment, a correction hovered on the tip of my tongue. There was a girl that'd really liked me in winter—a drummer from another school, whose texts I'd ignored for weeks—but I didn't feel like reliving my cruelty, or explaining myself to him. Not when he so clearly thought of me one way.

"Well, I lead a life of celibacy now. Interested only in my matchmaking service."

"And does the matchmaker miss the pleasures of the flesh?" Orion asked.

"Nope," I sang, which was a lie. His shoulder brushing mine, waiting for this strawberry moon, was sending shock waves through my body. I could reach out and wrap my hands in his shirt and pull him toward me, put his mouth to mine. . . .

What I didn't miss was seeing people I'd hooked up with over the weekend giving badly accented, halting presentations on the forests of Guatemala, and I'd just sit there, squirming with the too-intimate memory of them reclasping their bra or fishing in the sheets for their underwear. Sex wasn't the problem; it was everything *around* sex.

"Just don't tell me that you don't buy into love. We've already got one Liv in this town."

"I thought you were, like, a truthing disciple."

"I think her ideas are super interesting. But I don't one hundred percent agree with her."

This was news to me. I thought Orion bought everything that Liv was selling.

"Let me see if I can explain," he said. He brought one hand to his chin and rubbed the space beneath his lower lip. I could see his wheels turning, his sweet desire to say what he wanted to say correctly. He probably stuck his tongue out when he worked on homework. There wasn't anyone this earnest in New York—or, if there was, I hadn't been looking.

"I think she's right that there's some weirdness in your ancestors' story," he said at last. "No offense."

"None taken, for the millionth time."

"Liv thinks something dark and twisted was going on. But there's weirdness in everyone's story. Maybe Ransome and Fidelia were both just weird people who fell in weird love, but for them, it was normal. I don't know. Don't you think your great-great-great-grandparents loved each other?"

"It doesn't matter. They're long gone."

"What are you talking about? Love always matters." He'd fired back so quickly that I knew he'd spoken from his reptilian brain, from the most Orion part of Orion. Put him in a pot to boil and when the rest of him had cooked off, he'd leave behind this jammy-sweet truth. Orion *cared* in a way that made my chest ache: For music, for fish, for friends. For the moon and the ocean, for these forces that knit us together.

For me? I wondered, then wished, my thoughts circling like his beloved rays: *for me, please, for me.* There it was again: the romance channel static. He was so close to me, I could touch the gap between his teeth. He could put his mouth to my breast, a finger inside me, one, two . . .

"I mean, isn't that why you're searching with her now?" he asked. "To understand their relationship? What was really going on between them?"

"Her being Liv."

"Yes," he said, and he repeated her name, "Liv," like someone who was afraid they'd forget.

The clouds thinned over the moon and grew backlit, hazy pink and smoky, rippling like creek water. I felt Orion's gaze on my face, and I knew, if I turned to him, I could have what I wanted.

"Race you back to the car," I called, but I was already whipping through the woods, back to the road, to a van that was old and safe and not romantic, not in any way, shape, or form.

I beat him, but not by much.

∞

At home, I found cell service on the dock down the hill, and while looking at the sky—now cloudless, pink moon on prominent display—I sent my mom a two-word text: *the moon.*

She sent me back a yellow crescent, six hearts, and inexplicably, perfectly, a single fuzzy bumblebee.

LIGHTHOUSE

June turned to July, and Orion, true to his word, sent me to meet Liv on Saturday to show her the newly unearthed Lyric papers. She had to work, so I met her at the Lighthouse Museum way out on Bat Wing Point, past the center of town, and up a short, notoriously steep hill to get to the stubby lighthouse. During our family summers here, we'd always meant to go but we'd never quite made it, deterred by the walk and the lure of the beach.

The second I stepped inside, I wished we'd put in the effort, for Sam's sake. The place was brimming over with nautical plenty: lenses of every shape, size, and color, plus glass buoys and maps and ropes, charts for tides and celestial navigation. It was packed with people, too, though I thought it'd be deserted. Through the throng, I spotted Liv by a collection of mounted foghorns. She'd ditched the black for a slate-blue shirtdress and upgraded her sneakers to a pair of sharp-looking oxfords. All that remained from her uniform was her Portland Sea Dogs cap.

"You look so fancy," I said.

"Work drag. I'm the youngest person here, so I try to dress up. Sartorial respect is still respect, unfortunately. Is this the Joan stuff?" she said.

I handed her the folder and made a mental note to look up *sartorial*.

"How's your foot?" I asked.

"Healing nicely, thank you."

"Neosporin works wonders. Plus, you know, my magic hands."

Someone bumped me from behind—an older man, a grandfather, probably, gray-haired and rectangular.

"Sorry, there, fella," he said, and clapped me on the back.

"That's okay," I said.

On hearing my voice, he took a second look at me, standing six feet tall and almost bald in my dad's jeans and Toby's windbreaker. I'd thrown on lipstick, too, that morning—some tube from my mom's room so old that I'd probably poisoned myself just by wearing it. The color's name had rubbed away, so all that remained was INK. I wasn't sure I liked it, but then again, I hadn't taken it off.

"Not a fella!" the rectangle said. "Sorry, there, *hon*. What's a pretty girl like you doing with no hair?"

"Oh, you know. Just trying to make you, personally, confused," I said.

He said *ah*—and then went to find his family again.

"Guess it worked," I said to Liv, and she chuckled. "Is it always a zoo in here?"

"Sorry, yes, I thought it'd be slower by now. Mariah's mom—Anjali, she's the director—had us featured on a travel website that profiles off-the-beaten-path tourist sites, and we've *definitely* been busier this summer. She's *on* the social media thing. We try to send people to the aquarium, but that other one, well . . ."

"I never thought I'd hate a penguin so much," I said.

A woman with Mariah's nose and mouth and perfect lipstick came toward us. Anjali. I wondered if she'd taught her daughter how to do makeup, side by side in the mirror, or if Mariah had just learned by watching. If they had the sort of relationship where Mariah could tell her anything, or if there were secrets between them.

"Liv," Anjali said, "I know you're meant to be off at two, but would you mind doing the tour? I'm drowning in e-mail and still have to post about Summer Saturdays."

Liv looked at me. "We were supposed to . . ."

"I can wait," I said. I didn't normally like tours, but I wanted to see Liv's.

Anjali looked my way excitedly. "Are you the New Yorker? What's your name? Vi? Mariah said you were funny. Strong youth outreach, Liv. Let me get a picture of you two for social. We have a really excellent feed, no thanks to Liv. Look engaged with these foghorns, now, but candid, candid."

Liv gestured vaguely at a foghorn, and I pulled my hand to my chin, miming learning while making eyes at Liv over how ridiculous this was.

"Beautiful," said Anjali, showing us. Seeing us captured, I didn't mind having the photo taken anymore.

"Miss," someone called. "Are we going to get this tour started?"

"I'm distracting you. Bad boss," Anjali said, tucking her phone away.

Liv handed the folder to me, then turned to the crowd.

"Folks," she called. "We'll begin the tour in a few moments with the history of the lighthouse. If you'd like to gather round . . ."

I blended into the crowd, and my palms itched with the memory of my near-disastrous aquarium talk. But it actually had gone . . . *okay*. Maybe it was possible to grow out of the shipwreck gene, to shed it like a skin.

The tour was starting.

"The lighthouse was erected in 1910," Liv began. She found my face in the crowd and looked straight at me. I wasn't used to being in the audience and felt uneasy, unsure of whether to hold her gaze. It was too weird, I decided, so eventually I settled on memorizing the floppy fall of a loose button on the collar of her dress.

"The keepers lived upstairs until the fifties, when operations ceased."

I peeked at her face, and Liv was smiling. She was an ace public speaker, and she knew it. A slightly more professional version of herself: elegant and warm, clear-spoken, knowledgeable and articulate. *"Isn't she darling?"* the woman in front of me whispered to her husband, but that wasn't it at all. Liv was geometric, precise. She held her shoulders back and enunciated so crisply, a theater director would have thrown her a parade. What was more: she fucking knew some stuff.

She named six different types of foghorns, plus the names of the men who'd used them. She told a ghost story about the original lighthouse keeper and paused in all the right places. From there she talked about celestial navigation, sextants and the angle of the horizon, and then knots: cleat hitch, bowline, cat's paw.

She stopped in front of a massive lens that resembled a spaceship, glass and bronze, nearly as tall as Liv herself. She laid her hand atop the glass, rainbowed in the light.

"The Fresnel lens," she explained, "is a landmark in lighthouse achievements. Glass was assembled in concentric sections, allowing light to radiate farther than ever before. The hyperradiant Fresnel was the largest lens invented. One of the most famous, the Makapuu Point Light in Hawaii, is over forty-six feet tall, and has over a thousand prisms."

She met my gaze again and my heart stuttered. *A thousand prisms.* I imagined sunlight piercing a glass chest full of cut crystals, the light turning to Technicolor fractals as it passed through jewels.

Our last stop on the tour was a map of coastal Maine marked with pins. Liv took a breath. The crowd shuffled, waiting for her to speak. She paused a moment longer. The woman in front of me futzed with her hearing aid. My heart stopped. I recognized what Liv was doing. She was *gathering.*

"Our town is, of course, famously founded by the survivor of the wreck of the *Lyric*, Fidelia Rudolph, and her husband,

Ransome. While that ship remains undiscovered, there are many opportunities to see other wrecks along the coast."

I understood: each pin was a different shipwreck, a whole underwater disaster network. I'd thought—such a silly thought, once I had it—that our wreck had been the only one.

"If you're looking to see some that *don't* require submersibles, I'd recommend Aguecheek Bay, to the north, if you have time. Last year, a Revolutionary War–era ship became visible again on the beach up there. The ship's been coming and going for decades depending on tides and erosion. Lucky you, this year, the stars have aligned and the ship can be seen for the first time since the 1950s." She turned back to the map. "If you'd like, we can end the tour with a little game. Stump me, and you'll win a prize." Her eyes sparkled beneath her cap. "Violet," she called. "Pick a pin, any pin."

I approached her. According to the map, the coast was *riddled* with wreck sites. She couldn't possibly know them all. I pointed to a yellow pushpin south of Lyric.

"The *Bohemian*," Liv said. "1864. Passenger ship. Struck Alden's Rock in the fog and sank."

A wrinkled hand pointed.

"The *Gypsum King*. 1906. Tugboat. Stranded on a ledge. No fatalities there—the crew rowed to shore in a lifeboat."

"*Ulysses*. 1878. Broke loose from its mooring."

I thought a wreck was a wreck was a wreck, but I was wrong. Liv rattled off a million different reasons and just as many types of ships: fogs, brigs, ledges, gales, freighters, failed engines, schooners and steamers and mechanical breakdowns. I followed her voice through an underwater tour that till now had only been traveled by whales and sharks and anglerfish.

"That blue pin," said the rectangle.

"*Lady of the Lake*," Liv said. "1895. Filled with rocks and scuttled. That one, supposedly, is haunted."

It was amazing, all these wrecks.

But where was the *Lyric*? Where was my ship? My family's?

Nothing held us to the map. The *Lyric* was a great gaping hole in our family history, a terrible blank.

❦

The staircase up to the offices was cramped, woven tightly into the stone like a nautilus. The soles of Liv's oxfords echoed in the chamber with the pleasing click of a good tap shoe. I imagined the lighthouse keeper eating tinned ham and drinking nips of whiskey to warm himself, taking salt-spray-soaked walks in a yellow rain slicker. If he'd been here just a few years earlier, the wreck wouldn't've happened. All those people wouldn't've died; but I wouldn't be here either.

I was so dizzy when we arrived at the top, I leaned my head against the stone wall.

"You okay?" Liv asked, putting her hand on my shoulder.

"The thing with wrecks," I said, talking into the wall, "is that all these people didn't make it. I'm not sure I really *realized* that before. Fidelia lived, but no one else did. Sorry. I'm not trying to be a downer."

I peeled my head from the wall. Liv reached out and very lightly, with her fingertips, touched my forehead where the stone had left pockmarks. Light spilled through the office windows, and the gaps in Liv's braids seemed to glow.

"Ouch," she said quietly. A strand of her hair had come loose; I resisted the urge to weave it back into place.

She pulled her hand away and spoke with a small voice: "Should we look?"

"Yeah," I said.

One sheet at a time, she arranged the folder's contents in a grid across the floor. We were up high, and out the window, I watched sailboats glide across the ocean, the water calm and lovely. These boats could've been cruising over the wreck of the *Lyric*, and the tourists on board would have no idea. I shivered as I imagined them in their perfectly nautical outfits, sipping local craft beers and posing for sunset pictures, all while passing over skeletons of lost passengers.

Sam hated losing things. I did, too.

"Liv," I said, "has anyone ever tried to really find the *Lyric*? Conducted like a true search?"

"Not really. As I said, no one really cares past *Their Love*

Was Our Beginning. Besides, you need Funding, capital *F*, and Equipment, capital *E*. Beyond the blizzard, we don't really have a sense of where the boat might be. Oh, these are lovely."

She passed me two drawings, pen and ink on yellowed paper. The first was a deer, the second a black bear cub. The drawings weren't great—the animals were oddly proportioned, kind of lumpy—but even in their wrongness, there was a certain softness to them, a kind of care and affection in the line. Both were signed *RR* in spiky crab letters.

"Oh," Liv cried. "*OOOH!!!*"

"What? What is it?!"

"I've never seen a picture before! Look!"

She rushed to my side with a newspaper Xerox. The picture in question was blurry, ink-blotted, but showed two men standing in an empty wrought-iron cage. The accompanying story read:

LYRIC RESIDENTS TO EXPAND TOWN MENAGERIE
For the past few years, Ransome Rudolph and his wife, Mrs. Fidelia Rudolph, have sought to build a public menagerie for the residents of Lyric. Already in their custody is an orphaned black bear cub named Nanny, who famously eats from Mrs. Rudolph's palm, as well as two white deer, and Ruby, the scarlet parrot. Their first exotic addition, an Indian tiger, will arrive this fall. Mr. Rudolph hopes the tiger will have the same fondness for his wife as Nanny does.

"I'm sorry," I said, "but what the *fuck*?"

"You don't know about the zoo?" Liv said, as though it were the most natural thing in the world.

"*No*, I do not know about the *zoo*."

She squinted at the photograph. "I wonder if that's one of their sons. Hold on. I know there's a magnifying glass here somewhere. . . ."

Across the room, there was a metal cabinet that seemed entirely composed of tiny drawers, and she left my side to open them, one by one. I had the feeling we could be here awhile.

"Can you please explain about the zoo?" I said.

"Oh, yes. Sorry. That was the precursor to the aquarium. Short-lived, though."

I didn't like the sound of that. "Did they get the tiger?"

"To my knowledge, yes."

"And?"

"Well," she said reluctantly, "as I understand it, he didn't adapt well to a new land."

"What happened?" I asked, but part of me already knew.

"Well," Liv said. "Supposedly, that winter was very cold. . . ."

I felt suddenly nauseated. Porous, like Sam. The cold, homesick tiger cub. These drawings, still in my hand: had they died that winter, too, the bear cub and a deer? How had no one told me about this, this fat blemish on our family history? Why didn't we talk about *anything*? Why couldn't I figure out how to start with Sam?

I put the heels of my hands to my eyes and pressed so hard that a purple pink aurora bloomed beneath my lids.

"Violet?"

"I didn't know," I croaked.

"It was a long time ago," Liv said quietly. "In those days, it was a common status symbol to have a wide array of animals. William Randolph Hearst had zebras. They at least were trying to make theirs public . . . and Fidelia and Ransome really loved the animals, I think, the story is the bear cub was wounded and kept in their house for a while. . . ."

I'd taken my hands from my eyes, but the splotches were still swimming in my vision.

"Maybe I'm misremembering the whole thing," Liv said. "I'm probably wrong."

"You're *never* wrong," I said. I could hear myself getting worked up. I wanted to know, yes, but I also just couldn't see the point. The more I learned, the worse I felt. And Sam knew plenty, more than plenty, and he still couldn't figure out how to fucking *live*.

Liv squinted through the magnifying glass at the Xerox. "Okay, so, that's *definitely* Ransome, and they had three boys, Sterling, James, and Llewyn. Did you know you're part Welsh, on Ransome's side? The Welsh have some *really* interesting mythologies. . . ."

"Who cares! Who cares if I'm Welsh, or Irish or Martian? What's the point of knowing *any* of this? My brother knows tons of shit, too, I bet *he* can tell me what *sartorial* means and who William Randolph Hearst was and why it matters that he had zebras, but he still can't *do* anything. Like, what good is getting an A on some translation of Caesar if he still wants to jump off a bridge?"

I was yelling, I realized. She had frozen.

"I'm sorry," I said. "I'm not mad at you."

"Okay," she said, sounding unconvinced.

"Sorry. Really. My brother hates yelling, too. When my parents and I yell, he hides."

"Your parents yell?" she said.

"Is that weird?"

"No. Probably not. I've literally *never* seen my parents fight," Liv said. "Not even after Will died."

"God, I wish we were that way," I said without thinking. "I mean—I'm so sorry. I don't wish—I mean—"

"You don't wish your brother were dead? Let's just say it, okay? My brother's dead. Yours is alive. It's a fact."

She crossed her arms and we let this fact hang between us. The silence was so deep I swore I heard the air sacs in my lungs expand and contract. I didn't know what to say. I'd just have to wait, agonizing as it was.

"Sometimes I wish we yelled," Liv said slowly. "After Will died . . . like— Sorry, I don't like 'passed away.' It's what my parents say, like bike accidents are this gentle, floating thing . . . but that's just it. They don't like to look at things."

I'd barely even thought of Liv as having parents. I imagined her springing from her father's head fully formed, like Athena.

"So—last year, right after I got my license," Liv said, "I drove down to Portland for the day. I just wanted to be in a bigger place where no one knew me, where no one knew Will either, or what had happened. It was so nice to be in a city that I went back the next day, and the next day, too, and by the third night I was so tired from all the driving, I stayed down there overnight. I told my parents I was at Mariah's. But not a single person knew where I was."

"Where'd you sleep?"

"In my car," she said, and I ached for her. "Anyway, by that point, I'd missed half a week of school, and so my dad called, worried sick. On the way back, I had these visions of the fight we'd have. I'd tell them I'd been in Portland and—then they'd, like, finally fly off the handle? We have this china cake stand in our kitchen, the kind with a glass dome, and I had this image in my head that I would hurl it against the wall. I *wanted* to hurl it against the wall.

"But when I got home . . . they were both so *quiet*. They had this pot of tea in the living room, and my dad did all the talking while my mom just sat there not looking at me, and he said *they loved me* and *this wasn't me* and I just felt horrible, because here I'd been, thinking about throwing a cake stand, and here were my parents, just so sad, so worried, in so much *agony*."

"Your mom really didn't say *anything*?"

"No. For the week after, too, she was so quiet and I just slinked around her, like I didn't belong—and I left her these little offerings like a cat—like these jam cookies she likes, or this paper on Oliver Cromwell I'd done well on—but nothing. Eventually, things just went back to normal. But we never talked about it. She never even said it was okay."

"That's fucked," I said, and when she stiffened, I added, "I don't know your mom, obviously."

"It's just how they are," Liv said protectively. "Yours yell, mine don't. I don't even know why I told that story. The grass is always greener, or whatever."

"Well, yelling's not all it's cracked up to be," I assured her. "And, like, when I think of talking to Sam next . . . it's, like, all the websites say I shouldn't be mad at him. Just understanding. But he tried—let's just say it, right? He tried to kill himself."

I said it again, thick voiced: "He tried to kill himself."

What if he hadn't just tried? What if he'd succeeded?

My throat was suddenly swollen. It was the feeling I got whenever I tried to write him, like I'd swallowed a pomegranate whole, a fruit like a grenade, and now with the dead tiger and Liv alone in her car—

I felt like I had by the hospital vending machines, so cold, so blurry, so away—

"Violet?"

I didn't want this to happen again, I'd already had one I didn't need another please not two please not two my throat was like a python middigestion I was wheezing I hated this no—

I imagined Orion's hand between my shoulder blades, and the pomegranate eased, slightly, but the world was punching black—

"Violet, I think you should lie down."

Liv's voice. I listened. I starfished across her grid of documents, and somehow she was next to me, on the ground, breathing big exaggerated breaths. The ceiling above us was white with heavy wooden beams. I was so upset about the vending machines. I remembered trying to lie on the floor of a pool, pushing air out my belly, bubbles puckering surface-ward. I stayed on the ground. I matched my breathing with hers.

"It's good to be on the ground sometimes," Liv said.

"I hit on a grown man while Sam was in the hospital," I said miserably, through my pomegranate throat.

"I kissed Orion two days after Will died."

"I'm so mean to my brother, Liv."

"I bet you're not."

"I am."

"You can change."

"I'm not sure I can."

"You can," she said. "You know, I once put a fish behind Will's dresser."

I didn't expect to giggle, but I did. "A *fish?*"

"Well, not a whole fish. A tuna fish sandwich in a Ziploc."

"That's . . . serial killer behavior, Liv."

"It was genius. He couldn't figure it out for a month. His room reeked. He was being a jerk. He could be a jerk sometimes. He changed a lot, though. Would've changed more, probably. Wanna sit up?"

"Okay," I said, and we pulled ourselves upright. The room

didn't feel normal—it was possible a room wouldn't feel normal ever again—but I at least knew where I was, and who I was with.

"You all right?" she said. The gray of her eyes looked heavier than usual.

"My brain goes bananas sometimes," I said.

She nodded. "I think too much, too. Neurons fire, overwhelm. Racing thoughts. That kind of thing."

"Who's William Randolph Hearst?"

"It really doesn't matter," she said. Her neck had gotten splotchy, taken on the shape of countries.

"Your tour was really good," I said, and I imagined pushing back her braid and tracing my fingers, slowly, across the outlines of those countries.

"Thanks," she said. "Oh my God."

"What? Did I do something wrong?"

"No, no, not at all. That expression. When you looked at me just now, I . . ." She looked back at the Xerox, then back to me, her wintry eyes puzzled, then flashing. "Look at the person on the right."

She handed me the magnifying glass and the Xerox. I peered through the glass. A nose, a mouth, eyes, cheeks, and suddenly, the other face clicked. The supposed son's. His face was my own.

"I think that's *Fidelia*," Liv said.

"She didn't look like me in the other picture," I said.

"Wedding-day makeup, maybe. Or like—here she's in profile, and the other was head-on."

"But she was in disguise *before* they got married," I said.

"This suggests she was in disguise for much, much longer. Or maybe she wasn't in disguise at all! Curiouser and curiouser!"

"Maybe she just liked pants," I said. I took a second look: it wasn't just my face I saw, but Sam's and Toby's, too. From the side, she was all three of us.

"Point taken. Even so: this is something. Honestly, I never find anything, I've been working on this for years, and this is so exciting—calm down. Organize." She hopped to her feet. "Schedule work time first. Where's my planner?"

"How about we just block off Saturday afternoons for research?"

"'We'? You're interested in this?"

"It's kinda fun. If you don't mind . . ."

"Are you kidding me? I'm going to tell Mariah and Felix every single day that you said this was 'kinda fun.'" She grinned at me. "Saturdays will be for wreck hunting from now on. Standing date, okay?"

My heart swelled. Saturdays were for wreck hunting. I had a standing date with Professor Stone.

⌗

I biked home still thinking of the wreck. The *Lyric* wasn't an idea. It was real. A ship. Hands had made it, used rivets and bolts and sheets of metal to build a thing meant to last. For a time, like magic, it had floated. Then it sank. It couldn't be *lost for good*. It was somewhere on this earth, lying on the ocean floor, and I wanted to see it, suddenly, fiercely: what Fidelia had escaped. I didn't just want to—I needed to. For us.

A wedge had been driven between Sam and me, that was true. A wedge that I'd helped put there. Maybe I'd never be able to make up for it. But if I could do something big for him, to show that I cared . . . I imagined handing Sam a screw from the *Lyric*'s deck when we finally saw each other next, its ridges filled with salt and sea gunk, the size of a flimsy key chain with triple the weight. I'd say, *Here, have this.* I could give him proof that he mattered. That *we* mattered. If I could find our wreck, maybe I could start to put us back together again.

I'd find the wreck, and I'd make us whole.

That day I wrote him a letter, the very first one I sent:

Sammy:
Here's my new summer goal: track down the wreck of the Lyric. Seven-year-old you would be so proud of me.
I love you and I miss you.
Vi

I shoved my extra aquarium T-shirt in a box and sent that along for good measure.

MISSING PIECES

The next morning I was up before eight to set up wreck-searching camp at the Mola Mola, Toby's bakery. He'd named it after his favorite fish—the "goofiest fish in the sea," he claimed—and even that early, its mismatched wooden tables were filled with locals and tourists thirsty for coffee and hungry for baked goods. I spotted Joan in the far corner reading the paper with her husband, and I gave her a tiny wave as I hunted for a seat. It was starting to feel sort of nice, the feeling that in Lyric I might always run into a familiar face.

I tucked into the last available table, partially shielded by a plaster bust of a Greek goddess in a metallic-purple party hat. Here, in this secluded magical corner, I would track down the *Lyric*. I had a blueberry oat bar. I had *Diving for Sunken Treasure*. Most important, I had the ability to google *how to find a shipwreck*.

Scratch that.

"Do you seriously not have *Wi-Fi*?" I asked Toby at the counter.

"*Converse* with me," he said. "Have an espresso. Better yet, how 'bout you take a shift at ye olde register? I gave too many employees off and we're about to be overrun with the midmorning rush. I've never seen so many tourists in my life."

"Toby, *I'm trying to find a shipwreck.*"

"Ambitious."

"Just be grateful I'm not out getting pregnant."

"Are those really your only options? C'mon! Service will broaden your horizons in ways you've never anticipated!"

"Fine," I said, suspecting I'd regret it.

"Steel yourself for the onslaught," Toby said. "The good news is, everyone knows being a barista makes you infinitely cooler."

If by *infinitely cooler* he meant *homicidal*, he'd nailed it. The majority of patrons were painfully picky, forever on their phones, ordering the most complicated drinks I'd ever heard of. One woman asked if I could scrape the icing off a shark cookie because she "only ate sugar that had been baked." Toby, meanwhile, was like an octopus-wizard hybrid on the espresso machine, steaming milk with one hand, slicing bagels with the other, and somehow, still finding time to sing along to the Clash *and* have conversations with everyone he knew. No wonder he fell asleep by seven.

When we finally reached a lull, he shook his wrist out, and his bones crackled. "I need a more ergonomic profession."

"Why don't you take a break?" I offered. "Just, like, twenty minutes. Power nap."

"What a foreign concept. Just you up here?" He hesitated, then nodded. "Okay. Sure. You can handle it."

He gave me a crash course in how to pull thick, chocolaty espresso shots and foam milk to the consistency of paint. After five practice cappuccinos, he declared my drinks "passable," and retreated to his office. "Though I'm probably too amped up from your B-minus espresso now to actually *fall* asleep," he called on his way.

I had to remake my first few drinks—too thin and watery— but when I finally handed over a well-pulled latte, I practically glowed. Handing someone a warm paper cup was a nice feeling, even if they were a needy tourist.

Then the door swung open, and in came Frieda from the Lyric Pub.

In daylight, she seemed monolithic and unmovable. Black jeans and a Ramones T-shirt, aviators, a black bandanna holding back her hair. I couldn't envision her being anywhere, doing anything she didn't want.

I hoped I looked like her when I grew up, and I hoped she didn't remember me.

"Hey, boozehound," she said, pulling off her shades. "I was wondering when I'd see you again."

Well. There was that.

"You work here now?"

"Just today. Um. Look. I'm really sorry about your glass," I said, hoping to hurry her along.

"I don't give a shit about the glass. How are *you*?"

"Fine. What can I get for you?"

She drummed her fingers on the countertop, taking her sweet time. She was really savoring this moment. Payback.

"I'll have a small mint lemonade, please," she said finally.

I was expecting black coffee, tough and acidic. She'd brought her own plastic cup, which I filled to the brim, taking care to add extra ice.

"Thank you," she said. She slurped from the rim and made no moves toward the door. I prayed for someone else to come through and order a drink so complicated it'd take me centuries to make.

"You might be interested to know that Rus left town," she said. "Hopefully he'll get eaten by a shark."

"Ha. Um—thanks. Really. For that night. Calling Toby."

"It was nothing. Seriously. I've seen some shit at that bar."

"Well, I promise it won't happen again," I said.

She swirled simple syrup into her lemonade. "What are you, doll, eighteen?"

"Sixteen," I said, but I felt even younger as I answered.

"Huh. I bet people tell you you look pretty grown-up."

"Yes," I said, though *grown-up* hadn't been what they'd said, exactly. On Broadway, Mrs. Darling had looked me up and down and told me with a body like mine, I could really do some damage. I didn't understand what she meant until weeks later.

"They used to say that to me, too," Frieda said. She considered me for a second, then checked over both her shoulders and turned back, her voice low, eyes fixed on me. The room tunneled around us, and the intensity of her gaze made my blood rush. A lump formed in my throat. *Leave,* I thought, *leave, leave, leave.*

"I'm going to keep this real short because you and I don't really know each other. Just because you look grown-up doesn't mean you *are*, okay?"

"I know," I said.

"That's my whole point. *Don't* know it yet. *Don't* know anything. You're a kid. Be lost. Ask questions. Be safe but stupid. Listen."

I tried to swallow and failed. She made it sound so easy. Like I could be the kind of teenager who horsed around in shopping carts with their friends, or sneaked onto the roofs of buildings. The kind of teenager who got into *hijinks* and *mischief*, rather than bars and danger.

"I think . . ." I paused to gulp some air, and before I could stop myself, my voice curled to a squeaky question: "I think it might be too late for me?"

Frieda shook her head softly and spoke too kindly. "Hardly, doll."

I nodded, not because I believed her, but because if I spoke, I'd cry.

"Here's a secret, too," she said. "Most adults don't grow up all the way either. Only the best ones, like your uncle, figure how to make that look good. Thanks for the lemonade."

She tipped me twenty bucks.

❧

Toby emerged forty-five minutes later and told me, kindly, that I was fired.

"Great," I said. After my conversation with Frieda, I was desperate to get out of the Mola Mola. I threw my wreck research into my bag and headed for the door.

"Hey, kid," Toby called. "Seriously, thank you. You might try the library for the wreck. Strongest Wi-Fi round these parts." He rattled the tip jar at me. "Don't forget these."

Outside, the day was ludicrously picturesque, the sky cobalt blue and cloudless. The slow days at the aquarium had led me to believe that Lyric was a dead zone, but there were *lots* of people here, Main Street busy with some cheery July Fourth pop-up fair. People ambled amid sidewalk sales and face painters, a bicycle-decorating contest and information about tomorrow's fireworks, and I felt rickety and cold, detached from it all. What had even happened back there?

A young white guy in butter-yellow shorts came toward me, phone extended, and said, "Excuse me, miss, would you take our picture?"

"Um," I said, and he pressed his phone into my hand before I could say no. He arranged his arm about his eagle-faced wife, who was holding a grumpy-looking baby. Someone had slapped a red-and-blue hairband with a grosgrain rosette on their baby's head—so the whole world would know the baby was a girl, I guessed.

"Say 'cheese,'" the husband instructed his family. That hairband was so gross. They smiled plastic smiles and the baby shrieked mid-photograph, which made me feel a little tinge of pride. Less than a year old, and she was already working her sabotage muscles.

To get to the library and away from the crowds, I cut through an alley to the side streets, where the shops were sparser and a little more run-down. There was Lyric Records & Video, long since boarded up; Mona's Hardware; Lyric Yarn and Craft, which I now considered might be a front for drugs. I couldn't get Frieda out of my head. *Hardly, doll.* I wanted to believe her, but I felt like I'd lived a thousand lifetimes already, none of them particularly kid-friendly.

I was petting a black Lab tethered outside the copy-and-print shop, when two tan girls skipped by me in a fit of giggles. One was in lime-green shorts; the other one had streaks of fake red in her hair and was bouncing a fuchsia ball flecked with glitter. They might've been sisters or they might've been friends, I wasn't sure. They didn't look alike, but they had that same summer carelessness about them—peeling sunburns, salt-dried hair, mosquito-bitten legs.

"*Quickly, quickly, quickly!*" shrieked Lime-Green Shorts. What could possibly be so important? They were going in the opposite direction of the library, but that was fine. I wasn't in a hurry, and I wanted to see what they were after. It sounded important. Illicit, even.

They crossed a bridge over a river, then followed some old train tracks through a field to some woods, where they shimmied through a gap in a chain-link fence. We were drawing close, I knew, and I needed to see what they were after.

We came to a creek where a rope swing dangled over the water, and they waded in without hesitation. They overturned rocks and splashed each other; Lime-Green Shorts found a salamander and watched it skitter up her arm. I waited to see what they'd come for. Was someone meeting them, or—? But they just lollygagged in the creek, took turns on the rope swing, wading up and down, and then, slowly, finally it dawned on me. They hadn't been *going* anywhere at all.

I watched them play for a while longer, hoping they'd teach me something crucial I'd missed.

⁂

I made it to the library eventually, bramble-scratched and bug-bitten, and found some kind of rummage sale happening in the parking lot. Beneath pop-up tents, people ferreted through racks of clothes and pawed over electronics. One woman held a radio to her ear like a seashell. I skirted a tent's edge and made for the library's door, but as I watched a woman try on a pair of red cowboy boots, I felt a tug of jealousy. I'd liked the savage fluorescence of that little girl's shorts, too, and I had to admit I was getting tired of my Hanes tees. The day was still early. Ten minutes, I promised myself, then wreck research.

I was considering a royal-blue shirt that said RICHARD LI'S ORTHODONTICS, when I heard, "That's good. You can do better, though."

It was Mariah, in a poppy-colored sundress and look-at-me chandelier earrings that grazed her shoulders—the kind I used to wear. I was relieved to see a friendly face that wasn't Frieda's, plus Mariah'd been so nice to me the night we'd met. Now she greeted me with a warm, easy hug, like we'd been friends for years.

"Did Orion bring you?" she said.

I shook my head. "He's here?"

"Inside. Something about compost. Dude, I'm impressed you found the Missing Piece on your own. Lyric's finest fashion with the most unpredictable hours," she said. "Like, you obviously need this."

From the racks, she pulled loose an appallingly ugly patchwork vest embroidered with animals from Noah's Ark. The animals were tumorous and the sun had a stitched-on smiley face.

"Four dollars?" I cried, laughing out loud. "They'd charge eighty for that in New York."

"Some fool would buy it, too. You looking for something specific?" she asked, hanging the vest back up.

"Just . . . color."

"That's a task I can handle. We'll find you something downright kaleidoscopic," she said, and began to tick quickly, methodically through the hangers. I fell in beside her and watched rumpled T-shirts fly by, thrilled that, apparently, we were hanging out now. Mariah put me at ease.

"I met your mom," I said.

"That's right, Liv said you came by—and that you're, like, a truthing convert now. How was Mama C? Did she force you into some social media thing?"

"Yes, but she was super nice about it. And the museum was *packed*."

"It's *so* weird how much she loves that place." Mariah sighed.

"Has she worked there a long time?"

"Almost ten years now. We were in Boston till I was eight, but she's got a curatorial degree, and like four jobs exist in that field. There was cheaper rent here. My sister and I had our own rooms. Plus, my parents thought Indian kids in Maine was a pretty good hook for college."

I slithered halfheartedly into a denim jacket she'd selected for me. "Seriously?"

She shot me a pitying look. "I'm kidding, Violet. Liv told me you had a sense of humor." She held up a pair of blue zebra-print leggings. "If these weren't so threadbare in the knees . . ."

She shoved them back onto the rack. I envied her, how quickly she made decisions. I took a Lyric High School Hockey sweatshirt from the racks, the *R* missing so that it read *LYRIC B EAKERS*.

"No," Mariah said, and checked the price tag. "Especially not for eight dollars."

"But it's a good chemistry joke," I argued.

"It's at best a mediocre chemistry joke. And trust me, you wouldn't support the Lyric Breakers if you met them."

"Is your school really that bad?" I asked.

She ran the sleeve of a green faux-fur jacket through her fingers, considering. I'd look like a yeti in it, but she'd be able to pull it off. I wanted her to give me lessons in how to carry myself.

"Most people are okay. But the few that aren't . . . It's worse for Felix and my sister than it is for me. She's in college now, though, and it's fine. Felix and I try to laugh stuff off but . . ."

"Sometimes that makes it worse."

"Yes. Exactly." She dropped the sleeve of the coat and clapped her hands. "Nope. No. No more outerwear. Two more years, and then it's Hollywood for me."

"You want to be an actress?" I said. No wonder I liked her.

"Writing," she said. "TV. Comedy, preferably, though I'd settle for soapy doctor drama. As long as I never have to dig my car out of the snow ever again. Okay, normally I'd've found twelve thousand things by now, but you're distracting me. Look: eyes on the prize . . . we'll divide and conquer and hunt for each other, okay? I'll wear anything with sequins. Seriously. I'm a magpie."

I drifted through the racks, running fingers over the old T-shirts and reject sweaters, edging my way past other decisive shoppers clutching their finds. How did everyone have it all figured out? Oxford for Liv, California for Mariah. If I couldn't even decide on a T-shirt, how could I decide on a future? And Sam—what would he do?

I managed to find a sequined headband and an embroidered bag covered in little bits of mirror. And then—because, why not?—I picked up a long pair of sturdy flippers that I found over by the overcoats. One was dog-gnawed, but they looked otherwise passable.

Mariah came back with a royal-purple bundle in her arms, which she unrolled like Cleopatra from the rug.

"The cuffs are a little ratty, but . . ."

It was a crewneck sweatshirt that said LYRIC AQUARIUM MARINE MINGLE in white, screen-printed with the silhouettes of three dancing whales. It was, in a word, perfect.

"I *love* it," I said. I yanked it over my head, then hugged myself to myself, the whole of me a tight little ball.

"Pretty cute," she agreed. "I love that bag, but I hope those flippers aren't for me."

"Oh—um. Liv and I were talking about . . . hunting for the wreck?"

I waited for her to roll her eyes, but she just laughed. Her laugh was big, like my mom's.

"You're even more outrageously hopeful than she is. You know Felix's family has a porthole that they think is from the *Lyric*, right? It's in their store. Treasures of Atlantis?"

"Felix's family *owns* Treasures of Atlantis? I used to steal stuff from there!"

"Thief," scolded Mariah. "Yeah. I mean, take everything he says with a grain of salt, but he thinks it's from the *Lyric*. Maybe it'll get you somewhere. We could go look at it right now, if you want? I'm about to go meet Liv."

Her offer was tempting, but I'd come here to work, and I'd taken enough detours for the day. Potentially running into Orion wasn't even appealing at this point. I just wanted to crack the books.

"Next time," I said. "Tell her I said hey."

"I'm gonna tell her you bought flippers and leave it at that."

∎

Thankfully, Orion didn't appear to be in the library anymore, and double thankfully, there was an entire display devoted to shipwreck literature right where I walked in. Jackpot. I nabbed *The Principles of Maritime Archaeology*, a doorstop of a book, and then, to balance it out, I grabbed a slim book of poems from the same shelf. I'd recognized Adrienne Rich, the author, from school.

I picked the kids' section to read in, all primary colors and smelling of apple juice, even though the sign said under twelve only. Nestled in a waxy yellow beanbag, I heaved *Maritime Archaeology* into my lap, ready, at long last, to learn the secrets of wreck hunters.

INTRODUCTION

The quintessence of humanity is curiosity, which ushers us, undeviatingly, toward the liminal. We seek boundaries in an effort to more fully comprehend our being, epistemological and somatic, to elucidate and concretize our existence. At present, we find the last physical manifestation of the liminal in the "wine-dark sea," that horizon where philosophies and theories of mind gyre maddeningly in the attempt to reconcile . . .

Oh. My. God.

This was the *introduction*?

I needed a new brain to find this ship. Sam's brain, preferably. He read stuff like that and got it, whereas all I understood was *wine*. I tried the sentences a few more times, then decided I'd read the poems as a warm-up. I'd never minded poetry—at least, I didn't groan like everyone else when our teacher announced the inevitable unit. Most poems were mercifully short, for one thing, even if you didn't get them.

I started the first one:

Out in this desert, we are testing bombs,
That's why we came here

My nose panged, those lines hit me so hard.

How was there so much there—loneliness and danger and pain and seeking—in so few words? I read them again. Again. Again, and then I kept going.

Out in this desert, we are testing bombs,
That's why we came here

Sometimes I feel an underground river
forcing its way between deformed cliffs
an acute angle of understanding

"Miss, children only back here."

Orion, right on cue, flopping in the beanbag beside me. I wiped at my eyes surreptitiously and closed the poems into the book of marine archaeology, feeling suddenly protective of them.

"What're you reading? That's looks like an Andy-level book," he said. He was wearing a lavender T-shirt that said LILAC FESTIVAL 5K, the words faded from so many washings. I shouldn't have been surprised that he was even *more* handsome out of his aquarium shirt, but the color was really good for him.

I flashed him the cover and he said, "Wow, Liv really converted you to the cause, huh?"

"Light research," I said, the teensiest bit embarrassed. I hoped he hadn't noticed the flippers.

"Any updates on that front? With Liv? About . . ."

"About *you*?" I said, and now *he* looked embarrassed. "Yeah. Um. You know. We didn't get very far." Also known as *Liv made it expressly clear she does not want to date you, and I am stalling.*

"You might even think about broadening your horizons, Orion. I know it's a small town, slim pickings and all that, but maybe there's someone else out there for you."

"Maybe," he said cautiously, which I took as further evidence of his undying devotion to Liv. I didn't blame him. She'd been so nice to me in the lighthouse.

"I'm glad I ran into you, Violet," he said. "It was weird not seeing you these past few days, plus with the holiday . . ."

"Yeah," I said. "Nice to run into you, too."

It seemed for a second like he might hang around—or like he wanted me to ask him to stay—but for once, I held my tongue.

"Well," he said finally, "enjoy your reading."

I spent another hour alternating between the poems and staggering through the first few pages of *Maritime Archaeology*. When I stood up to stretch, my first thought was that he'd done it on purpose. Because really, how could he possibly miss it?

Orion's black wallet was smack-dab in the center of the beanbag, terribly obvious and just begging to be returned.

NIVATION HOLLOW **BLUES**

The trumpeting began as I was crossing the lawn to his house, coming from a shed in the trees I'd failed to notice. A warm, raspy note bull's-eyed the bridge of my nose and rocketed through the rest of me.

Notes burst, then ached; jazzy, slow then fast, slow again, great big surprising gaps around the sound that left me hanging on for the next note. The song was rough around its edges but inviting and sweet underneath, whispering in places. I just listened. This music made everything beautiful: the crabgrass beneath my feet transformed into a lush forest, and the burl in a nearby tree whorled into a new planet.

In school, there'd been no shortage of boys with guitars and basses, boys who wrote their own music, boys who met on the weekend to jam. Girls, too, like the spurned drummer. And sure, I'd heard trumpets at church on Christmas Eve (one more of Mom's misguided attempts to "rebuild the family"), but Lord almighty, Orion Lewis was playing music altogether different. I wanted to crawl into the music and live there. He played like he *cared*.

When he stopped, my ears filled with a tinny echo, whining for more.

From inside, Orion yelled *"Fuck"* so loudly I nearly jumped out of my skin.

"Hey!" I shouted, approaching the shed. "I'm eavesdropping on your artistic turmoil!"

The door flew open. Orion was holding a gold trumpet in his left hand, and his cheeks were bright red, rosy as apples. His mouth was on fire, the skin around it angry and inflamed, like he'd just spent hours kissing someone with a beard.

"What're you doing here?" he said.

"I got your address from your license," I said, and I held up his wallet. I'd snooped, of course, but the most scandalous thing he had in there was a Seafood Watch Do Not Eat card.

"Oh. I'm an idiot. Thanks." He glanced over his shoulder. "You want to, like, come in?"

I knew I should leave. I sensed the romance channel got great reception in the shed. I should leave, I should leave, I should leave. . . .

"Sure," I said.

The shed's floor was crowded with gardening junk and coated with sawdust, plus a record player and a few music stands. Over a mint-green canning table, a map had been covered in a few pushpins—the Caribbean. It hit me: this was the shed where they'd started building the boat.

There was a window in the back corner. Through it, I spied a blue plastic tarp, thrown over something the size—well, something the size of a small rowboat. I thought the boat hadn't been finished, but whatever was beneath that tarp looked solid. Real. Seaworthy.

We stood there awkwardly for a second. It was weird to hang out *not* at the aquarium. I suddenly understood why people made lists of things to talk about.

"Okay, so you've heard me play twice now," he said, settling onto a stool. "Your turn. Serenade me. I want to hear your voice, for real."

"You've heard me sing," I said.

"Singing 'Twist and Trout' with Andy does not count."

"But . . ." I didn't *really* want to sing. But I also didn't want to get locked into an argument where I eventually capitulated. That would have been too much buildup for the voice that I actually had. I was not a belter. My singing voice was low and a little husky. I always sounded a little sad. *Haunting* was the word that my choir director used. My voice wouldn't have lived up to the hype.

And part of me had been missing singing ever since I'd sung "Lobster Moon River."

So I sang the first song that came into my head: *"Happy birthday to you . . ."*

Orion pulled one hand over his mouth. Was he laughing? I searched for a smile but found none. On the contrary: he was taking me seriously. Really seriously. Because alone, without music, this song sounded *sad*. *Way* more emotional than I intended. I could have picked anything else. . . . I could have picked "Mean Mr. Mustard" or "We Welcome You to Munchkinland" . . .

"Happy birthday to you . . ."

Because wasn't this a sort of weirdly sexy song, too, thanks to Marilyn Monroe and JFK? I tried to look as platonic as possible. More than platonic: undesirable. I had a gnarly zit on my cheek and I turned that side of my face toward Orion.

"Happy birthday . . ."

I glued my gaze to a garbage pail filled with hockey sticks.

"Dear Orion . . ."

On a pile of tangled Christmas lights.

"Happy birthday to you."

I went to tuck my hair behind my ear and rubbed my head instead. I felt like the exposed nerve of a tooth.

"You've got a really nice voice," Orion said.

"Shut up."

"I'm serious. The timbre of your voice . . . it's *melancholy*. You know what a dying fall is?"

"Orion. Oh my God."

"It's, like, an emotional swoon in music. A sad one, where you have to sort of sigh and drop to hit a certain note. Like, 'Greensleeves.' You'd be good on that."

"Are we done here?"

"Or, 'It goes like this, the fourth, the fifth . . .'"

"'The minor fall, the major lift,'" I quoted back.

"That's you. That line, I mean. If that line were a person, it'd be you."

The air around us turned needle sharp. Orion looked shocked

at himself. I think it was the nicest thing anyone had ever said to me. I tucked my arms into Marine Mingle and nodded toward the window.

"What's that?" I asked.

"Oh. Remember the boat I mentioned?"

"I thought you said building the boat was just an idea."

"It was. But then . . . I finished it. I had a lot of trouble sleeping for a while."

I gaped back at the tarp. "You built a *boat*?"

"It's not much. Just a dinghy. A rowboat. Well, it's got an outboard motor, but still. The original plan had been a sailboat, but I couldn't hack it, at least not by myself and not the first time around. Liv's dad helped a lot. It's really not a big deal."

"Orion. Shut up. This is not the time for modesty. You murder on the trumpet, and you built a freaking *boat*. Does Liv know you finished this?"

He shook his head. "I'm not even sure I'm going to tell her."

"You're not going to *tell* her? As your official go-between, I feel this boat could be your ultimate wooing move. Few girls would be able to resist a boat. Play the trumpet for her, too, and she's all yours."

"Would you be able to resist a boat?"

"I'm off-limits, I remind you."

"Not *mine*. Just . . . someone's."

I hesitated. I could keep the romance channel firmly switched to off.

"My powers of resistance are legendary."

Resisted!

"But it's possible they might bend to a boat. Not *your* boat, of course."

So much for growing out of the shipwreck gene.

"Of course," Orion said. "I can show you something else, though. Requires a walk. Want to see?"

"*Yes,*" I said, perhaps overenthusiastically.

Orion's house was farther inland than Toby's, more deeply set in the woods.

We walked along a well-trodden dirt path through the woods. Trees closed above us and light grew dim. Far off, I could make out the sound of water. The hiking wasn't terribly tough: the ground was flat, but it was a hot, humid day, overcast with clouds, and buggy as we walked deeper into the woods.

"We won't go too far," Orion said.

Suddenly, like a typhoon, I missed New York. I missed things I'd never thought I'd miss: noise, traffic, the subway in the summer. I missed my parents. My brother. I was supposed to be finding the wreck today, and look where I was now: in the middle of the woods with some boy. I had terrible follow-through. This was Rus and the Karaoke Disaster all over again, just without the booze. Soon a whole summer would pass, and I'd have nothing to show to Sam but a new sweatshirt.

"Just up here," Orion said, pointing.

Set into the side of the hill was a gaping hole formed by enormous boulders: a stone crevasse like an opening to the underworld.

"It's really cool inside," he assured me, striding toward the opening.

"You want me to go *in there?*" I said. "What about bears?"

Orion just laughed and shimmied sideways through the gap in the rock. Not feeling reassured, I wedged myself through behind him. At least it wasn't a true cave, so my voice would carry if I were mauled. The tops of trees were still visible as we walked deeper into the split between the boulders, a wedge of humid gray sky always visible, ten, fifteen, twenty feet below the opening. It was *cold* down here.

"This is what I wanted to show you," Orion said.

He pointed to a rocky shelf where the split ended, set in shadow. There, even in the July heat, was a stripe of bright white snow.

"Welcome to the Nivation Hollow," he said.

I knew Orion meant for me to be amazed. *Dazzled.* Snow in July in a hole in the world: What was that, if not treasure?

But I missed home. I missed my brother. I felt like a fuckup. Why was I here in a hole in the ground with this boy, instead of checking in with Sam every single day?

Orion, meanwhile, was explaining geology. "It's also called a snow niche, and its formation is a periglacial process. Basically, this snow freezes and never fully thaws—so it's been around for centuries."

A bit of wall crumbled off in my hand. Little shards of shale clung to my fingertips, and I rubbed them against my thighs so they scratched.

"There used to be way more snow, actually. I used to come up here with a lunch box and pack it full in the summer. Put it in the freezer. I wanted to have snow in August."

Names had been scratched into the rock across the rest of the hollow: *John and Loretta, 1999. You are beautiful. Marie was here.* Some of the graffiti was even older—one was dated 1884, the year before the *Lyric* sank, the year before the town had been made official. I couldn't even believe that people had been coming here that long. There must've been so much snow there. What would I write? *Violet: Descendant of Fidelia and eternal fuckup.*

Something wet and cold slid down my back. I yelped and wriggled. A chip of ice fell from the hem of my sweatshirt.

"Couldn't resist," Orion said.

He packed a scratchy snowball, then tossed it my way. I caught it and whipped it back so hard it burst on the wall behind him. Orion dodged just in time.

"Could've broken my nose, Babe Ruth!" he said, laughing.

I wasn't in the mood. "I thought he was a hitter."

"Started out pitching."

"What time is it? I'm starving." My hands were red and rough, raw from the cold. I blew on my fingers to warm them.

"Here," Orion said. He stepped toward me and took my hands, then tucked them inside his shirt and flattened them against his stomach. Yes. *On his stomach.* His warm stomach that made my fingers tingle as they touched skin and a wiry happy trail that ran from his belly button to the lip of his jeans.

"I run pretty hot," he said.

I would've made a crack if I could—would've been a fucking layup—but I could barely open my mouth. Because I was *touching Orion Lewis's stomach* with my wet-snow hands—sad, homesick hands, hands that lost everything, hands that should've been googling *how to find a shipwreck*—but hands that were still connected to a person with a body. The romance channel came in loud and clear, playing *yes yes yes.* . . .

He leaned toward me. My heart pounded. His mouth was still red from the trumpet. He put cold fingers to my face; traced them over my lips. Instinctively, I shut my eyes. His lips brushed mine, just a little bit, so soft they might have been snowflakes.

I opened my left eye a sliver, just enough to see the ratty cuffs of my new sweatshirt on Orion's stomach.

I am sorry to report that was as hot as it got.

Because let's not forget my shipwreck gene.

When he put his mouth to mine, I spoke: "Liv."

Yes. That's right. Orion Lewis, Eyebrow God, the Certifiable Smokeshow, Dreamboat Builder of Boats, Player of the Trumpet, Serenader of Lobsters, tried to kiss me in a magical nivation hollow, and I said the name of his longtime lady love *INTO HIS MOUTH*.

I mean—not kissing was the original goal. So we can consider that a win.

Except it was not a win. Not at all. BECAUSE I COULD HAVE HAD PASSIONATE SEX IN A NIVATION HOLLOW WITH A GAP-TOOTHED EYEBROW GOD.

The walk back to his house was awkward. Orion was silent, pulling leaves from trees, shredding them from their veins. The situation grew even *more* awkward when I had to ask for a ride home. We rode in the Apogee in silence. I counted the empty bottles in the front seat: nine.

"I shouldn't have done that," he said. "I'm really sorry, Violet. I mean, there's Liv, and we *work* together, you know?"

Here is what I wanted to say: *Do that again! I'll kiss you back, I promise! You just caught me in a weird, melancholy moment!*

Here is what I said: "It's no big deal."

I couldn't believe myself. I had *never* turned down a kiss, not even if the guy had a soul patch or wore exclusively ironic T-shirts or if the girl had been smoking all night. But the second a nice, sweet boy made the moves on me: nope, no, shut it down, think of Liv, say Liv, Liv, Liv Liv Liv Liv!

Fuck the shipwreck gene.

Perhaps, said a feeble voice that didn't even sound like my own, *this wasn't a shipwreck gene, but a choice, that follow-through you so longed for, and now you're actually making good on . . .*

"You won't tell Liv, right?"

"I won't," I promised.

"Will this be weird?" Orion asked. "I really don't want it to be weird."

"It won't be weird," I assured him. That was one good thing to come out of the Year of Wild. Situations that required grace, nuance, and a proper empathetic response (see: *that's enough, Violet*) were a challenge, but pretending like a nonkiss in a magical hollow with my coworker had never happened?

That was totally in my repertoire.

INDEPENDENCE DAY

The next day, I celebrated our great nation's independence by not thinking about sex, and reading the letters of my great-great-great-grandparents. While googling *how to find a shipwreck* had gotten me nowhere besides demoralizing websites that talked about grants from NOAA, the letters had been easy to find: in a trunk in the attic, a whole bundle of them.

"How do you just have documents from the 1900s up there?" I asked Toby. "Shouldn't these be in temperature-controlled vaults? Or at least, like, plastic?"

Toby was unperturbed. "Some people have Caravaggios in the attic. This strikes me as fairly tame in comparison."

Finding the letters might have been easy, but *reading* them was a challenge. Toby had assembled nearly all of the Emerald City while I tried to make sense of Fidelia's craggy, cramped handwriting and Ransome's indecipherable scrawl. There weren't even that many letters between Ransome and Fidelia. Most of the letters seemed to have been written to their sons at college. The ones that *did* exist made heavy use of *my darling*, but mostly they were humdrum accounts of their daily life, descriptions of milk deliveries and what they'd seen on walks. Their marriage seemed dull. Normal.

Certainly not doing a whole lot to support Liv's theory that *their love was a whole lot weirder than people are willing to admit*—mostly it just seemed that they'd really liked each other.

Reading through these was a waste of time. I should have been wreck-hunting harder. At the very least, I should have been spending some quality time with Cousteau and *Diving for Sunken Treasure*. I cracked the book open and sighed, determined to finally understand the principles of marine archaeology and not just look at the pictures.

"Shouldn't you be off shooting illegal fireworks?" Toby asked, not looking up from the puzzle. He kept complaining that his back hurt.

"Shouldn't you not encourage dangerous behavior?"

"What happened to those kids you've been hanging out with?"

"Why do you care so much?"

"It's my job to care," Toby said. "You should at least call home. Your mom would love to hear from you."

"*You* call her. I'm busy." I waved the stack of letters at him.

"Make you a deal," he said. "You call, and I'll read the last of those letters."

I considered this. It was four in the afternoon, and she'd have the day off—she'd probably finished the crossword long ago, and was now trying to be *productive*, reorganizing the bookshelf or making the kitchen "more efficient." Her inability to sit still had always bothered me, but now the thought of her trying to find the best place for the pepper mill made my heart pang.

"Fine," I said.

"What am I looking for exactly?"

"Anything that shows *their love was weirder than people were willing to admit*, or any mention of where the wreck of the *Lyric* might be."

"So a needle in the haystack," he said.

"Essentially, yes."

⌘

"VisweetieI'msogladyoucalled!"

At the sound of my mom's voice, the pressure in my chest lifted. My heart unsnarled. I love my mom, I thought dumbly. It was that easy.

"We miss you!" she said.

"I miss you, too. I'm in your room, actually." I'd wandered into her childhood bedroom on the cordless phone, curled up in her blue canopy bed with her stuffed cat collection, and *missing her* barely covered it. I wanted to teleport into my mom's lap and never leave.

"How's Dad?" I asked.

"He's okay," she said. "Grilling."

Leave it to my parents to *grill*, even on the most fucked-up Fourth of July in family history. Perseverance, indeed.

"How's Toby?" Mom asked.

"Terrible at puzzles."

"Some things never change. He sent me your picture from the Lighthouse Museum's website. I can't believe you finally made it there! How was it? That lipstick made you look so grown-up."

"It was yours. Or, I found it in your room."

"Wow. I'm surprised it hadn't gone bad."

We both knew the next question. Neither of us wanted to ask it.

"I spoke to Sam," she said at last. "They're off to fireworks tonight. The whole group is, I mean. He's gained some weight, so that's good. He has privileges now to go into town, which means he's made progress."

"I sent him a letter. And an aquarium shirt."

"Good. I'm glad."

Another pause. I pictured my mom fiddling with the back of her earring. I took a raggedy white cat with ice-blue marble eyes into my arms.

"Your father and I are thinking of spending the last couple of weeks of August together in Maine as a family. You two are actually not that far apart, it turns out."

I was quiet. The last time we were all together as a family . . .

"It won't be Spain," she said cautiously.

"That sounds good."

"Good," she said.

We breathed. I tapped on the kitty's eyes with my fingernail. How did my mom and I have so *little* to say to one another, after all that had happened? This was the woman who used to tuck me into the folds of her coat and call me her koala.

"Mom, am I here because of the vending machines? Or because of what I said about the snorkel? Because I'm sorry for that, I didn't mean it, you have to know, I think I was just upset—you were so mad—"

"Snorkel?"

"I made an awful joke, and you were like, *That's enough, Violet*, and I'm so sorry. . . ."

"Honey, honey, stop. Breathe for a second. Listen to me. First of all, I can't even remember half of what happened that day, or that week, or the week before, and if I spoke to you sharply that day, I'm sorry, I'm so sorry. I know you were upset. I was, too. We all were."

I nodded and realized she couldn't see me.

"Second of all, you know your going to Lyric had nothing to do with Sam. Well, that's not true. But it wasn't *because* of Sam. We talked about this."

"What do you mean? Are you talking about the romance channel?"

"The romance channel? No. That was such a dumb thing to say, I regret saying that. No, when we talked—" And she sucked in her breath. "We never talked about it."

"Talked about what?"

"Oh my God, I'm a terrible mother. I guess—shit. Goddammit. Shit."

"Mom? What's wrong? Did I do something?"

"No, no. You didn't do anything. *I* screwed up. Oh, Violet. Oh, honey. Listen."

She explained as I held the stuffed animal to my face: how she and Toby had been talking more, in the spring, right after Spain. How he offered to have me come stay, just for a few weeks. In July, maybe. How the plan had been to involve me in the conversation, to ask me how that sounded, but with Sam, they'd made the decision for me.

"Toby wanted me here?" I said, wiping my face on the cat.

"Yes. *Yes.* You're so wanted. We want you here, too," she said. "Violet, do you want to come home?"

"What?"

"I wasn't thinking straight in June. Obviously. You must have felt so abandoned. Do you want to come home? You can. You're not missing anything, just me and Dad grilling, but maybe . . ."

I could go home?

I could go *home*.

I could pick up where I left off. Text my friends. Go to summer concerts. Wear glitter on my cheeks and run through the city at night, tipsy and giggling and warm. Just yesterday, I'd missed New York. Or maybe I wouldn't even fall into old patterns. Maybe I could just crawl into my mom's lap and stay there.

I'd never have to see Orion again. Or Liv. I could forget about finding the wreck, and truthing. How likely was it, really, that we'd find anything?

"I don't know," I said slowly. "It's just—I've been doing a lot of family research on Fidelia. Trying to flesh out holes. Understand the family a little more."

"Oh?" she said. She was trying to sound positive, but she just sounded hurt. She wanted me to come home. She missed me. She actually *missed* me.

"Have you found anything good?" she asked.

Responses ballooned in my chest. I learned that you basically raised Toby, and I didn't do anything to make your life easier. That you're so much stronger than I thought you were. That your life was so much more complicated than I thought.

"Not yet," I said. "Hey, Mom?"

"Hey, Vi?"

Another balloon joined the responses. *I love you, Mom.* It wasn't hard to tell her.

"Can I go through your old jewelry box?"

The balloon sputtered and deflated. My mom sighed.

"Sure. It's junk jewelry, anyway. Stuff I wore when I was your age." She waited another beat. "Anything else going on?"

Just missing Sam so much I can't breathe.

"Not really."

"Us, either."

We were terrible liars.

When we hung up, I laid her jewelry across the bed: the gold horse pendant, the crystal necklace, the fake diamond bracelet. My favorite piece was a silver pocket watch on a chain: broken, of course, and badly tarnished, but in the palm of my hand it was heavy and satisfying as a good skipping stone. A lone earring was tangled in its chain—the size of a clove of garlic and made of cut green glass—but I liked the way they looked together, like a makeshift charm necklace. In the mirror, wearing that necklace and the Ink lipstick, I looked a little bit, I thought, like my mom.

"Playing dress-up?" Toby asked, appearing in the doorway. "Oooh, you found the best thing. Your mom and I used to fight over that watch as kids. Our mom told us it was lucky."

"Sounds like a thing I should never take off, then."

"I wouldn't put a lot of stock in anything our mother said."

I tugged at the charm on the necklace. "My mom said I could come home."

"And you're staying?"

I nodded. I must've looked like I'd been crying, but Toby didn't mention it.

"Good. You're doing good here. Keeping me in line. Frankly, I don't know how your mother manages in New York. I left that place after a year."

"You were in New York, too?"

"Years ago. I did a stint in art school but had to leave. It made me too anxious."

"Art school? What? And you're not anxious."

"Past life. And if I'm not anxious that's because the meds are working. And because I like what I do. Why do you think I chose to live here, and not in New York?"

I'd never really considered anything in Toby's life a *choice*—I'd always thought of him as vaguely black-sheep-ish. But Maine, the house, the slow puzzling, the man bun—these were things that he'd chosen. Toby was leading the life he wanted. In spite of all his genetics.

I was descended from a survivor of a shipwreck, sure—but I also could make my own choices. I'd already chosen to stay in Lyric, hadn't I?

"I'm glad you're staying," Toby said. He pulled a letter from his breast pocket and passed it toward me. "Especially because your research assistant just made a big discovery. I take cash or check."

∞

November 1919

My darling boy,

Your father and I have received your most recent letter. We both ache for you and send you boundless love. Remember that your periods of sadness have come before and they have passed. Sadness moves like the tide, and this wave, like the others, will retreat. You say your brothers are stronger than you because they fought, but they hurt, my love, and they talk of you often, of your bravery. Remember to take care of yourself. See a doctor, take a tonic, eat a full meal. Sleep, darling. Sleep is important. Know that I think of you every moment of every day. I wish, darling, that this could be enough.

Do you remember the stories we told you when you were small? I think, in particular, of the story of the whale that delivered me from the wreck. How you loved this story! How you begged for me to tell it! Your brave mother rode on a whale's back to escape the sea. I delight, even now, in the wonder on your face.

Of course, my darling, you understand that this story is a story, nothing more. It has roots in truth, I suppose. It is true that I saw a whale. Through the peculiar haze that descended over the water, against a blinding wall of white, I watched his tail rise from the water. But he did not carry me to safety. I did not even want him to. When I saw him, I wished he would swallow me whole. Clinging to a shred of lifeboat, the screams around me, the bodies in the water, I did not want to live.

I thought living would be too difficult.

I washed ashore in a strange land. I was not brave. I despaired. I wished myself dead many, many times.

I tell you this because I am glad now that I lived. I am glad because of your father, and because of you and your brothers.

I would send a whale to you if I could, a great blue one that would whisk you away to safety. But you know that life is not so kind. These whales that save us are few and far between, if they come at all. And *if they do, they do not change us in the way that we think they will. Magic whales are just that: magic whales, gone in an instant, and your life stretches before you still.*

So, I offer you something far less spectacular than a magic whale, but more durable. I have begun to think of them as pebbles, small moments from each day that I collect and store in the corners of my mind. These are moments I hold fast to when I am in a period of sadness: a lump of sugar dissolving into morning coffee. Watching ink dry on the page. The smile on your father's face when we come across deer tracks in the woods; the way he knows the names of trees. Your handwriting on an envelope addressed to me.

These pebbles are there in your day, if you hunt. Find your own pebbles, my darling. Pebbles can make a beach, and a beach can save you. More so, even, than a magic whale.

All my love to you,
Your mother

⋇

My mind was racing. My great-great-great-grandmother was a *person*.

She wasn't just a story. She had handwriting. Words. Thoughts and feelings, advice for her kids. She wasn't all perseverance and luck. She'd been in a real wreck—the wall of white, that was the blizzard, and there'd been a whale and a lifeboat—and part of me was already thinking like Liv, wondering how I could use these facts as a springboard toward theory, but the other part of me just hurt. Fidelia had been sad and scared and lost.

I sat there on my mother's bed and the pain worked its way through me. She knew what to say to her son, and she knew what to say to Sam, and to me.

I wanted that to be my inheritance.

Dear Sam,

Happy 4th of July! You haven't even gotten my first letter, but I wanted to say hi. There is already progress in the wreck search. Whales are involved. Here's a drawing of you and me:

All my love to you,
Your sister

REPRISE REJECTED

Three days after our nonkiss, letters winging their way to Sam, I marched into the aquarium with a question guaranteed to make things between Orion and me as not-weird as possible. I had on my Marine Mingle sweatshirt, and my mom's pocket watch, too, and grains of salt, or whatever, but I kind of liked the idea that it was lucky.

"Orion, if you were a whale in March of 1885, where in the ocean would you be?"

I frog-marched him over to the animated wreck map. The red line stretched, exploded, and the stick survivor swam for shore, again and again.

"Fidelia saw a whale the night the ship sank. If we knew where whales usually were, I thought we could narrow down the location of the wreck. Track them."

"Man. I know Liv got in your head, but she *really* got in your head, huh?"

I said her name into his mouth.

I said her name into his mouth.

I said her name into his mouth.

"Sorry," Orion said, "trying to not be weird. Um, lemme think.

Whales are generally migrating by March. They calve in the spring in warmer waters. It's possible there were some here in the late spring . . . but . . . I mean, there *is* a feeding ground up here." He pointed so far north I imagined ice caps and polar bears. "Maybe the boat veered off course?"

"Maybe." Fidelia's *blinding wall of white* said differently.

"Violet, I've got a question for you, too."

Oh, Jesus. Couldn't we just pretend nothing had happened?

"Would you want to put together an educational concert series here? For kids? I don't know if you've noticed, but the aquarium's kinda struggling. Joan thinks the answer's in education. She thought your song workshop went so well the other day, she wants it to be like a daily thing. She mentioned that you wanted to get more involved."

I gaped like a bottom feeder.

"We already have a bunch of lyrics. We can just make them more school-y. It's not exactly penguins, but we could even do a show at the end of the summer to raise money."

I pictured the two of us singing "Cod Only Knows," getting lost in each other's googly fish eyes. I hadn't been on a real stage, in front of a real audience, since Broadway.

"We'd have to do a lot of work, but it'd be pretty fun. . . ."

"No."

His face fell. "What do you mean, 'no'?"

"I don't sing anymore."

"You sang for all those kids. You sang for me."

"The first time, I was desperate, and the second time, you bullied me into it," I said. I breathed in, trying to think of a way to explain this to him. "Look, you know I was in the Broadway revival of *Peter Pan*?"

"See? That's perfect. I knew you were good! You're a *star*!"

"No. I'm not. That's the point. *Peter Pan* ruined lives, okay?"

"What'd you do? Kill Tinker Bell?"

"Never mind." I retreated to the gift shop, but Orion just followed me, and then I'd accidentally cornered myself behind the Scrooge McDuck.

"Look. I don't believe that a Broadway musical ruined lives. And this—it's not going to be Broadway, just fish songs. I don't think you realize how good you are onstage. You come alive when you do it. You make *me* want to sing, and I haven't in forever. I wasn't going to bring this up, but"—he lowered his voice—"that's why I kissed you. Your singing."

As if I needed another reason to say no.

"Orion, just trust me about this, okay? Forget I sang. It's not a good idea. When I perform, it only ends in disaster."

ALL CHILDREN, EXCEPT ONE, **GROW UP**

If I had to put a date on it—the moment that Sam and I splintered—it was the night of my Broadway debut. My big break was our big break.

I was twelve; Sam was eleven. By then, I'd been Dorothy in *The Wizard of Oz* and Annie in *Annie Get Your Gun*, and the spring before I'd brought the house down with "Moonshine Lullaby." My theater director had a friend casting for a revival on Broadway, and he recommended me for an audition. Not to blame my director, but he made a critical mistake: he told *me* about the audition before he told my parents. And I told Sam.

That afternoon, my mom came home to find the babysitter exhausted and me and Sam leaping from couch to coffee table, shrieking, *I'm flying, flying, flying!* In Maine, he and I were deep-sea divers, but here in New York, we were *magic*. We flew! We'd cover the whole world, him and me, sea to stars.

"Violet's going to be in *Peter Pan*!" Sam screamed.

Like my mom even had a *chance* to say no. Especially not after I nailed the audition.

"I don't like this," I overheard my mom say to my dad that

night. "I'm worried about her missing school. And her taking the subway by herself?"

"You grew up in Maine, honey. This is what kids do in the city. She's happy," my dad said. "And did you see how happy *he* was, too?"

My dad had a point: Sam had been having a tough time recently. His tantrums were rarer, but more often teachers called home, noting that he'd seemed withdrawn and quiet. He was too thin and the doctor had prescribed a breakfast of waffles made with heavy cream to help him gain weight. There was talk of growth hormones, too, but there was still a chance Sam's body would catch up. "Hard to say what's physical and what's emotional" had been the doctor's line.

Through the wall between our rooms, there was the sound of fabric on fabric, then the noise of something wet. It took me a second to understand: my parents were kissing.

"This is professional theater," my dad said. "Nothing bad is going to happen."

Hence: *propriety.* On Broadway, things were wholesome, scandal-free—at least they had to be in my parents' understanding. When they asked how rehearsal was, I babbled about the tutor who taught us French irregular verbs, or the soy milk pudding we'd had for snack: nutritious *and* delicious. Or I talked about my friend Isla, *eye-lah*, fifteen and part Latvian, part Filipina, part Dominican, which meant, she said, she could play "almost any ethnicity." She had an *agent*, I told them, and—get this—her mom played Maria in the national tour of *West Side Story.*

The seedy bits I kept to myself. How the older Lost Boys compared blow-job tips with some of the pirates until they realized I was listening, at which point they switched to fisting. That the contents of Mrs. Darling's travel mug smelled more like nail-polish remover than coffee. The rumor that Wendy—poor, poor nineteen-year-old Wendy—was having an affair with the technical director, a man my dad's age with a ponytail longer than mine. Through her dressing room door, Isla and I listened for sex noises with an overturned glass like they did in Nancy Drew, giggling, and I had this petrifying thought that I *wanted* to hear sex noises, was *hoping* to hear them. With Isla, specifically.

I knew better than to mention this scene to my parents. Besides, Sam had pitched a fit in art class that day. He'd torn apart the painting he'd been making, and he'd hidden under the table for all of class. At least that's what I gathered from eavesdropping on my parents as we played *Peter Pan* in socks. They washed the dishes and I half listened, half taught him the lines I was learning, because it helped me remember.

"Isn't he a little young for medication?" my dad said. "Middle school's hard on everyone. What if we both just cut back on hours? Spend more time at home."

"College tuition doesn't grow on trees," my mom snapped. "I'm sorry. I just think—everything is so crazy right now. I'm at the end of my rope. Everything will be easier when *Peter Pan*'s over."

I let Sam sing the line about climbing trees and dignity because it was his favorite and he beamed through the lyrics.

The musical director—*not* the technical director—liked me. I remembered blocking. I could hit the harmonies. I sang when I was told and knew when to shut up.

"Thank God *someone's* listening," the director said. "Now *that's* a skill."

⟡

One afternoon, the director says he has a surprise for me. He sends me to the stage, and there, I find one of the flight techs, holding the harness. Flying by Foy, we all know the name of the company now, and how they're the "industry standard," they won't stop saying it. We've learned the word *aerography*, and I've nearly memorized Peter's aerial steps in "I'm Flying," watched her longingly from the downstairs screens, wished her part were mine.

"Ready to fly?" the tech says.

I'm going to fly, I think.

The tech helps me into the harness, thinner than I expect, but sturdy and complicated, crisscrossed with nylon straps and thick buckles. John complains the harness chafes. The tech's hands are a blur, buckling here, threading there, and then I'm strapped in, ready to fly.

Some of the Lost Boys and Tiger Lily's tribe are funneling out now, with their moms or their nannies, watching me, confused, because they've been told a thousand times that flying's only for principals, *it's not a toy.* Isla and I wave to each other. Milo's with her, too. He's sixteen and plays Michael. The three of us have been hanging out more.

The wires I'm connected to are sturdy, thick metal. As soon as I got cast, Sam got a book out of the library on flight, because that's what he does—he reads. We both love da Vinci's ornithopter, a flying machine based on the ribbing of bat wings. The da Vinci drawings are sketchy, red and brown ink. Flimsy and pretty. None of them worked. These cables that I'm clipped to now aren't pretty, but when you look close, they're made of thinner moon-silver cables all twisted together like a ropy medieval braid, or DNA, and when the lights hit the wires a certain way, there's a definite sparkle there—

"You can hold on to the wires," the tech calls from the wings, "they're not going to break."

One tug—

I hover, gripping the wires—

Two tugs—

I hold my breath, like I'm diving—

And then I'm zooming up, into the sky, the stage lights are suns and the seats are mountains, I'm Icarus with metal wings, I can stay up here as long as I want; Isla waves, I can see the part in her hair, and the Lost Boys are really lost now—

I swing left and right, the harness pinches but who even *cares* about the chafing—John's such a whiner! I point my toes, hold my legs in an arabesque, the buckles click-clack and it's the best noise I've heard. I land on the mantel like Peter (I really have memorized the aerography)—

Isla whoops in the audience and I let go of the wires. I'm holding on to nothing now. I'm seized with a sudden urge to sing, so I do. Peter's song, my voice, my song, bursts out of me, and the near-empty theater explodes with music and words of soaring, and flying, and higher and higher, and if I had my choice, I wouldn't ever come down. The last words I belt in a breathless rush:

follow all the air 'cause I'm about to disappear I'm flying

My toes skim the stage floor, my knees weak like when I got caught in a riptide last summer. The director looks at me like it's for the first time. Then he smiles and says, "You're going to make audiences very happy one day."

When I meet up with Isla, she kisses me on the cheek and tells me I'm a star, that I should've seen the look on Milo's face.

That's when I know: my performance will dazzle my family into *happiness*.

Opening night, an unseasonal heat wave strikes. The radio issues warnings for the elderly, citing last year's death toll. I worry about my parents. Sam is even more irritable than usual. Mom thinks he has reverse seasonal affective disorder. The school called last week about an outburst. They've been calling about my grades, too.

The theater is a blistering inferno. They use special primer for our makeup and an extra-strong hair spray. The twigs'll take years to pull out. Isla and I watch the audience gather on the TV screens downstairs. She's started touching me more, bumping my hip, telling me where to get waxes. I like her in the worst way, where I want to crawl into her skin.

"Violet. Break a leg." It's Milo. We've been talking more. He just got cast as Anna's son in *The King and I*, but made me promise to keep it secret.

"Somebody likes you," Isla whispers. "He's cute, too."

Isla's lips on my ear set off faraway whistles. I shiver.

Two Lost Boys sprint by. One of them has a ring of chocolate around his lips, leftover from that disgusting pudding. The other one Isla has a crush on. She even told me he had a cute ass, which I didn't even know was a thing you were supposed to say.

"Isla," that one says, "you gotta come see. This kid is like *freaking out* upstairs. Like screaming and pounding the floor and shit. Like, he won't move and they can't get the show started because he's blocking the aisles. They're calling security."

There's a plummeting in my body.

"Come on, Violet," Isla says, but I stay.

I've seen that show enough times to have it memorized. My mom's wrong: this isn't *just middle school*, and life will not be easier after *Peter Pan*.

My mom and Sam miss opening night. Onstage, we build a lovely little house for Wendy, and with the rest of the Lost Boys, I step-ball-change with brooms and help make a sloppy bed. Peter rhapsodizes about pockets, and I fluff fake-moss pillows. *We won't be lonely anymore*. I don't miss a single, meaningless beat.

We build the same stage-magic house we build every night,

this fake house full of fake shit that I, stupidly, foolishly, believed would save my very real family.

⁂

I'm supposed to go meet my family upstairs, but I've still got all these twigs in my hair, and I'm wondering if it's really possible to run away and join the circus when I hear my name. *Violet.* It's Milo, sticking his head out of a dark dressing room. He's holding Mrs. Darling's mug. "C'mere," he says.

Mrs. Darling's mug is full of vodka. Milo and I take turns drinking from it, sitting on a couch in the empty dressing room dark. We drain the whole thing. My lips sting. My scalp hurts from the twigs. Vodka feels like the faint hum of bees in my throat. I keep licking the edge of the mug, not for the taste, which is horrible, but for the sting. I like the sting. Milo doesn't notice. He won't stop yammering about *The King and I.*

"Being small for your age is a real advantage in this business," he says, like he's the authority. "No offense."

None taken. I already know I'm too tall, too big. The costume manager binds my boobs before each performance. Nothing to be done about my hips, she said. Everything about me is wrong wrong wrong. I lick the edge of the mug.

"You could play . . . like . . ."

"I don't give a fuck about theater," I say. Isla says that sometimes, and it's funny, but from my mouth, it sounds mean.

"I mean . . ." Milo's scrambling now, and I like it. Watching him flounder makes me feel powerful. "You're, like, *gorgeous*. You don't even, like, *need* theater. You're that kind of pretty."

"Shut up," I say. "Really?" What I don't ask: *I don't even need theater for* what?

"Uh-huh. Everyone says so. Even Captain Hook."

I can tell I'm supposed to find this flattering. Captain Hook has the hairiest arms I've ever seen. I imagine him sitting next to me instead of Milo and feel a little scared.

"Violet," Milo says, "can I kiss you?"

"Sure," I say, rolling my eyes like I've done it a million times, even though it's my first.

Then we're kissing. First one. That's it? I open my eyes and almost laugh because he's so *dumb-looking* he should see his own face. He tries to put a hand through my hair but can't with the twigs, so he just kind of cradles my head like a helmet. I tell myself to *feel*. I think about Isla and the overturned glass, but that's wrong, don't want to think about her, she's too special, she belongs in another brain, a second brain for all my sacred thoughts.

The kissing starts to feel good.

I like kissing Milo. I like it a lot.

Kissing Milo feels, like, *really good*.

I want more. I want years and years and years of this.

I'm on top of him then, flattening the length of my body against his, like I studied once in a movie, only the girl was meant to be on the bottom. My hips make hula-hoop circles, a mind of their own. I want this, I want more.

And then I'm away from him so suddenly that Milo kisses air with his eyes closed, looking dopey and vulnerable.

"I'm twelve," I say. In my memory, I'm sitting now, hugging my knees, but the thing is I don't remember moving. All we did was kiss. So why am I so scared?

Milo scrambles up to sit. He doesn't like what he's heard. "I thought you were Isla's age," he says, like I've betrayed him.

"I'm almost thirteen." *I* sound scared, too. I'm shaking. But I don't want to stop. I want to keep going. I think.

"You're *twelve*," he says, "and you kiss like *that*?"

Milo wipes his mouth with the back of his hand because kissing like *that* is not a good thing. Kissing me is gross and weird.

"I have to go," he says. He sounds even more scared than I am. I scared *him*.

"Bye," I say, like I'm cool.

Alone, I run my hand around the inside of Mrs. Darling's mug and lick my fingers, trying to get the sting back. I'm twelve, and I kiss like that. How would it be different if I were thirteen? Seventeen? How was I supposed to kiss?

I'm starting to feel a little sick. Bees are prickling in my brain. Is this what they mean, when they say *buzzed*? I list things in the room to remind myself where I am. I'm holding Mrs. Darling's empty mug. I'm in my street clothes. These are my shoes. There are sticks in my hair. I'm steady. In the mirror, I look the same, even though I know I'm different. My insides are a twister. I change the settings on the vanity, I get so close up that my face fuzzes out.

My parents are waiting for me upstairs. We're going to miss our dinner reservation. That's fine. Sam won't eat anything anyway. Soon he'll up therapy to three times a week, start on meds, ace his classes. Come fall, I'll hang out with Isla once or twice, but she'll bring her boyfriend, and it'll be so awkward that I'll cry in the bathroom and make some excuse to go home early. I'll bounce back strong, start going to parties where people are left breathless by the way I kiss, people who don't wipe their mouth like I am an ugly curse.

My hair looks kind of cool with those twigs.

I hate Milo. I hope he gets hit by a bus.

"I am Oz, the great and powerful," I say, lips against the mirror. "Ozzz."

I buzz like a bee, because I'm alone, and I'm mean, and I can. In the mirror, I pull my face steady, ice cold, and in a blink, I'm a marble statue, like at the Met. I make another face and I'm a blue-and-gold night, smeary constellations. Tourists will crowd around me and fight to take my picture, flashes like galaxies. Another face, another, another—

I'm me again. Sort of. I'm me and all the things, too. Me, boy, girl. Him, you. Powerful beautiful it. I kiss like *that*, like it's a *gift* and a *curse*. I leave behind a wake of splintered wood and broken buildings and scared, know-nothing boys.

TREASURES OF ATLANTIS

Orion didn't bring up singing again that week, and I was grateful. Instead, I had him arrange my meeting with Liv, following up on Mariah's tip about the supposed *Lyric* porthole. Saturday afternoon, Liv was waiting for me outside Treasures of Atlantis to investigate. It was kind of fun, getting together without a phone: each time we actually met up seemed a small miracle.

"Shall we?" she said. She pushed open the door, the bell tinkled, and I squinted like a reflex against the barrage of crystals and clutter and the silver science whirligigs. The Wonder Emporium was a just-as-crowded, fancier version of Toby's house, part new age, part antiques, and you could spend a lot of time and money here. My mom hated it.

"Friends!" Felix's voice came from the depths. "May you find everything you didn't know you needed! I'm back here, with the ship shit!"

"How does he know it's us?" I asked Liv.

"He's probably been saying that to everyone who's come in for the past hour," she said.

We twisted through slim aisles, careful not to knock anything over, until we spotted Felix, among lights in brass cages with red and blue lenses, an actual steering wheel—a helm, rather—and rusted metal bells that came up to my hip, all dredged from the sea. Felix pointed above a Liv-size wooden mermaid that leaned haphazardly against the wall, and there was the golden porthole labeled NOT FOR SALE.

"My dad's luckiest find. He was metal detecting at Seal Cove. Now, admittedly, we *are* amateur historians—and, like, don't go spreading it around, because metal detecting at Seal Cove's illegal—but we *believe* this comes from the *Lyric*. The make is consistent with what would have been found on the ship."

The porthole was a perfect brass circle. This had been on the ship with Fidelia. Maybe she'd even looked out this window, watched the blinding wall of white bear down on her, rubbed off condensation from the peculiar haze. I'd considered showing Liv the letter, but reading it had felt so personal. I wanted it to be just mine.

"We have to go to that beach," I said to Liv.

"And do what? Deep dives to the bottom of the ocean?"

"Maybe there's more debris!"

"I can get you the shop's metal detector," Felix offered. "It's a little wonky, but . . ."

"You just said it's illegal," said Liv.

"But if it's illegal to look there, maybe the ship's been hiding in plain sight, for years, like that Revolutionary War ship you mentioned. Seriously! It doesn't hurt to look. Another artifact could confirm the ship's location. Why not? Next weekend?"

"You've created a wreck-hunting monster, Liv," Felix said.

"This is what I get for asking people to consider things a metaphor," she muttered, but I could tell she was pleased.

I considered the porthole, tugging on the watch around my neck. I'd been wearing it since I'd found it in my mom's jewelry box, fiddling with the charms when I was thinking.

"That's quite a necklace, Violet," Felix said.

"It was my mom's. It's lucky, supposedly."

"Emeralds are usually cursed," Felix said.

"Oh. I meant the watch. And it's not an emerald. It's fake."

"Trust me," Felix said, tapping the space beneath his eye. "I know glass, and that is *not* glass."

"No *way*," Liv said.

Horrified, I ripped the necklace over my head. The green jewel knotted tightly in the chain sparkled back at me, looking suddenly realer and heavier that it had before.

"Holy *shit*," I said, "I've cleaned *tanks* in this necklace."

"Can I see?" Felix asked, holding out his hand.

"Definitely." I wanted to get that necklace as far away from me as possible.

"Tarnished," Felix said, clucking his tongue. "But there's a great design under here. You want me to polish this for you?"

"That'd be great."

"For a price." He looked at me hopefully. "One tea-leaf guinea pig?"

The last thing I wanted was an amateur clairvoyant poking around my brain, discovering my failed romantical foray with Orion. Liv claimed she wasn't interested in him, but my non-kiss with her nonboyfriend wasn't exactly a moment I wanted to *advertise*.

"I'll do it," Liv offered.

"I did your tarot a few weeks ago," Felix said. "You're not supposed to overdo someone's future. It dilutes the power of the reading. Besides, Violet, didn't you use to steal shit from the store? You owe me."

I groaned. "I really hate tea."

Felix clapped and disappeared through the aisles. "I'll put the kettle on," we heard. Liv pawed through a nearby tin of old postcards.

"Jesus," I said, "I really had no idea that was an emerald."

"Lucky you, I guess," Liv said. Her voice was a little brittle, I thought—or maybe that was in my head. She passed me a stack of cards. "These are silly," she said.

I flipped through them: women dressed as mermaids and posing on rocks, women swimming underwater, 1950s pinup girls with red lips, glistening scaled tails, and butter-yellow bathing suits. There was a note on the back of one in faded pencil.

Dear Stan, Caught this show at Weeki Wachee, hope Minnie's feeling better, we're sending you our love. Lois and Bill.

"I always thought mermaids would be more vicious," Liv said, passing me the tin. "Green skin. Sharp teeth. Not quite so . . ."

"Hot?"

"Sure," she said, betraying nothing. There were a few more Weeki Wachee postcards, and I took them, plus a few extras to send to Sam, my parents, maybe. Maybe to Toby, when I got back this fall.

"What does it say about me, that I'm a sucker for ladies with scales?" I said.

"Is that a rhetorical question?"

"Maybe I've just developed a fish fetish after all that time in the aquarium."

"Maybe." Liv cleared her throat. "Violet, can I ask you a question?"

"Shoot."

"Forgive me if I'm prying . . . but . . . would you say you're . . ."

Let me be perfectly clear: I knew exactly what Liv wanted to ask. I knew the moment she passed me the picture of the pinup mermaid. What was more: I wanted her to ask. Because I wanted to ask her the same question.

"Would I say I'm . . ." I prompted.

"I mean. How do you orient yourself? Toward others. In terms of attraction?"

"Are you asking me men or women?"

"If I'm prying . . ."

"I'm *teasing* you."

"Oh. That's very annoying. What's next, pulling my pigtail?"

She looked surprised at herself and quickly became busy straightening the lamps on a shelf into a neat row, dusting them with her fingertips.

"I'm whatever," I said. "Mostly boys in New York. But if a girl like that came along"—here I gestured to the mermaid—"ten out of ten. Who wouldn't?"

I watched Liv's face for a hiccup—a turn toward me, a turn away—

"I know plenty of people in Lyric, Maine, who wouldn't," she said, betraying nothing.

"I'm sorry—I didn't mean—"

"It's fine. I'm not mad at *you*."

She might not have been mad, but she was right. I was lucky. I went through life assuming that everyone else was in my boat. My comparative yacht, I realized, thinking guiltily of the emerald.

"Were your parents upset?" she asked.

"Upset? No. We hardly even talked about it," I said, watching my yacht grow larger. "What about you?" I asked.

"Me?"

"No, *her*." I pointed at the wooden mermaid.

"I *do* wonder how mermaids procreate."

"I always assumed they laid eggs. Though that makes them less sexy. Though maybe not! There's some weird shit out there. Tentacle porn."

Liv laughed. "I'm not whatever. Only boys. Definitely no ten-tacles. Not that any of that matters, compared to school. Oxford."

"Eyes on the prize."

"Can I ask you a dumb question?"

"Shoot."

"Why didn't you just say so?"

"Show up and scream, 'Come one, come all'?"

"Violet, give me a break, okay? Seriously. Why?"

I looked at Liv and I thought of that idiot in seventh grade who'd said, *You're gay or straight and everyone else is just desperate*, to a chorus of laughs; of the raven-haired girl who'd called me her "Litmus Test" after we'd hooked up last summer. How, after I'd got-ten in trouble for pot, the principal sang the praises of the queer student union, convinced she'd handed me the psychoanalytic eureka moment I'd been searching for my whole life.

I looked at Liv and thought, I just wanted this part to be folded in gently with the rest of me, like egg whites.

"I didn't want it to be the only thing you heard," I said.

"I get that." Liv returned to her lamps, all now at right angles, all facing the same way. "So, I go to church every Sunday with my parents," she said. "I know church is messed up. But I like it. Ours anyway. The ritual. I spend a lot of time looking at people's faces, how bored they are . . . I mean, I'll probably get struck by light-ning for saying this, but I'm on the fence about God anyway, and I'd definitely never say this to my parents, but . . . the faces. Some-times I think that's what church is about, not whoever's running the show, but just seeing other people and imagining what they're thinking. Or maybe Felix is *right* about the universe, and energy, and that's why the church burned witches, because they were taking out the competition. Classic capitalism. Because it's all the same idea. Some net beneath us. I probably sound crazy. I should just stop talking."

"You're not crazy," I said, "and you should *never* stop talking."

"You'd get sick of me," she said, but she was pulling the corners of her mouth down to keep herself from smiling. I wish she'd let herself.

"Why wouldn't you say any of that to your parents?" I said.

"I don't know. My mom teaches fifth-grade social studies, and my dad's a contractor. They're just very *concrete*, I guess."

The question bubbled up in my throat: Liv, are *you* very concrete?

Before I could ask, the kettle whistled loudly from the back room, beckoning us toward our future.

❀

"Tasseography," Felix announced, "or the *art of reading tea leaves*."

"You're doing this from your *phone?*" Liv said, aghast.

We were in the shop's tiny back office clustered around a small table. Felix had lowered the lights and lit a stick of jasmine incense. I coughed.

"Clairvoyants live in the digital age, too. Get with the program."

He passed me a steaming plastic travel mug of tea; it bore an illustration of Elvis crooning into a microphone.

"'I've Been to Graceland'?" I read from the mug. "I do not consider this auspicious."

"The vessel has no bearing on the reading," he assured me. "*Drink.*"

I drank and immediately spat my tea onto the floor.

"*Really?*" Felix said. He started riffling through drawers for a rag.

"That tastes," I said, "like bark."

I passed the mug to Liv for confirmation. Our fingers brushed. I tried not to think about it. I tried not to think about the fact that her mouth sipped from the exact same spot mine had sipped from. I tried not to think of this as a purposeful, by-proxy lip-lock. Especially since I had her answer: *Only boys. Not whatever.*

"No *sharing*! You're probably scrambling your destinies together," Felix scolded. He consulted his screen. "Violet, you can rip the bag into the shape of a cross. To represent the four elements. Strictly pagan."

I glanced at Liv, thinking about faces and church and boredom, and in spite of everything—the Elvis mug, the phone—I felt a little thrill deep in my stomach as the herbs slipped through my fingers, hot and foresty. Elemental.

"Oh, shit. You were supposed to be thinking of a question that whole time," Felix said.

"Amateur hour," Liv said.

"Not all of us can be professors-in-training," Felix said. "Just think of one now. About your future."

"My *future*?" I'd spent the past few weeks so buried in the past that it had barely occurred to me that I *had* a future. Me. Violet. I was a person moving through the world. This summer would end; I'd go home. Back to New York. To our apartment. To school. The same binders, the same hallways, the same bathroom with the too-bright fluorescents that Sam avoided. The same people I'd dropped at the beginning of the summer.

How could we possibly just resume our lives, after everything that had happened? How could we move *forward*?

"Ready?" Felix asked.

"Sure," I said.

He peered into the murk, then covered his glass eye with one hand.

"I *guess* that looks like a ring," Felix said. He scrolled through his phone. "The ring means marriage."

"I'm sixteen."

"Maybe it's an *O*," Liv said. "Orion."

My heart stopped. What was she trying to say? Did she know about the nonkiss? No. She couldn't. He made *me* promise not to tell anyone; no way he would have told her.

"Maybe *you'll* marry him, since Felix accused our destinies of being scrambled," I said.

"Don't make me repeat myself on that subject."

"What if it's a donut?" Felix said, forging fearlessly onward.

"Or a black hole," I said.

"How optimistic," Felix said.

"The moon, then," I said.

"The sun," Liv said.

"Both." I looked at her, and she blushed. What were we talking about?

"We messed it up," Felix said. "Here's the thing that's important to remember: things only have meaning if we grant them meaning."

"What a takeaway," Liv said.

"You're worse than Mariah," Felix said. "Shall we move on to the watch?"

He pulled it from his pocket, wrapped now in a strip of velvet. "The first thing I will say about this piece," he said, "is that it's got an incredibly strange energy."

"My uncle said it was lucky."

"I'd go more with haunted."

"Oh, fantastic."

"But look," Felix said.

He'd buffed the watch to a shine, lifting enough tarnish to reveal an engraved tree etched into the silver face. The tree was covered in tiny circles—not leaves, but the most basically rendered fruit.

"*Wow*," I said, "that's beautiful. Thanks, Felix."

"Second thing I will say: have you checked for watch papers?"

"Pardon me?"

"Most clockmakers put a piece of paper in the back case to protect the inner mechanisms from the elements. Back in the day, it doubled as free advertising." He flipped the watch over, twisted loose the back cover. A circle of paper fluttered out, yellow with age and crisp as a potato chip.

"*Bingo,*" Felix said. He held the paper out in his palm. There, printed with an ink drawing of an elaborate Celtic knot, we read in rolling, curlicued script: *Crane's Clockmakers, London, England.* He tipped the paper into my palm, and Liv leaned in toward me for a closer look. The brim of her cap caught me on the side of my face.

"Sorry," she muttered. She pulled her braid across her mouth.

"There's actually an inscription on the back, too," Felix said. He squirted some more silver polish onto the rag and buffed the back of the watch. "Jeepers, this is *tiny.*" He squinted. "Do you know an *S?*"

"My brother. Sam. Also my grandmother was Sterling, and her father . . ."

"Her grandfather," Liv corrected me.

"Were any of those people around in January of 1884?"

Felix passed me the watch. The tiny inscription read:

F.

MY APPLE, CLEFT IN TWO

S.

FEBRUARY 1884

My mouth fell open. First the emerald, now *this*? The watch papers put us in England, and 1884 put us in the right year, and the *F* . . .

"This is *Fidelia's* watch?"

"Unless you know another British *F* from 1884 whose antique jewels would be lying around your house," Felix said.

"That means she was wearing this *on the ship*," I said.

"You're the definition of flabbergasted right now, Violet."

Liv, as usual, was already three steps ahead of us.

"Someone gave this watch to Fidelia right before she left England on the *Lyric*," she said. "Maybe this *S* has to do with why she left. Maybe this watch was a going-away present. A romantic gesture!" She slapped the table in excitement. "I knew there was some weird reason she didn't write."

"I'm sorry. How did we get to a romantic gesture?"

"February, obviously. Valentine's Day. And the apple! The engraving must be an apple tree. A reference to Adam and Eve. Temptation. Forbidden fruit!"

"Isn't the apple knowledge?" Felix asked.

"*Biblical* knowledge," Liv said. She waggled her eyebrows suggestively. "But even without that part—*cleft in two*. They were clearly being split apart when she boarded the boat. How painful is that language? Could it mean anything other than heartbreak? Two lovers being wrenched apart?"

"*Their Love Story Was Actually Someone Else's Tragic Breakup*," Felix said.

"Say whatever you want," Liv said. "This engraving is so tiny! It wasn't meant to be *seen*. That seems highly suspect."

"Look out, Professor Stone's off and running," said Felix. She was, indeed. You practically see the cartoon lightbulb over Liv's head.

"Maybe she was pregnant with S's baby," Liv said. "The apple is *fruit*, after all. And maybe that's why she got married so quickly to Ransome!" She looked to me hungrily. "When did she give birth to their first child? Let's figure that out, stat."

"Your anti–love story is nearly as absurd as the *actual* love story, Liv," I said. "Let's back up for a second. Who else could S be? What do we know about Fidelia before she left England?"

Liv's face fell.

"Well, that's a problem. There's not that much on her, at least not in public records. Her whole history is sort of a blank." Her eyes grew wide. "But if she was having some torrid affair and then she was shipped off because of a shameful pregnancy, the whole thing would make sense. Her disguise here and her relationship with Ransome could be tied to *erasure* of her past. Maybe the earring is even part of it. The emerald," Liv went on. "Maybe she gave the other earring to someone else in England as a love token. Some people gave a lock of hair, but she was probably more aristocratic than that."

"The earring was just tangled with the watch," I said. "No evidence that it was Fidelia's."

"There's no stamp or mark on the earring," Felix agreed. "I checked."

"See, Liv? They're not related."

"That you *know of*," she said.

"And you think *tarot* is ridiculous," said Felix. "This is so far-fetched!"

"I'm *theorizing*, not reading things in a crystal ball!"

"For the last time, you *know* I think crystal-ball gazers are a racket."

"Violet. What do you think?" Liv said, turning toward me, eyes glittering. It was amazing, how quickly she'd jungle-gymmed her way to a full-blown theory. But also . . .

"It's kind of sad how much we *don't* know about her. Like . . . who's her mom? Why doesn't anyone care about *that*?"

"If it makes you feel any better, no one will care about us someday either."

"That does *not* make me feel better," I said.

"I know, but—what I mean is we should look, right? Carpe diem. You know that poem? Horace. *Tu ne quaesieris, scire nefas, quem mihi, quem tibi . . .*"

I'd never met anyone like her.

"Mariah calls *me* the show-off," Felix scoffed.

Hard to say which was more unlikely: that Liv would debunk the love story of my great-great-great-grandparents, or that I would find a shipwreck in the middle of the Atlantic. But Liv had the letter *S*, and now a theory. I had a beach. Felix had a metal detector.

"We have a start," I said.

I couldn't wait to tell Sam.

"Felix!"

"Shit. That's my dad."

"You better be tied up by robbers back there! I just watched two paying customers walk out the door!" The voice came closer and Felix, in a frenzy, hurried us to the back door and shoved us into the alley with the trash cans.

"Goodbye, thanks for coming, next time we'll do tarot!" he said, and shut the door abruptly.

Liv and I blinked. A lifetime had passed in the Wonder Emporium, but it was still daylight in the real world, shadowy-bright in the space between two buildings. From cracks in the asphalt, a rash of little purple and yellow flowers stretched up toward the sun.

"Did you ever do this?" I picked a buttercup and held it beneath her chin. The petals were so shiny and yellow they looked plastic, but a glow caught on the underside of Liv's skin, like a buttercup torch.

"You like butter," I announced.

"Oh my God, yes! Where does that butter thing even come from?" Liv asked.

"Who knows. Some secret girl network." I tucked the flower into her braid, taking longer than I needed. Her hair looked brittle like straw but it was as soft as the petals. Church bells chimed: 6:00 p.m.

"Hey, d'you want to come to dinner?" Liv asked. "I mean, unless you have other plans. I know I said my parents are concrete, or whatever, but they're actually super nice. They love having people over."

"I'm starving," I admitted. "Okay. Sure. Just . . ." I plucked a few flowers—weeds, really, dandelions and buttercups—and dropped them in an empty Campbell's Chunky Soup can that'd been licked clean by some rodent. "My mom would be really mad if I showed up empty-handed."

"You're *so* annoying. My mom is going to adore you." She plucked a fresh dandelion from my arrangement. "Did you ever do this?"

She scored the stem with her fingernail, and then, like a split end, she peeled the edges apart, revealing the flower's pale green insides.

"No. What's that?"

"I don't know. Maybe it's not a thing. I always just liked the way it felt. Feels."

I reached for one end of the flayed dandelion and ran it between my fingers. The insides were sticky with glucose, the stem already browning in places. We held it like a wishbone three days past Thanksgiving, thoroughly dried and ready to crack. I wanted to know what she was wishing for, but I wasn't brave enough to ask.

HAPPY FAMILIES ARE ALL ALIKE

I'd wished for Liv's parents to like me.

I knew it was just dinner, but I had the feeling in my stomach like I used to get before an audition. Wanting to nail it, suspecting that I could, and knowing, in all likelihood, that things could go horribly, horribly wrong.

"Hi, Livvy!" I heard as soon as we walked into the mudroom. The house smelled of basil and garlic; radio babble wafted from the kitchen. I'd never been in the house of parents who'd lost a child before, and I'd expected—I don't know. Coldness and severity, like a medieval church, an emptiness so vast it felt like fear.

Instead, I followed Liv into a cozy sunlit kitchen where her mom was slicing tomatoes into thick red slabs on a wooden cutting board. She was even shorter than her daughter, in a light blue T-shirt and cheap black flip-flops, a salt-and-pepper bob held back from her face with two tortoiseshell barrettes. Her earrings matched her necklace, purple glass beads, the sort of jewelry made at camp. I wondered if Liv or Will had made them for her.

"Dad's drowning in shucking duties. I got way too much corn, but it looked so good, I hope you're hungry. . . ."

"Mom, this is Violet. She's going to eat with us, okay?"

Liv's mom's eyes drifted from the tomatoes to me, and I worried about my hair, my height, the coffee grounds and fish juice on my jean shorts. This woman lost a kid, I thought, don't say the wrong thing.

"Of course, of course!" Liv's mom said, with a smile so wide it made me feel like she'd been waiting for me her whole life. "Hi, Violet, I'm Ann, no *e*, I'd shake your hand, but I'm covered in tomato juice. We can bump elbows. That's what we do with the kids during flu season, anyway."

We bumped elbows, mine scabbed and pale where hers was soft and tan. I bet, at school, she was the kind of teacher who developed a cult following, who kids hoped all summer they'd get next year.

"These are for you," I said, offering her my Campbell's soup can, feeling a little shy. The flowers were browning in places; there was some lingering soup gunk I hadn't noticed before.

"*Love* this," Ann declared. "We don't have a centerpiece yet for dinner. Go help your dad, will you, Livvy? There're cheese and crackers out there, too—help yourself to anything, Violet, and don't let him take you on the garden tour if you don't want to."

Their house was larger than it looked from the front, with a more complicated layout than I expected, and slightly treacherous—an unexpected step down here, an exposed beam there. Each room seemed to have secret little nooks or a windowsill for curling up with a book and a blanket. I felt a bit like I was walking through a very nice person's brain, labyrinthine and warm. Had I been alone, I would've gone around knocking on the walls for secret passageways.

Outside on a slate patio, Liv's dad was in an Adirondack chair pulling corn from its squeaky leather husk, the ground around him like the end of a day at a blondes-only hair salon. He was completely bald, with bright orange Crocs and Liv's eyes.

"Dad, I brought a victim for your garden tour," she said.

"I'm sure that's the last thing your guest wants to do," he said. He was soft-spoken and mild mannered; his T-shirt was tucked into elastic-waist shorts. "Tom Stone. How do you do." His hand in mine was warm and dry.

"I'd like to see the garden, actually," I said. I honestly did.

"Well, in that case," he said, looking like Liv when she had an idea, "my delphiniums *are* doing rather well."

We walked along the plots, and he pointed out bugbane, Russian sage, day lilies. Little treats were hidden among the plants, too: a family of stone rabbits, a warbling fountain shaped like a spouting fish. I'd learned that he'd designed the house himself, and the garden, and he explained to me about shade and water and light, so much thought and care behind where plants lived. Through the window into the kitchen, I saw Liv hug her mom, long and rocking, and somehow still casual, everyday. I couldn't remember the last time I'd hugged my mom that way.

"Try this," said Tom, handing me a tiny ruby of a strawberry from a bush. It was even sweeter than Toby's pies.

Liv and I set the table for dinner, ferrying a green glass pitcher and a stack of cloth napkins from the kitchen. Ann lit peppermint candles, which, she claimed, smelled better than citronella and still kept the bugs away.

"But if we get really desperate, I've got the napalm," she said, and she winked at me, like we were in on a secret.

"Cheers," she said when we finally sat down, and Tom said, "*Clink,*" when we hit every glass. We passed around corn, green beans, a salad of tomatoes and avocado, chicken with pesto. Toby made a strong showing on the dessert front, but with all this color in front of me, I felt like I had scurvy. I heaped green beans onto my plate.

"Violet, we hear you're from New York," Ann said. "What brings you to Lyric?"

"Her uncle owns the Mola Mola, remember?" Liv said gently.

"New York's a long way away. I bet your parents miss you," Tom said.

"Oh, they're thrilled I'm gone," I said.

"Trust me," he said, "they're thinking about you every second of every day."

"Gosh, New York." Ann sighed. "We went once for Christmas, remember, Tom? Back when we were just married, I must've been twenty-three, I was so excited, I thought it was going to be like the movies: skating, hot chocolate . . ."

"We had to leave early," Tom said. "The crowds."

"I'm not a city girl. Neither is this one," Ann said, wrapping her hand around Liv's, and I saw Liv give her a squeeze back in agreement.

"What about Oxford?" I said.

"Oxford?" Ann said, quizzical. "What's in Oxford?"

"Felix told me I probably lived there in a past life," Liv said, and the lie rolled from her easy as a marble. "Supposedly I was a countess."

"And I was—what was it?" I said, picking up where she left off.

"You were Amelia Earhart," Liv said, and even though it wasn't true, her words dropped into my chest, fist-size and muscle heavy.

Tom chuckled and helped himself to more beans. "Felix. That boy is certainly something else, isn't he?"

He said it fondly, but still. *Certainly something else* jammed between my ribs, right next to my new aviator heart.

"I did like the Met, though," Ann said. "In New York. That Egyptian room! It was so quiet and contemplative, full of grace, and we'd just gotten married, and I felt awful, of course I must've been pregnant with Will, I just didn't know it then, that's why . . . why . . ."

She faltered and reached for her necklace, worrying the beads between her fingers. I watched her search for words, and then watched her go elsewhere, somewhere I couldn't follow. Like that, the night turned brittle as spun sugar.

"Mom?" Liv said cautiously.

Ann played with her necklace, staring off at someplace over my left shoulder. I looked to Tom, willed him to help her, but he was concentrating on his green beans. My teeth chattered once, twice, and I gripped my jaw with both hands.

Tenderly, with great practice, Liv drew her mother's hand into her own.

"Mom," she said, "should we go inside?"

"What was I saying?" she said softly, looking only at Liv.

"The Egyptian room. Full of grace."

"Yes," Ann said, coming back more fully now. "It really was."

"Wonderful beans, darling," said Tom.

"They are," I said, just to chime in.

"They're the same old thing," Ann said, and with that, we kept on like nothing had happened. We talked about Ann's unit on the ancient Maya and Tom's concern over a tree that was losing limbs; her childhood in New Hampshire and his in Minnesota. How they'd met in college, and she'd followed him to Lyric after graduation. "It was the craziest thing I've ever done in my life," she said. "We were so young. But I'm telling you girls: when you meet the one, whoever he is, you'll know."

Or she, or they, or ones, I didn't say, because who was I to say that right now to this woman?

"And who knows," Ann said, "maybe you've already met."

Liv, in response to her parents' love story, was totally, completely without barbs. The night stayed as glassy smooth as the sea had been that day at the lighthouse.

After dinner, Liv led me up a sneaky back staircase, two plastic bowls of homemade blueberry ice cream in hand. Her room was compact, like her, with citrus-colored walls covered in pictures of her friends, a little white desk stuck with half-peeled-off stickers, a framed print from *Alice in Wonderland*. On her twin bed, a battered stuffed bunny had been tucked into a pink patchwork quilt so un-Liv-like I almost couldn't picture her sleeping there.

"So those are my parents," she said slowly.

"They're nice," I said, because they were. "How often does your mom—?"

"Go away like that? I don't know. Enough that I know what to say."

I nodded and traced a finger over the stitching of her quilt. "I've got to admit, Liv, I thought your room would be more of an intellectual monastery."

"Is that really what you think of me? That in my free time I just twiddle away on my abacus?"

"No," I said, laughing a little.

"Here, this'll blow your mind, too: I *love* TV," she said.

"Really?"

"Yes! Why is that so hard to believe? You wouldn't believe how much TV I watch! I think as a species we may have evolved to develop a genetic predisposition toward TV, and I am going to donate my body to science to isolate the TV gene."

"See, saying shit like *that* is what makes me think abacus."

"Just look." She opened her closet, walked into her clothes, and—this I didn't expect—took a left, where I thought there was a wall. I poked my head in. The closet smelled overwhelmingly of Liv, smoky and salty and slightly like SweeTarts, and went farther back than I realized. In the back corner, where the ceiling sloped, she cuddled herself into a neat raft of pillows around a black-and-white TV, smaller than one of Toby's nine-inch cakes.

"We weren't allowed to watch TV during weekdays growing up—I mean, I'm *still* not, technically—but they would set this up when Will or I got sick. I think they think it's lost. We don't get a lot of channels, but there's probably a movie on now."

"Does Mariah know about this?" My head brushed the ceiling as I stooped toward her.

"Of course. What do you think she and I *do* when we hang out? Ooh, *Thelma and Louise*. You seen this?"

I shook my head no and curled up on the pillows, taking care not to touch her. My heart was beating fast.

"We missed the beginning, but that's fine," she said. "Sorry it's so crowded."

"I don't mind," I said. My knee brushed hers accidentally and I thought about apologizing, but chose not to.

We watched. Our spoons made little clicking noises against the plastic like miniature pony hooves. Liv stirred her ice cream to milkshake consistency, like I used to do as a kid, and the whole thing was platonic, I told myself, very platonic.

"Brad Pitt's in this," Liv said, eyes glued to the screen.

"Oh," I said.

"He gives Thelma her first orgasm," she said, and I swear she inched toward me.

The volume was low; you had to strain to hear. My breathing was very loud. She smelled so good, and I had a sudden urge to kiss the back of her arm, the one that was holding her ice cream spoon. The nonkiss with Orion had made me insane, I decided. My arm brushed her arm, and my blood was replaced with pins and needles.

On-screen, Thelma gasped and gasped, and here, beside Liv, every inch of me was on fire. The stuffy air between us pulsed like a heartbeat. I looked at her, but her face was impassive. We were watching a sex scene. How could this be platonic?

"Seems like that went well for her," I said. I wasn't used to being this nervous.

"Uh-huh," she said.

"You have corn silk on your dress," I said.

I plucked a thread from her skirt, my fingers light as a dandelion cloud. Our eyes met, and there was a flickering in my body, an unfolding, a ladybug's secret wings taking flight. I wanted to bat her bowl of ice cream from her hand, feel her weight on top of me, reach a hand up her dress, wanted to know if she was as wet as I was, she looked like she wasn't breathing—

She'd called me Amelia Earhart—

She was straight—

Downstairs, I heard Ann call to Tom about Tupperware—

"This next part's really good," Liv said, head tipped toward the TV. "We should watch."

"Sure," I said, dry-mouthed. She was straight enough to not even realize what was going on. Which was better, anyway. I really liked being her friend. Orion's, too. I didn't want to be a hitch between them.

"Hey," I said, "I'm sorry I brought up Oxford."

"What?"

"At dinner. Oxford. Your parents. I'd just assumed they knew."

"Oh. That's okay." She pulled her knees up to her chest. We weren't touching now, and I knew we wouldn't, and that knowledge made me feel safer, like I could say anything without fear of ruining my chances with her.

"It's just that we haven't really talked about college," she said. "They both went to the University of Maine. It's like two hours away. I could come home on weekends. Tuition is cheap."

"But you want to go to Oxford."

"Yeah," she said, "but it hurts me less to go to the University of Maine than it hurts *them* for me to go to Oxford."

"I don't know. I think there's probably a world where you can have what you want, too. Don't they just want you to be happy?"

"Maybe," she said. She rocked her chin on her knees, and I knew we were both thinking of Will. How different would her life be if he were still alive? Would I even be here?

"Can I tell you an *actual* secret?" she said.

"Okay," I said, nervous for what was to come.

"I really hate being called Professor Stone."

That I wasn't expecting. The left turn felt like a welcome relief, as if she'd thrown open a secret window in this tiny space.

"Really? Why?"

"It makes me feel like a know-it-all. Obnoxious. Pretentious."

"You *are* a know-it-all."

"Thanks a lot, Violet."

"You didn't let me finish! I like that about you best of all. Seriously. You've got, like, an acrobat brain. But I get it. I'll stop."

"Thanks," she said. "That's, um—extraordinarily nice. What you just said about my brain."

"Not nice so much as true," I told her.

I stayed even after the movie ended. For the next hour, while another movie played, she made me guess how *Thelma and Louise* had started, and I dreamed up different beginnings, each one more outrageous and convoluted than the next. The night was the best kind of boring, and making her laugh felt even better than being onstage.

DISPATCHES FROM LYRIC,
NEVER DISPATCHED

July 13
Wednesday

Dear Sam,

Hard to believe I've been in Lyric over a month. Not sure if you've been getting my letters, but I wanted to give you some Wreck Hunting Updates. Last weekend we made good progress, all thanks to an old watch of Mom's that's maybe haunted, maybe lucky. And get this: this weekend, we're going to Seal Cove to sweep the beach with a metal detector. It's possible the wreck's been there all along, right in front of our eyes, where we used to swim.

Meanwhile, this girl I met is developing a theory about Fidelia's potentially sordid past: A love affair! A hidden pregnancy! It's all very scandalous.

This girl—the one with the theory—lost a brother a few years back. Her name's Liv. She knows how lighthouses work. My friend Orion described her as bright, which is accurate. She sparkles. Her brother died in an accident. Suddenly, is my understanding. I think, for her, it must've been one of those moments where you just can't believe what you're hearing.

Did you know, I wrote, *that I used to imagine you dying?*
I had never told anyone this, ever. I could barely admit it to myself.

There's this scene in Nancy Drew where she's being held hostage and signals for help with a lantern through a window. That's how I thought of you. A blinking light. SOS. Ever since I was little, I've imagined your funeral. I'd play this sick game, imagining the world without you, seeing if I could get myself to cry. Your funeral was very glamorous. I wore a black velvet gown and Mom was in a fur coat and Dad was in a tuxedo. We buried you in Central Park, spread your ashes from a rowboat in the lake. By the time I imagined that part, I was usually teary.

A drop splashed on the page, smearing my ink.

We got older. We heard stories in the news. Kids younger than me, than you, even, jumping in front of trains, taking their dads' guns. Once or twice, someone we sort of knew, someone from a different school, maybe, or a friend of a friend. One day there, the next day, gone. You and me, in a parallel universe. Every time I heard about someone, I'd turn this thought over in my head: Would Sam ever . . . ? Would I . . . ?

Where did he end and I begin? Was thinking the same thing as wanting? Trying?

When Mom called that day to tell me about you, my first thought wasn't surprise. I just asked, "Which hospital?"
I had no trouble understanding that you'd tried to kill yourself.
I saw it coming and I didn't do a thing.

I ripped the letter into tiny pieces, then shredded them in the blender for good measure. I sent him a dumb Weeki Wachee postcard instead.

ANAGRAMS

Seal Cove was a wide, flat beach bookended by rock forma-
tions ideal for cliff jumping and (I hoped) snagging ships and
drawing them into ocean depths where they'd stay hidden for centuries. When I arrived there Saturday afternoon to metal detect,
the beach was clearing out, families struggling over the dunes with
umbrellas and picnic baskets in tow. Some straggling sunbathers
still lounged on towels, and the water lapped calmly at the shore.
My heart fell. This beach was so tame and well-populated, it was
hard to believe that a wreck could have been hiding here for years.

A girl at the beach's far end was waving her arms in my direction. She looked like she was flagging me down, but I didn't
recognize her. She yelled louder. A fire was blazing in the pit
behind her. Was she all right? I jogged toward her, trying to make
out what she was saying.

"Violet! Violet!"

Holy shit. I *did* know her. Only I didn't. Because I was seeing,
for the first time, Liv without her hat.

Allow me, for a moment, a tangent on The Face.

My dad wore the same wire-framed glasses every day of our
childhood: gold-rimmed scholarly specs, dignified, simple. I had

never seen him without them, and I believed they were literally *part* of him—attached to his body as much as his kneecaps or the hairs on his toes. The first time I saw him without his glasses, I couldn't have been more than five or six, and legend has it, I burst into tears. Without his glasses, my dad was a stranger. His eyes were sunken and beady; his cheeks gaunt. His face looked watery, as though his features might slip off. Those glasses were glue, and without them, the pieces of his face went slipshod.

Seeing Liv without her hat was *nothing like* seeing my dad without his glasses.

It wasn't like I hadn't seen her face before. A hat can only hide so much. I knew she had gray eyes and straight ash-blond eyebrows. I knew that she had a thin red mouth; that her cheeks grew flushed when she was excited. I knew that she had acne along her cheek, in particular on the right side of her face. I knew she had a forehead. I assumed she had a hairline.

What I didn't know before I saw Hat-Free Liv was that foreheads and hairlines could *announce* themselves, say *Hey, look at me, I'm gorgeous!* I'd always assumed that she'd parted her hair in the middle, but in fact she parted it on the left, revealing a fine pale line of scalp. I thought her hair might have been dull after being hidden from the sun, but it was brighter than I expected, threaded with copper. And of course her braids were French braids, woven behind her ears and framing her face. Hers was the sort of face you wanted to look at, no matter what the owner was doing, whether she was smearing concealer under her eyes, or eating egg salad.

I would not have predicted that one could be so attracted to a hairline.

"Hello," she said when I finally reached her. She spoke in her museum voice, professional, precise. Then she brought one braid across her mouth. A small thrill coursed through me. This gesture was a habit. I wanted to know her other habits. I wanted her to know mine.

Behind her, the fire popped, shooting bright cinders into the sky. The prow of a ship careened through my heart.

Here's what I should have said: *I saw your face and the world was different.*

Here's what I actually managed: "Hey, girl, cool forehead."

There was a pause. I prayed for a freak wave to put me out of my misery.

"Oh," Liv said, her voice small. "Thanks, I guess."

"Where's everyone else?" I asked.

"Everyone else?"

"I invited Orion, and he was going to bring Felix and Mariah. . . ."

She had a little setup behind her, I saw now: a blanket spread with the metal detector, watermelon, and Oreos. Two flashlights.

"I thought it was going to be just us," Liv said.

"*Oh.* I thought . . . I guess . . ."

"Whatever. This is great. I'm sure Mastergoon Theater will have plenty of comments about how silly you look with a metal detector."

"Do you want . . ."

"Nope. No. This is perfect," she said, sounding just like my mom when I left crumbs all over the table after cleaning up from dinner. "Let's just hope they bring beer."

They didn't disappoint. Felix, Mariah, and Orion each arrived carrying a six-pack, whooping and hollering when they saw Liv.

"Hat-free, way to be!" said Felix.

"You look great!" Mariah said, and hugged her. Why couldn't I have done that?

Orion stared at Liv like he'd seen her for the first time.

"Are you going to say hi?" Liv said to him finally.

"You just look so good," he said. He was in love with her. Totally and completely in love with her. They were a saga. How could she *not* want him, when he talked to her like that? And sure enough, when they hugged, it was a long, swaying one, so much more than a hug between friends. Felix and Mariah made eyes at each other.

"Can I have a drink?" Liv said when they'd finally disentangled from each other.

"I thought you swore off drinking after you threw up behind that tree last winter," Felix said.

"People change," she said, hiss-popping open the top. *People change.* That was all the answer I needed. The hat was gone, and she wanted Orion.

Metal detecting was put off until dark, when there was less chance of getting caught. We sat around the fire pit, and somehow I wound up between Orion and Liv. I'd wanted to be in their vortex once, but now that I was here, I just felt awful. In the way, a

234

hideous rock in their babbling brook. Mariah and Felix bickered, but the three of us hardly said a word. Orion's knee bumped mine and I shifted closer to Liv, who angled herself toward Felix. Was she jealous? Orion only wanted her, obviously—

"Have you guys heard Liv's latest theory about *Their Love Was Our Beginning?*" I asked. Maybe turning the subject toward truthing would cheer her up. "She thinks my great-great-great-grandmother fled the country because of a torrid love affair with a mystery man named S."

"Sebastian," guessed Orion.

"Stephen."

"Sarah," Liv said. My heart nearly stopped.

"Saucy!" said Felix.

"Not saucy. It's possible S was a woman," Liv said.

"What about your pregnancy theory?" I asked.

"The math didn't hold up," Liv said dismissively. "Plus, if Fidelia had been having an affair with a woman, there's an even greater chance that she'd want to run away. And *stay* away once she landed. Not to mention that whole cross-dressing thing."

"They had three kids, though," I said.

"Sex means nothing," Liv said.

"That's *definitely* not true," said Orion.

Felix fanned himself furtively and glanced at Mariah. Orion had kissed Liv. She'd kissed him. *Grief second base,* she'd said, but maybe it'd been more. Maybe she'd been lying to me this whole time.

"Hey," Liv said suddenly to Orion, "why don't you and Violet sing for everyone?"

"What?" I glanced nervously at Orion.

"That's weirdly wholesome of you, Liv," Mariah said.

"I'm down!" said Felix. "Sing to us, you beautiful creatures."

"I don't sing," I said automatically.

"You sang for Orion," Liv said. "That's what he told me, at least."

I shot daggers at him. *Seriously?* Even after what I'd said about Broadway?

"I'm sorry, Violet, but it's true! You *do* have a nice voice," said Orion. "It's, like, moody and unique. . . . I have my harmonica. . . . We could do 'You Belong to Me' . . . that's your favorite, right?"

"Yes, yes, yes!" said Felix. "It'll be a real live campfire experience, like sleepaway camp!"

"Summer camp was miserable," said Mariah.

"Then this'll be *better*," said Felix.

"I really don't want to sing," I said. I had the feeling that when Orion and I played music together, we'd look really, really good. If Liv was upset with me—if she thought I was moving in on Orion, or if she thought—

She'd wanted it to be just us, I thought.

"It's a short song," Orion said. "Please?"

"Please!" said Felix.

"Please," said Mariah.

Liv lit a cigarette, already bored. I wanted her to look at me so badly I thought I'd burst.

"All right," I said, "let's sing."

What else could I do?

∝

Romeo and Juliet once had a conversation that became a sonnet. Alone, they were good; together, they were art. I always wondered what that would be like—to be so in sync with someone, you create.

I confirmed right then and there what I been suspecting: that Orion Lewis was my musical soul mate. Music at the aquarium was lo-fi, but here, now, on this beach, this was serious.

I took a deep breath and sang:

"See the pyramids along the Nile
Watch the sunrise on a tropic isle . . ."

Orion punctuated the words with his twangy, bluesy notes, and I looked skyward at first, because that was easier than looking at their faces. I tried hard not to impress anyone, just to remember how much I loved this song, throaty and sad with lyrics that sparkled, each one its own moment of discovery.

"Send me photographs and souvenirs . . ."

My tune double-helixed with Orion's and I chanced a look at Mariah, who was dreamy-eyed. Felix was swaying. I wanted to look at Liv so badly, so badly, to see her look at me, to watch me the same way I'd watched her in the museum. . . .

"Fly the ocean in a silver plane
See the jungle when it's wet with rain . . ."

I looked at her, finally. She was looking at him.

"Just remember till you're home again . . ."

In the final lines of the song, I willed her gray eyes my way, and when her gaze didn't budge, I looked skyward again. My voice was overly thick with feeling, Orion's notes panging blue, and I sang the last line looking up at the stars. *You belong to me.*

It didn't matter where I was looking, though. From the start, I'd been singing only for her.

Orion played his final notes, and I recognized the silence that followed as that of an audience transported. It hadn't been a sonnet, but it felt close. I wasn't even sure Liv cared.

Felix was the first one to speak. "You two would make the most handsome musical babies."

Mariah whacked him on the shoulder. "You guys are obviously amazing, but that song is jacked. How 'bout *you belong to no one and are free to make your own choices?*"

"Doesn't have quite the same ring to it," said Orion.

I looked to Liv, stared at the new fact of her face. For the first time, her eyes met mine, and looking into their somber gray depths, I wanted to hear everything she thought, to hear her use a word I'd never heard, to give me some weird fact about Old Algiers, to compare my voice to some obscure singer that I'd listen to and fall in love with.

"Not bad," she said.

Then she snatched Felix's beer and took a long, long drink.

◌

By the time the tide was low enough for metal detecting, Liv was drunk.

Is she okay? I mouthed to Mariah as Liv fumbled with her lighter.

Take her with you, Mariah mouthed, miming metal detection.

"All right, Violet," Felix said, picking up the metal detector from the sand. "Crash course in how to use this sucker. It's the cheapo kind, but still."

The contraption was basic, a thin rod with a sensor at the bottom. Wires maypoled up the handle to a control box, which was supposed to beep-beep loudly if the sensor picked up any metallic traces. When I took the wand, the detector immediately went haywire, sending shrieking beeps into the night. Liv dropped her latest beer on the sand.

"We got it secondhand," Felix said apologetically. He punched a few buttons on the control panel. "Truth be told it's always been finicky."

Haywire and cheap as the metal detector was, when I swung it over the sand, I felt powerful, like I was holding a magic wand. I'd find pieces of the ship that would help reveal the location of the wreck. I'd write my brother and tell him *we found the* Lyric. I couldn't wait.

"You look intrepid," Orion said. Liv rolled her eyes. *Take her,* Mariah urged again.

"Liv, are you going to come with me?"

"You know you're not going to find anything," she said. "Especially not with that piece of junk."

"All this booze is making you uncharacteristically negative," Mariah said.

"I'm not saying anything she doesn't already know," Liv said. "There are over three million wrecks in the ocean. You really think you're just going to roll up to the beach with a metal detector and stumble upon the *Lyric?*"

"The power of positive thinking, Liv," Felix said.

"Yeah, that's gotten me so far in life," she said.

That shut us up. In the quiet, she slurped her beer. I'd lost track of how many she'd had.

"I thought we were in this together," I said. My voice sounded small.

"So did I."

"Then come with me."

"Make Orion go," she muttered.

"I'll go with you if you want," Orion offered.

"What a knight," Liv said. Felix and Mariah exchanged uncomfortable glances.

"That's really okay," I said. "I'm good on my own."

I set off across the dark beach, swinging the metal detector in front me like an absolute idiot. And what did I care if Liv came? She was just drunk. Besides, she was right: in the first half hour, the only treasure I'd dug up were soda-can pull tabs and oxidized pennies. Not exactly the clues I needed.

I'd made it to the end of the beach, when I heard Liv's voice behind me.

"Find anything good?"

She'd brought a flashlight and shone it on me. I uncurled my fistful of treasures: corroded scraps of metal, some nuts and bolts, the green pennies.

"Kind of a disappointment," I admitted. I waited for her to disagree. To tell me that the nuts and bolts looked promising, to offer me a theory entirely based around the way these rivets had corroded. She said nothing.

The detector beeped. I looked at the sand.

"Go ahead," Liv said.

I dug, fast. An old-fashioned house key.

"Kind of pretty. You want it?"

"Do I want your trash?" she said.

"I didn't . . . That wasn't . . ."

"Orion told me you kissed."

Oh, shit.

"It was more like a half kiss," I said, backpedaling furiously. "He told me not to tell you."

"Why didn't you just tell me you liked him? Instead of— whatever speech you gave me? Whatever—objective observer? Instead of prying for all sorts of personal stuff and letting me ramble on about *anagrams* and my family? Was that, like, recon? Get a read on how fucked up she is, report back?"

I was so stunned I could only choke out a "*No, never,*" before the metal detector exploded.

"Go ahead. Dig away. I know you want to," she said.

She shone her light at my feet. About a foot and a half down, the shovel scraped against something hard. In the beam of Liv's flashlight, I pulled loose a pair of binoculars—opera specs, really— corroded with salt, covered with barnacles, but there, nevertheless, in my hand. They looked *ancient*. They looked *amazing*. They looked straight off the deck of the—

"You have *got* to be kidding me. Forty-five minutes with a broken metal detector and you've got *artifacts*? I've been looking for *years* and I've got nothing. You get the zoo picture. Your emerald! Do you have any idea how much that must be *worth*? How much the rest of us would kill to find something like that?"

"Have it!" I said, waving the binoculars at her. "Take the emerald! And, Liv, seriously—Orion—that's not even a thing!"

"It's all so easy for you, isn't it? God. I'm so pathetic. For a second I thought it could be easy for me, too. Like I'd take off my hat and *poof*. Some dramatic makeover, I thought! I'm still the same. I'm still me. Same problems. Same everything. I won't ever get what I want. And you always will."

I reached my hand to her, because she was drunk, and hurting—

"What is that?" she said. "Am I supposed to hold your hand now?"

"No. I don't know. I just . . ."

"Don't hold my hand. I'm not *tragic*. I'm not *cool*. Death isn't *cool*. Fidelia's this party trick for you, and my dead person is *literally across the hallway*. We're not the same, you and me."

"No—we're anagrams, I thought—"

"DO YOU EVEN KNOW WHAT AN ANAGRAM IS? They're completely different words! *ICEMAN* is not *CINEMA*. *ORCHESTRA* is not *CARTHORSE*. Your family's missing a *WRECK* and my family's missing a *PERSON*. You smoke like an idiot at your fancy private school and get suspended and think that's the end of the world, and he'll kill me for telling you this, but Felix lost an *eye* in sixth grade and that wasn't the end for him, he almost left school last year because the bullying was so bad! And your brother! God! You don't even call him! Do you know how many times a day I wish I could call my brother? *It's so fucking easy.* Your whole life! So fucking easy!"

I stepped back. She was so angry. And she was so *right*.

"You are ungrateful," she said. "Deeply and truly ungrateful."

I didn't think it was possible to be blindsided by a truth you've always suspected, but there you have it. As it turns out, it's devastating.

I couldn't hear any more. I set the metal detector down at her feet and then ran down the beach, past the fire, past the chorus of shouts. They were Liv's friends, not mine. She needed them.

When I got home, there was a letter waiting for me on my bed. I recognized the handwriting.

⚮

Dear Violet,

I've got a picture of the family on my dresser here. Unfortunately it's the one you hate, from cousin Margot's wedding, the one where the photographer put you on the end to "account for height" (please don't say you look like a behemoth. I know you're thinking it). Whenever people see that picture, there's always a moment after I point you out where they say That's your sister? *I think they're going to talk about how pretty you are. People usually do. But today, someone said:* You guys look identical.

I don't know if you remember that wedding. It was last summer, right before things got bad for me, or worse than usual, and bad for you, too, I guess. The band was so loud I couldn't even be in the room with all the dancing. The cousins were so scary—so big and so adult. Half of them had kids! Dad told me to relax, that they were family, which was true, but that didn't help. Then he disappeared to talk to cousin Adam about baseball, and his need for a sports-oriented son was so blatant that I wanted to hide in the back with the caterers. I tried to be brave, but I just wanted to leave.

You knew.

"Let's take a break," you said.

There was that pond out front, with green plants and leaves and swans. You and I spent the whole time making boats out of leaves. It was really, really nice of you.

We're not identical, not in the slightest. You're like this Amazon. You're brave. Only you would think it would be possible to find a ship-wreck. Only you would try! I've wanted to be like you my whole life. Instead I'm me: terrified of my own cousins and made of jelly. Afraid of everything. I should have been a snail. I'd always have a hiding spot.

I know I can be a lot. I know I'm not the easiest brother to have. I'm not the easiest person to be. You're a good sister. I just wanted to say that. I love you, and I want to see you soon. I hope Maine is okay, and if it's not okay, that's okay, too. Vermont is fine. I feel a little better, but I wish I were there with you. I wish I could help you find the wreck.

Love,
Sammy

PS: Not a single person who's seen that picture says you look like a behemoth.

PPS: Mom said you shaved your head?

I did not feel like an Amazon. I felt like trash. Ungrateful, Great-Pacific-Garbage-Patch-size trash. I owed Sam a letter. A proper one. I couldn't put it off any longer.

I took a deep breath. I sat down at my desk and finally, finally wrote what I should have written long ago.

Dear Sammy,

Thank you so much for your letter. I'm so glad to hear from you. I'm sorry it took me so long to write something other than a wreck update. I didn't know what to say.

I've been thinking a lot about how we wound up here—you in Vermont, me in Maine. Genetics? Family curse? Bad luck? Broadway, maybe. The epicenter of all badness.

I have to admit now that part of what happened was my fault. Maybe I helped you build leaf boats that one time. But come on. That was one time out of a million. I'm sorry about all the times I walked by you in the halls at school. All the times I chose a romantic circus over hanging out with you. I'm sorry about Spain. I'm sorry I was nothing but mean.

You say you want to be like me. Here's the thing: I want to be like you. You have an endless well of patience, goodness, and love. You're kind. You have a sensitivity that can't be taught. You should have been the older brother. If you were older, you would have taken care of me.

I should have done more to protect you. I'm so grateful you're alive. I'm so, so grateful you're my brother.

Love,
Vi

ps—the search is going okay. A few minor hiccups. I wish you were here, too. In the meantime, I'll try my best for both of us.

HOW TO FIND A SHIPWRECK:
AN AMATEUR'S GUIDE

First things first: blast your relationships to smithereens. You may feel lonely, but loneliness is *good*. Loneliness means you can focus.

Loneliness is the natural state of the wreck hunter.

Focus. The weekend you destroy your relationships, review your primary source documents: a pocket watch engraved with a tree, an emerald earring frustratingly tangled in its chain; a letter describing whales and a *blinding wall of white*; a newly found set of opera specs. Examine the binoculars and cross-reference the maker's stamp; discover that the business did not exist until 1920. Understand these binoculars were not on the *Lyric*. Don't worry. Every wreck hunter experiences setbacks.

Sit on the floor and arrange your clues in a circle around you. Wait for an epiphany. Consider holding a séance to ask your great-great-great-grandmother, *Hey, Fidelia, where were you wrecked?*

Sleep with the pocket watch under your pillow. Perhaps, as if by osmosis, the wreck will present itself to you in a dream.

At work that week, be grateful for the spate of thunderstorms that drive thick crowds indoors, demanding your attention and your quick fingers on the cash register. Always toilet paper to replace, always someone to ring up; there is no time for music chatter. At the end of a shift, you feel *scrubbed*. Days pass. If the boy asks what happened between you and the girl that night (which he will, he's always so freaking *nice* and *interested*), point to the line at the gift shop, say you'd love to chat, but you've really got to ring these folks up.

When he drifts away, hurt, stay the course. Remember: loneliness.

Nights, surrender to the internet vortex. Note that wreck hunters do not have very advanced websites. They favor clip art and neon buttons that encourage you to "click here!" And yet: they are *highly technological*. They are not teenagers with zany plots. They are oceanographers, physical geologists, marine archaeologists, and they say finding a wreck requires a boat, GPS, and sonar. Cameras and floodlights. Scuba certifications. Underwater submersibles. Robots that *swim*.

Discover a blog called *The Adventures of Wreck Bros*. These are your closest friends: Steve and Trent, who go for *sick dives*. It's fun to hate them for a while, but then you start *liking* them, really wanting them to succeed. Trent's got a background in oceanography. Steve quotes a lot of poetry. They go up to Fabian's Bluff to see that Revolutionary War ship the Fresnel Lens Girl mentioned. Close the window.

Seek a quainter approach. Turn to *Diving for Sunken Treasure* for inspiration. Read three pages before you are overwhelmed by the cost, the gear, the effort that goes into finding a wreck—even one with a known location and see-through water.

Mr. Cousteau says nothing of pocket watches and whale migration.

Begin to despair.

One day after work, make a visit to the library. The librarian helps, contagiously eager and excited, sets you up with microfiche and a dusty machine in a hot, cramped side room. You find an article that describes an 1885 blizzard as *the storm of the year*, but discusses the resulting effect on fishing more than conditions on the water. Compare maps of the bay against the wreck's trajectory, a bay in which there are over three hundred unidentified islands. *Three hundred islands to check*, and that's assuming the ship is near land.

Suspect you've bitten off more than you can chew.

That afternoon, wander the coast in your backyard. Stare blankly at the sea, your eyes humming against the bands of blue. There are over three million wrecks in the ocean, but from where you stand, you can't see a single one.

Get sidetracked. Spend that night drafting a musical, tentatively titled *Cousteau!* Set it partially in a submarine. Include a singing whale. Singing whales are crucial to the wreck-hunting process.

After a week of searching, and writing one half of a terrible musical, face facts: You are a selfish sixteen-year-old with a broken pocket watch and a family history of mental illness. Your strengths are jazz hands, parody songs involving crustaceans, and DIY hairstyles. You have no friends. You wanted to give your brother proof the two of you mattered? Yeah, right.

Know it once and for all: wrecks, not discoveries, are in your blood.

THE WORLD BLOOMS UNEXPECTEDLY

A week passed without Liv, a week where I'd hardly spoken to Orion, or anyone, for that matter. At the end of the workday, Boris got tangled under my feet, and I hit the ground hard. Boris, contrite, attempted to lick my face. I shoved him away with two hands and said, louder than I needed to, "Stupid dog!"

He gave a piercing, wounded whine and split for Andy's comforting arms. From the touch tank, a mom and her son stared at me.

"That lady was mean," the boy said.

"She sure was," her mother said. "Does she *work* here?"

Orion helped me to my feet. "Are you okay?"

"Fine."

"No—I mean—are you okay? You've seemed a little off today."

A *little off* was generous. I was a terrible sister, and a terrible wreck hunter. A failure, through and through.

"I'm super," I said, my voice cracking.

"Very convincing. Why don't you take a break? It's almost the end of the day, anyway."

Upstairs I slouched into the fat maroon sofa, trying to forget every single detail of my life. I pulled a pillow over my face, listing ways to improve myself. *Stop causing so much trouble. Stop fighting with people. Stop ignoring your brother. Stop feeling sorry for yourself. Stop being so pathetic. Perseverance.*

A half hour later, Orion plopped down next to me and tap-tapped at the screen of his phone.

"I'm sorry I made such a scene. I know we're hurting for patrons. You can leave me alone, though. I promise I'll behave better."

"Just watch," he said, holding the phone between us. "But more important, listen."

A humpback whale appeared on the screen, barrel-rolling in deep waters. At first I heard just water gurgling, but then another sound emerged: A creaking. A keening. A strange and ugly noise.

"They're whale songs," Orion said. "They're supposed to calm you down."

"These do not sound very soothing."

"The grief counselor I saw recommended them. Definitely not for everyone, but . . . they're kind of comforting after a while. I thought you'd be into them. There's a pattern there, if you listen long enough."

"You saw a grief counselor?"

"Sure. After Will passed away? We all did. I would have kept going, if it weren't so expensive." The humpback rolled again; another whale creak filled the silence. "They remind me of you.

Of your voice. Sorry, I know singing only ends in disaster, or whatever. I won't bring up your voice again. I'm sorry I made you sing the other night, too. I know you fought with Liv, and I'm worried it's my fault."

The whale groaned.

"It's not," I assured him. "Should I take that comparison to my voice as a compliment?"

"Yes. Just listen."

I closed my eyes, listening to the echoes and creaks of this strange new music. Slowly, the ugliness loosened. Orion was right: a pattern emerged, and the whale's song, as unfamiliar as it was, became recognizable though ancient, like language before language. Like the voice of someone who hadn't spoken in a while, but now they were cleaning the rust from their instrument.

"I feel like I'm failing at life," I said to Orion. "I fuck up every time I turn around. I fuck up in New York, I fuck up here . . ."

"Violet, all you did was get angry at Boris. It's okay. He'll forgive you."

I shook my head. Boris might forgive me, but Liv would never, and I doubted Sam would either. Orion didn't know just how badly I'd screwed up with my family, and I couldn't bring myself to tell him. The whole story was so long, so complicated. But I could start somewhere.

"Broadway was a disaster," I said. "Not a *total* disaster. I also got to fly."

"Uh-huh," said Orion.

"I didn't kill Tinker Bell. It's just hard for me to think about singing, though, because singing reminds me of Broadway, and parts of it were great, but parts of it were so hard. I don't know how two opposite things can be true at once. You know?"

"You can like two things at once," Orion said slowly.

"No, this isn't like liking two people. It's like hating and loving the same thing. Or, like, different parts of the same thing."

"Uh-huh."

"I have all this research to tell Liv about. I, like, miss her. Is that weird?"

"Yeah, Violet, it's really weird to miss your friends after you fight. *No*, it's not weird. You should tell Liv you're sorry. I bet she's sorry, too. She's not good with conflict. That's what my mom says, at least."

The whale song creaked. I thought of what he'd said the other day: when I sang, I came alive. Singing had always made me so happy. Even this past week . . .

"I started writing a musical called *Cousteau!* It's really goony and ridiculous right now. But what if we did *that* instead of the concert series? Performed part of it?"

"You're kidding."

"Alas, I am not."

"Can I hear a song from it?"

"The melody's not perfect yet, but . . ."

I adopted my best French accent and sang:

*"Zere is nothing quite so très jolie
As a sparkling dive beneath ze sea,
You hold your breath, and one, two, three,
Ze world blooms unexpectedly . . ."*

Orion looked appalled, and I buried my face in the couch.

"It's horrible! I knew it! I can't even read music!"

"No—Violet. This sounds *awesome*. I'm so in. We can build props and I'll talk to Joan about opening up the space at night, we can make it an event— Wait," he said. "I don't want to distract you from the wreck."

"I'm still working on the wreck. You can like two things at once, right?"

The door of the break room edged open. I saw a black nose, a gray snout, a set of woebegone eyes, and wiry, mangled eyebrows. Honey dog.

"Boris," I said, getting on the floor and opening my arms wide. "C'mere, baby."

On the ground, he was the perfect height for a hug. I wrapped my arms around his dog body, threading my fingers through his coarse coat. *"I'm sorry,"* I whispered into his ear. He rumbled, wanting more. *"I'm sorry to Sam, too."* Whether it was the whale songs or saying the words out loud, I already felt lighter.

Arrghghrhghr, went Boris, and struggled beneath my grasp.

"Okay, you're over it," I said, and released him. "Sorry. Orion. What were you going to say?"

"Don't even remember," Orion said slowly. On the floor and covered in dog hair, I must've looked like a total weirdo, because that's how Orion was staring at me. Fair. I *had* just given Boris an extremely aggressive hug.

"You sure? What we were talking about? Props?"

"Nah," he said. "Gone completely."

"It'll come to you," I assured him.

AT OZ

Joan greenlit *Cousteau!*, set a performance date three weeks away, and announced the event on the website. Overnight, the musical was *real* and the pressure was on. During the day, Andy helped us build paper-plate tambourines and Kleenex-box guitars, a cardboard submarine, papier-mâché fish. Nights, I worked on lyrics while Toby worked on the puzzle. Dorothy was really coming together, minus a wormhole in her cheek, the puzzle lines across her forehead like sloppy Frankenstein stitches.

"Ann Stone's daughter came into the coffee shop today," Toby said. "She was there all afternoon until we closed."

"Hmm," I said. It'd been pouring all day, and I was scratching away at a particularly annoying crossword, taking a break from a rhyme I couldn't work out about Cousteau's diving saucer. I wondered if Liv was still working on the wreck, or the motto, or if like me, she'd quit.

"I can't believe Ann lets her smoke." Toby sighed.

"Ann doesn't know. Wait, how do *you* know that?"

Toby's face looked more disappointed than when he'd dropped me off at Club Tentacle. "She smells like a chimney, kid. You really think people don't notice?"

I didn't know what I thought about Liv anymore.

"This cheek piece is driving me *nuts*," Toby said. "You haven't been stealing pieces, have you? That's what your mom used to do, that way she could always finish the puzzle."

"That's *so* mean," I said.

"Older sisters," Toby said.

I plucked at my necklace and stared at the crossword. I didn't wear the watch outside the house anymore, for fear of losing the emerald, which I couldn't untangle, even though I'd tried everything: needles, mineral oil, baby powder. A website I'd looked at said I'd also need "patience (not pictured!)," which I found extremely condescending.

"What the heck is *atoz*?" I said. I'd been staring at that word for what felt like hours. It made no sense, but I couldn't figure out which letter was wrong.

"What's the clue?" asked Toby.

"'The whole ball of wax.'"

"Oh," he said. "Not atoz. A to Z. Three separate words. A phrase."

I stared back at my own letters. Atoz. A to Z. What had been one word fractured into three. A different way of reading, seeing. Atoz. At Oz. Emerald City: a city of prisms so luminous you'd have to shield your eyes against it.

My brain skitter-stepped, crab-walked backward across an ocean floor, and surfaced to radiant, dazzling daylight.

"The blinding wall of white," I said.

"Is that a lyric?" Toby said.

"No. Toby. Oh my God. Fidelia. The *blinding wall of white*. I thought she was talking about the blizzard, like, she was speaking metaphorically. Like, snow. But maybe she meant something else?"

"I don't follow."

I scrambled in my heap of crosswords and legal pads for her letter. Why was I so careless? Where was it? Why hadn't I put it in a safer place—

Blinding wall of white
The whale
I watched his tail

The watch—2:48—not necessarily night—

"What if she was just talking about the *sun*? Or the sun on the water, or glare from snow, how bright it was . . ."

"So annoying when you leave your sunglasses behind on a sinking ship."

"Oh my God. Steve and Trent. Steve and Trent!"

"Who? Are you having a stroke?"

I threw the printout ineffectually to Toby.

"'Epic trip. Thank God we remembered our shades hashtag-brotime hashtag-theroadlesstraveledby hashtag-frostisdope?' Who *are* these people, why are they dumb enough to be kayaking by Fabian's Bluff, and why are they misquoting Robert Frost?"

"Fabian's Bluff," I repeated. "Fabian's Bluff . . ."

Old Sow Whirlpool. The Desert of Maine. I scrambled for the training manual, flipping wildly to the section of Maine's natural wonders. *Fabian's Bluff, limestone cliffs known to locals as "The Little Cliffs of Dover," extend over a mile and rise nearly one hundred fifty feet above the ocean.*

"We've been looking in the wrong place!"

"Why are you *yelling*?"

"Toby! The wreck! It's not here! It's *there*!" I said, pointing frantically at the printout.

"I don't want to crush your dreams," Toby said, "but Fabian's Bluff is *really* far north of here. Those cliffs are up in Aguecheek Bay."

"Where that Revolutionary War ship is?!"

"Again with the yelling."

"It's just too perfect! Of course the wreck is there! Oh my God, Toby! The whales! The feeding ground!"

"Ah, yes," Toby said slowly, "the whales."

"Toby," I said. My voice was steady. "I know this makes no sense to you. It barely makes any sense to me. But just—look, could you give me a ride? I need to go to office hours."

"Office hours? What professor have you been bothering?"

"No professor. Sorry. That's not what I meant. I just need . . . I need to go talk to Liv."

⟨⟩

Ann Stone was happy to see me. She gave me a towel to blot at my rain-soaked clothes, and handed me a mug of golden tea to take upstairs to Liv, so spicy-sweet-smelling that even I wanted to drink it after I'd declined a cup.

Upstairs, Liv was tucked into bed with a copy of *Charlotte's Web*, red hoodie up so that she was all face. She was wearing glasses, and beneath the lenses, her eyes seemed magnified. The warmth from the mug in my hands spread to places I'd never been aware of before, like where my neck met my brain, or the shallow beside my anklebone.

"I didn't know you wore glasses," I said.

She looked up, her eyes vacant, then scared. "What're you doing here?"

"Bringing you tea. Can I sit with you?"

"Okay," she said uneasily.

I perched on the edge of her twin bed, feet on the floor, feeling oddly like I was tucking her in. She set her book beside her and reached for a braid, but there was none.

"Who's your favorite?" I asked.

"Charlotte. Yours?"

"Templeton."

"He's good, too."

I handed her the tea, and our fingers brushed. I knew why we'd fought, I thought, but maybe I didn't know everything.

"Liv, I'm so sorry," I said.

"No, Violet, please. I was so mean. I keep replaying the things

I said, and I was so drunk, and I was wrong. Of course you know what an anagram is! I mean, that's not the point, obviously. Felix was so mad at me, too, that wasn't my story to tell, I like *used* him, and it's not a competition for who's saddest. . . ."

"You were upset," I said. "Not to mention *right*. I wrote to Sam. A real letter. I am—*ungrateful*."

At that word, she winced, but I shook my head.

"I needed to hear it," I said.

"I'm still sorry," she said.

I took a deep breath, considering whether I wanted to say more. It didn't matter what I said, I decided.

"I think you're great, Liv."

"I think you're great, too."

We stared at each other, the tea unspooling steam between us. My body was humming a low melody, familiar, like a song I'd maybe heard once. Only, I hadn't heard this particular melody before. This wasn't the romance channel. This was a new station with music so lovely, so frightening, so foreign, I hadn't even known to search for its signal.

"We're friends, right?" she said, and the music was over.

"If that's what you want," I said.

She nodded too quick and my heart broke.

"I'm so glad you're here, actually," she said, propping herself up against her headboard. I pretzeled my legs, feeling a whole lot less maternal. "I've been thinking so much about the apple. *Cleft in two*. It's a little far-fetched, but I've been reading about these hidden orchards in London, a lot of them beneath hospital grounds, or psychiatric institutes from like that exact time period, so maybe Fidelia had an affair with the orchard owner. . . ."

"Liv, as much as I hate to crush your dreams, I really think their love might have just been *love*. Their letters are so boring."

"You found *letters?*"

"A while ago," I admitted.

"You could've told me!"

"I know! I'm telling you now! Liv. I think I know where the wreck is."

"You don't."

"I do! I do! Listen. In her letters, Fidelia mentions a *blinding wall of white*. At first I thought she was talking about the blizzard, like being metaphoric. But what if she was speaking literally?"

"I'm listening," said Liv.

"Okay. So I found this blog by these two dudes, and it got me thinking. Maybe the ship veered off course to avoid the blizzard, and wound up far north, near Aguecheek, near that Revolutionary War ship. And the *white* wasn't snow, but *limestone cliffs*, Fabian's Bluff, and it was too bright, like *February*, too, imagine the glare off the snow, so . . . I don't know . . . it blinded the captain and he ran aground. Or not, the ship just sank in daylight for whatever reason, but still, Fidelia couldn't see because it was so sunny!"

"The cliffs as reverse lighthouse," Liv murmured, and I wanted to kiss her, taste nicotine, bad breath, the aftertaste of tea I'd never tried.

"It's certainly poetic," she admitted.

"I think we should go up there," I told her.

"And what? Metal detect? I don't think I have to remind you what happened the last time we tried to metal detect. Besides, it's, like, *weird* up there. We used to camp there as kids. We stopped going because Will was convinced there were ghosts and he got so freaked out. Every year there's some story about someone getting lost or drowning in the fog."

"The *peculiar haze*! How did you not mention this before?!"

"Because you didn't tell me about the letter! And didn't you hear a word I said? *People die.* And what about the porthole at Seal Cove?"

"Maybe everyone was just looking in the wrong spot," I argued. "We should still go!"

"Violet, your evidence hinges largely on a blog."

"So what! Why are you so obsessed with evidence anyway? People find stuff every day! There's a sunken ship in Lake Michigan, d'you know that? A passenger galleon under a jetty on the Jersey Shore. A boat in the Connecticut River! Just this past week, there was this diver in Florida, nearby where my dad used to go with his parents, the guy found treasure from Spain from the 1700s! There's all this stuff *out there*!"

"Yes, and don't forget THE FOURTEEN HUMAN FEET that have washed up in the Pacific Northwest over the past few years! There are bodies, Violet, people hacked up into tiny pieces! Not everything you find in the ocean is sparkles and rainbows!"

I was breathing very hard. So was she. Downstairs I heard a sink running, Ann calling to Tom over the noise of water. I wondered what Will's voice had sounded like, calling from room to room.

"Rationally speaking," Liv said, and I wanted to punch rationality in its stupid fucking face, "even if the ship *were* there, you think Fidelia would've made it all the way from Aguecheek to Lyric, post-shipwreck, frozen, 1895, no roads, all wilderness? People get hypothermic from *this* weather."

I stared out the window at the pelting rain. Liv slurped her tea. She was so frustrating. This whole thing was so frustrating. Why did I even care about a shipwreck, anyway?

"You know what? *Fuck* Fidelia," I said.

"That escalated quickly," said Liv.

"I don't even understand why she felt compelled to tell people she survived this wreck! She was planning on hiding. But she didn't. She could have just lived her whole life as someone else, and then her descendants could have been totally normal. Instead of cursed with a shipwreck gene."

"Don't you think you're being a bit dramatic?"

"I think I should quit."

"Violet, this is research. It's boring a lot of the time. Walls and giving up are part of it. Then you reroute. You try a new approach. Do you think Orion built that boat in a day? Do you think he knew what he was doing every step of the way? Definitely not. But he chose to keep going."

"Orion showed you the boat?" I said.

Liv shrank a little, hiding behind her mug. "We went out in the boat, actually."

I pictured them, *Little Mermaid*–style, floating in a blue lagoon. Knowing Orion, he'd probably conjured four fruit-colored moons for the occasion and trained a team of eels in matching swim caps to perform a water ballet. Few girls, a moron once said, would be able to resist a boat.

"It was nice," she said.

"Uh-huh," I said.

"I'm—I'm trying to think of how to say this to you, Violet. Orion and I are friends. More than friends. I know I spent a lot of time saying I didn't want him . . ."

Well. Shit.

". . . and I still don't . . ."

Oh my God. Ohmigod.

". . . so if there's anything going on . . ."

This wasn't happening. This wasn't happening. Could it be happening?

". . . between you and him, you should let that happen. I don't mind, at all. I want him to be happy. You too. And I think he likes you."

"Oh." That was how she felt toward me: apathetic.

"Thanks, I guess."

"Don't quit looking for the wreck," Liv said. "Not if you're invested. Choosing to try is all there is sometimes."

"But *you* won't try," I said.

"I need more to go on before I get in a car and spend money on gas and drive into the wilderness," Liv said. "Plus, I promised my parents I'd help them clean this weekend."

There were so many things I could say. Please. It'll be fun. It's not that dangerous, it's not that far. We might find something cool. Hadn't you felt what I felt, in that closet, looking at that strand of corn silk? I want to grow clammy and sweaty and panting with you on this bed, broad daylight, touch you, taste you, then tuck us in and read to you from *Charlotte's Web* with your head on my chest, and I'll even do the characters' voices.

"Cleaning can be really satisfying," I said carefully.

"It is," she said, and I swore I caught a hint of ruefulness in her voice. "You can still go, you know. Without me. I bet Orion would take you."

"You know I want to find the wreck for Sam," I said weakly.

"I don't think you need to find a shipwreck to show your brother you care about him," she said. "But keep at it. If you have something real, the universe will start giving you gifts."

"You sound like Felix."

"That's because it's some dumb thing he told me once. But dumb things are comforting. Like, here, take this. Felix gave it to me once upon a time. Maybe it'll bring you luck."

She twisted the purple ring off her finger and handed it to me, like a fashionable consolation prize.

❦

The first thing Orion said to me the next day was: "Liv said you found the ship!"

I was up in the break room, putting finishing touches on the cardboard submarine. I'd gotten there super early, and made good progress—I'd started painting on an intricate control panel, red buttons, and levers. I'd tried to make it clumsy, like Ransome's drawings, but more likely it'd just look sloppy. I hoped no one would come to the show.

"Holy shit," said Orion, "you're almost done with the sub! You're like me with the boat!"

"Ha," I said weakly. Liv's ring was clunky on my finger, and it hurt to look at, but I couldn't take it off. He didn't know what we had in common.

"So this means you're friends again, right? And we're gonna go up there?" said Orion.

"Liv has to help her parents clean. And I'm not even sure I found it."

"Yeah, her parents need her around sometimes. But we can still go, you and I. And Felix and Mariah. We can take the boat, even—that was the whole *point* of building the boat. For adventure times. We can think of it as like a musical brainstorming retreat. . . ."

"I dunno, Orion. My theory's pretty shaky. Plus, Liv told me all this stuff about severed feet. . . ."

"I mean, we don't even need to look for the wreck if you don't want. You've barely seen anything besides Lyric. Aguecheek's so cool, it's like wild, and edge-of-the-earthy. . . ."

"Liv made it sound kind of creepy," I said.

"Liv is terrified of anything that doesn't involve TV or books," Orion said, and I really *liked* that about her, I realized. "Seriously. Why not? Isn't this what you wanted the whole time? To find this wreck?"

He was so *game*, so eager. I twisted the ring on my finger, looked at the ring on his inner arm. He had a point. Why was I making this so hard? What had Felix said? *These things only have meaning if we grant them meaning.* I wanted to find the ship for Sam, and that was that.

What did it matter how I got there?

"Sure. We'll go," I said simply, and Orion smiled like I'd just solved climate change.

⚮

to: samuel.alan.larkin@mail.com
from: violet.rudolph.larkin@mail.com

Sam,

I thought I'd be more excited to write this. Basically: I think I found the Lyric. And we're going, this weekend. Mariah's got a plan to get pirate rum, and Felix's threatening to make us glitter eye patches, and Orion's been working on a secret mixtape all week. It has all the makings of a Cousteau-ian deep-sea-diver ADVENTURE.

But Liv's not coming. Neither are you.

I'm still excited, I guess, and I'm trying not be ungrateful. This is what I wanted all along. But, I don't know. I just wish you were here. Wreck hunting's ours. It always has been. I don't think that'll ever change.

I miss you a lot.

Violet

GOOD SIGNS

July turned to August, and those first days of the new month spooled away in a haze of fish songs and wreck dreams. The Friday night before we left for Aguecheek Bay was cold, but I was down on the dock texting my mom. I was wearing Marine Mingle, Toby's windbreaker, and I'd brought a blanket down from inside, but it was the only place I got service. We'd added my dad to the thread, and I was just about to add Sam when a new number popped up: *Where r u Im at ur house its Liv Orion gave me ur number*

Backyard dock, I typed. Why was she here?

She came over the hill carrying a milk crate, flip-flops smacking on her heels, arms and legs totally bare. She must have been freezing.

"You text worse than my mom," I called, standing up.

"I found you, didn't I?" she said.

"Aren't you cold?"

"Not really." Her flip-flops were fuchsia, with a big cloth sunflower where plastic ribbons met over her toes.

"I like your shoes," I said.

"They're my mom's," she said, and set the crate down between us. "Okay, so you're not going to believe this, but I went to the

Missing Piece with my dad today, and *look at all the shit* we found."

She pulled out a pair of tattered wet suits, an enormous flood-light, and a few sets of extra-long snorkels.

"This is an underwater floodlight, it was broken, but my dad got it working again, and this is an underwater camera—the only thing I could think was that someone gave up free-diving recently. I mean, we're not qualified to free-dive, obviously, but maybe one day . . ."

What was she *doing* here?

"Wait," I said, "you're coming now?"

"Yeah. If that's okay? It just seemed like a sign."

I more tackled her than hugged her, wrapping the scratchy-soft blanket around us both. Maybe this was a sign for her, and it was a sign for me, too, and I'd count them . . . five seemed like a good number. Five, and then I'd tell her.

"Ow, yes, hi, thank you, ow." She extracted an arm and patted me gingerly, passionlessly on the shoulder.

"One more thing. I got you this, too."

Good sign one: a present.

She handed me a photograph from her pocket where she usually kept her cigarette butts. I looked at a woman in black and white. She was in the ocean, wearing a sort of white hazmat or space suit, holding on to a barrel.

"*Ama* pearl divers, Japan, you see, earliest recorded in 700. Literally it means 'women of the sea.' We have to go visit, one day. . . ."

Good sign two: a trip being planned years in advance.

"They hunt on the sea ground for abalone and seaweed and

urchins in order to feed their villages. Women supposedly did it because they have a higher percentage of body fat that kept them warm, and they used to dive naked. . . ."

Nudity was definitely good sign three. They'd piled up so quickly. We were almost there.

"They started using wet suits in 1964, all because of this pearl tycoon, but that's a different story. They learn to dive when they're fifteen. Isn't that incredible? They reminded me of you. Well, us, I guess."

Good sign four. What would I say, though? I'd use my words, like a grown-up. *I like you. I'd like to kiss you, but I'm afraid that's not what you want.* The woman in the photograph was smiling so big. Fireflies were twinkling around us. Could that be the fifth good sign? No. That was cheating.

"How do you *retain* all that?" I asked.

"That's just reading. What you do? Singing. Dancing. I can't stop thinking about you singing the other night. I know I flipped out, but you have a really good voice, Violet." She paused. "Orion won't stop talking about you."

It would have been the last good sign, but her mentioning Orion felt like a setback. I'd have to subtract one. So we were at what now? Four? Or three?

"Liv," I said, "can we not talk about Orion for one minute?"

"Okay. I'll time us."

She looked at her watch. It had a plain black band and a white face. How had I never noticed this watch before? It was a good cheap watch. Two black hands quietly ticked round and round. The watch was a little big for her; there was space between her wrist and the plastic. Space enough for me to slip two fingers there, and hook them around the band of the watch. Which is exactly what I did.

Her pulse quickened.

My pulse quickened.

I kept my fingers there, hooked around her watch.

Fuck the signs.

I pulled her toward me, and then, finally, finally: I kissed her. *Kissed.* Kissed, kissed, kissed.

I kissed her kissed her and I thought I'm kissing her and then I realized *she* was kissing *me*, like, OH MY GOD SHE WAS KISSING ME BACK, the fullness of her lips, the slight taste of cigarettes, smoke and fire catching in my ankles, her hand pressed against my jaw, so I pressed my hand against her jaw and her skin bumped like the seafloor under my fingers, what was this, what were we, an eel that'd just grown legs, walked on land after spending our whole life in a dark reef? A mermaid who'd traded her voice and soul for this? For the scrape of her teeth on my lower lip and the slight push of her tongue, worth it, holy fuck, so worth it, no voice for her mouth, her mouth, her mouth, we were bacteria crawling from primordial ooze, now we had soft blanket bee fur, just like I wanted this whole time and *knew* but I didn't, not even a little bit—just as long as it never stopped—

A foghorn blared far off. The ocean lapped at the rocks; a ghost crab scuttled across the sand yards away. Clams breathed bubbles beneath the sand, and I swear I heard a firefly shuffle his wings. Liv pulled away and tectonic plates moved beneath us; under miles of ocean, the seafloor split.

My fingers were still threaded through her watch and her skin, and I was only now realizing that her hand was wrapped hot around my hip, it was a wonder my hip bone didn't blast to smithereens from the shock, and this close up, I couldn't tell if I was looking at her nose or my nose or both our noses layered together. She moved back and her face sharpened into focus, and I looked into the world's only satisfying fun-house mirror. Liv. Mine.

How has this taken so long? I thought.

"How has this taken so long?" she said.

I ran my fingers over her lips. I thought of the arch of her foot and the zip of her thigh and her smell. I thought about kissing her again, and kissing her just now. Liv stared at me, quaking and gentle and bewildered and dumbstruck. She tucked her fingers through my belt loops and tugged, nervous.

"Are you okay?" I asked.

"I thought you liked Orion." She laughed. "I'm so stupid! That's all. Just. Very. Very. Stupid."

"The opposite."

She tugged my hips toward hers with my belt loops until our mouths met again. I'd never kissed anyone before her in my life. I'd never had a conversation like this. I could feel the muscles in her calves tighten where she was stretching up tall enough to meet me, her hands were moving, I should move my hands, too, why hadn't I moved them, touching neck, earlobe, chest, stomach.

I could kiss her neck, it occurred to me.

Liv tucked her face against my collarbone, Marine Mingle between us, our bodies mashed potatoes together, sweet potatoes, the kind with marshmallows on top. She was so soft, she thought she was all edge but she wasn't and neither was I.

"I didn't know . . ." I said at last. I kissed her forehead, left cheek, her right temple; her skin was soft, her cheek cold.

"I didn't know!" she said. "Not until you came here. Or I knew, but I didn't know. I still don't. Even when I thought, it was impossible, that you could think of *me*. . . ."

I could rest my chin on her scalp and I loved that, I wished I were even taller, a giantess, so I could put her in my pocket and take her wherever I went. I wanted to tell her all sorts of *big* things—all these thoughts about time and history and scope and bees that swim, my body was Fresnel-lensing again, light beaming and refracting and rainbowing. . . .

"You should really wash this sweatshirt," she said into my chest.

I giggled and she looked up at me. I hadn't ever seen her from this angle.

"If we go inside, will it be over?" she asked.

"It's not a spell," I said.

"Promise?" she said.

"Yes," I said.

The South American coast from Peru to Chile experiences a yearly period of coastal upwelling. Colder, nutrient-rich waters suddenly rush to the ocean's surface, and with that comes an overabundance of fish in search of food. Who knows what this *actually* looks like, but when I read about it in the Lyric Aquarium information packet, I imagined schools of fish filling the waters, creating a silver bridge from sand to horizon. A phenomenon that transformed the dark, cold sea into a walkway near solid and sparkling. A rare sort of aquatic alchemy.

Side by side. On the couch. Her body against mine and mine against hers. Hands on ribs, stomachs, up in hair. I squeezed her earlobe just because I could. Kissing like that for days. Hours. Minutes. Who knew? Fresnel lenses don't tell time.

Her dress rode up. I put my hand on the outside of her bare thigh and she spoke.

"I've never had sex," she said, frank, soft, scared.

"We don't have to have sex."

"But you have, right?"

I nodded and my nose grazed hers.

"Both people?"

"Yes." I felt like crying, scared and happy, like in the instant before I set foot onstage.

"Do you care that I haven't?"

I shook my head no. "We don't have to," I said again, but I wanted to. With us, it was right. I knew that. She knew that. And still, part of me wished this moment between us could stay perfect and set, like sea fossils in the desert long after the water had gone.

Her breath mixed with mine. We weren't fossils. We were changing, alive, and I wanted her.

"I . . . I want to. With you. If you do?" she said.

Her mouth on mine was so warm I shivered. I dipped my hand under her dress, traced the comma of her hamstring to the edge of her cotton underwear, and she made a throaty noise I'd hear in my dreams for years to come. Did I want to? I wanted to. It wasn't a question.

"It's okay," she whispered.

I was too nervous. She was real. She had edges. I propped my fingertips on her stomach, my hand tented like a little four-legged creature. Then, slowly, I flattened my hand against her skin, a deer splayed on ice.

Her breathing quickened. God, I was so nervous. Why was I so nervous?

I wasn't ginger. I was trembling but deliberate. I imagined my hand sinking through her skin, every cell on my hand touching every part of her ribs. I marveled at the sturdiness of her rib cage and the strength of her breath. Her heart was frantic and her skin was cold. My middle finger skimmed her bra's cloth and wire edge. I opened my eyes, and her lash line was purple, like tattooed eyeliner. I slipped two fingers beneath the bridge of her bra and kept them there, feeling for her pulse between her breasts.

She put her hand under my shirt and laid her palm flat on my heart. Eight limbs between us, two hearts each beating in their own rhythm, and her eyes warm and constant as pilot lights. She smiled and, so gently, took my hand and guided it back down.

"Now, please?" she asked, so very polite.

✣

At one point, someone stifled a yawn. Me too, the other one said.

"I've got to go home," Liv said. Her hair had fallen out of the braids and was sticking every which way, matted in the back. The next time I'd see her it'd be brushed and rebraided, all evidence of what happened between us undone with a shower and a comb. We weren't fossils, but we had memories, and we had each other.

"This happened, right?" I asked, sitting up beside her.

"I think so. No. I *know* so."

"Maybe that's why people give each other love tokens. It's, like, proof."

She touched my face. "Is it okay if we don't—if we don't tell anyone here?"

I thought of her parents and Felix. That man who'd yelled at me from the car window. We could do what she wanted. This was her home.

"Could I tell Sam? Not in graphic detail, but just about you?"

She ran her fingers over my UFO tattoo, considering.

"You can tell Sam," she said finally.

"Okay," I said. "But we can—we can do this again, right?"

She kissed me. *She* kissed *me*.

"This happened. It will happen again." She looked at her watch. "I'm picking you up in six hours to go look for this wreck, so you're stuck with me all weekend anyway."

∞

As soon as she walked out the door, time shifted. Second hands eked their way around the clock. My entire life revolved around waiting: waiting for it to be morning so then I could see Liv again. To kiss. To kiss, and kiss, and kiss, and kiss.

I couldn't sleep. Possessed by an inner effervescence, I cleaned the shit out of my grandmother's house. I organized the attic. I did laundry. I scrubbed toilets and sinks and showers. I swept. I busted out the mop. As I cleaned, Liv was a scrim that came down over everything, a show always playing on the wet curve of my eyeballs, a contact nestled up close to my pupils, my irises.

"Jesus Christ, are you on *drugs*?" Toby asked, lurching into the kitchen at 4:00 a.m. on his way to the bakery.

"Not anymore!"

This was better than drugs. Every object I touched felt *new* and *old* all at once. I felt connected to everything: I was bathing in this collective well of *love* and *history*, like I'd invented this feeling, or discovered it. But *this this this* was much bigger than me, too, much bigger than Liv, much bigger than *humans*. When I'd folded T-shirts, I felt not the fabric but the original cotton blooms that had been harvested to make them; when I'd shined the surface of the dining room table, I understood its former life as a tree, saw the forest it grew up in, felt the waxy greenness of its summertime leaves.

"I know I'm absent at best, but I really didn't peg you for a speed freak," Toby said.

"I just mopped! Careful!"

"What are you doing awake? Where did you even *find* a mop?" He put his hand to my forehead. "Are you feeling okay?"

I shook him off. I hadn't felt this good in a long, long time.

After he left, I worked on the puzzle. All that was left was a cornfield, blue sky, the gingham of Dorothy's dress—the hard parts that everyone left for last. There were just the edges of each piece left to guide me, no pictures to give me clues, but I knew I could do this. I could do the hard parts.

Around 7:00 a.m., the doorbell rang. *Liv.* She was back, I knew it. She couldn't wait to see me either. I was going to open the door, and I was going to grab her. I wanted to pull her braid across my mouth. I wanted to pull her black dress over her head. I wanted to press my body against hers. I swung the door open, my heart leaping from my chest.

It was Sam.

PART THREE: SURVIVAL

PORTRAIT OF A FAMILY

The year is Wild. This is a Family.

Every day, the Parents wake up at 5:00 a.m. The Mother spends all day cutting open sick children, tinkering with their parts, and sewing them back together. Sometimes, despite all her herculean efforts, she must report to their completely strung-out parents that she did her best, but little Marcus/Chloe/Roberto didn't have the strength to pull through. Her job is truly the stuff of nightmares. The Father does something complex with numbers and taxes and *businesses*. The Daughter imagines an abacus, though she doesn't *really* know, because she's never asked. Instead of "Dad," she and the Son sometimes call him the "Finance Department," which can't feel good. The Father has so much paper in his office that when she was little, the Daughter used to worry that he'd be crushed in an office avalanche.

Both the Mother and the Father average a fourteen-hour day. All this so they can live with their family in a fancy-ass apartment on the Upper West Side and send their offspring, their complete *lemons* of children, to private school. The Son was always . . . *complicated*, but the Daughter actually used to be okay. The worst she did was sing, very loudly, at the dinner table. Once she demanded their presence at her one-woman-revival of *My Fair Lady*, which she staged in their living room.

Now, though, the Daughter is sixteen and a force to be reckoned with. She looks about twenty-five. She stays out late. There are boys. There are girls. She scares her parents. They look at her like they can't believe they made her. Is she actually *theirs*? The Son they understand: he is wasting away in front of them. There is a physical manifestation of a murkier mental problem. He's in desperate need of treatment, medication, doctors. But the Daughter? They're at a loss. She scares them so much they stop asking questions altogether. They know something is *wrong*, but it's also easier not to know what time she came home and what she got up to over the weekend.

One day, though, the Parents get a call. The Daughter has been caught smoking weed in the middle of the day a block away from school grounds. The school has no choice but to suspend her. The Son, it should be noted, frequently hides in an unused school closet because the lights are too fluorescent and the voices are too loud and the world is becoming such a horrible place that all he can do is not eat and read. For him this is more or less standard behavior, plus he's still acing his classes. The Daughter's suspension, however, is a real breaking point. They can no longer ignore the brewing catastrophe.

So the Parents come up with a plan. The spring before the Son's suicide attempt, they all take an expensive vacation to Spain to "rebuild the family." Days, they sightsee, bake in the heat, and struggle with the language barrier. Nights, the Daughter smokes hashish and drinks rioja with the young Spanish hotelier from the front desk while the Son reads alone in their room. The Son doesn't ask her to stay, but the Daughter notes he doesn't fall asleep until she returns.

The Son is having a bad time in Spain. He hates potatoes and mayonnaise, cannot stand the vastness of cathedrals, finds the language abrasive and loud. He cannot take the sun and the heat. He doesn't understand why there's no *water* in this city. At a particularly grim lunch at an outdoor café, where flies keep landing on his anemic salad of iceberg lettuce, tuna, and mayonnaise-slathered tomato, the Mother admits that maybe she didn't think this trip through. The Father reminds everyone they're descended from the survivor of a shipwreck and they're in *Spain*, for Christ's sake, can't we all just have a good time? The Son, obviously guilt-ridden, takes a bite of a tomato and gags. The Daughter fantasizes about the waiter fingering her in the bathroom.

The Parents persevere. They must. They see *Guernica*. They take the high-speed train to Granada and tour the Alhambra, forcing the children to pose with stone lions. The temperature drops, rare for this time of year, but the cold snap is a welcome relief for the foreigners. They catch a flamenco show in a cave, and after, the Father sweetly embarrasses himself trying to re-create the moves. He pulls the Daughter into the street for a dance, and she lets him. This, though small, turns out to be the beginning.

After that night, the Son asks for plain white rice: the first food he's requested in months. The family winds up eating in a lot of grimy Chinese joints as a result, and the three-way lost-in-translation farce that invariably ensues is enough to make all of them laugh, plus the servers, all at the same time, so much so that the Father weeps a little bit and props his glasses on his forehead. The Daughter remembers, oh yeah, Dad is *human*—we all are. That night, the Daughter stays in with her brother. They perfect their Jacques Cousteau impressions. The brother admits he missed her this past year. The Daughter says, yeah, I know. They work on crossword puzzles. They finish two Saturdays and an acrostic.

The next night, the four of them take a good family photograph at the top of San Nicolas at sunset, the orange light bouncing off the Alhambra, making it glow from within like a lantern. The Daughter has learned that Granada means *grenade*, yes, but also *pomegranate*. She loves this fact: this city feels ripe and red and mythical as the fruit itself. Hippies play homemade instruments, and the Daughter and her brother dance a tango to the music of wood flutes. The Parents kiss, a long one. *It's working*, everyone thinks, but is too scared to say aloud. That's how tenuous and unbelievable the whole thing feels: their happy family floats cautiously, like a shimmering soap bubble.

And maybe, maybe, the trip to Spain would have worked, were it not for the Table Incident.

After the photograph, the family heads to dinner. It's still early by Spanish standards—ten p.m. The restaurant is empty. The Son can't figure out what to order. The Daughter is bothered by the quiet. The Mother wants to know if she's okay. *I'm fine,* the Daughter snaps. They'll be heading home in a few days: their return to New York looms over her.

The Mother says she has a question.

Uh-oh, the Father says.

The Mother, in a gesture of goodwill and advice straight out of parenting books, asks the Daughter whether she might like to, when they get back to the city, take a visit to the Son's expensive therapist. They haven't talked about the suspension, not really, but the Mother thinks the therapist might be a good place to start.

The Daughter grows resistant, but not mean. Not yet. The Mother soldiers on, undeterred by the Daughter's terse, one-word answers. The Mother has been buoyed by the familial closeness of the last few days. She thinks now she has an opportunity to reach her daughter. *It's just been so nice to see you smile these past few days,* she says. *I cannot remember the last time you smiled.* The Mother has left her small patients dying on the other side of the world so she can be here, with her miserable, fucked-up family in this empty restaurant, too early, with her Daughter who never smiles and her Son who never eats. The Mother is obviously at her wit's end, huge bags under her eyes, mascara flaking her cheekbones like freckles on a corpse.

Even though the Daughter thinks privately that therapy would do her a lot of good, she can't swallow the Mother's kindness. She misses the rush of New York City. She wants to get high. She wants to have sex. She doesn't want to go to therapy. She doesn't want to get better, because getting better would mean there's something *wrong* with her.

So she spits back: just because I'm a slut doesn't mean I'm unhappy.

The Mother, of course, starts to cry.

The Daughter glances at her brother, looping his spoon through his soup, his other hand clenched in a fist. She cannot remember the last time he ate a full meal. His veins are blue and his cheeks are gaunt. His blond hair is falling out, but his arms have grown downy. The Daughter is suddenly furious. She is *so tired* of this, *so tired* of eyeing his plate and seeing how many bites he takes, of the constant monitoring, so angry to have eaten in so many Chinese restaurants when there are mountains of jamón ibérico and goat cheese and honey and paella to be inhaled. How hard is it, really, to suck down some fucking gazpacho?

The shipwreck gene roils in her stomach. The Daughter looks her Mother in the eye.

Besides, the Daughter says, Sam's been in therapy since birth, and look at how well *he's* doing.

The Son stops playing with his food. He puts the dripping spoon on the table, leaving an archipelago of stains behind. He stands up. He walks across the restaurant, gets down on his hands and knees, and crawls beneath another table. He disappears entirely from view. The waiters glance at each other nervously. The tablecloth flutters, then goes still. *Curtain.*

The Father congratulates the Daughter on making half the

family cry. He'd join in, he says, if he weren't so dehydrated. He signals for the bill.

Thanks, Finance, the Daughter says.

The Daughter knows she must change. More than anyone else, more than the rest of the family combined, she is disgusted with the person she has become. She knows it's not hard to say a kind a word. To say, *Thanks, Mom, I think you're right, and I appreciate your noticing.* She knows when she and the brother get back to the room, she should crawl under the covers with him, hold his hand, and tell him that things will get better, that she's there for him, she promises.

Instead, when they return to the hotel, the Daughter sneaks out with the guy from the front desk. His name is Elio, and in his seamy apartment there is a black futon and three heavy, stoned roommates and a huge burgundy wall hanging, ripped across the center to reveal a beige stucco wall behind. By the Daughter's feet sits a pearl-gray cat with an ear that's being eaten away by some kind of fungus. A naked patch behind the cat's ear is furless and scabbed. The Daughter contemplates this patch on the ear, points it out to Elio. Elio says the cat's just a street cat, no big deal. They smoke.

When the hash takes hold, the Daughter *flips*. The cat needs antibiotics. She tells this to Elio, who says again, the cat's just a street cat. She insists that the cat needs medicine. The cat is in pain. She calls Elio a *terrible pet owner*, which at the time is just about the meanest, cruelest thing she can come up with (which, given what you've seen of the Daughter, is pretty weak, but also explains just how high she is). At least it is spat with venom and vitriol. Elio stares at the Daughter. The cat mews. The Daughter's ears ring, she's been screaming so loud. She wasn't aware she'd been yelling.

There is silence. Then Elio starts to laugh.

In her mind's eye, the Daughter sees herself from above: a girl yelling about a street cat in a stranger's apartment in Granada, while her family does not sleep in a hotel a mile away.

When she gets back to their room, her brother is gone.

APPARITION

Seven a.m. on a misty August Saturday, bleary with lack of sleep and lovelust fireworking in my chest and expecting to be greeted with *Liv, Liv, Liv, Liv*, I at first mistook my brother for an apparition—not of *my brother*, or even of a ghost, but of *myself*. Dumbly, I figured that someone had propped a mirror in front of the door, and my own reflection was staring back at me, sandy short hair wacky from a cleaning spree, eyes love-twitchy and sleep-deprived, heart thumping beneath the thin cotton of my Lyric Aquarium T-shirt.

Then my reflection *moved* and *spoke*.

"You can't tell Mom and Dad. Are you mad? Don't be mad."

"*Sammy?*"

"Hi." He curled his fingers in a cautious wave, smiling the close-lipped smile he'd been smiling since he'd gotten braces. Nearly two years had passed since I'd gotten a good long look at his teeth.

"Violet?" he said. "Are you mad?"

I still wasn't convinced he was real. When I reached for him, I half expected my hand to pass through his body. But he wasn't a ghost: Sam was here, on this chilly Maine morning, pressed to me, taller, almost my height now. I hugged him and he smelled like pine trees and sweat and Diet Coke. The wing of his shoulder blade was sharp under my fingers. My brother was here. *My brother was here.*

"Ow. Violet. You're breaking my ribs."

I let him go. He looked the same and he looked different: same scuttling green animal eyes, pigeon-toed feet and crunched-up shoulders. But his hair was longer, curling around his ears and the nape of his neck, and his elfin face was fuller. New freckles spattered their way across the bridge of his same rabbit nose.

"You're so tall," I said.

"I'm only like an inch taller than when you saw me last."

"What? That's impossible. You're, like, almost my height."

"I'm five nine and a half. I was five eight and a half in June."

"No, that can't be true—"

"They measure us, okay? Every week. At weigh-ins. You probably just didn't notice before I left." He pulled his fists inside his hoodie, looking anywhere but at me. My brother was here, all right.

"Sam, what's going on? Are you in trouble?"

"No. Probably. I'm probably in trouble now that I'm here. It doesn't matter."

I was halfway inside the house before I turned around and saw him still there, in the doorway.

"Sam," I called, "come on. Come in."

"Are you sure? Is Toby there?"

"What do you mean, am I sure? Were you planning on hanging out in the driveway all morning? *Come in.*"

In the kitchen, we stood on opposite sides of the island counter. Sam looked tired beneath the too-bright lights, the skin under his eyes puffy as marshmallows, but he wasn't flickering like normal. He looked bigger. Stronger.

"It smells delicious in here," he said finally.

"Cupcakes," I said. "Funfetti."

I wanted to hug him again, squeeze him so tight he'd never leave. When he'd run away that night in Spain, he'd taken a cab to the airport. The Guardia Civil found him there, trying to change his ticket home. He just wanted to be, he said, somewhere he knew.

"Sam, how did you get here?" What was he—a delinquent, a runaway?

"I took the bus." Sam could barely manage the subway to school, let alone an unfamiliar bus route across state lines. "It's not a big deal, Violet. I just bought a bus ticket. My roommate's covering for me. No one will even notice I'm gone until midmorning. What is all this stuff? Is this for the *Lyric*? You're going this weekend, right?"

He pawed through Liv's crate. He brought a sleeve of the wet suit to his nose and grimaced, then lifted out the chewed-up flippers. There was a knife on the counter that winked at me. I'd have to Sam-proof the house, hide the blades and the pills. At least until I figured out what the hell I was going to *do*. At least until we called Mom and Dad.

I had to call Mom and Dad.

Sam slipped the flippers over his hands like a sea lion. "Do you think you'll actually go on a dive? Like, get in the water and swim to the ship?"

We were only a year apart, but he looked so very young. Something inside me snapped like a twig.

"Sam. *Stop.*"

"Are you mad?" he squeaked, and I knew he was in danger of retreating then, curling into himself, away from me.

"Sam, it's okay. Just *talk* to me. I want to know what you're doing here."

"That place bored me," Sam said finally. "Not bored like uninteresting. Bored like boring a hole. It was good, at first, and I felt better, and, like, eating feels more normal, so that's good, but then I was ready to leave. I'm better now, I think." His voice cracked; it was more gravelly than I remembered.

"Is that what your doctor said? Why didn't you just *talk* to someone? Tell Mom and Dad?"

"Is that what you would have done?" he said, and he didn't even let me answer. "Then I got your email. I hadn't even been checking my email—it's all, like, dumb school stuff—and then—bam—this email from you—everything just clicked. You sounded so sad. I wanted to be here with you, too. And then I realized I *could* be. All I had to do was buy a bus ticket." He shrugged, gazing at his feet. "So here I am."

"We've got to call home," I said.

"No, Vi, please, they'll freak out."

"They're going to freak out anyway when they notice you're gone!"

"You wanted me to come, didn't you? It'll be what, a day, tops. You get to have an adventure. I want an adventure, too. I've already missed so much—just because"—he shook his head—"I was born with this brain instead of yours."

I studied my brother's pleading, desperate face. I'd wished for him to be here, hadn't I? Finding the *Lyric* was about Sam. And now here he was. . . .

"What bus did you even *take*?" I asked.

He *lit up*.

"Well, it was three different buses, actually, all these little commuter buses. The first one picked me up behind the bank, the second one picked me up outside a mall, and the third one, that was weird, they just, like, dropped me on the side of the highway, almost. *That* scared me. But this other guy showed up, and I asked him about Lyric, and he was like, yeah, don't worry, this'll get you there."

He was still wearing his flipper hands. I loved him so much.

"Then—get this—I asked him *where he was going* and he was a lobsterman, it was so cool, and he told me all these stories about being on the fishing boat—he wasn't creepy, don't make that face—and then the bus CAME! Like a miracle, and then we sat separately, it wasn't even a big deal, it wasn't awkward, but then he handed me his card when we got off the bus and he told me they needed smart people, so, I dunno, maybe I should do that next summer, Violet, stop looking at me like that, I grew up in New York, too, you know, and I know what creepy feels like, probably even better than you."

He crossed his arms defensively. I flicked him, hard, right in the center of the *r* on his Lyric Aquarium T-shirt.

"*Ow,*" he said, rubbing his chest with a flipper hand, "what's wrong with you?"

Good. Sam was real. He was in there. I hadn't lost my marbles.

"The whole trip cost six seventy-five," he said with pride.

"We've gotta call Mom and Dad."

"No, Violet, please—"

A car crunched in the driveway. *Toby.*

"You have to hide." I grabbed Sam by the wrist and we flew upstairs to my bedroom, spilling flippers on the stairs. We'd barely made it inside, when we heard the front door slam. Toby's voice echoed through the house: *"Violet! Where are you?"*

"In here," I hissed, pushing Sam into my closet.

"What are all these fur coats?" he said, pawing at the minks on hangers.

"*Violet!*" yelled Toby.

"I don't know, Sam, storage, shut up!"

I swung the door closed just in time. Toby strolled into the room, wild-eyed and sallow-skinned, still wearing his bakery apron.

"I just got off the phone with your mother," he said. "You haven't heard from Sam, have you?"

Toby was only breaths away from my closet, and the door was swinging open. From where I stood, I could make out the shape of my brother, crouching amid the hanging furs.

"Sam didn't show up for breakfast in Vermont. I guess he left a note about catching the bus. To New York. Everyone's trying to reach him, and we're calling the people at Greyhound, but—and I don't want to scare you—but it's not good, when someone who's just attempted suicide disappears. He didn't say anything to you, did he?"

"Nothing."

"Shit," Toby said, hitting the *t* hard. I remembered what he'd made me promise in the car that dark morning in front of the aquarium: that if I ever needed his help, I'd tell him. This was the moment he'd meant.

"Sam's always disappeared. Remember Spain? He's a good hider. He was always the last to be found in sardines. I think he's probably okay. He just doesn't want to be found."

I'd said this to make Toby feel better, but he looked at me piercingly. Did he know I was lying?

"Look, I have to get back to the bakery, okay? But just keep your phone on. In case he tries to get in touch with you. If you hear from him . . ."

"I'll tell you," I said.

"Violet," he said, "this is really serious."

Toby didn't know. He was petrified. My parents must've been beside themselves. I nodded, not trusting myself to speak, and watched my uncle go.

There was no way Sam was coming with us to find the ship. I didn't care how badly he wanted an adventure, or how unfair the world was. Sam would be disappointed, but I'd already disappointed him time and time again. What was one more to add to the big, fat pile?

I opened the closet doors and switched on the light. Sam was squashed against the hanging fur coats, and he was smiling. A full, openmouthed smile.

"It's like Narnia! See, Violet, this is already so much fun!"

His teeth caught the light, and his silver braces glittered like jewels. He'd taken three buses. He wanted to work *on a boat*. I could give him the thing he'd only read about.

"Also, I'm starving, can we eat those cupcakes?"

Absurd, really, the things that'll make you change your mind.

Dear Mom and Dad and Toby,

We're safe. Please don't be mad.

Sam's not in New York, but we're together. We're going up north and we'll be back by tomorrow afternoon. I promise we'll call soon. Sam agrees that we can be grounded for life when we get back. It's just that right now . . .

Right now, we have to go find something. We're not sure if we'll find it—it'll be hard, maybe too hard—but we think that if the two of us look together, with two sets of eyes and two good brains and two adventurers' hearts—we think that maybe, maybe, we might be able to track that something down.

We love all three of you a lot. We're sorry to scare you.

Love,
Sam & Violet

PS—Mom, go easy on Toby. This isn't his fault.
PPS—Toby, go easy on yourself. This isn't your fault.
PPPS—Did you know that the ocean is full of faults?
PPPPS—That was a geology pun.
PPPPPS—I'm sure we'll all laugh about this someday . . . she says, fingers crossed.

"You've overthinking this," Sam said. He snatched my pen and scribbled over the stack of PSs, then placed the note on top of the puzzle, where Toby would be sure to see it. "Aren't you supposed to be good at sneaking out?"

"I haven't slept. I'm off my game."

"You should always sleep. Do you know what not sleeping does to your brain?" Sam took a huge bite of my cupcake, sprinkling crumbs all over the puzzle and my work. I wondered if there was such a thing as being *too* okay.

He reached for the latest printout of the script for *Cousteau!* "What's the 'The Calypso Tango'?"

"God, don't *read that*." My voice was sharp.

"Sorry," Sam said, hands up like a criminal, crossword floating back to the table.

"Sorry. You can read it."

"I won't read it." He picked up a piece of the puzzle—the sky—and clicked it in place on the first try. "You were such a good Dorothy," he said, looking at the puzzle.

"I was *twelve*. No one can be good. Except for Yael Dwyer,

who remains to this day the best scarecrow I've ever seen."

"You were the one on Broadway, though," he said, clicking another piece. "Remember when you took me backstage . . ."

"What? No, I didn't."

"Not on Broadway. At school. You took me backstage and we watched the Wicked Witch of the West take off her makeup, and she had an extra set of fake nails, so you put one hand on me, and I put the other on you. That's what I remember best. Those black nails. I had to turn the pages of books with my palms," Sam said. "You know I still have your ruby slippers?"

"You do not." I needed coffee.

"In my closet. Mom taught me how to walk in them. They don't fit anymore, but, I don't know, they're pretty, and they make me think of you." He pointed at the pocket watch, currently serving as a paperweight. I'd taken it off with Liv, and dropped it on the table when she left. "Can I look at that?"

"Yeah. See if you can get that knot undone. I'm gonna make some coffee."

Sam's face brightened. Good. Once a caffeine fiend, always a caffeine fiend.

I set up the Mr. Coffee in the kitchen. My stomach felt like gears grinding. The Wreck. We were going. Sam was here. He was better? He looked better. And we were going. I'd had sex with Liv. Liv. Wreck. Liv. Sam. Sex.

"Why didn't you sleep?" Sam asked, beside me suddenly.

"Um." I assumed he'd heard things at school, but we'd never really spoken about my love life. For the first time, I really wanted to tell him.

"I was with a girl," I said finally.

"Is she hot?"

"Sam!"

"Is she?"

"I can't believe you just said that!"

"Why? It's a good question." Sam reached into his pocket and pulled out a pack of Doublemint gum. He stretched it toward me, smiling shyly. "You'll need this, if you're dating a babe."

I stared at his outstretched hand. "Aren't you not supposed to chew gum with braces?"

"You don't have a monopoly on being a rebel, Violet."

The coffeemaker gurgled in agreement. I took a piece of gum and slipped it into my back pocket. "For later," I said. "You can't say anything to Liv. She's like . . . She's in the middle of things. Her family situation is complicated. Her parents are . . . *nice* . . . but . . ."

"Mom and Dad are really the best, you know?"

I knew.

"I think this is the first time you've ever told me a real secret," Sam said.

"We'll have to build a monument to celebrate," I said, thinking of the pebbles from Fidelia's letter. First secrets. A melted stick of gum. Sam's teeth. Enough and we'd build a secret beach that was just ours, one not even the shipwreck gene would destroy.

Sam sat on the floor, leaning against the island counter and gripping his ankles. "So there's Liv. And Orion, you mentioned him in your letter."

"And Mariah and Felix."

"That's a lot of friends.

"Four." I wasn't sure if I was agreeing or disagreeing.

Sam peeled away some loose rubber from his sneaker. "At the Center, there was this group of three girls that'd sneak into town and smoke. The Threebies, they called themselves. They hoarded all the embroidery thread from the rec room so they were the only ones who could make bracelets, and I know that doesn't sound like a big deal, but trust me, it was, like, a violation of community, or whatever."

I stared at the coffeemaker. I didn't like where this was going.

"I told our house coordinator during one of my personal check-ins that I felt a little left out," Sam said. "Just mentioned it. No big deal. Next thing I knew, she'd called this house meeting about cliques. She kept pronouncing it *cleeks*, like she was so smart and French. *Cleeks* are detrimental to our healing, *cleeks* aren't part of our community."

"Those girls sound like bitches, Sam."

"Don't say bitches, it's such a mean word," Sam said. His voice had gotten higher, familiar. I wished he'd go back to being a stranger. "So one of the Threebies, the captain or whatever, raises her hand, and she's got bracelets from her wrist halfway down to her elbow, and she says she doesn't see *cleeks* but friends, and *friends* are important to the healing process, and then she looks *right at me*. And everyone else just goes, 'Yeah, we're friends,' and the house coordinator keeps saying, '*Some people don't agree,*' and of course everyone knew right away that *I* was the problem."

I left the coffee and curled up next to Sam. The pebbles were gathering in our pockets, heavy, real.

"They hated me after that. The Threebies." He volleyed the watch from hand to hand.

"You're not hateable, Sam."

"Yeah, Mom and Dad always say that, but you don't understand, the way . . ." He tucked his chin and spoke into his knees. "They reminded me a little bit of you, actually."

The seams of my pockets strained and burst, no warning at all. The pebbles flew everywhere. One went under the stove, gone for good. "What does that mean?" I said.

"Nothing. I don't know. I'm sorry."

"You mean I'm a bitch."

"No, *don't say that word*—one of them was nice, sometimes, if you got her alone. . . ."

"Sam, I *want* you here. Didn't you hear how scared Toby was? Mom and Dad are *freaking out* right now. I agreed not to call them, I'm doing everything you ask. . . ."

Sam shrank, hugging his knees tighter, a hermit crab trying to scuttle back into his shell. "You're mad. Please don't be mad at me, Violet, I hate when you're mad."

"*You're* the one who's mad at *me*."

"I shouldn't have come." His knuckles were turning white, still clenched around the watch.

"Sam, no. That's not what I meant. Don't freak out—"

He pulled his hood over his head.

"I'm sorry I said that, Violet, really. I'm so sorry—"

"Sam, take it easy."

"I shouldn't have come, I shouldn't have come." His voice was muffled and wrenched. "I'm sorry. I'm sorry. I'm so sorry."

"Sam . . ." I put my hand on his hunched shoulders and spread them as wide as I could, an Orion-size wingspan. Sam had been up all night. I had, too.

"*Shhh,*" I said, my voice a mixture of Mom, Dad's, Toby's. "Please," I said, to whom or what, I wasn't sure.

"Please, Vi, I didn't mean it. Just leave me alone."

"I'm scared to leave you alone right now," I said, the words falling from me. I didn't know where they'd come from.

"I won't move," Sam said. "I swear. Please. I promise. I'm different."

"Ten minutes," I said.

I pressed my fingers into his back before I took my hand away, like a tree frog powering from one branch to the next, leaving behind slime and fairy dust and coffee grounds, a magic mixture that'd make him feel okay, now and for always.

Fresh air felt good. Quiet was nice. Maybe I liked quiet even more than Sam did.

Six minutes into my ten-minute time-out, Liv's car came into view, and I didn't care if I had to live in Times Square for the rest of my life. I'd opened the passenger door and slid inside before she'd even turned the engine off.

"I don't think I've ever seen you move that fast," she said.

"Hi," I said, peeling her hand from the steering wheel and lacing her fingers through mine. "This happened, right? I mean, it's happening. You and me."

"It's happening," she said, giving my hand a squeeze. "I know, because that was the longest five hours of my life."

I leaned toward her and pulled her to me at the same time. The gearshift got me right in the stomach just as when her lips met mine, smoke and coffee-y and minty-toothpaste descant, my body went liquid, melting, the two of us butter-mouthed and soft and real. During the Year of Wild, kissing anyone twice was rare, and kissing anyone sober—that list was so small, I could count them on one hand. Twice *and* sober? Yeah, right. I'd known a lot of lips, but I hadn't ever known *one set* intimately: the meat of a lower and the daintiness of an upper, the shape of the space formed when the two separated.

"You taste like sugar," she said.

"I made cupcakes."

"A regular Betty Crocker," she said, and I nipped her lower lip.

"I want to memorize your face. Your mouth, specifically."

"I'll give you an inventory. A map of my mouth. The left corner droops. And I have a recurrent zit on the edge, right here, that's been with me now for over a year, so I hope you get used to it."

She kissed me again, pecking, fast. That was fun, too, these little giggly ones, especially when they got serious, when our mouths met and I'd give anything to keep kissing her—anything—go away, Sam, go away, let this be the only thing in the world, this *Liv*, this feeling of having found yourself in another person—

I stopped kissing her.

This wasn't real. Real was my brother, quaking in the kitchen. Real wasn't just kissing. Real was hard, and it took work.

"What is it?" Liv was breathless. A jolt in my stomach: I'd made her breathless.

"My brother's here," I said.

She pointed at the floor. "*Here* here?"

"He's coming with us to Aguecheek. My parents wanted it to be a surprise." I didn't like lying to her, but the alternative seemed altogether too complicated.

"Good thing Orion has a minivan," she said, and then she touched the thin skin beneath my eyes—surely puffed and purple. "You okay? Is it good to see him?"

"Yes. No. We're already fighting. He seems good—but it's worse, because he's different, and I'm different, and we both know we shouldn't say these horrible things to each other, but we still do."

With her other hand, Liv scratched at her clavicle. I'd never seen her do that before. She'd left red streaks behind on her own body that I wanted to smooth away with my thumb. I wanted to learn everything about her.

"I want you to meet him," I said.

"I want to meet him, too," she said.

"He's really shy." In fact, he's probably still hermit-crabbed on the ground.

"I know he's been through a lot," Liv said.

"He may not even say anything to you. Just don't take it personally, okay?"

"I won't," she assured me. I wanted to believe her.

"I'm worried I'll never say the right thing to him."

"Maybe there is no right thing. Maybe there are just *things*, plural, and you have to try them all."

❦

Sam wasn't in the kitchen. The world exploded. Then Liv took my hand.

Three buses. Deep breaths. Easy.

"Sam?" I called carefully.

"In here," he called from the dining room, and everything Mary Poppins–ed back into place. "I fixed it!"

"Fixed what?" I called back.

"Should we go see?" Liv asked, and a horrible thought struck me: what if Sam and Liv didn't like each other? Or worse: what if Liv took one look at me with Sam—real me, bad sister me, New

York me, ungrateful me—and decided she didn't want any part of this minefield she'd stumbled upon?

"Violet?" Sam called.

We walked into the dining room. Sam wasn't a hermit crab anymore. He was at the dining room table, hunched over, and he snapped up when he saw us. He had Fidelia's watch in one hand, and the earring in the other. Separate from each other. Untangled.

"*You did it,*" I breathed. Sam's eyes were bloodshot, his bunny nose was tinged pink, but he was up. Talking. He'd de-lumped, and he'd unsnarled the knot.

Sam's eyes darted behind me. "Are you Liv?" he asked.

"Yes. Hi. Sam." She stuck out her hand to my brother. Sam'd never liked handshakes—*awful to be expected to touch strangers*, he said, *and germy*—but cautiously, he took hers, and shook.

"You, my friend, have got a great handshake," Liv said.

"No dead fish," Sam said, and Liv laughed.

"Sam," I said, "how did you undo that knot? You don't understand, I've been trying to untangle those all summer."

"You're exaggerating," Sam mumbled. His voice was more muted around Liv, but he was still *talking*. "You don't have the patience for that."

"She's so impatient!" Liv agreed.

"She can barely finish a book," he said.

"You should have *seen* how quickly she wanted to quit on the *Lyric*! She never would have done it without us." Liv let the earring clatter to the table and held the watch up between them. "If I believed in omens, I'd consider this a good one. Felix claims the watch has got a weird energy and Violet claims it's lucky, but I'm just pretty sure it's yours now. You should wear it. It's got an *S* on it, after all."

She held the chain open and Sam ducked his head through the loop, as though he were being knighted. The watch thumped against his chest, and Sam—I couldn't believe this—*posed and batted his eyelashes*.

How was this all going so—what was the word—*well*?

"Resplendent," she said. "Ready to go? The Apogee awaits."

He nodded and tucked the watch under the shirt. "Who's S?"

"You're asking all the right questions. C'mon. I'll give you the lecture." She linked arms with him and walked him out the door, babbling away, as though talking with him were the easiest thing in the world.

We found Orion balanced on the Apogee's bumper, red-faced and trying to get the rowboat lashed more securely to the roof, directing Felix and Mariah, who seemed more interested in sword fighting with bungee cords. Sam and Liv had spent the drive over gabbing about wreck hunting and I'd sat in the backseat, stunned. It was the most I'd heard my brother talk to anyone in months. Between that and seeing his teeth, it'd already been a banner day.

"Wow," said Liv, looking at her friends and the boat, "we're really going, I guess."

It had hit me, too, with the weight of a prophecy. Sam was here. Liv was here. The stars had aligned, and the *Lyric* was ours.

Liv bounded from the car and Mariah and Felix shrieked.

"I thought you weren't coming!" said Mariah, squeezing her into a hug.

"They all look so old," said Sam.

"Orion's going to be a senior, and everyone else is my age."

"So I'm the youngest," he said.

"You don't *look* the youngest," I said, feeling impatient. Now that we were here, I wanted to *go*. We were going to find the wreck—didn't Sam see that? If he came, we'd find it, and Liv would get into Oxford, and maybe Orion could save the aquarium . . . and we'd be fixed. Sam and I would be fixed.

"They won't hurt you," I said.

"Maybe I shouldn't go," he said. I needed Liv back; she was like the Sam whisperer. Maybe I needed a mantra. Mantras were a thing that calm, centered people used, right? *I will be as kind as Liv, I will be as kind as Liv, I will be as kind as Liv. . . .*

"Look. If it's overwhelming, you should just ask Liv to tell you more about Lyric history. And everyone will groan and she'll give you a private tutorial, okay? Say it now."

"Like, practice?"

"So you learn the lines."

"I'm depressed, not *five*."

Whoever came up with mantras was clearly an only child.

"Please come," I said. "I want you to come."

Somehow, that pushed him over the edge. He got out of the car: phase one complete. I never thought standing in a driveway would feel like such a victory.

"Everyone, this is Sam, Violet's brother!" Liv said. "Sam's the whole reason we're wreck hunting! Sam, that's Orion, and this is Mariah and Felix."

Sam had time to murmur a barely audible *hi* before the conversation came like a crush:

"More Fidelia spawn!" cried Felix gleefully.

"Field day for Liv," said Mariah.

"You have no idea," Liv said.

"Oooh, can I read your tarot?" cried Felix, and Mariah wrestled him into a bungee-cord restraint. I thought of my first night with them: how close they'd seemed, how afraid I'd been that they'd never let me in.

"They're nice, I promise," I whispered to him.

"Could someone help me with this boat, please?" Orion called, straining to fix the rowboat in place. I rushed to the other side of the van and tied a knot as best I could, centering and securing the boat atop the Apogee. We hopped down and Orion said, "What's this I hear about you having a brother?"

Had I really not told Orion about Sam?

"Hi, Sam," Orion said, and Sam blanched. No one was safe from the Eyebrow God's beauty.

"You guys look so much alike," Mariah said to me.

"Fraternal, yet same-egged," Felix agreed.

God bless them: when we were little, Sam loved telling people we were twins.

"People actually used to confuse us. Right, Sam?" He hadn't said anything yet, and I just wanted him to start talking, to supply the details: our identical bowl cuts, matching backpacks, coordinated outfits.

But Sam wasn't interested in telling the story. He wasn't even looking at me. "Liv," he said, his voice small, "can you tell me more about Lyric history?"

As predicted, Felix and Mariah groaned. Liv grinned, and slid open the Apogee's back door. "Step into Professor Stone's office."

I opened the Apogee's front door, ready to shove aside the familiar pile of trash, but there wasn't any. The trash was gone. The seat and the floor were vacuum-streaked. The car smelled fresh and lemony.

"Speaking of surprises," Orion said.

"I cleaned all last night, too," I said.

"Great minds," Orion said.

You have no idea what's going on with me and Liv, I thought.

"Let's go!" screamed Mariah from the back. "Before someone we know sees me getting into a strange boy's van and tells my parents!"

"Ready?" Orion asked.

Sam was talking to Liv. He was fine. The only thing holding us back was me.

"Ready," I said.

The last familiar sight I saw was Frieda, four miles outside town, with her head held high, jogging back toward Lyric. Then she was a spot in the distance, and then she was gone, and then we were *going*.

"We're going!" I drummed the dash, swiveled in my seat, and screamed to the back, *"We're going!"*

"Don't distract the driver!" Orion yelled through the applause and cheers.

"What if we *actually find the ship?*" I said, still fighting the seat belt to face backward.

"Wait, we're actually looking for the ship? I thought this was just an excuse to drink," said Mariah.

"Of course we're looking for the ship!" said Liv. "We have Orion's boat! Wet suits! Fins!"

"Someone one hundred percent peed in that wet suit," said Felix.

All good? I mouthed to Sam, and Sam rolled his eyes like I was Mom.

"The way I see it, if we don't find the ship, no loss," said Liv, "and if we do find it . . ."

"Oxford, here you come," Orion said.

"Oxford!" Felix yelled. "Try Hollywood! Dream big, Liv!"

"I'm game for Hollywood, but are witches supposed to be so fame-hungry?" said Mariah.

"We *do* live in a capitalist society," said Sam.

Felix burst into applause. "YES! Even witches need to get paid!"

"What'd you tell your parents you were doing?" Liv asked Mariah.

"Staying with you," Mariah said. "You?"

"Camping with Orion."

"Classic. Ann hand you condoms on the way out?"

In the rearview, Liv blushed furiously. I stared out the windshield, hot with the memory of her body on mine. Keep your eyes on the pines, eyes on the pines, don't think of her mouth, her hands, where they touched you—

"C'mon, Mariah," Orion said. "That's not cool."

"Yeah, sorry, I know you're more like her dad," said Mariah.

"He's *super* dad-like!" Felix poked Sam on the shoulder. "Just wait'll you hear his jokes."

"They can't be worse than Violet's," said Sam.

"Sick brother burn!" crowed Felix.

"I'll allow it," I said. In the rearview, Liv's blush was fading. Good.

"I'm not a *dad*," Orion muttered. "Violet, you like this song?"

He'd turned on the radio—his secret mix, I realized. The song was bubblegum punk, lady voices singing about cheap whiskey and sour candy. *Picking flowers on LSD. This song's good and it sets me free.* In the rearview, Liv and I caught eyes, and I let myself remember last night, let my memories linger with hers.

"It's good," I said. "It's really good."

✐

An hour south of Aguecheek Bay, we stopped for provisions at a ramshackle gas station that advertised seventy-five-cent coffee and fresh bait and tackle. Thick, wet fog had rolled in, and when we hopped from the car, I shivered in Toby's windbreaker. We'd been jabbering in the car, hopped up on sugar and music and each other, and the feeling of fresh air and mist made me realize how *tired* I was. I'd gotten *no* sleep.

"You know they call this the Ghost Coast," Felix said.

"Yes, Felix, we all grew up here," said Liv.

"We didn't," said Sam.

"I have to pee *so badly,*" Mariah said, pushing Felix out of the way.

"We should get some real food besides cupcakes," I said.

"More coffee," said Sam.

"Coffee, yes," said Felix.

I followed them toward the shop, and my phone buzzed a million times, all texts coming in, thanks to a rare patch of cell reception. I thought what I always thought when I got a lot of texts at once, that there'd been a shooting or a terrorist attack or someone I loved had died in a plane crash. It was a string of increasingly panicked texts from my parents and Toby. *Call us now. Violet, where are you? Violet, answer us. Violet. We're getting on a plane.*

I texted: *We're safe.* Then I switched my phone off for the first time since June.

"Secret admirer, in addition to secret brother?" Orion asked.

"Just my parents," I said, feeling a little woozy, taking a seat on the Apogee's bumper. I needed a turkey sandwich. Protein.

"Hmm," Orion said. "Everything okay?"

"Fine." My parents would never forgive me, likely. But I was giving Sam an adventure.

"I hope your brother's having an okay time," Orion said, sitting beside me. "Hey, Violet? Why did I not know you had a brother?"

"What do you mean?" I said.

"I just feel confused," Orion said. "Like I told you all about Liv . . . and Will . . . and Louise and whale songs . . . and *love* . . . I mean, Jesus, Violet, you know practically everything about me. Do you think I have those conversations with *everyone* I meet? I mean—you're special, obviously."

I looked quickly at the ground. I wasn't special. I was lying to him. There was an oil splash on the pavement by my feet: iridescent, amorphous. If I touched it with my toe, maybe I'd mutate, hideous, repellent. He'd see what I really was.

"Look, I'm not trying to pressure you into sharing your deepest, darkest secrets. Sometimes I just feel like . . . you keep me on the outside on purpose. You obviously have all this stuff going on . . . like, your panic attack, and freaking out that day at the aquarium . . . You can tell me. Didn't you think we were getting close? Or was that just me?"

"Not just you," I said dumbly. Maybe I didn't want to kiss Orion anymore, but he was right: we had gotten close. Or he'd gotten close to me. I'd gotten close to Liv.

"Violet, I really didn't have plans to say this to you now, here. . . ."

That tone of voice: it was the death knell.

"But sometimes I think you should just say these things when you feel them. . . ."

Stop. No.

"I really like you."

My heart fell from my body and hit the pavement hard. The muscle, beating outside my body, meaty and gross, more beautiful than the oil spill. Electrical. Liv's.

"I freaked you out in the nivation hollow, I know. I freaked myself out. But this is different. And I know this is a lot, and not the right time, it smells like gasoline and we're about to get back in the van, but I had to say something before I exploded."

"I know the feeling," I said, because I did.

"You do," he said, altogether too-relieved, and what could I do, *correct him*? He was my musical soul mate. I didn't want to hurt him.

Liv and Sam emerged from the store wearing new hats, practically skipping with good fortune. Hers was a teal beanie embroidered with a pink moose and topped with a pink pom-pom, and his was a foam trucker hat that said THE PINE TREE STATE. The neediest, most scrabbling part of me hoped they'd gotten one for me.

"I know you don't want to be with anyone right now," Orion said, "so I really don't expect anything, really, but . . . do you think you and I could ever . . . ?"

They posed by the bait-and-tackle sign with their new hats, and Sam snapped picture after picture. How hard was it to say no to Orion? *I want to be your friend, nothing more.* Why did people have to get hurt? Why did I have to hurt him?

"I'm not sure I can think about this right now," I said.

He nodded, falsely stoic. I'd softened my answer, but I still hadn't said what he wanted to hear. I watched Sam and Liv horse around and I just wanted everyone to have a silly new hat and a fucking happy ending, Orion included.

"But maybe when I'm a gnarled old hag," I said.

"I'll carve you a cane," he said back, so warmly that I knew instantly I'd made a mistake.

I couldn't blame him and I couldn't blame the shipwreck gene either. This looming disaster was all mine.

❧

Our campground was deserted, at the end of a ribboned, unmarked gravel road and on the edge of the pine-dense, definitely haunted forest. The ocean lay just through the woods, but the fog was so thick we could barely see two feet in front of us. Birds sounded through the trees, and I imagined them fanged, the size of koalas. I felt the way I'd felt at my first six sleepovers, when I'd cried so hard that my parents had to come pick me up in the middle of the night. I wanted the aquarium and Toby and my own bed. I wished we were doing the puzzle with Liv and Sam. Why did adventures have to happen away from home? Couldn't the puzzle be an adventure, too?

"It's so peaceful here with the fog," said Sam.

"You're a forest bather, aren't you?" said Felix. "Oooooh, we should go skinny-dipping later."

I stole a glance at Liv, but she was looking at the trees.

"God, it's bizarre being back here," said Liv. Of course: she was thinking of her brother. What was wrong with me, that I didn't know that?

"I think Will'd be happy we came back, don't you? You're, like, conquering his fears for him," said Orion, and I was amazed how he could do that, just let him into the woods with us.

A cave cleared in the fog, revealing a pair of middle-aged white folks, already set up with tents and a Coleman stove and two kayaks leaning against trees. The woman waved brusquely, but the man just glared. They were clearly not happy about the company of six teenagers.

"Should we tell them we're mellow?" Felix whispered.

"Mellow but rowdy," Mariah said, waving a bottle of rum in our direction. "Yo, ho, ho."

"Yolo, ho," Felix said, and Mariah kicked him in the calf.

I turned my phone on, just to see. No service. It was just a weekend. We'd be back tomorrow. These were my friends. I missed my parents. I felt so *homesick*. I understood Sam's impulse to run, to just get away.

Liv pointed toward an opening in the trees past the kayakers' camp.

"You can't see it now, but there's a path. Take it to the right, and you'll follow a trail that'll take you to the good lookout spot. You'll finally be able to see that Revolutionary War ship, Violet."

I tried to cling to this perk: a pebble, I thought, this Halley's Comet ship, this hike with Liv and Sam.

"You're going to come with us, right?" Sam asked Liv.

She shook her head. "I've seen them. And you've seen me hike, Violet, I'm a nightmare."

She didn't want to come. Had she changed her mind about me? She said it'd been real, but maybe she was lying. I lied all the time. . . . Maybe she'd seen I was a liar, and saw now that I was near tears for no reason, she saw what a baby I was, that I was ugly, a bad kisser, too much too fast—

"Lemme pee first," Sam said.

"Don't wander off," I called as he trekked off into the woods, and he flipped me the bird.

"You two are so *cute*," Mariah said, going to help Orion and Felix with the tents.

The fog thickened again, so densely that I was alone with Liv. *She doesn't like you. You're a bad sister. A bad friend.* The voices of the Ghost Coast were so mean.

"You're really not coming?" I said.

"You two should go. He came here to see you."

"I know . . . but . . ."

"Violet? You're so sad. What's going on? Don't you think it'd be good for the two of you to have some together time?"

She furrowed her brow. She smelled like smoke, even though I hadn't seen her light up all day.

"I do," I said. "But . . ."

"But?"

"But this morning was a nightmare before you got there. Plus . . ."

"Plus what?"

"He likes you more," I said, barely able to say it.

"*Violet,*" Liv said. "He came here to see you."

"I know . . . but . . . you have matching hats."

She took the hat from her head and fixed it on mine, one hand lingering on my cheek, the other tugging on the zip of Toby's windbreaker. A charm of hummingbirds beat their wings against my throat.

"Violet. It's just a hat. It's easy for me because I'm new, so I don't know him the way you do. But you're his sister. We're all

322

on the same team. This isn't a competition," she said. "Love isn't *finite*."

I nodded. The hat was cozy and smelled like her hair, and muffled the voices of the ghosts.

"Just go with him," she said. "Trust me, he wants you right now. It's a short walk, and I'll be here when you get back, promise."

In the fog, she kissed me once, very quickly, and it felt like courage.

In the forest, the air was wet and the trees were giants. The higher Sam and I climbed, the more the path became a cliff walk: the land on our left fell completely away, a sheer drop to the ocean. The path was steep, but it'd be worth it, I knew, to see the Revolutionary War ship, the ship that came and went like an eclipse.

"Are you and Liv in love?" Sam asked suddenly. "Sorry. Is that too personal?"

I gulped pine air. Here, among the trees, it was easier not to bristle. "It's *different* with Liv. We talk, for starters."

"I like her."

"Thanks."

We were quiet again. Sam's breathing was labored. Had he eaten anything today besides sugar and coffee? I should have been keeping better track.

"I read your musical," Sam said, slightly winded. "*Cousteau!*"

"I told you not to!"

"Um, no, you said I could, remember? Anyway, you were never going to *show* me. You're so private."

"I'm not private."

"Yes, you are, Violet. You don't say half the stuff you're thinking. You're so introverted. You've got all these secrets."

"I'm not introverted. Mom says I take up space."

"That doesn't mean anything. Think about how tired and weird and sad you are right now after being trapped in a car with your loud friends. We're more alike than you think, you know."

Had Sam always been this perceptive, or was I just that obvious?

"You should keep working on *Cousteau!* It was funny," he said.

"You should help me. You've actually finished *Diving for Sunken Treasure.*"

"You didn't finish it?"

"When have I ever finished anything?"

"I don't understand how you passed ninth-grade English," he said.

"Do they find any treasure?"

"Not really. Mostly junk." Classic.

The trees thinned, and the trail opened up to a lookout over the bay. At the edge of the clearing, there was a bench made of great stone slabs, and Sam and I stood there to look out over the water. The fog was clearing, revealing a stretch of islands that peppered the bay, each with its own set of cliffs and craggy coastline.

Across bands and bands of blue water, way off in the distance, rose the white limestone cliffs of Fabian's Bluff.

My heart sank. This bay was *enormous*. There were so many islands, so many hiding spots. There was no way we'd find the *Lyric* in all this ocean.

"Are those the wrecks Liv was talking about?" Sam said, pointing down the beach to an old tugboat, a dirty red-rusted thing sprayed with pink graffiti. Even *this* beach had so many hiding spots—the coastline curled and dipped, disappeared into pockets of rocks, and unfurled, creating a series of hidden coves and inlets.

"Revolutionary War era, remember?"

"Not the tugboat. In *front*."

"Next to the driftwood?"

"No—I'm saying the boat *is* the driftwood."

I pulled out the opera specs from my pocket, the ones I'd found that night at Seal Cove. The picture was cloudy, the glass badly scratched. It didn't look like a ship. It looked like a set of stumps, rising from the sand like a huge set of rotting, gaping teeth. Time had worn the vessel down to its nubbins.

I'm not sure what I'd been imagining. Maybe in the back of my brain I thought the ships would move: like after all this time, they'd plow through the sand, like great ghost ships.

I felt so silly.

Of course these wrecks weren't magic. Of course the *Lyric* wouldn't be, either.

Finding the *Lyric* wouldn't fix Sam and me. We were going to take more than that. I'd known it all along, hadn't I? I was just afraid to really *know* what that meant. Afraid to know, because knowing meant work.

"Kind of a letdown," I said.

"Really? I think they're cool," Sam said, taking the binoculars from me.

"On the way back into town, we can ask Orion to stop up close," I said.

At the mention of town, Sam hopped from the bench. Long grasses grew on the edge of the outcropping and he picked a few, then began to braid the sticky threads together. The wind blew and ruffled his hair. His skin was pink from the hike. My parents told us they loved us all the time, but I didn't know if Sam and I had ever said it to each other. *I love you, Sam.* Why did that feel so hard?

"Wrist, please," Sam said. He tied the grass braid in a gentle, loose knot around my wrist. A tiny beetle crawled along one of the fronds, then toward the crook of my elbow.

"Make one for yourself, too," I said.

When he finished the second one, I helped tie the bracelet around his wrist. His veins were exceptionally blue under his skin. I shivered, thinking about how thin his skin was there.

"Perfect," I said.

"No, it's not," Sam said, twirling his bracelet. "I know we're both pretending it's fine. *I'm* fine. But everything's a mess. Everything will only ever be a mess."

"It'll be okay, Sam."

"No. No, it *won't*. Stop saying that. You don't understand, Violet. You're *good* at things. You're funny and tall. You make friends wherever you go! I couldn't even make friends with the other lunatics."

"You're *not* a lunatic."

"You just pull it off. *Living.* Two months here and you have a girlfriend."

"Dating doesn't matter."

"Dating *does* matter! It's insulting to say it doesn't. Normal people date. Normal people go to high school. Normal people grow up. Can you even imagine me as an adult? What would I even be like?"

"No one knows what they'll be like."

"It's different." He shook his head. "All I see in my future is being this way. Forever."

My heart went weak and heavy. For the first time, I felt the weight of my brother's sadness in my own chest. He was a jellyfish being asked to float on land. Maybe life, for him, would always be hard. Maybe I couldn't argue.

"Sometimes I wish Fidelia hadn't made it," he said. "Maybe if she'd drowned, everyone would have been saved a lot of trouble."

"*Sam.*" I wouldn't say the right thing. I couldn't *ever* say the right thing, because the right thing didn't exist. All that mattered was that I said *something*. That I kept trying.

"I used to think shipwrecks were a recessive gene. Like Mom and Dad were always talking about *making it* and *perseverance*."

"We're descended from *survivors*," Sam said, pitching his voice in a perfect imitation of Dad's. For a second, he was him, minus the glasses. We were all so painfully, beautifully related.

"Thanks, Finance," I said. "I never saw it that way, though. I thought we'd inherited disaster. That we were cursed."

"And this summer showed you that we *weren't*?"

"No, I think maybe we *are* cursed! Seriously. But, like, maybe a curse doesn't always have to be *bad*? Maybe it's, like, a promise in disguise. Because that other stuff—luck, perseverance—that's in there, too."

Neither of us spoke. Maybe that was okay. Maybe listening was a way of trying.

"Everyone has thirty-two great-great-great-grandparents," said Sam at last.

"What?"

"It's exponential growth. Four grandparents, eight great-grandparents, sixteen, thirty-two. Fidelia's just one of thirty-two great-great-greats."

I tried to branch out the tree in my head, splitting and splitting from both our parents. Who knows what our great-great-great-grandparents on Dad's side were like? We were made up of so many people.

"That's insane," I said eventually.

"It is," Sam agreed.

There was quiet again. I tried to listen for the voices of the Ghost Coast, but I heard nothing. Just me and Sam breathing, and the sounds of waves. Fidelia had heard these same sounds. She'd pulled herself from this very ocean on this very beach and then walked, in the cold, all the way to Lyric.

"Sometimes," I said, "I think what's amazing is not that Fidelia survived, but that she *chose* to tell people."

Sam said nothing.

"I think she was intending on keeping it a secret. But then— she changed her mind. Who knows what it was, or why, but she chose. She didn't want to be a normal person. She wanted to be a person who survived a shipwreck. She *chose*: that was the story she wanted. You're a person who can *choose*."

"I don't just get to pick to feel better," Sam said.

"Of course not. We're all sorts of DNA and bad genetics and scrambled shit in there, too. But I'm saying our choices matter. Choosing to try . . . that's not a small thing." I grabbed him by the shoulder, strange and strained, but necessary.

"Sam, the world is a big place. There's space for you in it."

He gave a tiny, almost imperceptible nod. He'd been crying. We both had.

"I'm glad you survived. Now you just have to *keep surviving*."

It was the first time I'd said *survival* aloud. Sam had survived. He'd *survived*, and I'd survived, too. Now we would survive together.

The fog had rolled back in, obscuring the bay with clouds.

"You think we'll find the *Lyric*?" I asked.

Sam pursed his lips. "Well. Our equipment seems a bit out-of-date."

I couldn't help laughing. He'd answered me seriously, but the whole idea was so incredibly absurd: that our floodlight and pocket watch and snorkels would successfully guide us beneath the ocean to a wreck that'd been hidden for more than a century. So I laughed, and then he did, too: a beautiful, looping cursive of a laugh. I loved that noise. So much time had passed since I'd heard it. We laughed until we were punchy and our stomachs hurt. A moment passed where we were just breathing, inhaling and exhaling together, hiccuping, wiping our eyes with the backs of our hands.

"You asked earlier about Cousteau," Sam said finally. "What they find."

"Go on."

"He's not even interested in the treasure. The whole point is the adventure. At least, for his crew, that's the point. The last true poets of the sea, he calls them. People for whom *discovery*—like, the concept of the journey—is the treasure itself."

"The quest," I said.

"If you want to be dramatic about it."

"I usually do."

Singing wouldn't fix Sam. Neither would finding the *Lyric*, nor would my saying the right thing. No one thing could fix us, because no one thing was wrong. The fixing would be in keeping going, in trying. Survival was its own quest: we needed to choose to survive over and over again. We had to wash up on shore, and we had to choose to keep washing up every single day. We had to let the survival accrue, pebble after pebble, building a beach from a million tiny moments until suddenly we stopped, looked around, and thought, on a Saturday in Maine, *I'm glad we're here.*

"I'm glad we're here, Sam. And I love you."

"Me too," he said.

Sam taught me to put thick blades of grass between our thumbs and whistle, so that we sputtered until we were dizzy and light-headed. The sun got low in the sky. We strained our eyes looking for sea life against the remaining wisps of fog, convincing ourselves that we'd seen a whale cresting out of the corner of our eyes. Surely, something was down there, if only we looked hard enough. Surely there was life, if we just kept searching.

"Hey," Sam said, "if you squint, doesn't that rock out there look like a whale?"

AFTER ALL THAT...

"No *way*," Orion said.

We'd gathered on the beach, sans Felix and Mariah, who'd volunteered to cook us dinner, and Orion was peering out across the bay through the opera specs. Sam stood over his shoulder, jittery with excitement. A breeze had picked up since we'd hiked down from the lookout.

Sam snatched the binoculars and passed them to me. There it was, far off the beach, rising from the water: a rock shaped like a whale's tail, waves breaking around it, sending spray skyward, then crashing to thick foam. I understood that the whale-shaped rock was one of many boulders in a string, and together, these rocks formed a jagged barrier far off our beach. The rocks were a reverse moat, almost, dividing the calm waters of our bay from open ocean.

"If you were over there by that rock, you'd be able to see the bluffs perfectly," Sam said. "The *blinding wall of white*."

"The currents are certainly moving the right way," Orion said. "Whatever debris from over there would wind up here."

I passed Liv the specs. I could hardly believe what I was about to say.

"I think we may have found it."

Liv sucked in her breath. She looked so good with binoculars. "We may have found it, indeed."

Beside me, Sam hopped with excitement. "Can we go right now?"

"Past those rocks, in *Orion's* boat?" Liv shot him a glance. "No offense. It's great for river rides, but . . ."

"None taken," said Orion. "It's a dinghy. Not meant for the open ocean."

"But it has a motor! And isn't that what we came here for?" Sam said. "To find the *Lyric*? Violet?"

I bit my lip. The waves looked pretty big. The water there must have been deep and treacherous, if it had hidden a ship for nearly a century.

"Orion? Tell me what you think. It's your boat."

He shook his head. "We'd be like an eyelash out there. Especially if this wind picks up."

"But . . . we're still going to go," Sam said, his voice full of disbelief. "That's the whole point. That's why we're here. Violet?"

I looked at the three people standing beside me. A brother, a beloved, and a friend. The whole point wasn't the wreck. The whole point had been getting here, and what we were, now.

"Orion's right."

My brother's face fell. "But . . . *why?*"

"Because first of all, it's too dangerous, and second of all, we don't need a wreck. You know that." Sam didn't need an adventure. He needed dinner. He needed our parents. They needed us.

"But I came all this way." Sam's voice ached with disappointment.

"Remember the quest? Cousteau?"

"You untangled the knot, Sam. You found it," Liv said. "You did what we couldn't."

His face crumpled in that familiar way, and I saw a tantrum unfold—and then he pulled his hands into his sleeves, and said, "This *sucks*."

"Indeed," said Liv.

"It's still an adventure," I said. He was okay. He really was.

"I'm going to help Felix and Mariah with dinner," he mumbled.

"I'll go with you," Orion said.

They shuffled off, leaving Liv and me behind.

"Are you okay?" Liv said, watching them go. "Is he?"

"We talked. It was really, really good. He's not *okay* okay, and I'm not either, but we will be, I think."

My brother and Orion disappeared through the pines.

"Well," Liv said, "what should we do now?"

It was almost dark enough that we were hidden. There was a rise in the dunes. We kissed and my heart turned into a wave and my edges eroded. We kissed and we were salmon flashing upstream.

"There's still all this shit we don't know, like about S, and Fidelia. . . ."

"Violet, shut up."

She was great at kissing my neck.

"It doesn't bug you, though? That no one wants to turn the rock over?"

"No. You're bugging me, right now."

Her hair smelled smoky.

We were lying down.

Our bed was kelp pods.

"We should stop," I said.

"No we shouldn't," she said.

Her weight on top of me, her hands, reaching—

"Liv?"

Mariah's small voice.

Liv and I were apart. Mariah was *right there*, her arms full of kindling.

There was much more sunlight than we said there was, I realized now.

"I'm sorry—I wouldn't have—the kayakers were staring over here. I thought they'd like—seen a moose or—sorry. Should I go? I'm going to—?"

"Don't go," said Liv, and she grabbed my hand to say *Don't go either.*

Mariah didn't move, and I loved her for it.

"Livvy," Mariah said finally, "you know I don't care who you kiss."

"I would have told you, only, this just happened, literally, last night, don't tell anyone, please. . . ."

"Why don't we sit," Mariah said evenly.

We sat, the three of us on the sand, touching knee to knee to knee, like witches, or little girls pretending to be witches. Liv had my hand in a death grip.

"Livvy, what if I'd been Orion? He'd be crushed."

"No, we talked. He and I. He's not interested in me anymore. I swear."

"So why not just tell him?"

"What would I say?"

"That you're . . ."

"I don't know what I am! That's the problem!"

"Okay . . . so just . . . tell him about . . ."

Mariah gestured between the two of us. Liv tipped her head back; a dry reed was tangled in her hair and I pulled it loose.

"I know I should," she said. "And I know that intellectually, I know what I'm about to say is ridiculous. Intellectually, I realize this. I'm a smart person."

"We'll give you a pass on this one, Professor Stone," Mariah said.

"But—what if I tell Orion and he doesn't like me anymore?" Her voice was the smallest it'd ever been.

"Oh, Liv," Mariah breathed.

"What if the possibility that we *might date* is the only reason he's still around? He was a minor meathead! Will was a minor meathead and he didn't care, probably, but it's more like . . ."

"Will knew?"

"I think so," said Liv.

Mariah broke our knee circle then to hug Liv. It was a long hug. I counted 256 grains of sand, and I lost count a few times. Liv pulled away and wiped at her face with the back of her hand and took my hand with the other.

"What did you say to him?" Mariah asked.

"It was so dumb. There was this stupid reality show we liked with this really pretty girl on it and then one day point-blank he was like, *Liv, would you make out with her,* in that way of his and I was just like, yeah, but I was also thirteen! That was all we said, so maybe he didn't really know. . . ."

"Liv. It sounds like he knew and loved you."

Liv's mouth squirmed on her face.

"You know Orion would, too," Mariah said.

I thought about all the times *I* could have told him. Had I wanted him to think I was straight? I'd loved the attention so much, *his* attention. It wasn't that I didn't want him to like me less: it was that I didn't want him to like me differently. I'd wanted to keep his affection the same, unchanging, like summertime jars of blueberry preserves.

"What if you're wrong, though?" said Liv. "Orion—I know it doesn't make any sense, but what . . . what if I lose him, too? What if my *parents* lose him? And don't even get me started on Tom and Ann, when Felix came out they just kept talking about how hard it must be for his parents, and Ann will *hate* me, she has *no* idea . . ."

"Ann would *never* hate you," said Mariah.

Liv shook her head. "And then there's Felix, he had this all figured out when he was ten, and had to go through all that shit, but, like, maybe I'll date a guy next, who cares, but, like, right now I just like Violet but I'm still an absolute morass!"

"Is that like a moron-ass hybrid?" I asked.

"No, it's a mess. A bog. A wetland."

"My mistake. If you're a bog, then be a bog. 'Are you gay?' 'Nah, I'm more like a bog.'"

Liv considered this. "I'd rather be a fen," she said finally. "They're less acidic."

"How 'bout we're all just *people?*" Mariah said. "And I'd like to add, first and foremost, that Felix does *not* have it all figured out. Remember how he thought Allyson Wilson was Mata Hari reincarnated and he used to make me go buy movie tickets from her because he 'couldn't handle her beauty'?"

Liv choke-cry-laughed.

"Second of all, I get that Ann and Tom are, like, delicate. But, like . . ."

"You're their kid," I said, thinking of Frieda, of Fidelia.

"Yeah," Mariah said. "Third of all, and you already know this, but Orion won't care. I think the smoke and mirrors will make him more upset than anything else." Mariah bit her lip. "Also . . . not sure if this makes a difference, but, uh, I'm pretty sure he's into Violet now?"

"Confirmed, unfortunately," I said.

"I'll fight him," Liv said.

"He's a pacifist," said Mariah.

"I was *joking*," said Liv.

"Violet," Mariah said, turning now to me, "I, for one, am *not* interested in you, though I'm in awe of your sex magic. Especially given that you've been wearing that sweatshirt since literally the day you bought it."

"I'll give you sex-magic lessons," I said.

"Not in that sweatshirt, you won't."

"In Toby's windbreaker, then."

"Surely that windbreaker has the reverse effect."

"Liv, is this working?" I asked. "Are you feeling better?"

"Not really," she said.

"Okay. How 'bout this?" said Mariah. "I'm not going anywhere. Neither, apparently, is this weirdo."

"I don't know what to, like, *do* now," Liv said. "I just . . . don't want tonight to be about this. Or this weekend to be about this."

"What would you like it to be about, Liv?"

She shook her head. "I don't know. I just want it to be normal. I know that word is meaningless, and that's what I want. Stupid shit that doesn't mean anything."

I held my hands out to both of them and they stared at the fact of my palms.

"Did you two ever play energy?" I said.

"Oh my God, *yes!*" said Mariah.

"Is that like pulse?" Liv asked.

They both knew how to play slightly different versions of the same game. We figured out our own set of rules and squeezed a pulse around our circle until we saw our friends lugging a rowboat to the water.

∽

That was how the six of us found ourselves pushing Orion's dinghy into the summer-warmed waters of Aguecheek Bay as the sun set. We opted for oars over the motor. We weren't trying to find the shipwreck of my great-great-great-grandmother. We weren't journeying across the sea. We just wanted to swim.

Our motley crew consisted of two childhood friends, two lovers, two musical soul mates, two long-lost siblings, an amateur psychic, and a *really good friend*. The memory of a brother and a best friend, of a great-great-great-grandmother and a great-great-great-grandfather. There were secrets between us, and stories we didn't fully understand. But in the water our wires weren't *tangled*. They were *knit*.

Orion and I stood calf-deep in the shallow water, holding the boat steady for Sam and Liv as they climbed aboard. The water turned orange, then pink, then gold.

"Push on three," Orion said. "One, two . . ."

We pushed. Sam rowed my beloved out to sea in my friend's boat. Felix threw himself beneath the waves and popped up, seal-like, beside the boat. Mariah burst out laughing.

"*Ooh,*" he cried. "Refreshing!"

Mariah, Orion, and I swam after them, Mariah and I still in our clothes, for now, paddling around the boat in a ring, dolphin-like. Beyond the stone whale the waters were churning and dangerous, but here, in this bay, they were safe. I swam underwater alongside the boat for as long as I could hold my breath, amazed at how good the ocean felt. How had I not *swum yet* this summer?

I surfaced. A set of hands hooked under my arms and pulled me over the lip of the boat. Orion cannonballed off the side; Sam followed, Mariah was in the boat, then out. I could hardly tell who was where, it was all happening so fast. The boat tipped and everyone was fine.

I had never had friends before, not like this.

In darkness, we built a fire and warmed our hands. Orion played the harmonica, and Sam and Liv leaned against each other. Felix read Mariah's palm. ("Career line strong, unbroken—and westward," he declared. Mariah bit back a satisfied smile.) Liv smoked five cigarettes, drank no beer, and winked at me once, which was enough. I had some whiskey. My brother ate a s'more, then another, and I wiped the marshmallow–graham-cracker goo from his face.

"To the wreck hunters," Orion said, raising his water bottle. "And whale songs."

"To truthing," said Liv.

"To tea leaves," said Felix.

"To pickup trucks," said Mariah.

We kept toasting: To Fidelia and Ransome. To the rest of the *Lyric* passengers whose bones had been picked clean by fish. To adventures. Our voices overlapped and were indistinguishable: To baseball caps, to Patsy Cline. To whiskey and blow jobs and cunnilingus, birth control, treasure, no treasure, sleeping bags, bug spray, headphones, and crosswords.

"To family," I called.

"Surviving," said Sam.

"Please can you keep it down!" yelled a voice from inside the kayakers' tent.

"To angry, reluctant chaperones," Mariah stage-whispered.

We all collapsed into stifled giggles, then put out the fire and trekked down the beach to stage an impromptu, perfectly imperfect reading of *Cousteau!* by cell-phone light. Sam had brought the latest printout of the script with him.

That night, it didn't matter what had come before and what was going to come after. In that moment, we were the last true poets of the sea, and what mattered more than anything else was our quest.

THEFT

"All right, hooligans."

I woke to a strange, sharp voice, and the darting beam of a flashlight. At the last minute, we'd abandoned the tents and slept outside, and when I opened my eyes, it took me a second to remember where we were. Night was just beginning to lift, the sky above me turning from black to navy. A few stars peeked through the clouds, and the moon's shine was dull, like the dry rind of an orange. *Ghost Coast*, I thought dumbly.

"What the hell did you do with our kayak?"

Orion was stirring, shielding his eyes against the flashlight's strong glare. "What's up, man?"

"Our kayak is gone. Don't make me say it again. We put up with the noise. The shenanigans. The underage drinking, the fire for which—I'm betting—you did not have a permit. We're not interested in whatever prank war you kids are pulling."

We'd slept with our heads in the middle. Mariah lay next to me in a sleep mask embroidered with cerulean eyes; Felix was flopped flat on his stomach like a manatee; Orion; then Liv, beautiful Liv, next to me, still sleeping, her braids fuzzy with flyaways.

Only—where—where—?

"To say nothing of the two of you *necking* on the beach. There wasn't supposed to *be* this Girls Gone Wild stuff up here. There was supposed to be solitude! So tell me again: where's our kayak?"

"Where's Sam?" I said, to no one and to everyone.

The angry man shone his flashlight in my face. "No," he said. "Where's my *kayak*?"

"*Girls Gone Wild?*" Orion repeated, shaking himself loose from his sleeping bag.

"Those two! *Girls Gone Wild!*"

I shook Liv awake. In the moment before she recognized the panic on my face, she looked at me so dreamily, happily, that I wanted to live inside that look forever.

"Sam's gone," I said.

"He's here," she said automatically, immediately awake. "He must be."

"No, Liv," I said. "He's not. He runs away. This is what he does. He did this in Spain, he ran away from Vermont. . . ."

Felix and Mariah were groggily pulling themselves from sleep by now, grouchy and confused. Orion was trying to calm the man down, but he just would not shut up: "Are you going to help me find our kayak or not?"

I knew where Sam was.

"He's looking for the wreck," I said.

Liv scrambled loose from her cocoon and yanked a sweatshirt over her head. "He's not," she said. "I'm sure he's here. . . ."

"He's out there in the ocean in a kayak. Liv—he's not *okay*. I lied to you. My parents don't even know he's here. He's not thinking straight. We've got to go after him."

"I'll go with you," she said, putting her hand in mine. "Orion," she called. "Orion. *Orion*."

Orion turned his gaze toward me and Liv, and she didn't let go of my hand.

"We need to take the boat," Liv said. "Sam's gone. To the ocean."

Orion's gaze flicked between the two of us, down to our gripped hands, back to our faces. His expression went from puzzled to blank, and then, in the flat light of the moon, I watched a wave of understanding wash over him. The hurt on his face made me think of newly unpeeled fruit, raw and tender.

He opened his mouth—and then, simply, he nodded.

"I'll go with you. The boat's still on the beach. Liv, get the floodlight and the life vests from the van. Violet, help me with these oars. We'll bring them just in case. We'll lift on three and then through the woods, okay? One . . ."

The man was shaking his head violently. "You kids can't go out there—it's dark, and dangerous—"

"Two . . ."

"What's going on?" said Mariah, pulling off her sleep mask.

"Three," he said.

Of all the ways I'd imagined Orion learning that Liv and I were together, I'd never predicted this. I'd underestimated him, and I was ashamed.

He was a good person. A good friend. I'd been ungrateful for that friendship, and now there was no time to explain.

∝

The wind had picked up during the night, and the bay had turned so angry that the dinghy threatened to tip at any moment. Waves socked the sides of the boat. We were soaked in an instant. I held the floodlight in front, and its beam faltered through the gray light. We could hardly see for the wind and the spray. Liv shivered beside me, but I hardly felt the cold. The three of us had life jackets, but I wasn't sure Sam did. He was a good swimmer, but the ocean was unfathomably large, the water beneath us blacker than black. If the kayak tipped . . .

Liv put her hand on my shoulder. Her face frozen with worry, braids undone, hair plastered against her forehead. She yelled to me over the noise of motor and surf. I understood that her mouth was forming the words, that she was telling me he'd be okay, but I felt only fear.

A horrible thought occurred to me: What if Sam wasn't just *looking* for the wreck? What if he was trying to join it?

"Can we go any faster?" I shouted, turning back toward Orion.

"We don't know what's out here," Orion called from the stern. "Plenty of rocks to snag us."

"We'll get there," Liv said. "We *are* getting there. Look."

She pointed. The whale-shaped rock was closer than it'd been just moments ago, stretching taller and taller into the lightening sky. I craned my neck to see its full reach. The binoculars hadn't even begun to convey just how formidable these rocks were, this backward moat: in the pockets between the boulders, waves crashed and churned, forming a series of aqua eddies hungry for small ships. Getting past them would require deft navigation, and once we passed the rock barrier, we were in open ocean. In a dinghy that was filling up quickly with salt water.

To find the wreck of the *Lyric* was to invite another.

A wave crashed into us, and the boat pitched wildly; Orion grabbed the straps of Liv's life vest to keep her from tumbling out. There was a horrible sound that sounded like scraping. The early morning smelled like gasoline. The spray from the rocks and wind lashed my face, and I strained to see beyond the whale-shaped rock, to the ocean, to just ocean.

"Keep going. We've got to get past those rocks."

Orion kept one hand on the motor, trying to steady us in the waves. "Vi. What you're seeing—that's only the tip of the iceberg. There are so many rocks you can't see below us. We'll get snagged for sure."

"We don't even know he's here," Liv said. Her voice was as gentle as it could be against the noise. "We don't even know he took the kayak."

"If he did he probably got scared and turned around," Orion said.

"We've got to go back," Liv said, and I could hear how her

voice had changed, turned pleading, desperate. "It's not safe."

"Violet," Orion said. "The boat's not meant for this."

No one understood: Sam wanted to undo all the surviving we'd managed, all the way back to Fidelia. I held the underwater floodlight steady, and traced my eyes along the length of its beam, scanning the black ocean beyond the rocks. They needed to go back. But I couldn't. My feet were anchors.

"Violet," Liv called.

"*Violet*," Orion repeated, louder.

"Stop saying my name like that! What if my brother's there? What if—"

That's when I spotted it, in the beam of light: a vessel floating beyond the rock barrier. A flash of yellow. Then it disappeared, subsumed by the waves. The stolen kayak had tipped, emptied of its thief.

Without even deciding to jump, I was in the air. Then the water went over my head with a cold, sharp slap.

✧

Underwater, I was blind. The current wrenched me in every direction, tumbled me under and up and over. I was a strong swimmer, I'd escaped riptides, I had a life vest, but I had no breath, and which way was up, and all I could do was hug the light to my chest and hope. My shin was sliced; my head was knocked, banged, split; my forehead burst with pain. I flailed and surfaced and gasped, before a huge swell swept me under again.

How had Fidelia survived this? How would Sam?

Beneath the waves, my ears filled with black noise, horrible engines of water in a torment around me. The world had turned all to water, loud, angry water—

Then there was a different noise, small but distinct. I could scarcely hear it at first: it whined and scratched across an underwater frequency, piercing the rush. It was a voice. Not human, but a whale song of a voice that spoke to me through the water, ancient and creaking and primal. It wasn't language, exactly, but the meaning was as clear as if I'd thought of it myself:

Kick, the voice said.

I kicked. My feet were flippers, and I imagined I was Fidelia, pulling herself through the cold. I kicked, and kicked, and kicked, and then, even though I hadn't known which direction was up, I surfaced.

The water was calmer, here, and it took me a moment to realize why—I'd passed beyond the rock barrier. I was on the other side of the whale-shaped rock.

I squinted against the salt, searching for my friends, but I couldn't see beyond the rocks anymore.

There was nothing to do now but kick, swim away from the rocks, toward where I'd last seen the kayak. In all this ocean, I hardly even knew where that was.

I swam.

My body stung with cold. My lungs felt squeezed in an enormous fist, and I kicked uselessly. The water was deepening below me, I felt it, and I knew the continental shelf had fallen off. My heart took flight, battered its wings against my throat. As a child, I never swam out too far for fear that a fish or worse was lurking out there, waiting to gobble me up, and that same sensation swept through me now.

My body understood before I did. Something was there. A presence. Solid.

I ducked below the surface and shone the light below me. Through the heavy curtain of salt and dark I saw a slow, ominous form take shape.

The wreck.

I'd have to swim down there to find Sam.

My life jacket buoyed me back to the surface. I'd have to take it off to get deeper.

I unbuckled it and shimmied my shoulders loose. The jacket bobbed slowly away from me, and as I watched it ebb, I grew tiny and scrabbling, feeble and squeaking. My legs pedaled furiously below the surface.

I took a deep, deep breath, and ducked back beneath the waves.

Don't, I heard.

The water was crushing, dark, dangerously cold. I ignored the whale-song voice and swam deeper. The currents seemed to help pull me down. They rushed together like a great slide, shuttling me deeper and deeper to the shape that I'd seen. It was coming into focus in the beam of my floodlight: a mast, cracked in half, and beneath that, a mossy deck.

Sam, Sam, are you here? I wanted to scream, to cry out—

My vision was blackening—the pressure was cracking my head open, there was a whining between my ears—how did these currents rush me so deep so quickly?—I couldn't swim toward the surface, now, if I tried. . . .

The whale-song voice was speaking again: *Forget the wreck. Look up.*

I fought against the current, corkscrewed the whole of me, shone the beam toward the surface. Above me, a form slipped like a seal, and in the beam of my light, there was a radiant sparkle of silver.

The pocket watch. Fidelia's. Sam's. He'd been wearing it.

Swim up, said the whale-song voice.

I tried, but the current was dragging me toward the wreck. There was no way out: I was trapped in an underwater vortex and running out of air. The ocean was too much. The wreck wanted me. I didn't have the strength to try.

Drop the light. Swim up.

The light.

Drop it.

Swim!

I let the light fall, and struggled against the rush—

I was so tired, my body was giving out, my lungs were collapsing, the pull was too strong, everything around me squeezed and squeezed and squeezed until a single word vibrated within me:

Up.

I kicked with all my might, and popped free of the current. I was loose, suddenly, swimming up, toward the silver glimmer in the water. Was it Sam? Everything was spangled now, spots dancing in front of my eyes—was I drowning?—I needed to breathe so badly, but something else was coming into view and I was so close to the surface—

UP.

I was so near to the surface, and the shape looked almost human—was it someone I knew? They looked so familiar—I reached out my hand—

The whale-song voice overtook me, until there was only buzzing.

I was coughing. More than coughing. Vomiting. Heaving. Salt water tore at my throat. A hand pummeled me on the back; something long and black, like a bootlace, slithered up my throat. I coughed onto the sand, and I swear an eye looked back at me, white and jellied as a pearl onion.

"Oh God," someone was saying, "oh God, oh God, oh God."

I hacked up bile and salt and sand. My throat burned. I was alive. Was I dying? I'd died. This was how people died. There was a pile of sea stuff in front of me. Sea stuff that had been inside my stomach, now on the black sand. My face hurt. My body hurt. The tide rushed beneath me and I retched again. Someone thumped a hand between my shoulder blades.

"Violet, Violet—" the voice said. "Are you okay? Can you sit up? I just wanted to see it for myself—I thought I could make it back before morning—I thought I could give the kayak back, but it was so windy, and so dark, I forgot the light, so I thought I'd just stay by the rocks—I'm so, so sorry, I just wasn't thinking—"

Sam, leaning over me, eyes rimmed with salt, skin angry from the thrashing waves. Sam, alive. I touched the side of his head, and he touched mine. When he pulled away, his fingers were dark with blood. He hid them, like he didn't want me to see.

I spoke. "Where are we?"

"I don't know. A sandbar. I saw you, out in the water, and you floated this way—I just swam to you, I still had the life vest on—"

"I heard a voice. A whale song. Speaking."

Sam nodded. "Telling you to swim up?"

"How did you . . ."

"I heard the same thing. Why weren't you wearing a life vest? Why aren't you?"

Fog closed around my brother's wet face: or was that just me, drifting away? The world spangled. God, I was so dizzy. Everything was buzzing, and shapes were going cloudy. I heard a voice again, words buzzing not from the ocean, but from deep inside me: *Him, her, a whale, you, what does it matter? You both saw the wreck, and you both swam up.*

TRAVELING MUSIC

A show in progress. A story unfolding. The theater goes dark for a scene change.

The orchestra, though, continues to play. A riff on the show's dominant melody fills the house—somber or suspenseful or sweepingly romantic—and the tone of the next scene starts there, with the music. In the dark, the crew storms the stage, scurrying to place props and flip panels with the authority of blind, tunnel-dwelling mammals, creatures that know their way home by feel. Even without light, there is complete control. The music swells and leads the audience by the nose—the very sound tells you what comes next, what you should expect.

Here is the music I woke to, frenzied, dissonant, unknown voices:

"He's still freezing—"

"She's like ice—"

"Luckiest kids alive—"

"More like dumbest. No one's safe yet."

"Is she still bleeding?"

"Less."

"He's not getting warmer—"

"Another blanket, here—"

"We've got a while till harbor, yet . . ."

"Never thought I'd say it, but thank God we were lost—"

"Sam?"

I recognized that last voice. It was my own.

"She's up."

"Keep her awake. Talk to her."

A woman's face was before mine, suddenly—white-haired, round, wet brown eyes—and her hot, hot hand was on my forehead.

"Hon?" she said. "We've got you."

The room took shape around me. I was in a dark-wood nook, creaky and damp. There was humming—was it the voice again, a whale song, speaking to me? No—it was mechanical, sputtering, and that gasoline smell was back. An engine. I was in the belly of a boat, I realized, lying down in a tight bunk. I tried to move but couldn't: I'd been burrito-wrapped in a blanket, arms pinned by my sides. I smelled cedar and wet wool. A kettle shrieked from another room, and I raised my head slightly. Through the door, I could make out a tiny galley of a kitchen, and lying horizontal on a cushioned bench, being tended to by a baseball-capped man, was Sam. He wasn't moving.

"Keep her awake, Pat," the man called.

The kettle was still screaming on the heat.

"My brother," I said, but I was foggy, marble-mouthed. My throat burned.

"Easy, there. Try to stay awake, now. . . ."

I tried, but the world around me flickered. I heard the static of the radio and the man's voice from the other room. A sip of burning-hot tea nearly split my throat in half. The woman clapped her hands inches from my face, like cracking, angry applause. I wanted desperately to sleep.

"Focus, dear. Stay awake. Talk to me, if you can."

I tried. I know I did. I remember trying. But my memory of the boat is patchy, moth-eaten. What comes back to me now in wincing, lurid detail is the summer afternoon of Sam's suicide attempt, when I was a little bit high—daytime high, nothing too aggressive—but just high enough that the world became super saturated, doubly memorable.

I was lolling in Central Park with friends, playing round after round of Fuck, Marry, Kill when my mom called. Our conversation lasted less than a minute. I left my friends without saying goodbye and I hailed the first open cab: Taxi 7N25. I memorized numbers because I lost things in cabs so often. The driver, according to his medallion, was Edward Rhee. The cab had squeaky brakes. On the sidewalk, a dog was yapping. A song I hated was on the radio, and I thought of traveling music then, how shitty this song was, how this couldn't possibly be the song that began our next scene.

"Pretty day," Edward said.

"Yup," I said.

We squeaked to a stop sooner than I would've liked. I paid Edward Rhee twelve dollars. The bills were sweaty from my pocket, crumpled, but I was grateful to have cash; I never did.

With my hands, I broke the seal of sweat that'd glued my thighs to the leather seat. I did not get out of the car.

"You okay?" Edward asked.

No response. I didn't know the answer.

"You want me to wait?" he said.

Maybe.

"My brother tried to kill himself," I said.

Edward Rhee sucked in his breath.

"I can wait." His voice was so kind, so careful. "No trouble at all."

"That's okay," I said finally.

Edward Rhee, of Taxi 7N25. I should write him a thank-you note.

Rather than go straight into the hospital, I looped around the block. I passed a deli, a nail salon, a bagel shop. That dumb song from the radio was stuck in my head. I couldn't go in the hospital with a song that I hated stuck in my head. I needed a different song, comforting, before I went inside the hospital. A better song for me, and for Sam. That song would be my own version of a prayer.

I took another loop and willed the words to come. A deli, a nail salon, a bagel shop. My mind went blank. Nothing came. I knew hundreds of songs, but my mind was wiped clean. I was so afraid, dumb and stoned, alone and scared. I missed Edward Rhee's cab with its squeaky brakes. The sidewalk was littered with dark polka dots that I realized, suddenly, like a fool, was chewing gum, turned black with dirt. Sixteen years in the city, and my brain had chosen *now* for this epiphany? I couldn't even do traveling music right.

The man in the boat was speaking.

"He doesn't look good, he doesn't look good at all—"

The music on this boat—these fearful voices, this buzzing radio, these clapping hands—this music was no good for our next scene. Sam and I needed a different tune. Through my own fog, I tried to hum. The song hadn't come to me that afternoon in the city, but I had it now, lying here in this boat. This song was a good offering. The Emerald City glitters on the horizon, and four friends and a dog sprint across the poppy field, and before there's snow, before there's sleep, there are voices in celebratory chorus, high, trilling, bright.

There was only air at first, breathy and catching in the back of my throat, stinging where I'd retched. I tried again and managed a few feeble peeps—an animal dying, an animal in bliss. The notes weren't audible, but if I kept trying, they formed a weak heartbeat in the back of my throat. I couldn't remember what the song was called, but everything else, I knew. The lyrics were about holding on: to breath, to heart, to hope.

SURVIVAL

I was warmer when I woke next. My index finger was in the alligator mouth of a heart monitor, and the noises from the boat were gone, replaced with sterile beeps and jangling carts. I was tucked tight in a bed, but bright midday sun spilled through the window, and the world sharpened when I blinked. Midday. Sunny. A window. My mom was in a chair beside me, eyes closed, cardigan draped over her like a blanket. She looked exactly the same: a stubby brown ponytail, tiny gold studs, no makeup. She was so *little*. Had she always been that small? My mom was here. But where . . .

"Where's Sam?"

"*Vi*," my mom gasped, eyes springing open. She shot from her seat and wrapped her arms around me. I'd dwarfed her since I was twelve, but her hug still made me feel small. Taken care of. I hooked my nose into the crook of her elbow and breathed. We were in a hospital—I'd figured that much out—but my mom still smelled sweet and bready, like her morning self.

"Mom. What's going on? Where's Sam?"

"You're back in Lyric, Violet—oh God, we were so worried. . . ."

She clutched me so tight I could barely breathe.

"Sam, Mom," I said. She wasn't answering fast enough, and my teeth started to chatter. It wasn't enough. It hadn't been enough. Maybe we had everything we needed—luck and perseverance and heart and hope—and maybe that still hadn't been enough, maybe we weren't as strong as Fidelia, or maybe we were—but there were no guarantees in life, it was all so incredibly arbitrary, a piano could fall on us tomorrow, and where was Sam, why wasn't she answering, where was he—

"There," my mom said, pointing.

My dad and Sam were in the doorway, holding hands. Sam had a black eye and a sliced-open cheek, but he was there, standing.

My family was here in this room.

"Hi," I said to everyone.

My dad had gotten new glasses.

That's when I started crying. Like I hadn't cried since I was a kid, snot everywhere, spit flying from my mouth, tears coming hard and fast. The weight of *living* poured out of me: the Year of Wild and Spain and Rus/Gus, *Peter Pan* and the rays and my tea leaves, finding Sam and Orion's stunned face and the love of Liv. Life could be so very much.

"I've got you," my mom said.

"Where's Liv? Where's Orion?"

"They're fine," Sam said.

"A little freaked out," said my dad.

"Understatement of the century," my mom said. "They were

severely hypothermic and traumatized, clinically. You too. All of us."

"What happened?" I said, running the back of my hand across my wet face. I remembered a shrieking kettle and someone clapping, and poppies, but beyond that, everything was fuzzy.

"The couple from the campground—they had a satellite phone," my dad said. "After you went out to sea, they called the Coast Guard, who put your disappearance out on the radio to any boats at sea. A couple found you guys on a sandbar—they'd been out fishing, gotten turned around. If they hadn't been there . . ."

"I thought you . . ." I looked at my brother. The boat came back to me, and the song I'd sung like a prayer, and then, like that, I had it, the knowledge that'd escaped me—

" 'Optimistic Voices'!" I cried. "That's what that song is called. 'Optimistic Voices.' "

"She's still confused, I think," my dad said.

"I'm not. I'm good. I just . . . remembered."

"We're so lucky they were lost," my mom said, almost to herself.

"We owe them a kayak," Sam said. "The couple from the campsite, I mean."

"We owe them a little more than that," my dad said, rubbing Sam's back. "I'll tell you, though, it's sort of a miracle you both found that sandbar. That couple, too. All that ocean, and just that one spot . . ."

Sam and I glanced at each other. Everything before the boat

rushed back: the whale-song voice, the wreck. *Swim up.* The sand-bar. Had it been there all along?

"How?" my dad said simply. We were all thinking it.

"I just swam," Sam said finally. "One stroke at a time, and then I saw Violet, and then we swam, together. Until we found the sandbar."

"I don't even remember swimming," I said.

"You did," said Sam. "You kicked like crazy."

"So lucky," my dad repeated. "So *stupid . . .*"

"Years of swim lessons," my mom said.

"Strong, too," I said.

"Both. All. Stupid, strong, swim lessons," Sam said.

I was so grateful to have them. So grateful that we were all *here* together.

Except—

"Where's Toby?" I said. "Oh my God, Mom, did you kill him? It's not his fault. Promise me you're not going to blame him. Blame me."

"Toby's fine, Violet. He wanted to give us a minute. And believe me when I tell you that we've moved very far beyond blame. What we're dealing with in this family, it's just . . . altogether too complicated for blame. There will be no blame, okay? We'll have to just . . ."

She struggled to finish, and glanced to my dad for help. I wondered, too, what we'd have to do.

"Persevere?" I suggested.

"Fuck perseverance," my dad said.

"*Alan!*" my mom squawked. Sam laughed through his fingers.

"Jesus, Dad, tell us how you really feel."

"I *am* telling you how I really feel," my dad said. "We'll get to perseverance, I'm sure. But today, fuck perseverance, and fuck it tomorrow, too. Fuck it for the whole next week. The next year even. We'll talk about perseverance until the cows come home, I promise you. But today, I think we should just *be*, and have that be enough. That's all we're gonna do, okay? *Be.* Together. Here."

In the silence that followed, my dad looked a little shocked. I didn't blame him: it was the most adamant I'd ever heard him. My mom gaped, openmouthed. But she didn't say he was *wrong*.

"Being works," Sam said. He flopped next to me on the bed.

"Being sounds really good, actually," I said, scooching to make more space.

My mom picked up the remote from my bedside table and held it out to my dad, an olive branch for our time. "I guess we should start with terrible hospital TV?"

My parents gathered on my bed, too, altogether too cramped and too hot, but not wanting it any other way. During a commercial break, Sam and my dad fetched us coffee and Oreos. Together, we grimaced through sips of vile coffee and shouted the wrong answers at *Jeopardy!* until our collective volume rose so loud a nurse popped in to ask if all was well.

"We're great," I said. And so for the moment, we were.

We finished *Jeopardy!* and then, even though my mom can't

stand Pat Sajak, we worked together to solve the puzzles on *Wheel of Fortune*.

In this very boring way, we began a long and difficult survival.

⊶

Later that afternoon, my mom showed me her research.

My family had decided to eat dinner in shifts so that no one would have to be alone. Sam and my dad had been gone only a few minutes when my mom said she needed to show me something.

Almost shyly, she pulled a thick manila folder from her bag. "After we talked on the phone last time, and you were telling me what you were finding out about the family, I got inspired. I did one of those website things, but that wasn't much use, so then I contacted a genealogist." She passed me the folder. Inside was a thick stack of paper: photocopied newspaper clippings from the library archives. A copy of the *Lyric*'s ship manifest, and there she was, her name highlighted, *Fidelia Hathaway*, and right below her . . .

"*Septimus?*"

"Fidelia was a twin," my mom said.

It all made such sudden, crashing sense. *My apple, cleft in two.* Not temptation. Not knowledge. An apple: the fruit of a shared seed. Split down the middle into identical parts.

"They grew up in a foundling hospital," my mom said. "An orphanage, sort of. For abandoned children. That's why it's so hard to find any information on them—they were adopted, eventually, and I didn't learn much, but their life seemed okay. Says a lot that the parents wanted to take in both children, I think. Or I like to think."

"The hospital was an orchard," I said.

"Yes," my mom said. "Did you just—guess that—or . . . ?"

"And he . . ." I said, looking back at the manifest, my heart pounding. "He was coming over with her."

"They were eighteen. Around there. They didn't quite know her real age."

"He didn't make it," I said. It wasn't a question.

"No," my mom said, "he drowned."

"Maybe that's . . ."

The names on the manifest were small and blurred. *Fidelia Hathaway, Septimus Hathaway.* The letters swam before my eyes and their names bent to ours. A life without Sam: I didn't want to imagine it, but it was possible. A life without me: possible, too. My favorite possible was both of us, timeworn, bickering on a long-distance phone call. Who knew? The not-knowing hurt, but there was wonder coiled there, too: in a snail's shell, or in a grass bracelet.

"Maybe that's what?" my mom asked.

"Maybe that's why Fidelia didn't write to her family," I said. "Maybe it was too hard to tell them. That she'd lived, and he hadn't. Maybe it was easier to just . . . disappear."

I closed the folder. My mom was wiping at her eyes with the

back of her hand. Through everything—*Peter Pan* and our fights and her long nights in the hospital, worrying about her patients, her own kids—I'd never seen her cry. Her tears didn't scare me. They felt like a relief.

"Mom, I'm so sorry. I've done so many bad things. I'm a bad daughter."

"Violet, *no*. None of this is your fault."

"I had a panic attack in June. I worry all the time. I see catastrophe everywhere. Sometimes my mind just goes and goes and goes and I can't stop it. I'm so scared, always. Is that normal?"

"You get that from me," she said. "Try not to worry."

"I can't. I worry all the time. I didn't know you had such a hard time growing up. I didn't know about your mom, and everything you did for Toby, that must have been so hard—"

"Shhhh," she said. "We'll talk about it. But we're just being today, remember?"

She brushed my bangs back from my forehead. Her hand was warm—maybe the only doctor of which this was true.

"I'm liking the short hair," she said.

"I might grow it out."

"So contrary."

My mom smiled, then glanced over her shoulder.

"Violet," she said, nodding toward the hall, "do you know that person?"

I looked. Liv was pacing the hallway, sneaking a look in my

room each time she passed. She was holding a vase of bright blue hydrangeas.

"I do," I said. "You ready to meet someone important?"

My mom glanced between me and the nervous, flower-wielding girl.

"That's a thing I've never heard you say before," she said.

"Just don't be weird, okay? She matters."

I waved to Liv, beckoning her in. She stepped over the threshold, but lingered in the doorway, unsure of herself.

"Hello," she said formally. She was so nervous.

"Liv, this is my mom. And, Mom, this is Liv," I said. "She's the best."

My mom walked toward her, hand outstretched.

"Nice to meet you, Liv. Wow, that's a firm handshake," she said admiringly.

"No dead fish," Liv said. My mom laughed.

"Mom, can you . . . ?" I said.

"Can I, like, *leave*? Of course," she said, in the ever-so-slightly-embarrassing voice of someone who wasn't born yesterday. "Your dad and Sam probably miss me anyway. I'll just wait outside like . . . like . . ."

"A gargoyle," Liv suggested.

"Yes," my mom said. "That was exactly the word I wanted."

She disappeared down the hall, but Liv still stayed far from me, lurking inches from the doorway. Behind her, a nurse pushed a patient in a wheelchair, and doctors buzzed down the hallways. Pagers went off and sneakers squeaked. Liv wasn't coming closer. Maybe, with everything that had happened, she'd decided—she'd chosen—she thought things would be easier if she and I just—

"Are you real?" I asked her.

"Real," she affirmed. She set the hydrangeas down on my bedside table and perched in the chair next to me, crossing her ankles and folding her hands in her lap. She was real, but she looked so far away. It was the first time she and I had been in public together, since . . . Could I touch her? Was I allowed? I reached for her hand just as a nurse bustled in, and Liv pulled away from me, startled.

"Family only," the nurse chirped.

"She's staying," I said. "Please don't argue."

The nurse raised his eyebrows, looking between the two of us.

"Just this once," he said.

"Thanks," Liv said to him. "Thanks," she said to me.

"Did you bathe in cigarettes?" I asked.

"I was stressed."

"As much as I want you to quit, I actually missed that smell."

She smiled and my heart trilled.

"Liv, I'm so sorry."

"I was so scared," she said. "You can't do that again."

"I promise I will never jump off a boat into the open ocean ever again."

"I'll hold you to that."

"How's Orion?" I asked.

"Physically, fine. My mom doesn't really understand what happened out there, so I just told her we got swept away, okay?" she said, and bit her lip. "Orion doesn't really understand why it took so long for me to tell him. I don't either, really."

"It took so long to tell him because it was hard."

"He feels like a fool. I don't think he'll come to see you. He doesn't really do hospitals. I barely do, to tell you the truth." She crossed and uncrossed her ankles. "I also talked to my parents. About fens. I wasn't even planning it, I just started *talking*. It was like jumping out of the boat, I think, instinct took over."

"What'd you say? What'd they say?"

"*Wellll,*" she said. "It didn't go great."

She squished her mouth to a little bud. She must've been making that face since she was a child, thinking through the letters in *Australia* on a third-grade spelling quiz. I loved her. Yes. I loved her.

"Well, I started by talking about Orion," she said, "and then I brought in the fen part, not even about me yet, and my mom was like, '*Mmmm*, boys are complicated,' and I was like, '*I'm* complicated.' So *then* she got so nervous and started talking about feeling 'prepared for physical intimacy' and I was like, 'No, Mom, *I'm* the fen,' and she *must* have realized something was up, because she started talking about Back Bay Fens in Boston, and asked my dad whether the Red Sox had been mathematically eliminated."

"What'd he say?"

"Well, he was half watching golf, so he just said they were still in it."

"You had this conversation while they were watching golf?"

"I was trying to be casual!" she said. I definitely loved her.

"I'm going to have to have this conversation with them a million times, you know. I might wait a while for the next one." She plucked at the hydrangeas, avoiding my eyes. "Part of me thinks it'll take years."

"You've had the first one. I think it'll get easier."

"I wish . . ." she said, trailing off.

"I wish, too." For her, I wished everything.

"Later my mom—um—she, um, told me that she wasn't sure you were a good influence?" She pulled loose a petal and arranged it over her thumbnail. "But she also sent you these, so."

"It's a very nice arrangement," I said slowly.

"Good blues," Liv agreed.

I wanted her to crawl in bed with me. I wanted to tell her I loved her. That her parents would come around, that it wouldn't always be this hard, this complicated. But I couldn't say any of that for certain.

Instead, across the thin hospital sheets, I offered her my index finger. She hooked her finger with mine. Tiny, minuscule, a grain of sand split in half, but right then, the link between our fingers was the truest thing I knew.

AND

"Do you care to explain why we had to make a twenty-minute detour to the nice seafood store?" Toby asked as we pulled into Orion's driveway. It was the first place I'd asked to be taken once I got out of the hospital.

"You have better places to be?" I asked him.

"I should be off trying to make things right with your mother, for a start," Toby said.

"One day at a time," I said, patting him on the knee. "If anything, you can thank me for bringing you two closer together."

"Remind me to do that later," Toby said, rolling his eyes.

I got out of the car with my leaky bag of shrimp. I slammed the car door shut, then rapped on the window. Toby lowered the glass.

"Thank you," I said. "I'm very glad you're my uncle."

"I'm very glad you're my niece."

I walked around back to Orion's shed, following the noise of a trumpet. I stood outside and listened, letting the notes wash over me. My body hummed with the music. This mattered, this music. Whether he forgave me or not: this had mattered.

I knocked and the door of the shed swung open. Orion poked his head out.

"Violet," he said, reciting my name like a stale fact.

"Hi," I said. "Can I come in?"

He didn't look thrilled at the idea, but swung the door open anyway, disappearing back inside. I followed him, keeping a fair bit of distance between us, standing while he perched on the stool.

"How are you?" I asked finally.

"Fine," he said. "Liv told me you were okay. I'm sorry I didn't come to the hospital, it's just . . ."

"Please don't apologize before I can, that's the whole reason I'm here. Seriously. You have nothing to be sorry for."

Orion rubbed his forearm. I watched his tattoo disappear and reappear like magic. My first day at the aquarium felt like a lifetime ago.

"I got you a seafood-of-the-month club," I blurted. "And shrimp! Well, not *you*. The rays. The guys at the seafood store thought I was the absolute weirdest. They don't really do that, it turns out, but they wrote this down on a receipt for you. . . ." I passed him the slip of paper that the cashier had written up for me and set the bag of shrimp at his feet, pathetically, like an offering.

" 'Fish for a Year'?" he read skeptically. "Are you trying to buy my friendship?"

"The *rays'* friendship. You get an apology."

Orion crossed his arms. "I'm listening."

"We should have told you," I said, sounding out the words the way I'd practiced. "We were careless with your feelings."

"Yep," he said. Well. He wasn't going to make my job easy. Good thing I had more apology memorized.

"I'm not used to having friends," I went on. "Good friends who are good people. People who sing to lobsters and pick up trash off the beach. Not that that's an excuse. I'm just . . . out of practice. I think sometimes I come off flirtier than I intend, and I'm sorry if I led you on. But, I mean, that's not even the problem. I'm sorry I kept you on the outside. I want you to know me."

He waited. That was all I'd rehearsed.

"I didn't set out to . . . I hope you don't think I . . ."

"Used your dumb go-betweening shtick as a way to get to Liv?"

"Orion, God, *no*. I watched you both that first night, and you two were so close—and I'd just never been that close to someone. I wanted to be around you both, but I seriously thought you belonged together. Honestly I was kind of into Mariah, or I thought she was like the prettiest person I'd ever seen, at least, don't tell her that, though. What happened with Liv and me took me completely by surprise."

"Me too," he said. "You could've told me, you know."

"She didn't want me to."

"No. You could've told me about you. That you're bisexual. I wouldn't've cared, you know? I mean, I *don't* care. You're still you."

"I know," I said. I'd never liked that term for myself—but it seemed kind of a trivial point to argue in the face of Orion's kindness. I'd school him on the nuances later. "Sometimes it, like, still surprises me. How hard it can be to tell people."

"I get that," he said, "though I've got to admit, I feel like an idiot."

"You are *not* an idiot. You're this jack of all trades! You build boats and play music and you understand thermohaline circulation. . . ."

"Thermohaline circulation isn't even complicated, Violet. Meanwhile, I fell for two girls who fell in love with each other." He held up two fingers, and repeated himself, just in case I missed it. "*Two.*"

"That doesn't mean you're an idiot," I said. "That means you have this incredible capacity for love. Not to mention excellent taste."

"What a skill set."

"It *is*! You wouldn't be this good at music if you didn't have it. And the rays wouldn't be as well-fed, and the aquarium would be dead in the water—you *care*, and that's so special, it's like a *gift*. I have *loved* playing music with you this summer. No matter what happens with you and me. I want you to know that. It really, really mattered."

I wanted Orion to get everything that he wanted in life: To go south on a boat and play his music. To find a girl who loved him, even if it took years. To be rewarded in some way, for his goodness.

"For me, too," he said.

"And thermohaline circulation *is* complicated."

He snorted. "Thanks, I guess."

"Do you still want to do *Cousteau!?*" I asked.

"I think we should get rid of the exclamation point. I don't know how to say it."

"Sorry, nonnegotiable. Just throw in jazz hands if you need emphasis."

"And I really think in the lyrics in the third stanza of 'Calypso Tango' . . ."

"I'll get rid of the joke about the three-way."

"But I mean—the flyers are already up. People are coming. We should probably work on it. Now that you're here, actually—I memorized the first song. Will you listen?"

"*Yes,*" I said. There was nothing I'd rather do more.

He took a deep breath, and I suddenly remembered.

"Wait!" I cried.

"You have a real problem with interrupting people, you know that?"

"I know. I know. Just. Do you know how we're saving manatees? At the aquarium."

"Violet, you worked there for two solid months."

"I know . . . I just . . ."

"I'm so glad we didn't pay you," Orion said. "It's not like it's some great mystery. We donate to a wildlife rehab clinic in Florida.

Like, for manatees who've been sliced up by propellers or tangled up in nets. Just a few dollars here and there, but . . ."

I finished the sentence for him. "Every little bit helps."

$$\infty$$

"To what do I owe the pleasure?" Felix asked. "Former thieves, come to repent?"

"We need your paranormal expertise," I said, hardly believing what I was saying.

"There's a sucker born every minute," said Mariah.

"*Fun*," Felix said. "Does this have to do with a haunted pocket watch?"

"Sort of," Sam said.

We explained to Felix about the whale-song voice. We told him about the magic sandbar, and the Ghost Coast, and Septimus, and the presence of the wreck we both felt beneath the waves.

"Can you, like, séance Septimus using the watch and ask him if the wreck is really there?" I said.

" '*Séance him*'?" said Felix.

"God, don't make me ask again, Felix!"

Felix cracked the watch like a flip phone and held it to his ear. " 'Hey, Septimus, how's ghost life, you still at that same wreck?' "

"You read my tea leaves from your phone! How is this any more ridiculous?!"

"I mean . . ." Mariah said. "I'm kind of curious, too. Don't you want to know if the wreck is there?"

"*Yes,*" said Sam. "We both, like, *sensed it.* But who knows what we actually saw, the whole thing was so confusing."

"Lack of depth perception will really fuck with you," Felix agreed.

"But that voice. We both heard it."

"That you could probably chalk up to stress," said Mariah.

"I kind of agree with her," said Felix. "The brain does weird things sometimes when it goes into survival mode. When I lost my eye, I like really, really thought I was dying, but I also knew I was going to live. I heard all sorts of shit. But maybe the voice was just *you.* Haven't you ever heard a voice in your head that didn't sound *exactly* like your own?"

Duh, said a voice. *Shut up,* said another.

"I can't just call Septimus on a watch. First of all, maybe he's on a ghost date, and second of all, I'm kind of scared to chat with the dead. I might get addicted." He slid the pocket watch across the table.

"Okay," I said slowly. "But is there a way—I know you think crystal balls are a racket, but there must be another way. We just want to know. Was the wreck there?"

Sam, Mariah, and I stared avidly at Felix, waiting while he considered.

"Do you want to know what I think, or what I think?" Felix said.

"Are those things different?" Sam asked.

"Well, I'm of, like, four minds, that's kind of my point. Brain One says no wreck. Brain Two says yes wreck. Brain Three says I *hope* they found it, and Brain Four is thinking about whether I should have a hot dog for lunch. Who knows who's right? I mean, Violet, do you think it's there?"

"Sometimes. Sometimes not."

"*See?*" said Felix. "Maybe that's your answer."

"Schrödinger's cat is the answer?! That's *so shitty*," said Sam.

"Well, okay," said Mariah. "Let's say you found the wreck, and then you brought in a team of scientists, and they dredged it from the water with the crane, and you made it a houseboat and lived there. Then what?"

"I'm going to regret saying this, but she's right," said Felix.

Mariah threw her arms skyward and screamed, *"I've waited my whole life for this day!"*

"She didn't even make a point," said Sam.

"She did," said Felix. "Finding it . . . that's not where the story ends. I one hundred percent found a shipwreck, and . . ."

"And what?" said Sam.

Felix shrugged. "And I dunno. That's what I'm trying to say. And it's up to you."

POETRY

My family had two August weeks together in Lyric. We barbecued and watched TV, we read books and picked blueberries and waded, but didn't swim. Joan told me I could take August off, but I did half days. We petted the rays and Boris. Orion sang "Kelp!" for us, with Andy soloing on the tambourine. Sam and I walked along our coast in the afternoons, and in the morning, our parents did the same. They came up over the hill one morning, their hair damp with mist, and I saw they'd hooked their index fingers together.

Toby finished the puzzle and started a new one the very next day.

We *talked*, too. Not every conversation was a revelation. Sometimes we just talked about how delicious the asparagus was, or remarked on the weather. Sometimes we weren't patient with each other. Sometimes we snapped. But none of our conversations had a sense of finality. If we snapped, we came back to apologize. We all were beginning to understand the importance of *and*.

And there was Liv.

A few days before we returned to New York, she and I were lying in the bed at her house while her parents were out.

"I don't want you to go back to New York," she said.

"I know. It feels like the beginning of *Grease*. Soon I'll take up smoking and wear leather pants."

"I'm serious. Don't joke."

"I don't want to go back either," I admitted. There was so much to be scared of: my mom had spent the morning placing calls to colleagues, making a list of therapists that specialized in family sessions. Getting help was the right thing to do, but the year ahead of us was going to be work. There wasn't going to be *magic healing*; there'd be only a string of *and*s on which we'd thread our survival.

"I don't want to be different on my own," Liv said.

"You're not on your own. You're my anagram." I reached for her hand, worrying her ring around her finger. "Do you remember that day with the tea leaves?"

"You think your future was leading toward me because I wear a purple ring?"

"No," I said, thinking of Felix. "I think our futures intertwined because we wanted them to. Besides, that ring could have meant *anything*."

"The moon," Liv offered.

"The roundness of an apple."

"Things coming full circle," Liv said. "An end, and a beginning."

"A whole note."

"The world."

I put my head on her chest and clung to her. I wrapped my legs around her like a barnacle. I pressed my skin to hers and felt woozy, drifting along on this feeling. I couldn't be close enough. What would happen to us? I didn't know. I fretted; I squeezed her closer; I didn't want to leave, I was already mourning going—

"I love you, Violet," she said, "have I told you that?"

She hadn't, but I had a feeling. I loved her, too. I told her so.

"Promise me something?" I said.

"Anything."

✁

Cousteau! was an extremely well-attended fiasco. Joan had sent flyers to the penguin aquarium, and they'd *promoted the shit* out of it—organized tour buses, even, for loads of tourists, plus their whole staff. Andy's parents came. Felix and Mariah, their parents, their siblings. Joan's family, husband, three kids, and her sister. The librarian. A couple of kids from Lyric High, who Mariah was convinced were just there to heckle, but they didn't.

We performed outside, and Orion, as Cousteau, *nailed* the opening number. He was the only one who memorized his lines, while me, Felix, Mariah, and Joan bumbled through with scripts in hand, all the songs and scenes nearly illegible with my last-minute notes. We gave Boris a shark fin and people loved that. Thankfully, between Orion and Boris, the overall impression was good, because by the third scene, the rain began: our cardboard submarine was a pulpy mess before we even got aboard.

We tried to do the show inside, but everyone was freezing and our props were soaked, and finally Boris lay down in the center of stage as if to say, *Enough*. The show must go on, but sometimes the show musn't go on *right now*.

"Intermission," Joan called. The reception, at least, was banging, catered by the Mola Mola and the Lyric Pub, dark and stormy mocktails and cocktails that were super easy to swipe, and an epic cake Toby made in the shape of an octopus, its tentacles wrapped around a tiny ship.

Liv brought me and Orion each a single rose. She tucked his rose behind his ear, and mine into my lapel.

"That was amazing," she said.

"Spare us," Orion said.

"You should try out for the musical this year," Liv said. "Seriously."

She twirled off toward Sam at the cake. Orion and I watched Sam feed Liv a bite of cake, and I didn't think there was space in me for all the ways I was feeling.

"Well, we did it," he said.

"Sort of." I'd worn a spirit-gum mustache to play the first mate, and I ripped it off, seething through my teeth with pain and pressing my hand to my mouth. Later, bubbles would develop on my skin, allergic and raw.

"*Ow*," Orion said. "You could try to be gentler with yourself, you know?"

I knew. But when he said that, I launched myself at him for the hardest, least-gentle hug I could muster, chest to chest, pressing so hard we might fall through one another. He was better than a magic whale: he had helped save me, and then he'd stuck around.

⚬

I've heard it said that love—good love—feels like finding your missing puzzle piece. Here's the thing, though: I'm not sure the person who came up with that has done a lot of puzzles.

Take, for example, the most conventional jigsaw in the puzzle-verse. A Ravensburger thousand-piece, picture on the box, kitschy drawing of Yosemite, maybe, or bicycles in Amsterdam, sunset nonnegotiable. Some lush jungle, fuchsia flowers, and birds of paradise soaring past a waterfall and dappled light on a shadowy ocelot's coat, overwrought, bathetic.

One puzzle piece actually has *four* different ways to connect, not just two. That means four different ways to fit with someone else. Even if you're a corner piece, so statistically very rare, a real fucking weirdo in this particular puzzle—you're *still* going to connect in at least two places. Which means, theoretically, that as the *special-est, strangest, rarest* piece, you fit with not just one person, but *two people*.

What about one of those wooden puzzles my dad gives my mom for Christmas, the kind he claims are "*actually* very nice puzzles" but are *actually* just a huge pain in the ass? There aren't any edges, and there's no picture on the box to help, so you just have to *start* and hope for the best. Last year's was circus-themed, acrobats and clowns and a lion tamer, tightrope walkers in red tutus, trapeze artists mid-flight, a seal balancing a ball on his nose.

The pieces were laser-cut in the WACKIEST shapes, like little countries, or bacteria. A bajillion different ways these pieces could connect to each other. It's trial and error, your back aches and your eyes tear up from the work of hunting for that piece you think you need, the wooden pieces leach oil from your fingertips, each one thirsty for touch, and this puzzle is a freaking *joke*, it's too hard, forget this, I quit.

&

Quit, for now.

Let yourself be stuck.

Stare out the window, maybe. What do you see? Inky darkness? Maybe it's daytime. Maybe it's hot, the hottest day of the year. Leave the puzzle. Go swimming. Bring a friend. And on your way home there's salt on your skin and you're sitting on one towel and your brother's sitting on another. A big black dog leans out the window of a passing station wagon, his silky ears blowing back to reveal bunny-pink insides. Maybe he looks like a bat. Maybe he reminds you of being eight years old when you believed you could navigate by echolocation. You pitched tennis balls across the park and, with your eyes closed, listened for the sound when they landed.

Maybe, if you close your eyes now, you'll remember the tennis ball's Velcro fuzz and the lingering new-can smell. How your shoulder cracked when you hurled the ball across the lawn. Maybe you'll even hear the muffled sound of the ball landing, even in New York City. The soft-but-sure sound that announced itself as your guide.

$$\propto\!\!\!\!\!\!\!\!\!\!\!\!\!\!\!\!$$

Days later, or ten minutes later, you're back at it. Clarity. It's always the last piece you think you need (of course it's the last piece you try, because you don't keep looking after you find it). Then it's a cavalcade, hands moving before your brain gets there, Ouija board puzzling, muscle memory now, and all the hearts interlock with the spaces where hearts should be.

Except you're missing a piece. You can't find the seal's face. He's a faceless seal balancing a whole lot of nothing, a scoop taken out of the puzzle, an important one, too. It never won't bother you, but that's part of it.

The puzzle's an incomplete circus, the pieces touching each other in all these ways, and there's a hitch in your back from where you've hunched, but you've done it. You've put this thing together. Seams like veins pump blood through this cobbled-together catastrophe, this broken, beautiful mess.

STONES

Our last night in Lyric, Sam and I biked to get lobster rolls.

"Do you want to invite Liv?" he'd asked, buckling his helmet beneath his chin. "I don't mind."

"Let's have it be just us."

"Are you sure?"

"*Yes*," I said, rapping on his helmet. "We'll go to the touristy place, okay?"

The lobster shack was crowded with vacationing families, the air thick with salt and fried clams and ketchup. In line, Sam asked me, "Did you ever think that other people survived the wreck, maybe?"

I'd never thought that, but once he'd said it, I knew there was a chance.

We sat with our lobster rolls on a picnic table that faced the water, squeezing in on the end. Sam took slow bites of his roll, even the bun. He didn't finish the whole thing, but progress was still progress.

The night was beautiful, but something was still bothering me.

"Sam," I said cautiously, "when you went out in the kayak—what was going through your mind?"

"I wanted to see the wreck," he said. "That's all."

The pause between us was painful and searching. Should I ask what I wanted to ask? Kids dashed by us, running for the playground, screeching with delight. My brother looked down at his plate. His eyelashes were so long; his freckles so sweet. He had so much longer to live. He wanted to, didn't he?

I hadn't said what I'd needed to say—I needed to say more—to convince him—

"Sam. No matter what happens in the future. If you ever feel like you did in June—I want you to talk to me. I'm here for you. You're needed."

A long time passed before Sam spoke. "I swam up, Violet. We both did."

After, we walked down to the beach and skipped stones. Sam helped me perfect my form, showing me how to whip my wrist just so.

"The trick's in the rock, though. You have to get a good, smooth, flat one. Big, but not too big."

"Let's keep doing this in New York," I said.

"Skipping stones?"

"Brother-sister dates."

"You don't have to do that," he said. "I just mean—it's okay. If you get a better offer."

"I *want* to," I said. "You're my brother. But I want to be your friend, too. If that's okay."

"It's okay," he said. "Thanks for letting me come on the search."

"Thanks for coming," I said, "thanks for being here."

The sun grew orange over the water. Maybe we'd come back here next summer. Maybe Liv and I would last. Maybe she'd go to Oxford and meet some dashing British chick with glasses and a tweed blazer, or some bloke who played the organ. Maybe Sam and I would have our own families one day, bring them here, to this very spot. Maybe neither of us would have kids. Maybe the seas would rise so high that they'd lap at the back door of our grandmother's house.

"Seven skips!" Sam said, bursting into a grin. "Did you see that?!"

I wouldn't worry, not tonight. We'd come back here one day, when we were old. We had a long way to go, but by then we'd be so knowledgeable, so wise, that between the two of us, we'd be able to name all the constellations.

EPILOGUE

NEW FOUND LAND

Two weeks later, New York City was a blistering September inferno. Sam and I stood at the top of the subway entrance, headed home from our third appointment with Dr. Blank. I liked her, as much as one could like the stranger who'd seen you cry the first three times you'd met them. I didn't feel grown-up around her. I felt like a baby. Feeling better would be slow, hard work— but at least Dr. Blank had great shoes and an excellent listening face. At least Sam and I were in it together.

A train thundered into the station below, and heat gasped up the stairs. Sam grimaced and started down, shielding himself against the current of ascending travelers. I looked at my watch. We weren't in a hurry.

"Sam? Let's walk."

We took my favorite route in Manhattan and strolled along the west side of the park, the shore where the city meets nature. We walked beneath the shade of leafy trees, the cobblestone sidewalk hilly and broken in places where roots burst through brick. We passed two middle-aged men, hands intertwined. A mother held her toddler close and crooned to him in Spanish. Far down the path, a handsome, lumbering Newfoundland paused to sniff the base of a tree.

"*Look*," I said to my brother.

"He's like a *bear*," Sam agreed, amazed.

A bear to Sam. A friend to his owner. A big, slobbering dog to anyone else. To me, the Newfoundland was a pebble landing in my pocket, smooth and flat as a good skipping stone.

My phone buzzed as we waited to cross the street toward our apartment. It was a picture from Liv: her bicep sporting a nicotine patch. *Day two,* she'd written, *somehow even harder than day one.*

She was keeping her promise. A second pebble clacked against the first. Two before noon: I was on a roll.

Another buzz. *PS Orion wants to know when you'll have the next draft of Cousteau!*

"Sexts?"

"Gross, Sam. Liv and Orion are just asking about *Cousteau!*"

"Did you tell them that I'm making you finish the book before you go any further?"

"I'm telling them that you're helping me with critical research, yes."

My phone buzzed again before I could text back. For a self-proclaimed Luddite, Liv had seriously swift thumbs.

PPS I miss you and I can't wait to see you at Thanksgiving.

The third pebble was bigger than the others, and heart-shaped.

"Violet," Sam said, and he reached for my hand. "We're crossing."

A few blocks from our apartment, I caught a glimpse of my

reflection in a storefront widow. Growing out my hair had been far more challenging than I'd anticipated—my hair grew quickly, but the awkward phase was lasting an eternity. I thought about cutting it all the time, but then I'd just be back at square one and where would that leave me?

I didn't know what to do.

I still don't.

But it's just hair, I guess.

Hairs plural.

Each one grows, like love or trees or anything good.

ACKNOWLEDGMENTS

I'm so grateful to all the people who helped bring this book into existence.

Thank you to my agent extraordinaire, Pete Knapp, who believed wholeheartedly in this story after reading an early, messy draft. I so appreciate your patience, your spot-on feedback, and your dedication to this project.

I could not be more grateful to Laura Schreiber, my wonderful editor, whose insight into this story was so startlingly perceptive that I suspect she might be magic. Thank you, Laura, for helping me write the book that I always wanted to. Thank you to the rest of the team at Hyperion for your unmatched enthusiasm and hard work, especially Holly Nagel, Danielle DiMartino, Seale Ballenger, Christine Saunders, Sara Liebling, Marci Senders, and Emily Meehan. Big thanks, too, to Jenna Stempell-Lobell and Katie Vernon for the gorgeous cover art.

I'm lucky to have had so many wonderful teachers over the years who believed in my writing. Special thanks to Betsy de Luca, who taught me in eleventh grade to think a little harder, and to Gene Bell-Villada at Williams College, for always being so supportive of my writing and my thinking. Thank you to Elissa Schappell and Deborah Eisenberg, whose words I think of often when I write, and thank you to Stacey D'Erasmo, who told me "this book is going to work." And eternal gratitude to Jim Shepard, who changed my life for the better. A big thank you to Sue Mendelsohn and the Columbia University Writing Center for throwing me a much-needed lifeline, and to Joe Cross and Kathleen Ross, for helping me through the first-year-teacher wilderness and for chatting with me about this book in its infancy.

All my thanks to Sasha Berger for helping me find my way.

For reading this book at different stages, and for making me a better writer: Dan Grossman, Chris Fox, Jesse Gordon, and John Magary. Special thank you to Jonathan Draxton, who read several drafts of this project and gave me excellent feedback. Thank you to workshop members at Columbia who read faint, sketchy versions of this novel and encouraged me to keep going.

I'm grateful to the Sitka Fellows Program, where I revised a good chunk of this book in the summer of 2017, and to the marvelous Fellowesses, whose work and camaraderie kept me motivated: Hannah Brinkmann, Sarah Chadwick Gibson, Muira McCammon, Sylvia Ryerson, Madeleine Welsch, and Lauren Wimmer. Thank you also to the Sitka Sound Science Center for being a wonderful resource when I needed some aquarium inspiration.

Thank you so very much to my wonderful students over the years, especially the hugely talented, fiercely inspirational Ireland writers of 2017 and 2018. Thanks to BJ Love and Chris Catanese, actual poets, for traveling and teaching alongside me, and for seeing me through some very long days.

A big thank you to the Mittelstead family for your

generosity and encouragement, and for making me sweet potatoes on Thanksgiving. Thank you to my friends, with whom I have celebrated and commiserated: Katherine Tandler, Jane Tandler, Noah Fields, Ariel Hubbard, and Mikaela Dunitz. Big hugs to the SF Thursday Night Crew for the beers and the raccoon inspo. Thank you to the whole of Combo Za for making me laugh till I cried, and for inspiring me with your wit, weirdness, and creativity.

To my very best reader and even better friend, Clare Fielder, who believed in this project when it was just a "what if . . . ?": you are the reason this book exists. Thank you for your writing, your reading, and most of all, for your friendship.

Thank you to my brother Nat, whose hilarious and beautiful writing always gave me something to aspire to, both growing up and now. A herd of sea horses to Madeline Miller for your love and support. My multitalented brother-in-law BJ Thompson is the genius behind *Kelp!*, and he took my author photograph *and* he saved an early draft of this book from a deep dark technological abyss: thank you. Thank you to my sister and mostly companion Tina, who designed my website, advised me on all matters oceanographic and/or mathematical, and read this book many times over. I'm very, very lucky you're my sister.

To my parents, Catherine and Jonathan Drake. There seems to be nothing I *can't* thank you for, and that includes throwing a wedding for an invisible hamster. Thank you for always believing in me, and for always being there.

And to Nick, who helped me through the hardest parts—I love you. You're it.

Julia Drake

grew up outside Philadelphia. As a teenager, she played some of Shakespeare's best heroines in her high school theater program, and their stories would stay with her forever. Julia received her BA in Spanish from Williams College and her MFA in creative writing from Columbia University, where she also taught writing to first-year students. She currently works as a book coach for aspiring writers and teaches creative-writing classes for Writopia Lab, a nonprofit that fosters a love of writing in young adults. She lives in San Francisco with her partner and their rescue rabbit, Ned.